Praise for *The Sacred Cipher*, The Jeru

"I wasn't sure at times if I was reading a novel . . . or the newspaper. Except that *The Sacred Cipher* was a far more fascinating read. If you read one book this year, make it this one."

—Wanda Dyson, author of *Judgment Day* and *Obsession*

"More historically and biblically accurate than *The Davinci Code* and just as adventurous as an Indiana Jones movie, *The Sacred Cipher* combines action and mystery to draw readers into a world of ancient secrets and international escapades."

—*Christian Retailing*

Praise for *The Brotherhood Conspiracy*, The Jerusalem Prophecies #2

"Terry Brennan meticulously crafts stories of intrigue and action. His ability to weave archaeological and historical detail into a riveting plotline is simply amazing. Both *The Sacred Cipher* and *The Brotherhood Conspiracy* could step off the front page of any newspaper tomorrow. You'll find them captivating!"

—Mike Dellosso, author of *Fearless* and *Frantic*

"*The Brotherhood Conspiracy* weaves a beautifully intricate web of intrigue and suspense. Painstakingly researched with powerful characters, it takes the reader on an exciting and thought-provoking adventure. Brennan brilliantly meshes an internal struggle of faith with an epic story about a world on the brink."

—David E. Stevens, former Navy commander and
F-18 fighter pilot, author of *Resurrect*

"An international mystery thriller with a rapid-fire plot . . . Readers who enjoy the creative juxtaposition of history, religion, and geopolitics will find in Brennan's work a feast for the senses."

—*Publishers Weekly*

The Jerusalem Prophecies
The Sacred Cipher
The Brotherhood Conspiracy
The Aleppo Code

THE
ALEPPO
CODE

A NOVEL

TERRY
BRENNAN

Kregel
Publications

The Aleppo Code: A Novel
© 2015 by Terry Brennan

Published by Kregel Publications, a division of Kregel, Inc.,
2450 Oak Industrial Dr. NE, Grand Rapids, MI 49505.

Published in association with the literary agency of WordServe
Literary Group, Ltd., 10152 S. Knoll Circle, Highlands Ranch,
CO 80130. www.wordserveliterary.com.

Scriptures quotations are from the Holy Bible, New International Version®, NIV®. Copyright © 1973, 1978, 1984, 2011
by Biblica, Inc.™ Used by permission of Zondervan. All rights
reserved worldwide. www.zondervan.com

ISBN 978-0-8254-4389-3

Printed in the United States of America
15 16 17 18 19 20 21 22 23 24 / 5 4 3 2 1

To my wife, Andrea
Your smile and your spirit sustain me.

ACKNOWLEDGMENTS

For a guy with one idea to come up with an adventure trilogy—well, you know it's not been a solo journey.

First—always—I give thanks to God for the gift. Nothing is impossible for you.

On this earth, I am deeply indebted to my family for their love, support, and encouragement. Andrea, my wife, has helped keep my eyes on God and my feet on the ground for thirty-six years. You have made me whole. And to Meg, Azizi, and Matt—thanks for all the round-table discussions and debates that helped sharpen my writing and broaden my characters. Particularly for Meg, a fountain of logic and good sense—and great ideas. You'll write your own someday.

Thank you to Kathy Vance, who helped put life to the one idea; to Wanda Dyson, who believed in the idea, and in me; to my accountability partners—MO, FA, MP, JL, MM, SV, and MW—who held me to a higher standard as a man, husband, and father. Thanks to Stacey Ashton, for thoughtful insight.

And, as always, a rich thank you to the inspiring and talented team at Kregel Publications—Dennis Hillman, Steve Barclift, Dave Hill, Noelle Pedersen, and my editor, Dawn Anderson . . . I notice a lot of mistakes in the thrillers I read. Dawn, you are the best editor of the bunch. And so gentle with the whip.

PROMINENT CHARACTERS

The team that discovered the Third Temple of God
hidden under the Temple Mount:

Tom Bohannon. Executive director of the Bowery Mission in New York City; former investigative reporter.

Joe Rodriguez. Curator of the Periodicals Room in the New York Public Library's main building on Bryant Park; married to Deirdre, Tom Bohannon's sister.

"Sammy" Rizzo. Director of the book storage and retrieval system in the Humanities and Social Sciences Library on Bryant Park at 42nd Street in New York City; colleague of Joe Rodriguez.

Dr. Richard Johnson Sr. Managing director of the Collector's Club in Manhattan; former chair of the Antiquities College at Columbia University; fellow of the British Museum.

*** *

Annie Bohannon. Tom's wife of thirty years; photographer.

Baqir al-Musawi. President of Syria.

Benjamin Fineman. Messianic rabbi and custodian of Jeremiah's Grotto.

Bill Cartwright. Director of the Central Intelligence Agency; President Whitestone's longtime friend and accountability partner.

Chaim Shomsky. Chief of staff to the prime minister of Israel.

Connor Bohannon. Tom's son.

Deirdre Rodriguez. Sister of Tom Bohannon, wife of Joe Rodriguez.

Dr. Brandon McDonough. Provost of Trinity College, Dublin; expert in biblical archaeology; and Richard Johnson's boss at the British Museum.

Eliazar Baruk. Prime minister of Israel; lives in Tel Aviv.

General Moishe Orhlon. Israeli defense minister.

Jonathan Whitestone. President of the United States; Republican; evangelical Christian from the state of Texas.

Kallie Nolan. Masters candidate in biblical archaeology; friend of Sammy Rizzo; assisted the team in finding the Temple.

King Abbudin. Ruler of Saudi Arabia, fifth of the Saudi kings, secret leader of the Muslim Brotherhood.

Latiffa Naouri. Chief historian of the Iraqi Antiquities Commission, former colleague of Annie Bohannon.

Mike Whalen. Ex–Navy SEAL, leader of the *National Geographic* crew in Iraq.

Roberta Smith. Leader of the Demotic Dictionary Project at the University of Chicago's Oriental Institute, expert on the Demotic language.

Rory O'Neill. Commissioner of the New York City police department.

Sam Reynolds. Career diplomat of the US State Department; assisted the team that found the Temple.

Sergeant Jeremiah Fischoff. Battle-tested veteran of the Israel Defense Force, wounded in the rescue of Annie Bohannon.

Sheik Khalid al-Kabir. Head of the Anbar Awakening, the nomadic tribes in western Iraq who joined forces with US Marines to fight Al Qaeda; old friend of Annie Bohannon.

Stew Manthey. CFO of the Bowery Mission; colleague of Tom's.

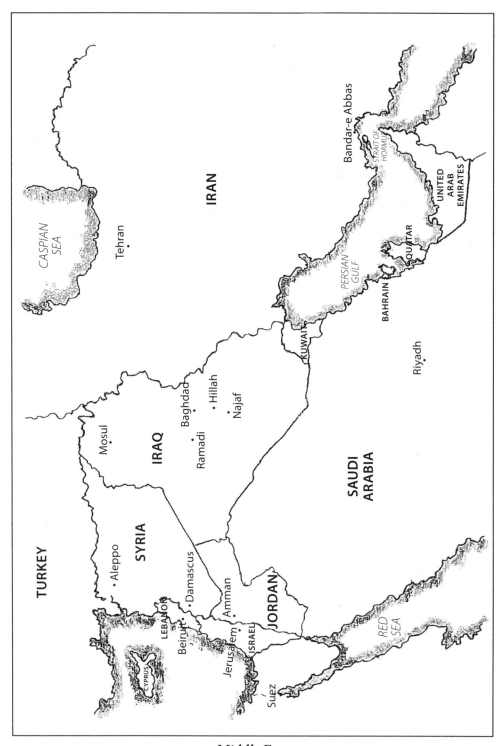

Middle East

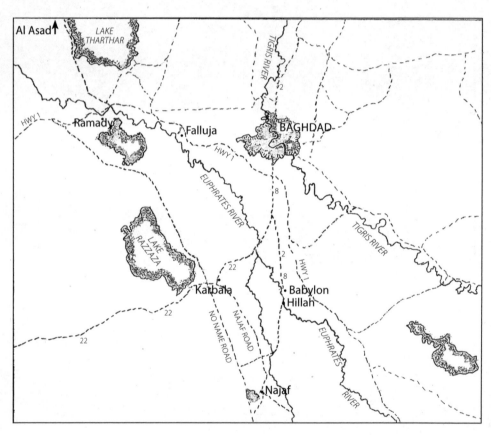

Central Iraq

PROLOGUE

1896

Edward Elgar not only felt like a fugitive, he acted like one. He believed his life depended on stealth.

Elgar's mind was no longer on the lecture he had just completed to the aspiring composers at the University of Westminster, nor was he conscious of his own shivers as he bundled his wool greatcoat tightly around his neck and pulled his hat down snugly over his thinning hair. He wasn't as interested in staying warm, protecting himself against the biting December wind that whipped across Paddington Street Gardens, as he was determined to be invisible.

Walking briskly along the east side of the gardens, Elgar kept his head tilted down, obscuring his face as he peered under the brim of his hat, scanning the street in front of him. He kept to the side streets, avoiding the easier walk on the Marylebone High Street in return for the shadows on gaslit Aybrook Street. Elgar regularly changed directions, glancing over his shoulder each time. At Manchester Square, he completely circled the square once, then half again, searching the shadows for movement and praying for his nerves to quiet.

Building a reputation as a composer, chiefly from his works for the great choral festivals of the English Midlands, Elgar would have normally felt foolish orchestrating these cloak-and-dagger maneuvers. But there was the break-in at his home in Great Malvern one week ago, in which his study was completely ransacked, and the two knife-wielding assailants who cornered him on a side street three nights earlier after he'd attended a concert at the Crystal Palace.

Were it not for the two constables who intervened and captured the foreign-looking criminals, Elgar could have lost his life.

Elgar didn't need to see their amulets to know that the killers were back, that he was their target, and that it was critical he contact Sir Charles Warren. Waiting three days for Warren to return from the Continent nearly destroyed his constitution.

Exiting Manchester Square, Elgar momentarily regretted his decision to help his good friend and renowned English preacher Charles Haddon Spurgeon unravel the cipher that protected the mysterious message on that confounded scroll. When Charles dispatched the scroll into the safekeeping of his colleague Louis Klopsch, the New York City publisher of Spurgeon's evangelical newspaper, both Spurgeon and Elgar felt released from their fear of the men who pursued the scroll—the men with the amulets. Spurgeon returned to preaching in his packed New Park Street Chapel in London, and Elgar returned to his work composing the Pomp and Circumstance Marches and his masterpiece, the "Enigma" Variations. But years ago, just prior to his death, Spurgeon had sent an odd warning for Elgar to notify Warren if his life were ever threatened like this. Combined with the report he recently received about the burglary in Klopsch's New York City home . . . well . . .

The Palestine Exploration Fund, the organization that funded Warren's 1867 excavations under Jerusalem's Temple Mount, occupied a four-story building constructed in the late 1700s in the Marylebone Village, its entrance tucked into the thin, short alley of Hinde Mews that turned off Marylebone Lane. Hard to find, but the rent was reasonable for an organization that Elgar knew was constantly scrabbling to maintain its funding.

After surveying the darkened streets once more, Elgar entered the side door and trundled up the steep stairs, shaking the chill from his coat. The attendant asked his business as he reached the second floor and pointed him up the stairs to the reading room on the third floor, where most of the fund's meetings were held. Elgar found the room warm, well lit, and inviting, a fire in the generous fireplace keeping out any chill.

Any Englishman who read a newspaper could have recognized Sir General Charles Warren, who sat hunched deep in a leather armchair that flanked the fireplace. Warren's face was a front-page fixture in the *Times*—and the more disreputable rags that claimed to practice journalism in London—not only for his many heroic military exploits in Africa but also for his daring, unprecedented explorations under the Temple Mount in Jerusalem. And then there was Warren's unlikely, but remarkable, three-year tenure as chief commissioner of the London Metropolitan Police from 1886 to 1888, when he was the lead investigator in the Jack the Ripper murders. Warren's face was often published more than the queen's.

Elgar crossed the room and extended his hand. "Sir Charles, thank you for seeing me on such short notice."

Warren's face was thinner than Elgar's, but both carried the high forehead of intelligence, the thinning hair of middle age, and the mustache that was nearly obligatory for an English gentleman—though the thick, bristly hedge that overwhelmed Elgar's upper lip was of a different magnitude than Warren's. Starched collar, thick cravat, wool suit and waistcoat—Elgar's brown, Warren's gray—completed the uniform of the day.

Warren stood and took Elgar's hand. "My pleasure, sir. I've enjoyed your music and was fascinated by your association with the Reverend Spurgeon."

"Which is why I am here tonight, I'm afraid." Elgar took off his coat, hung it beside the fireplace, and settled into the leather armchair opposite Warren's. "Charles urged me to contact you if I ever believed—"

"That your life was in danger?"

"How did you know?" Elgar was stunned by Warren's question, but even more shocked by his subsequent answer.

"I know, sir, why you believe you are in danger, and I agree with your assessment. When you contacted me, I inquired with a former colleague at the Yard. I know about the break-in at your home and the attempt on your life. I know you've come to me for help and protection. And I also know I'm going to disappoint you."

"But . . . I . . ." Elgar stammered, trying to find traction for his thoughts.

"Mr. Elgar, forgive me. I have looked forward to making your acquaintance. Sadly, it appears to be under strained circumstances, and more so, I have very little time this evening. I fear we will need to be brief and to the point. Please, allow me to begin.

"I met the Reverend Spurgeon during my time as commissioner of police, and we continued that relationship until I was assigned to command the garrison in Singapore. During that time we spoke often and at length, both about my experience exploring under Temple Mount in Jerusalem and also about the scroll the two of you deciphered that claimed a third Temple had been built, and then hidden, under Temple Mount prior to the Crusades.

"It is not because of the message on the scroll that you are being hunted, Mr. Elgar—"

"Please, call me Edward."

"Yes . . . Thank you . . . It's not the scroll, but rather because of a message contained in the mezuzah itself. A message that confirmed things I had discovered under Temple Mount, things that I have divulged to no one else except the Reverend Spurgeon. Two years after Charles died, on my return from Singapore, I took a ship north, crossing the Arabian Sea and Persian Gulf to the land route through Persia and Palestine. A longer trip, but necessary to support what Charles and I suspected."

With a momentary look around the room, Warren leaned in and closed the distance to Elgar. The composer became even more nervous.

"I joined an expedition from the British Museum at the site of the ancient city of Babylon in Assyria. My friend Hormuzd Rassam led the expedition. He was looking for cuneiform tablets. What I sought, and found, Edward, you will not be able to verify because the proof is in two far-off places, New York City—protected and safe, we can only hope—and under the sands of the Persian desert.

"I have kept this information in my safe until this night. I believe that you are one of the few living souls who can appreciate and understand its critical importance. Unfortunately, this information, were it to be discovered by others, would only increase the danger under which you now live."

Warren reached into the inner pocket of his suit coat, revealing to Elgar the pistol that rested in a holster under his left armpit. His anxiety already growing during Warren's comments, Elgar's heartbeat spiked at these last words and the sight of the weapon.

"You should think about getting one for yourself," Warren whispered. He held out a small envelope and kept it suspended between them until Elgar took it in his hand.

"I know you are very fond of ciphers and codes," said Warren. "On the paper inside this envelope are a series of directions from a point in Babylon to a portal. These directions, if combined with other, coded instructions that were hidden in Spurgeon's bronze mezuzah, would lead to the most astounding archaeological discovery in the history of man. And it's a discovery which we must never allow to happen."

Elgar's mind was as overloaded as it was on the first days of creating a symphony. "But . . . Sir Charles . . . I've come to *you* for help, for protection for my family. These men are now pursuing me."

Sir General Charles Warren, commander of the Thames District of the British Army, hero of the Boer War, drew himself upright in the leather armchair, facing Elgar directly and unveiling the full magnitude of his military bearing and presence. He leaned in closer to the composer, his voice low but brimming with authority.

"Mr. Elgar, I sympathize with your plight . . . I do. But what we face today—what Charles and I faced every day since that trip to Persia—is the very real prospect of the most powerful and destructive weapon in the history of the world falling into the hands of bloodthirsty killers who would use this weapon not simply to further their nefarious ends. No, these men do not seek riches. What they seek is the destruction of Western civilization as we know it, the subjugation of the Christian world, and the overthrow of its precepts."

Whether from the heat thrown by the vigorous fire, or from his own growing sense of dread, Elgar was perspiring heavily under his wool suit. His breathing was shallow, and his mind searched the corridors of his wisdom, looking for a door through which to escape the responsibility Warren was entrusting to him.

"I could be reassigned at a moment's notice," said the general, "dispatched to a part of the world where those directions would be even more at risk. No, I regret to say, Edward, this burden must fall to you. You understand codes and ciphers. Take what I've given you and make its secret secure. Use that code you deciphered from the scroll. Whatever you do, hide this secret and hide it well. If these directions are never deciphered, that would be an acceptable outcome."

Elgar was astonished to see the envelope still in his hands. He looked at the fire and wondered if that would not be a better fate for this fearful slip of paper.

"I know," whispered Warren, close now to Elgar's shoulder. "I've often thought the same thing myself. Why not just destroy it?"

"Why not?"

"It was the Reverend Spurgeon," said Warren. "He convinced me there was a spiritual, supernatural purpose for these directions. That someday, someone would need to know the way. He told me, *'When the day of reckoning comes, the*

day evil is defeated will be the day God's arm will stretch forth, and in his hand will
be his power.'"

A chill filled Elgar. "What are these? What are these directions?"

Warren leaned over, took the envelope out of Elgar's hand, and stuffed it into the inside pocket of Elgar's jacket. "They lead to the birthplace of man. And to the manifestation of the power of God. Hide them well, my friend."

———

The envelope in his jacket pocket felt as if it were burning a hole in his chest as Elgar traveled home by train to Worcestershire and the town of Great Malvern. He was thoroughly exhausted and at his wit's end after staying up all night in his London hotel room, working on the cipher. In the carriage from the station, the closer he got to his home, the heavier his burden became. Elgar had no safe at home, no secure place to hide such dangerous information. He recalled hearing someone speak on the advantage of hiding things in plain sight, but his thoughts were as chaotic and random as discordance theory. Nothing made sense.

Alice was standing on the front steps as the carriage pulled up the drive. He paid the driver, rushed up the steps with his bag in his hand, and barely acknowledged his wife as he hastened inside and went straight to his study. This was the room recently ransacked. What was the chance they would come back to it again? He looked frantically about him as Alice called his name from the doorway. Her steps started down the hall.

Elgar noticed his box of stationary on top of his desk. Of course. In with the note paper and cards, it would be nearly invisible. Elgar slit the envelope and took the single sheet of paper in his left hand. With his right, he lifted the lid on the stationary box, thumbed through the contents and, as Alice walked into the study, slipped the paper between two pieces of card stock. He would deal with it later.

"Edward . . . what is wrong with you? You look as if you've stared into the face of death."

PART ONE

JEREMIAH'S CALL

FRIDAY, AUGUST 28

Annie could see that guilt, like a ravenous cancer, consumed more of her husband with every heartbeat. The dead just kept piling up around them—Winthrop and Doc were dead. Now Kallie. Even Annie herself had narrowly escaped the same fate. Tom rubbed at his hands as if the blood would never wash away. Annie feared that the violence torturing Tom Bohannon's sleep and haunting his days was expanding beyond his capacity to cope.

Chiseled rays of the late-day sun sporadically pierced the wisteria that twisted over a wooden trellis tucked into the corner of Rabbi Ronald Fineman's garden in the Nahla'ot section of Jerusalem. A few hours earlier, Annie, Tom, and other friends who held Kallie Nolan dear had endured her memorial service, paying their respects in the land she loved, where she had lost her life, before sending her body back to her family in Iowa. Emotionally spent, the friends were seeking respite from their grief in Rabbi Fineman's garden. But respite was not on the guest list.

Annie kept her eyes on Tom as they all struggled to process what they had just been told by Sam Reynolds.

"But who would try to assassinate the president of the United States and the prime minister of Israel, both on the same night?" Tom asked. The last few months had dropped pounds from Bohannon's fifty-eight-year-old body—high anxiety and times of near-starvation had taken a severe toll. Now the awful burden of responsibility along with the weight of regret was evident as his six-foot frame hunched over a small table in a corner of the garden. "Who has that kind of power . . . that kind of reach?"

Under the trellis, the shade was full. Tom sat across from Annie, holding her hand. Tom's brother-in-law and sister, Joe and Dierdre Rodriguez, occupied a bench on the far side, Dierdre pressed closely against Rodriguez's side. In the rear, on a raised, shaded section of stone patio, Rabbi Fineman was engaged in hushed conversation with archaeologist Brandon McDonough.

"Radical Islam is behind this," said Reynolds, as he concluded his update. Despite his loose-limbed, Texas-cowboy looks, Reynolds had the sharp mind and dapper dress of a career diplomat with the US State Department. Annie was grateful that Reynolds had quickly become Tom's friend, ally, and protector over the past several months. "We see the Muslim Brotherhood's hand at work throughout the Middle East. We can only guess how far ISIS reaches. And your guys with the amulets seem to be involved, too."

Annie pulled her hand free from Tom's and shoved her chair back, a bolt of rage driving her to her feet. "God help us. Aren't we ever going to be rid of these people?"

Annie could feel that she'd become a different woman since she and Kallie were kidnapped by the Prophet's Guard, since Kallie had been murdered and Annie rescued on a dark road near Gaza. Her inner peace, which kept her balanced, had been replaced by a smoldering reservoir of anger that refused to cool. She wanted revenge. "Why can't you guys wipe out the Prophet's Guard and give us our lives back?"

"But—" Reynolds stammered.

"But nothing," Annie snapped. "You and the president and all his power have been nothing but bystanders watching from the sidelines as we—as Tom and Joe and Sammy—risked our lives, our families, chasing after the messages on the scroll. We need—"

A voice from outside the shade entered the conversation.

"They were never after the scroll."

Sammy Rizzo stepped under the trellis. Today Rizzo had shed his characteristic Hawaiian shirt for a stark black suit tailored to his four-foot frame. Sammy's grief—honed by a desired romance that would now be forever unrealized—bled from his eyes

He walked up beside Annie, took her hand in his, and looked into her face. "We were wrong," Rizzo said. "They wanted what the scroll, the mezuzah,

THE ALEPPO CODE   23

pointed to. And it wasn't the Temple or the Tent. The guys who got me out of the monastery—the Temple Guard guys—they told me what this is all about. They showed me. I think it's why so many have died. Why so many more may die."

Rizzo stroked Annie Bohannon's hand, his eyes on her fingers. "You know, Kallie was so excited about this treasure hunt of ours, she was willing to sacrifice anything to be a part of it."

Annie knelt down on the flagstones and looked directly into his face. "I'm sorry, Sam. It's okay—"

"No! It isn't over. What they're after, they'll never stop until they find it or they kill us all."

Annie reached out her right hand and placed it on Rizzo's shoulder. "Then you and I will stop them, Sammy. You and me, Tom, and Joe, if that's what it takes. God knows I'd rather go home and be normal. But we can't live the rest of our lives like this, running in fear from these killers. And we can't rely on the authorities to keep us safe. Can we, Sam?" She glanced at Reynolds who simply looked down at his polished shoes. "The Prophet's Guard is ruthless and relentless. Richard wasn't safe. Kallie wasn't safe. They even went after Caitlin."

She closed her eyes and shook her head.

"You know, I almost forgot this." Annie turned her head to look at Tom. "If God's hand is in this—and I believe that with all my heart—then he's called us to be in this to the end." There was no rebuke in Annie's words, only resignation. She turned her attention back to Rizzo. "No matter what it is that the Prophet's Guard wants."

Rizzo took a deep breath, holding eye contact with Annie. "They want to control the world," he said. "And they think they can use God's power to do that. That's what they're after."

"I don't understand," said Dierdre Rodriguez. "What do you mean, use God's power?"

Rizzo turned his head to face her. "They're looking for a weapon," he said.

"That is what we suspect." From the raised section of the patio, where he'd been in deliberations with the rabbi, McDonough now joined them, carrying a large sheet of paper.

"I traced these images," said McDonough, "from the cover of a sarcophagus in what I believe is Jeremiah's tomb." On the sheet of paper were traced two large, angelic beings, their wings upraised, flaming swords held aloft in their hands. Behind the angels stood a huge tree. Below the angels and the tree was a shepherd's staff.

"We believe they are looking for this." McDonough pointed to the staff. "The most powerful weapon in the history of man . . . And I think I know where we need to look: in the place where man's history began."

In the ensuing silence, Annie could hear the wings of an insect humming in the garden. From inside the house came the voices of Rabbi Fineman's other guests as they made their farewells.

A ringing cell phone shattered the stillness.

She looked to her right, where Reynolds was digging a phone out of his hip pocket.

"I must admit you've piqued my interest to hear more about the greatest weapon in the history of man, but"—he raised the still-ringing smartphone— "this is one call I've got to take. Don't get into the good stuff until I come back, okay?"

Reynolds took two steps out from under the arbor and stopped, his back to the group in the shade. The conversation was brief. Reynolds took one more step away from the group, then straightened up and stuck the phone back in his pocket. Hands on his hips, he stood motionless in the sun for a moment and then turned back to the shelter of the arbor.

"I'm sorry. I think I need to hear this story, but I've got to go," said Reynolds. He looked at Annie, but his eyes were distant. "Where will you be tomorrow?"

"Kallie's apartment, probably," she said.

"Good. I'll see you there . . . early." Reynolds glanced around the group. "And you had better start packing. It's time to leave."

Annie's inner cauldron began to bubble; but before she could object, Reynolds had done an about-face and was out of the garden.

"Good luck with that." Rizzo took off his jacket and draped it over the back of a chair. Was it defiance or resolve that creased Sammy's face? "I'm not going anywhere," he said. "This thing is still not over."

Bohannon rubbed his temples and snorted. "Maybe it's not over for you, but I've just about had enough." His words dripped with the poison of regret.

Annie walked over to where Tom was sitting and put her hand on his shoulder. "I think we need to listen." Her voice was firm, but her words were a plea. "We at least need to listen."

Rabbi Fineman stepped into the midst of the group, steadying the yarmulke that covered the thinning hair swept back over his head. "Let's go inside," he said, glancing in Annie's direction. "Get out of the heat. I think it best that we all get a bit more comfortable. This is going to be a long story."

⸏⸏⸏

Fineman's wife was in the kitchen, washing dishes. The rest of the house was empty, the rabbi's guests having departed one by one in his absence. The team gathered in his small parlor, a well-worn air conditioner trying valiantly to defeat the afternoon heat. Bohannon paced in the confined space.

"You're telling me that we never understood what this was all about, not even from the beginning?" After all they had discovered and endured over the last few months, after all their amazing and awful experiences, Tom Bohannon hadn't expected to be surprised by anything ever again.

But now he was stunned by what he heard from his colleagues.

"I do not believe it was possible for us to understand," said Professor Brandon McDonough. He still held the large piece of tracing paper in front of him. "We did not have the full story . . . probably still don't have the full story. But now that we have more of the pieces, well, I'd say we're moving closer to the truth."

"So why don't one of you," said Bohannon, sweeping a hand in the general direction of the rabbi, McDonough, and Rizzo, "tell us what's going on? You three seem to possess some information that the rest of us haven't been able to figure out." Bohannon threw himself into a soft, upholstered chair but then perched on the edge as if waiting to be launched.

"Well, Tom, you have to understand that for more than a thousand years, only a handful of people have understood the true story behind the mezuzah and the scroll." Rabbi Fineman sat on the sofa opposite Bohannon, his hands entwined, his face a roadmap of wrinkled concern. "You can't blame yourself for not seeing the truth—as if that would have made any difference in the things that have happened."

"You and McDonough figured it out." Bohannon flung the words into the crowded parlor as an indictment. "I should have seen it. I should have figured it out. Maybe then . . . maybe then . . ."

"Maybe what?" Carrying a plate of sandwiches, Annie walked in from greeting Mrs. Fineman in the kitchen and sat on the arm of the upholstered chair. She put her arm around her husband's shoulders, but her smile didn't reach her eyes. "And maybe then Doc wouldn't be dead? Maybe Kallie would still be alive?"

Self-pity rode into Tom's heart on the back of Annie's words, slicing deep into his confidence. He was the leader. It *was* his fault.

Twice over the last three months, Bohannon had been torn from his position as executive director of the Bowery Mission in New York City and thrown into a maelstrom of geopolitical crisis and intrigue in the Middle East. The first time, his unlikely team of archaeologists and amateur adventurers had thrust themselves into dangerous and uncharted waters to chase down a secret message decoded from an ancient scroll. Their young friend and colleague Winthrop Larsen was massacred by a Prophet's Guard car bomb in New York City, and the rest of them had nearly died in the caverns underneath Jerusalem's Temple Mount. The second time, Bohannon and his team were relentlessly recruited by the president of the United States to pursue any additional clues on the ancient scroll or the mezuzah that carried it.

While the inscrutable brass mezuzah finally did reveal a second secret that led to the discovery of the biblical Tent of Meeting in a desert cave along Scorpion Pass in the Negev, the cost of the adventure had been devastating.

Dr. Richard Johnson, former chair of the Antiquities College at Columbia University, was murdered by the Prophet's Guard in a fourth-century monastery in the Red Sea desert of Egypt, where Sammy Rizzo narrowly escaped with his life; Kallie Nolan and Annie Bohannon were kidnapped in Jerusalem by the same group of Muslim fanatics; Tom and Sammy were part of a headlong race by Israeli soldiers who intercepted the fleeing kidnappers, but not in time to save Kallie Nolan's life; Joe Rodriguez, shackled as a prisoner after unearthing the Tent of Meeting, watched in horror as Muslim fighters massacred a troop of Israeli soldiers on top of Temple Mount, then desecrated and torched the ancient Tent, after which the entire Mount platform was destroyed once again—this time by a pillar of fire.

And that was just the personal cost.

An improbable peace treaty between Israel and its Arab neighbors had been shattered as deeply as the Temple Mount; tension between Israel and Islam had risen to epic proportions; the Muslim Brotherhood was pursuing and consolidating power throughout the Middle East; the Israeli government of Prime Minister Eliazar Baruk was crumbling at just the time Israel was desperate for capable, moderate leadership; and an ultimate conflict over control of the Temple Mount appeared to be inevitable.

Now, Bohannon was being told that his quest to decode the sacred scroll and unlock the mysteries of the brass mezuzah—which led to the discovery of an eleventh-century Jewish Temple constructed under the Temple Mount and, later, the unearthing of the original Tent of Meeting—was not the objective of the relentless, murderous pursuit of the Prophet's Guard.

Tom's eyes flashed with anger as he looked up at his wife. "And maybe Jerusalem wouldn't have been devastated by an earthquake and thousands killed. Maybe . . ." He shook his head and looked around the room.

McDonough and Fineman sat alongside each other on the sofa, as mismatched a pair as one could imagine. Dr. Brandon McDonough, provost of Trinity College in Dublin, was round and portly—stereotypically Irish—while Rabbi Ronald Fineman, a messianic rabbi from New York City who had befriended Bohannon and his team in Jerusalem, was long and thin. Joe Rodriguez left his wife, Deirdre, on an inhospitable futon and forced his six-four body into a sitting position next to Rizzo on the floor. Rodriguez was speaking softly into Rizzo's ear while Sammy, his eyes downcast, absently folded and unfolded a piece of paper.

Bohannon brought his attention back to the rabbi on the sofa. "Maybe I haven't had a clue about the ultimate meaning of what we've found, and what we've experienced. But I do know it's important. And I suppose I'm not surprised there's more to come. So why don't you—all of you—tell us what you know. Then maybe we'll have some idea of what to do next."

Fineman looked left and right, his goatee bobbing on the end of his chin, sighed, and unfolded his hands as if opening a book.

"Three pieces are woven together," he said. "You know the first two, the mezuzah and the scroll—one ancient code after another concealing secrets as old as the Bible. But there is a third piece to this labyrinthine puzzle, a piece that leads to the weapon, a piece that burst into my consciousness just this afternoon. Let's start with the book. You need to know about the book, and then we can move on."

Bohannon was puzzled. First there was a weapon. Now there was a book. "What book?"

The response came from the floor. "A book I was shown in the Egyptian desert."

Rizzo kept his focus on the folded paper in his hands and, as he unfolded it once more, Tom noticed that it was the pamphlet distributed at the memorial service. Kallie's picture was on the cover.

"It's a book with all the answers," said Rizzo.

2

Eight Days Earlier

It was a large cavern, well away from the sandstorm that wailed across the cave opening on the desert ridge far above. Dual-mantle, gas-fired lanterns not only lit up the space but also added heat that kept the dampness at bay. Within the cavern resided a small tent city—canvas-covered, sparsely populated, adobe-walled structures randomly scattered around the circumference of the cavern and a larger, open-sided tent in the middle of the space with a cooking pit in the center flanked by tables. A dog barked off to the left. The rich, thick aroma of hay and animal stalls hovered in the open space. Straight ahead, as the Jeep carrying Rizzo and his two rescuers entered the cavern, was the community's main structure—an adobe building the size of a large church—the headquarters of the Temple Guard.

The two guard members in the front of the Jeep were dressed in the iconic outfits that appeared to identify their members—red-checked keffiyeh held in place by two black ropes, their ends trailing onto the leather vest they wore over a white, muslin shirt. Well-worn, blousy blue pants, kept in place by a wide red sash, were tucked into calf-high leather boots. The leader, Hassan, pulled the Jeep in front of the main building. He turned in his seat.

"Welcome to our modest home," said Hassan. "Few have seen this place who are not of the guardians."

The night before, Hassan and his cousin had rescued Rizzo from St. Antony's Monastery in the eastern Sahara Desert and from the clutches of the assassins of the Prophet's Guard who murdered Doc and had the same plans for Rizzo.

29

Through the night, their Jeep had raced across the desert, reaching this cave moments before a sandstorm obliterated visibility.

Hassan jumped out of the Jeep and picked up the book that rested between the front seats, the book they had rescued from St. Antony's Monastery along with Rizzo. "Come, we will show you what you seek to know."

Both Hassan and his cousin had a rifle slung over their shoulder, a bandolier of cartridges strapped across their chest, and a short scimitar tucked into the sash.

In any other circumstance, in spite of the weapons, Sammy would have been comforted by the genuine warmth and concern that radiated from Hassan's face. A black mustache, the size of a forest, exploded under his prodigious nose and dropped off each side of his mouth to frame his chin. His eyes were as black as the ocean depths but filled with the fire of life and a gladness of spirit. A ragged, screaming pink scar ran from his left cheek, across the eyebrow of his left eye, above his nose, and across his brow until it disappeared beneath the keffiyeh.

But in this circumstance, with Doc's lifeless body left lying in that cold, monk's cell, there was comfort neither in Rizzo's escape nor in his rescuers.

"I don't care what you have to show me," said Rizzo, dragging his battered body from the Jeep. "It just doesn't matter anymore."

"Perhaps. Come," said Hassan. He put one hand on Rizzo's shoulder and led him into the great hall.

Inside, Hassan turned to the left and entered a small, low-ceilinged room. In the center was a wooden table, with a book resting on a stand in the middle of the table, enclosed in what looked like a glass box. Hassan laid down the book he brought from the Jeep, lifted the glass, removed the other book and put it beside the first. Rizzo pushed up against the top of the table to get a better look.

Like an archaeologist sifting sand, looking for a buried treasure, Hassan caressed open a page of one book then did the same to the other. With the utmost care he turned page after page. Suddenly, with an audible sigh, he stopped and turned to his cousin. "They are identical, in what they contain and in what they are missing. We are no closer to the answer."

In spite of his despair, and the bruises inflicted by the ancient Jeep as it careened across the desert, Rizzo was drawn to the futile resignation of Hassan's words.

"What's this all about?" asked Rizzo. "Why have you brought me here?"

"Because of this . . . these books," said Hassan, waving a hand at the leather-bound books on the table. "You and your friends have been searching. This is what you have been looking for. Here . . . let's sit." Hassan's cousin dragged a wooden bench from the corner of the room up to the edge of the table and then left the room.

"Both the Prophet's Guard and Temple Guard possess copies of this book," said Hassan. "They are incomplete copies. Combined with what we know of the mezuzah and the scroll, these books have kept us locked in relentless battle with the Prophet's Guard for nearly a thousand years. Here. Let me explain."

Hassan swept the red-checked keffiyeh from his head and dropped it on the table. Scratching his head, he settled into the corner of the bench. Rizzo hopped up into the opposite corner.

"More than nine hundred years ago, some Crusaders came to St. Antony's Monastery. Part of a lay order, the Brotherhood of Saint Antony, they were on a pilgrimage to fulfill a vow. But they brought with them a scroll holder, or mezuzah, which they left at the monastery.

"The Coptic monks who occupied the monastery knew the scroll was written in Demotic, an ancient Egyptian language, but none of them could decipher what was on the scroll. Two hundred years later, another pilgrim made his way to the monastery, a Coptic skilled in ancient languages and a lover of puzzles. It took five years but this man broke the code and revealed the message."

Rizzo was startled. "You know . . . they knew?"

"You are not the only men to solve this puzzle. The monks of St. Antony's Monastery knew for seven hundred years there was a Jewish temple hidden under the sacred mount in Jerusalem."

"But why not reveal the secret?" Rizzo asked, his mind rebelling at the new information.

"How? They were here, stuck in the desert. Who would they tell? Jerusalem was over three hundred kilometers away, a two-month journey. So instead, they hid the mezuzah and its scroll in a small crypt carved into the foundation of the library building.

"Ultimately, the few brother monks who knew of the mezuzah formed a group of guardians; the Temple Guardians they called themselves. They swore on their faith in the cross of the Christ to protect the scroll, its mezuzah, and its message—to keep it a secret until the right moment, the right time to reveal the existence of this hidden temple.

"But the monastery is isolated. Even after the monks built their massive, defensive walls, St. Antony's was an inviting target for bandits and nomadic Bedouins. Soon the Temple Guardians became more warriors than monks, determined to keep the mezuzah safe, and secret.

"Eventually, knowledge of the mezuzah and the scroll—most importantly, of its message—came to a follower of Islam. No wall could deter that man and his Muslim brothers. The scroll's message was a threat to the Haram al-Sharif if knowledge of a hidden temple became known. These Muslim men also took a vow, to serve the defiled cross. A Coptic cross, like ours, with a lightning bolt slashing through on the diagonal.

"These warriors, who called themselves the Prophet's Guard, attacked the monastery, massacred the monks, and stole the mezuzah."

Rizzo was looking down at his boots, swinging his legs back and forth as he assimilated this new information. A critical question crashed into his thoughts. "Wait . . . once the Prophet's Guard got ahold of the mezuzah, why not destroy it? Get rid of the evidence?"

Hassan nodded his head. "A shrewd question, my friend. Destroying the mezuzah and its scroll would have solved one problem. But there is much about the mezuzah we have yet to learn, other clues to an ultimate secret all of us still seek. So our enemies hid the mezuzah while they continued their search."

"But," said Rizzo, "I thought the Temple Guard brought the mezuzah to the Bibliotheca de Historique in Suez?"

Outside in the larger cavern, a dog barked. Hassan lifted his head, peering out the entrance to the small chamber as if looking through the thousand years.

"Many generations have killed and pillaged in pursuit of the scroll," said Hassan, "and it changed hands many times. Nearly two hundred years ago, my ancestors of the Temple Guard captured the mezuzah once more and took it to the French, where it was held in great secrecy, where they thought it was safe. But the Prophet's Guard once again learned of its hiding place and raided the Scroll Room, killing many of my brothers. For over one hundred years, we heard nothing of the scroll, though we monitored the movements of the Prophet's Guard closely. It wasn't long before we discovered they no longer possessed the scroll, either. We thought it was lost to us forever."

Rizzo ran his mind through the rest of the story—how Charles Spurgeon purchased the mezuzah and its printed silk cover while wandering the streets of Alexandria; how the Prophet's Guard followed its trail to London; how

Spurgeon dispatched the hunted mezuzah to his friend Louis Klopsch at the Bowery Mission in New York City.

He looked around the nearly empty room, turned to look out the door into the bleak reaches of the cavern. "And you've been living here for a hundred years . . . waiting?"

Hassan shook his head, a smile rising under his mountainous mustache. "No, I'm afraid we're not that gallant. A few months ago we received word that the Prophet's Guard was once again in pursuit of the scroll. A call went out to my brothers of the undefiled Coptic cross, who began to gather here in hope."

An overriding question kept interrupting Rizzo's thoughts.

"But why do you still care? What difference does it make to you, or to the Prophet's Guard, who has the scroll? Not only has the message been deciphered but the Temple has been found and destroyed. What good is the scroll to you? Why . . . why are you here?"

Hassan's smile held no warmth. "It is not only the scroll we seek. In that you are correct. But there is a greater treasure, a treasure of which you have not dreamed." He turned toward the table, lifted one of the books, and pulled it close. "A treasure whose secret may be held within these books."

3

AUGUST 28

7:18 p.m., Rabbi Fineman's home, Jerusalem

"So what were these books?" asked Bohannon. "What was this treasure?"

Rizzo got up off the floor, his legs tight after relaying the story of the Temple Guard. He pushed his shoulders back, stretched his neck, put the much-folded pamphlet into his jacket pocket, and looked at the faces staring back at him.

"The books were incomplete copies of a book called the Aleppo Codex. The rabbi knows more about it than I do, but the Aleppo Codex is supposedly the most accurate representation of the Jewish Torah in existence. Why it's important to us is because of a message that is apparently contained in the margin notations. It's a message that completes a link between the mezuzah, Jeremiah, and Aaron's staff—the shepherd's staff symbol that we found on the mezuzah, in the St. Antony exhibit at the University of Pennsylvania, carved over the doorpost of the library at St. Antony's Monastery, scratched into the wall of Jeremiah's Grotto here in Jerusalem—"

"And on the sarcophagus I found in Jeremiah's tomb in Ireland," reminded Brandon McDonough.

"Right," said Rizzo, "and in Jeremiah's tomb. Think about this. We know Abiathar sent two messages to Meborak in Egypt—that the Third Temple of God had been constructed and hidden under Temple Mount and that the biblical Tent of Meeting was concealed by the prophet Jeremiah in a cave in the Negev Desert. Abiathar knew he would need one of these two objects to restore ritual sacrifice for the Jewish people, return the presence of God into the Temple, and reestablish Israel as the Chosen People. But, in order to complete the circle from ritual sacrifice to the presence of God, Abiathar needed more than just the Temple or the Tent. He needed power . . . the power of God. Either the mercy seat, the symbol of God's presence in the Holy of Holies; or the Ark of the Covenant; or, more importantly, the power that radiated from the Ark, the power that went before Israel into battle, the power that conquered the Promised Land.

"The story written in the margins of the book of Jeremiah was Abiathar's third message: where to find the power.

"The Ark of the Covenant was not powerful in itself. What was inside the Ark provided the power . . . the shepherd's staff . . . the most powerful weapon in the history of the world." He looked across the room to the sofa. "Rabbi, I think you better take it from here."

<hr/>

Bohannon was tired and frustrated, his body sore from the damage inflicted during the chase to save Annie and Kallie from their kidnappers. He wanted answers, not a long-winded lecture. But Rizzo's mention of the world's most powerful weapon grabbed his attention. Fineman wouldn't let it go.

The rabbi spun a tale of the codex, a book written in the tenth century that contained the most accurate compilation of the Tanakh, the twenty-four holy books of the Hebrew Bible. It was captured by the Crusaders, ransomed by Jews in Egypt, hidden for centuries in a cave under the main synagogue in Aleppo, Syria, and returned to Israel 850 years later, in 1958. But, by then, only half remained intact.

While the book's history was interesting, it was the story in the margins of the book of Jeremiah that brought Bohannon fully alert.

Fineman was staring through a darkened window, gazing absently into the Jerusalem night. "Did you know it was Aaron's staff specifically that brought forth six of the ten plagues against Egypt?" He turned from the window and crossed the room to a bookcase, speaking as he searched the shelves. "Moses or Aaron stretched out their hand and used the staff to call down the plagues of blood, frogs, gnats, hail, locusts, and darkness.

"It was Aaron's staff that Moses waved over the Red Sea to part the waters and lead Israel to safety, the staff that called down fire from heaven to destroy the rebellious Hebrews as Israel wandered in the desert for forty years."

Fineman removed an old book from the shelves, carried the book across the room and laid it in Bohannon's hands. "In rabbinical literature, particularly in this Haggadic Modification, it is taught that this staff has been handed down from generation to generation throughout the biblical history of man. That it passed through the hands of Shem, Enoch, Abraham, Isaac, and Jacob. Ancient Jewish authors claim that Joshua used the staff to part the waters of the Jordan River and to hit the walls of Jericho before they came crashing down; that David used it to slay Goliath; that Solomon used it as his scepter when he sat on the throne of Israel; and that when Messiah comes—when the Temple is rebuilt and sacrifice returns to the Temple—Messiah will receive Aaron's staff as his scepter of authority."

"The Temple?" said Bohannon. "We're back to the Temple?"

"Getting pretty interested now?" asked Rizzo, patting Bohannon on his good arm.

There was a glimmer of light flickering at the edges of Rizzo's eyes, a sliver of that impish smile nudging the corners of his mouth. Life, struggling for space. For the first time in days, Bohannon felt hope.

But Fineman's words, about the origins of Aaron's staff, seized Bohannon's attention once again.

"Rabbinical literature asserts that this staff was delivered into the hands of Adam when he was driven out of Paradise. The story is told that Aaron's staff is a fragment of the Tree of the Knowledge of Good and Evil, severed from the tree by God, for man to carry until the Messiah returns."

"You're kidding, right?" Bohannon slid forward in his chair, holding the book in front of him.

"Aaron's staff was part of the Tree of Life?" asked Rodriguez.

"No," said Fineman, returning to the sofa and sitting next to McDonough. "There were two trees in the garden—the Tree of Life and the Tree of the Knowledge of Good and Evil. It was the latter that God commanded Adam and Eve not to eat. When they sinned and God exiled them from the garden, God severed the staff from the tree and gave it to Adam. From there it passed down through the ages in the hands of Israel's leaders."

Bohannon looked at Fineman and McDonough. "Okay. So what does this Aleppo Codex book and Aaron's staff have to do with us?"

"Only half of the original Aleppo Codex remains intact," Fineman said. "Over two hundred pages have either been lost or destroyed, including a segment from the book of Jeremiah. But the Masoretic notes surrounding what remains of the book of Jeremiah tell a story that Jeremiah was the last person known to have possession of the Ark of the Covenant, the Tent of Meeting, and Aaron's staff. We know what happened to the Tent. We don't know what happened to the staff or the Ark."

"Aye, and there's the rub," McDonough cut in. "For a long time, I wondered why there were so many recurring images of a budding shepherd's staff in all the messages and clues left behind by Jeremiah on the mezuzah, in the grotto, and in his tomb. The purpose or meanings of the other symbols—the Tau symbol, and the scorpion and the others—have all fallen into place. But why the shepherd's staff? What did Aaron's budding staff have to do with finding the hidden Temple, or uncovering the burial place of the Tent of Meeting?"

"Which is where we come in," said Rizzo.

"So where . . . I'm sorry," said Bohannon, "but I still don't see how the codex or Aaron's staff is involved in the search for the hidden Temple, or the Tent of Meeting."

Rizzo grabbed a sandwich off the plate on the table and pulled a red-handled Swiss Army knife out of his back pocket. After carefully cutting the sandwich in quarters, he turned to face Bohannon, wiping down the blade with a napkin.

"Before Doc was killed," he said, "he was in his room, talking with the old man we met in the library of St. Antony's Monastery. When I gave up and went to bed, they were going through an old book. The two guys from the Temple Guard who rescued me grabbed that book and brought it with them. It was an incomplete version of the codex. This Aleppo Codex thing is what got Doc killed.

"Here's what I think," said Rizzo, taking a bite and chewing heartily. "Hey . . . Missus Fineman! This is great. Thanks." He turned back to the group. "I think Jeremiah was trying to tell us something. I think there was a third message on the mezuzah, a message from Jeremiah, something about Aaron's staff. That's what the guys with the Temple Guard believe—what they told me the Prophet's Guard believes. That Jeremiah was the last guy with this awesome weapon and that somehow—whether through the scroll, the mezuzah, or the scribblings in the margins of the Aleppo Codex—they will find the clues to reveal what Jeremiah did with the staff, where he hid it. Jeremiah was big into hiding stuff. Why wouldn't he hide the staff, too?"

An audible rustle circulated around the room. Bohannon could feel the excitement level ratcheting up.

"I asked those guys why they didn't reveal the secret before—the secret of the Temple, the secret of the Tent, or now of the Staff," said Rizzo, leaning against the door leading to a small dining area. "They said they knew they had not fully discovered all the secrets. They knew the message that was on the scroll, from when the code breaker came to the monastery, and there appeared to be other clues. Their incomplete copy of the codex told them about the power of Aaron's staff but not what happened to it. That's why they are not giving up, why the Prophet's Guard is still hard on our heels. They want Aaron's staff, and they want its power."

For a heartbeat, silence joined them. Tom was about to raise an objection . . .

"Hang on," said Annie. "I hear the history and I hear the legends. But there is one thought I can't escape. It's God's power. We're not talking about a stick's power, or an Ark's power. We're talking about God's power. And God's not going to allow his power to be used for evil. Who cares if the Prophet's Guard gets the staff? In their hands it will be a dead piece of wood."

"Yes, you are right," said Fineman, inching forward on the sofa. "All power is in the hands of the Creator. Yet, there are many things we humans don't know. None of us can see God's ultimate plan or understand his ultimate will. Isaiah has written, "'For my thoughts are not your thoughts, neither are your ways my ways,' declares the LORD. "As the heavens are higher than the earth, so are my ways higher than your ways and my thoughts than your thoughts.'" Perhaps the staff will have no power in the hands of God's enemies. But then, tell me, why has God brought you here? Why all these clues about Aaron's staff from so many different times, different places, different people, all coming to completion in this group of people? You *have* been called. So, *why* have you been called? What is your role and purpose? What is God's purpose."

He looked around the room and his eyes settled on Bohannon. "We don't know," said Fineman. "We do know that the Prophet's Guard has searched for centuries and risked everything to gain possession of the staff and that their adversaries, the Temple Guard, have fought just as earnestly to protect it. Both groups believe the staff could have power inherent in itself. We don't know."

Fineman turned his attention back to Annie. "This is no coincidence, no accident, that you are here. If it were, your friends would have perished in vain and I don't believe that's true. I believe God's plan is at work in the world and you were enlisted to bring part of that plan to fruition. I don't know why you or what part—and neither do you. I don't know if the staff itself has any power. I don't understand it all. But what am I confident about is that all you have experienced these last several months has been orchestrated by God. And now, I believe God has called you to find Aaron's staff."

"But, wait a minute," said Bohannon, shaking his head. "Sammy just said nobody knows what happened to the staff, right?"

"Well, me bucko, that may no longer be true," said Brandon McDonough. McDonough had the quick wit and the acerbic tongue all so familiar to the Irish, but his edges were softened by a passion to protect the downtrodden and a love of words, art, and beauty. "As me sainted mother used to say, 'If God sends you down a stony path, may he give you strong shoes.' I showed you the rubbing I made from the inscriptions carved into the top of the sarcophagus of Jeremiah's tomb. When I got here, the rabbi and I began sharing information. I believe that the carving on Jeremiah's sarcophagus was his last communication to us. It's a statement about what he did with Aaron's staff—that he brought it home . . . back to the garden of Eden."

The guttural rattle of the air conditioner ricocheted around the room. There was no other sound. Even each person's breathing seemed to be muted.

"Okay, I'll ask," offered Rodriguez, piercing the silence and indicting McDonough's logic with reasonable doubt. "The garden of Eden? I've heard some pretty crazy stuff over the past few months, but this is probably the most bizarre premise any of us have thrown on the table thus far. I'm sorry. This is crazy."

Fineman got up from the sofa and stretched his back. "You are correct, of course," he said. "The existence of the garden? No, it's just not possible."

"There. Thank you, Ronald, for agreeing with—"

"Only one thing. No, three things." Fineman stood in their midst and waited until all eyes were upon him. "First, on the last page of the Aleppo Codex are the names of some of the scribes involved in the project. At the head of those names are two hallmarks: Elijah, the man who was in charge of the final stages of its creation; and his son, who was the man who received the completed Codex—our old friend, Abiathar, head of the Jewish community in Jerusalem. Second, Elijah and Abiathar are direct descendants of Jeremiah the prophet."

"But that's not enough—"

Fineman's raised finger stalled Rodriguez's interruption.

"And the third thing are the notations in the Aleppo Codex around what is now considered the twenty-ninth chapter of Jeremiah—one of those missing from the original in the Israel Museum—where Jeremiah writes a letter to the Jewish exiles in Babylon. Those notes confirm what we know from rabbinical history, that in the year 594 Jeremiah traveled to Babylon at the request of King Nebuchadnezzar. Significantly, both Daniel and Ezekiel were exiles in Babylon at the same time, and Daniel was in charge of all facets of Nebuchadnezzar's government and continued as one of the most powerful men in Babylon during the reigns of the emperors Darius the Mede and Cyrus the Great.

"But this is most important." The rabbi looked around the room like a magician about to pull a rabbit out of a hat. "Following the flood of Noah, Babylon was the first city built by man. It was founded and built by Noah's grandson, Nimrod. The Masoretic notes surrounding Jeremiah twenty-nine attest that Nimrod built Babylon—which literally means 'The Gate of God'—directly over the location of the garden of Eden as a memorial to his family's salvation from the flood. And that Jeremiah brought Aaron's staff with him on his journey to Babylon for the express purpose of returning the staff to the garden of Eden, where it would be safe once again—until Messiah comes."

Tom could hear Mrs. Fineman singing a Hebrew song in the kitchen, the laboring air conditioner syncopating to her voice. One word kept buzzing in his mind. *Again? Are we really going to do this again?*

Across the room, Brandon McDonough held up the heavy paper containing the rubbing. "And I believe that is the same story being confirmed by this carving on the lid of Jeremiah's sarcophagus in Cairn T—that Aaron's staff has been returned to the Tree of the Knowledge of Good and Evil, guarded by archangels of God, in the garden of Eden.

"This staff is the last and only connection to the garden of Eden—Paradise in which man would live a perfect, content life in communion with God. The place of eternal life."

Rizzo pulled himself away from the doorjamb and crossed the room to where McDonough held the long piece of paper. He tapped the symbol of the staff on the drawing. "This is what the Prophet's Guard is hunting. They will stop at nothing to get their hands on it. It's the only way they can guarantee victory for themselves. Right now, they don't know where to look to find it." Rizzo turned back to the room. "How long will that last? And can we risk that they won't figure it out? Padre, why don't you tell them the kicker, what you told me."

Fineman tilted his head and scratched the back of his neck, a squirrely grimace twisting the edges of his mouth. "While there is much we know," he said, choosing his words with care, "there are still many unanswered questions about the staff and its place in prophecy. Many believe that the plagues of Egypt are the same as the plagues that will be released during the Tribulation period. That the plagues of Exodus will be the same as the plagues of Revelation. But, assuming the staff *is* the power of the Ark, will the staff need to be returned to the Ark before the events of Revelation can transpire? Now, with ritual sacrifice having returned to the Temple of God on Mount Zion—albeit only once—it's possible we are in the end of days. The return of Aaron's staff to the Ark of the Covenant could be another of the precursors to the events of Revelation. Or would the resurrection of Aaron's staff itself, whether used for good or evil, be enough to accelerate the end-times prophecy of Scripture?"

Deirdre Rodriguez rose from the futon and stretched her body from her red curls to her toes, attracting attention. "If I was an Islamic militant," she said, her eyes surveying the room, "the last thing in the world I would want is for the power of the Ark to be returned to its home. These Islamists read the Bible, too. They know what is prophesied about them and their future in Revelation. Why would they take any chance that the Bible may be accurate?"

Tom shook his head and stretched his left shoulder, almost as much to sort out his thoughts as to ward off the weight of weariness that hung on his bones more heavily every hour. "So this is why none of us understood what we were involved in? This . . . quest . . . mission . . . call it what you will. This assignment that has us all in its grip and won't let us go. It's much bigger than the mezuzah and the scroll. It's much bigger than anything we could have imagined. These relentless thugs, the Prophet's Guard, and now whoever is behind the Muslim Brotherhood, are not pursuing the Temple under Temple Mount or the Tent of Meeting. They're after Aaron's staff—the true power of the Ark of the Covenant and potentially a weapon of unimaginable force. And we remain square in the path of these murderous fanatics."

Bohannon twisted to the left to look at his wife. "It's still not over."

Annie, who had sat quietly beside Tom through the entire narration, was now on her feet. "Ronald, how do you know all this? You told us that nearly half of the Aleppo Codex was destroyed, including a good bit of the book of Jeremiah. How do you know what was written in the margins of a section that was lost?"

Fineman walked over to Tom and took the old book he had put in Tom's hands earlier. He looked at its cover and hefted its weight. "Because there is a complete copy of the Aleppo Codex in existence. And I've seen it."

The team all blurted out questions at the same time. Fineman held up the book as if trying to fend them off. "Wait . . . wait. It's much too late to go any further. I'm an old man. I need my sleep. So does my wife. Tomorrow. I have something to show you tomorrow."

"Reynolds is coming tomorrow," Annie reminded them. "And for some reason he wants us packed and ready to go home. Rabbi, we'd better make it early."

4

1:04 p.m., Washington, DC

The president and prime minister sat on opposite sides of the world, on either end of an encrypted, secure broadcast, but they were of one mind. Their revenge would leave a sovereign nation's economy a wasteland for generations.

"When someone targets two of the most powerful men in the world for assassination—one in his own home—then that someone needs to pay, and pay dearly," said Eliazar Baruk, the prime minister of Israel.

Jonathan Whitestone felt older than his years. The constant tension of the last few months, the attempted assassination, the gun battle outside Senator Green's home in Virginia, the panic as a human wall of Secret Service agents hustled him into a safe room in the senator's basement, now the final go-order for this destructive and dangerous raid on Iran—all took an exacting toll on his weakening heart. But there was no weakening in his resolve. The Iranian government was out of control, megalomaniac fanatics who had finally moved from empty denials of their nuclear intentions to a clear and present danger to Israel, the United States, even to world peace. Sanctions failed. Direct action was needed. Iran must be stopped. The assassination attempts on Whitestone and Baruk three days earlier interrupted their original timetable, but they still had in motion the means to devastate Iran's economy, its capacity to threaten anyone.

"Some may be more than a trifle suspect when we strike back this quickly," said Whitestone. Bill Cartwright, promoted to national security advisor when Whitestone purged his cabinet members following the near disaster surrounding the Tent of Meeting, was the only eyes and ears who would ever know of this conversation. They were locked into a secure communications room—with no recorders—deep in the bunkers under the White House.

"Let them speculate," Baruk responded. The normally unflappable and dapper prime minister looked as if he hadn't slept. His clothes were rumpled, his eyes heavy. "It took a few days, but there is now enough evidence in place to connect those hooded assassins to the Iranian mullahs."

"Are the teams still in place?"

Baruk pushed back his shoulders as if to wish life into his bones. "Three teams at Abadan, three teams at Bandar-e Abbas—the refineries will be ash in minutes. All the necessary items are in place at Fordow and the national treasury in Tehran. We have even managed access to certain portions of the Natanz facility. Don't worry, Jonathan, in twenty-four hours Iran will cease to be a threat to anyone. And their new president may have trouble keeping his position."

Cartwright leaned in around the president, an old friend, and pressed toward the camera. "Mr. Prime Minister, what about the teams on the ground? What are their chances?"

"The chance of success is high. The chance for survival? The teams at the refineries we hope to pick up by submarine in the gulf. The devices are nearly all in place in Fordow and Natanz. They are set to go off at the same time. Our assets will be far away when the explosions occur. The gold depository . . . well, the gold depository is another story.

"We've been planning for this day for quite some time," said Baruk, "long before you or the international community joined the call for Iran to cease its nuclear operations. We've sabotaged their centrifuges, taken out their scientists, even managed to deliver inferior grade concrete during their building boom at Natanz and Fordow. Those things slowed down the Iranians. But we knew this day was coming, and we've been patient and meticulous in the planning."

Baruk ran a hand through his thick, curling hair. "But the team at the Central Bank . . . we just don't know. It's the most difficult assignment—near impossible to gain access, more difficult to get out. You don't want to make it easy to leave a gold depository, do you? We tried hiding the devices in Iranian gold bars, but we couldn't get the weight right with the bars bored out, and the gold is so dense it would muffle a good bit of the explosive, limit the contamination. There's no place else to hide the devices in the depository.

"This has to be an inside job. The men are all native Iranians . . . long-time employees at the Central Bank. The devices are timed for just after shift-change, when the men are making their pickup inside the vault. There will be no time to escape. They knew the risk, the probable outcome. They volunteered anyway. Anyone inside that vault is a dead man."

Whitestone was well into his first term when he and Cartwright came to the same conclusion: the Iranians were unyielding in their determination to create nuclear weapons. And to use those weapons against Israel. Whitestone was an early champion of economic sanctions, which crippled the government in Tehran and impoverished its people but failed to deter the mullahs in control. It was in Whitestone's second term, when convinced only force would cripple the Iranian rush to nuclear capability, that he and Baruk began laying the groundwork of this most clandestine operation.

American B-2 stealth bombers were already in the air from Incirlik air base, circling over eastern Turkey, waiting for orders if they were needed. Their "bunker buster" bombs would not fully penetrate the facilities at Fordow or Natanz, but if the Israeli devices didn't fire properly, the bombs could destroy some of the underground labs and leave a pile of rubble forty feet thick, enough to hold in any radiation that would be unleashed in the deeper labs.

More importantly, the federal courts and federal banking system were on notice to be prepared for immediate action. What action, they didn't know. But before this day was over, every Iranian asset in the United States would be seized or frozen and evidence presented that Iran was behind the attempted assassinations of both Whitestone and Baruk. With the right amount of pressure, European banks would follow suit. And the Iranian government would be bankrupt.

5

Bohannon needed to clear his head and unburden his heart. His memory was plagued by the dead, and the guilt was so stifling that at times he felt his lungs would simply stop working. Now Rizzo, Fineman, and McDonough had revealed this fantastic story about a book and a staff. It appeared as if Jeremiah—or whoever was at the root of this mystery—wasn't finished with them yet. There was just too much to absorb.

"I'm not waiting for the cab. I'm going to walk back," said Tom as they departed the rabbi's house through the courtyard.

Joe Rodriguez's arm was protectively wrapped around his wife's waist. He looked back over his shoulder at his brother-in-law. "Do you think it's safe?"

"We're not safe in our own beds at home. What difference does it make?"

"Kallie's place is on the other side of town."

"Just a little over a mile as the crow flies. Look, I need the air. I need to think. And I can cut the distance by going through the market."

"Well, I'm no crow," said Rizzo. "I'm taking the cab."

"If you're walking, I'm walking." Annie came up to Bohannon's side. "We can talk on the way—try to make some sense of all this."

Deirdre didn't have the right shoes for walking. Joe pulled her into an embrace, kissed her gently, then separated himself from her, standing sentinel by Fineman's gate. "Don't think I'm going to allow the two of you to wander off by yourselves. People out there still want to do us harm."

Dr. Brandon McDonough was laboring with jet lag, and elected to wait with Sammy and Deirdre for dispatch to send the rare taxi driver who worked on the Sabbath.

Tom, Annie, and Joe crossed Tavon Street to begin their circuitous route through the random streets of Jerusalem to the Bar Lev Road and Kallie's apartment near Ammunition Hill.

From Fineman's house, they had two choices. To make a long loop east, on Bezalel Road, across King George V Street, through the Ben Yehuda pedestrian mall, and down the Jaffa Road to skirt the Old City on the Hatzanhanim to the Bar Lev Road; or to cut through the vast, but closed, Machane Yehuda open market to the Hanevi'im, which would reduce their walking distance by half.

Bohannon moved at a brisk pace, his feet keeping tempo with the thoughts rampaging through his mind. While the theory about the staff was fascinating, the dominant images were snapshots of Kallie Nolan's lifeless body in Sammy Rizzo's arms and of the plain wooden casket, covered with an American flag and mounds of flowers, in the tranquil pathways of the Garden Tomb.

When they reached the Agrippas Road, Annie and Joe came alongside as they waited for a solitary delivery truck to pass, then crossed together, entering the quiet and empty open market, headed northeast.

When two men dressed in black stepped out from the side of a darkened vegetable stall, the veil of grief and guilt was swept from Tom Bohannon's mind.

Bohannon nudged Joe with his elbow, grabbed his wife's hand, and plunged deeper into the shadows and echoes of the empty Machane Yehuda.

"C'mon, this way. Quick."

Running, his damaged shoulder in a sling and his battered body objecting to each stride, Bohannon led them down a narrow alley between the stalls.

"Tom . . . what are . . ." Annie's halting words were trumped by Rodriguez.

"I saw one of them."

Bohannon skidded to a stop as the alley opened to one of the main thoroughfares of the massive, covered market. "There are two more." Breathing deep to slow the flood of adrenaline surging through his veins, Bohannon peeked around the corner of the empty stall in one direction. Rodriguez cast a glance the other way.

"Maybe I'm being paran—"

A man in black appeared at the far end of the aisle. Behind them, from the alley, they heard a whistle.

"Go!"

Rodriguez now in the lead, Bohannon pushed Annie in front of him as they raced across the aisle and dove into the darkness of the alley on the far side. Their pounding feet echoed off the shuttered stalls, but they heard other footsteps, as well.

Bohannon's brother-in-law was pushing on every door he passed, the former basketball player barely breaking stride. When one door on the right yielded, Rodriguez nearly fell through it.

"Here, quick."

With his good arm, Bohannon pulled his wife into the darkness that smelled of fish and salt as Rodriguez pushed the door closed behind them and fumbled for the latch.

"We can't stay—"

Running feet passed the door, Rodriguez's shoulder keeping it firmly closed.

During the day, and well into most evenings, Jerusalem's sprawling Machane Yehuda market and its covered aisles overflowed with bodies jockeying to avoid collisions with each other and bulging bags of produce and fish, bread and cheese that hung from the end of almost every arm. Far removed from sunset, it was now Sabbath in Israel and the shops were long closed, the aisles empty, the shadows silent. The running feet had stopped.

"We need to find a way out," whispered Rodriguez. Pressing the rusted bolt in place, he pulled over a large wooden box that was next to the door and wedged it under the doorknob.

"Over here."

Bohannon turned in the direction of his wife's hushed words. Annie stood leaning against another door in the middle of the back wall of the stall. "It's quiet."

They huddled together around the metal door. "Probably not a main corridor," she whispered.

"We've got to chance it," said Bohannon. "They'll figure out we ducked in somewhere along that alley."

Annie nodded, turned to the metal door, caressed the bolt to slip it out of its latch, and cracked the door open so Bohannon could peek outside. It was a narrow little passage, barely four feet wide, nearly impenetrable because of stacked crates alternating on either side. "Storage space," he whispered. "Looks like it runs behind this entire row of shops."

"A way out?" Annie's lips brushed his ear.

Someone rattled the other door.

Annie was out first, squeezing her body through the tight space as she moved to the left, uphill, away from the alley. Bohannon followed closely behind and, his hand on her arm, edged around Annie in the dark. He was hoping for an escape route and hoping not to knock over any of the assorted boxes standing in precarious rows.

Ahead of him, the darkness lightened, and Bohannon could see the mouth of the passageway. Twenty feet from the end, he stopped behind four barrels that smelled of pickles and pressed his back against the wall as first Annie and then Joe came to his side.

"That should be Jaffa Road," Bohannon whispered, tilting his head to the opening. "If there are pedestrians out, they'll be on Jaffa Road. And there's the tram."

"Not this late," said Joe. "Not on Sabbath."

"Well, it's our best chance to get where there are other people. Look, once we break out of this alley—no matter who's out there—turn right and run down-hill. If we can get to Zion Square, to the bottom of Ben Yehuda, there should be pedestrians down there. Maybe we can find a cop."

Bohannon turned to his left and caught a glimpse of Annie's eyes through the gloom. "Be careful . . . and run fast."

"You run fast." Annie put her hand on the sling cradling Bohannon's dam-aged right arm. "And don't worry about me. I'll probably be there first."

"Well, then tie this thing tighter," he whispered, turning so she could tighten the sling. His right arm secured against his chest, Bohannon cast one more glance toward the end of the passage, then stepped toward the opening. Like a runner during warm-up, Bohannon stretched his long legs with each step, picking up speed. As he reached the end of the passage, he burst into the street, turned hard to the right and started his downhill sprint, hoping all the hours on his bike would now pay off.

And confusion erupted around him.

Shouts ripped the silence—one from up the hill, another from down the hill, a third behind them. Tom glanced back over his shoulder—Annie was a stride behind, closing fast. A black shape emerged from a darkened alcove on the right, intent on intercepting Bohannon. But Joe flashed by on his right, slammed into the man's unprotected side, drove him back into the alcove, and kept running.

Annie and Tom now ran side by side. He prayed something would be open on the King George Road.

There was no stopping now, no holding back against the headlong, down-hill momentum. If these guys had guns, they were dead. But guns weren't the Prophet's Guard's MO. They were looking for hostages, bargaining chips—not bodies.

As they approached the darkened intersection of the King George V Road, a black van pulled across Jaffa Road, a door slid back, and two more black-clad men jumped into the street.

"Right!"

Joe yanked on Bohannon's damaged right arm and dragged him under an arch where they bounced off a stone wall. Tom's vision blurred, he felt sick to his stomach, and his knees started to buckle. "Don't you dare fall down," Joe hissed as he propelled Bohannon down the narrow alley into an open court-yard filled with dozens of cats and an acidic assault of feline urine. They ran headlong down the left side of the courtyard, dodging stray bowls of indeci-pherable matter, and into another alley and across a gravel parking lot before they burst into a small square, thick with hedges and darkened by a copse of huge trees. Joe and Tom collided with a hedge, and were thrown to the ground. Even in his pain-wracked mind, Tom rolled over on his back to get out of Annie's way.

But Annie wasn't there. No one was there except Joe. No one followed. They were alone.

⌁⌁⌁

She knew . . . as soon as the black van entered the intersection, slowing down, all her mother's intuition, all her protective instincts, kicked in. Before the van stopped, Annie Bohannon glimpsed the tiny street opening on her left. She cut left and was sprinting across the four empty lanes of the Jaffa Road when she heard the shout behind her.

"Right!"

Annie's heart jumped into her throat as she plunged into the narrow, cobble-stoned street. She was focused on her feet, determined not to trip on the uneven stones, and frantically trying to remain calm. She was on her own. Tom and Joe were running in the opposite direction. And the men in black were sure to be close behind. No going back now. Escape . . . she had to find a way to escape . . . and to get off these cobblestones.

She turned into a passage barely as wide as her shoulders, ran through somebody's darkened garden, and emerged onto another small street. She darted a look left—and saw the warning sign.

"Please Dress Appropriately in the Me'a She'arim."

Annie had reached the ultra-Orthodox neighborhood of Me'a She'arim, a walled-in community that shunned not only westerners but also other, more secular Jews. Only the ultra-Orthodox with their ironclad dress codes were welcome in this section of Jerusalem. In her form-fitting pants and short-sleeve shirt, Annie realized no door would open to her. But she would be much harder to find in the district's maze of crisscrossing streets. And the men in black wouldn't be welcome here, either.

Moving through the shadows, Annie came even with an opening in the wall on the far side of the street. She looked in both directions. The street was empty and silent. She burst from her hiding place. At the same instant, a black shape launched from a shadowed doorway up the street. She heard the running feet, restrained the urge to look, and raced under the arched opening. Just inside the wall, a tree-shaded lane curved down to the right. Annie ran down the lane, turned left into the next opening, sprinted across a small courtyard, turned into a dark opening, and stopped.

Enough.

Annie quickly looked around. In a darkened corner was a large trash bin. She could hide. But hiding was not in her thoughts.

Instead, Annie pulled the round metal lid from the bin and hefted it in her hands. It would do.

She flattened her back against the wall just inside the passageway, waiting. Part of her felt like a fool. But more of her felt determined, felt empowered. She wasn't going to run anymore.

Soon she heard running feet, the sound growing louder as they approached the entry to the courtyard. Then they stopped.

Her heart beating louder than the man's steps, Annie struggled to control her breathing. But her hands, and her resolve, were steady. She strained her hearing out of the passageway and into the courtyard. No sound . . . but a shadow fell across the face of the passage entrance.

She waited, lifted the metal cover, tightening her grip.

The change from shadow to substance was subtle. Had she not been so keenly concentrated on that dark shape, she could have missed it entirely. But it was substance, not shadow, that leaned into the passageway.

With a force that surprised even her, Annie swung the lid down onto the man's head and shoulders. The thud, and the man's grunt, echoed down the passageway. The kickback from the lid sent shivers of pain through her wrists. But it was the crack of bone that turned her stomach. The man in black lay crumpled at her feet. Annie leaned back against the wall, looked hopefully along the length of the passageway, and was about to drop the lid and run, when she heard the noise. More feet running . . . voices this time. Getting closer.

She pressed back into the dark, felt the lid slip in her perspiring hands. Then realized the black-clad man's body was half in, half out of the passageway entrance.

Annie hesitated. *I should pull him in.* But the running feet were in the courtyard.

She raised the lid once more. *Maybe I'll have one chance. Maybe . . .*

A shadow fell across the motionless body. Something moved. Annie flexed the muscles in her forearms, braced her legs, and shifted her weight to once again bring the lid down with all the force she could summon.

A whisper. "Annie?"

Tom's voice. The metal lid slipped from her grasp as she tried to stop its momentum. It clanged against the far wall.

"Annie!"

He was over the fallen body before she could react, hugged her tight with his one good arm. "Annie."

She pulled back to catch her breath. "How did you find me?"

Joe ducked under the arch and stepped over the body. "Good work. But no time for explanations." Rodriguez put his hands on their shoulders and urged them farther into the passageway. "C'mon. They're still looking. We're not out of this yet."

Running feet echoed off the walls of the passageway as they pressed north, out of the Me'a She'arim. Three pairs of feet, running for safety.

6

Mohsen Kolabi closed the door to the maintenance closet and put his weight behind the overloaded metal cart. On the level below him, the insolent North Korean scientists still worked at a feverish pitch, trying to bring the last centrifuge cascade online. But up here, the level with the testing labs and administrative offices, the lights were dim and the corridors quiet.

Administrators at Fordow didn't work the night shift. Just maintenance men, the many guard posts, and rude North Koreans in lab coats.

The uranium enrichment plant at Fordow, operational in 2011, was a series of chambers on multiple levels, built into the side of a mountain just outside the sacred city of Qom. The facility was comprised of multiple blast-proof doors; hardened, double-concrete ceilings with earth in between; and twenty-centimeter-thick concrete walls. All of it burrowed under the protection of ninety meters of mountain. The Iranians considered it impenetrable.

Mohsen Kolabi had this level and one more to finish. He strained to move the cart across the uneven, gray-painted concrete floor, down the long, gray-painted corridor between the darkened labs. He came up to where he had left his stepladder propped against a wall, just under the huge photo of the supreme leader, Ayatollah Ali Ghorbani.

He opened the opposite door and flipped the light switch for the enrichment lab. The white, plastic sensor on his lapel came to life, pulsing with sickly, yellow light. Warning. Kolabi carried his stepladder into the lab, then went back and hauled the heavy cart into the room, closing the door and closing his mind to the meaning of the warning light. It was too late for him, anyway. His cousin, the doctor, told him there was no hope. But his family? His six children? Who would take care of them?

So Kolabi was here in the enrichment lab, working another man's shift for the extra money—and for the opportunity. The opportunity to take care of his family for the rest of their lives.

Scrawny thin, five feet tall, wisps of salt-and-pepper hair on his round head, Kolabi opened his stepladder under one of the old light fixtures, climbed the rungs with his tool pouch hanging from his right hip, and disconnected the old fixture. The new ones were better. They provided more light with less electricity, yes. But they did not have a very long life span. Not much longer than his.

He could have worn the lead tunic under his clothes as the Jew had instructed. But his cousin, the doctor, had informed Kolabi that other radiation had already taken its toll. He felt his way down the ladder, turned to the cart and removed one of the new fixtures from its packing. The fixtures were manufactured in Russia. How the Israelis intercepted the shipment, he didn't know. He did know these fixtures were heavy. The explosives, detonators, and radioactive cores—small but powerfully destructive—added extra pounds.

Kolabi hefted the fixture onto his right shoulder and struggled back up the ladder. One more level. He must finish. Tonight damnation would erupt throughout the Fordow facility. All four levels with the new, lethal light fixtures—three above and one below the banks of centrifuges on the level under his feet—would be destroyed. The Jew believed the reinforced concrete floors would breach under the power of the massed explosives and the resulting radioactive contamination would make Fordow uninhabitable for the life of a thousand suns.

He would be here to feel the eruptions, to watch the panic. Perhaps he would die tonight instead of in a few months, weeks. But he must be here. The ayatollahs were no fools. Anyone who did not report for duty or who left early would be suspect. They and their families would be judged without trial. If mercy reigned, those poor souls would spend the rest of their lives wasting away in a labor camp. But mercy seldom reigned. No. Kolabi would be here, protecting his family. Their future was also protected, the funds provided by the Jewish agent safely and secretly invested in a chain of food markets.

Kolabi completed installation of the light fixture, checked the wiring once more, flipped the switch to activate the timing mechanism, and hobbled back down the ladder.

One more level. Freedom called him on.

11:10 p.m., Abadan Oil Refinery, Iran

Colonel Avi Migdol released the four clamps holding the back panel in place. He pushed on the lever and cracked the panel open. Light filtered into the belly of the oil tanker truck, barely denting the impenetrable blackness they suffered through for the last several hours. The hazmat suits were claustrophobic, holding temperature and moisture against their skin, soaking their uniforms. But their respirators kept them alive during the long drive from Turkey, and the suits protected them from the burns their skin would otherwise suffer from the oil residue that coated the tanker's interior.

Colonel Migdol had twenty soldiers at his back. Sabra, mostly. Field-tested, hardened, combat veterans. More importantly, for all of these men this assignment was a calling, a moment of divine intervention, an answer to whispered prayers, and the chance to avenge a lost loved one. They may die. But they would not fail.

Peeking through the opening in the rear panel of the oil tanker, Migdol watched the outside darkness for moving shadows. He slipped the visored hood from his head, held his breath, and listened. Still and quiet. He held up a gloved hand, keeping his soldiers in place. The colonel eased the back panel farther away from the truck's body, just enough that he could slip through the opening and drop to the ground outside.

In the shadow of the tanker's belly, Migdol's black hazmat suit was invisible. In a squat, he pulled apart the strips of Velcro, and the top of the suit dropped around his waist. The Uzi was strapped against the black Kevlar vest on his chest. For a heartbeat, Migdol held the machine gun close to his heart, remembering why he was here. Then he turned its barrel away from him. Time to go to work.

He swung the Uzi in an arc as he quickly swept a three-sixty circle. Nothing moved. Off in the distance, the sounds of the refinery were distinct, carrying through the silence. The overnight shift, which kept the refinery's pumps moving, the kilns and crackers cooking up more Iranian crude, paid no attention to the tanker trucks parked in this far corner of the refinery.

Migdol motioned with his left hand, his eyes ever searching the distance where he knew the workers toiled. Two soft, barely discernible thuds. He edged along the length of the tanker's body as more soldiers dropped out of the belly of the beast. Certain of his cover, Migdol pulled apart the Velcro on the legs of the hazmat suit. He was free. Soggy, but free. He moved farther along the bottom of the truck until he came to the end of the shadow. He knew his men were behind him. It was his duty to lead.

The colonel and his men were alike in many ways—born in Israel, career soldiers in a nation of reservists, trained in stealth and destruction. And each had a personal reason to exact this revenge. Migdol's mother and father were on the way to market, on the Egged bus to Kiryat Shmona. The bombers came across the border from Lebanon, with Russian weapons and Iranian explosives. Twenty-eight were murdered—blown apart or burned, no one knew for sure. There wasn't much left to determine how they died.

Avi Migdol joined the army that day. He trained and waited. He fought in Lebanon and waited some more. Tonight the waiting ended.

Far southwest of Tehran, along the northern edge of the Persian Gulf and hard against the border with Iraq, the oil refinery of Abadan was Iran's largest. Over 320 thousand barrels of oil flowed through its pipes and onto tankers every day, only half the amount that it did before the West imposed economic sanctions on the recalcitrant regime. Even so, the oil pumped from Abadan and Iran's five other major refineries was the life's blood of the staggering Iranian economy. Without the income from this oil, even more Iranians would suffer. Without the hope that someday these refineries would return to full capacity, the new president, Hussein Rakhsha, and the supreme leader, Ayatollah Ali Ghorbani, would be in greater risk of losing their death grip of fear and reprisal. Iran could fall.

Migdol's team of demolition experts carried a new generation of phosphorous chemical explosive, like napalm on steroids. Once the charges were in place, the sequential detonations would build, one upon the other, sucking the Iranian oil into an expanding conflagration that would melt the metal catwalks and leave the refinery a molten, smoking disaster. Another assault group was at Bandar-e Abbas tonight, the nation's third-largest refinery, with the same mission. They were the only two refineries on the Iranian coast, but accounted for more than forty percent of the nation's oil capacity. Two parts of what Migdol surmised was a larger plan—a plan to destroy the government of Iran and its capacity to pose a significant threat to Israel.

Tonight was the night he had waited for.

Migdol knew exactly where he was in the refinery. He had memorized every pathway, tank farm, and building. He scanned the landscape, the narrow spires of metal chimneys and ductwork illuminated by hundreds of bare red and white lightbulbs, large pipes sidling through the spires and catwalks like an endless, giant gray snake. No alarm—no running feet, no shouting voices. Only the rhythmic clanging of chains holding the tanker ships at anchor in the gulf.

He pointed right, and seven soldiers padded off, skirting the pools of white and red light, moving to the refinery's edge nearest to the harbor. Migdol watched their backs and tilted his head to the left. Seven more melted into the night toward the far eastern fences—three demo experts, two snipers, and two gunners lugging Dror .30-caliber machine guns. That team needed to be on time. They were the fuse lighting off the chain reaction of the explosives that would rip through the refinery from east to west. If they acted too soon, some of his men would get fried before they could escape. Too late, and all of them would be exposed in their most vulnerable position.

Migdol patted his chest, pointed forward, left the lee of the truck body, and double-timed it across a gravel berm that fell away into a dirt ditch, part of the dugout surrounding one of the refinery's storage tanks. A forest of these circular tanks ran along the northern flank of the refinery, each one surrounded by a square, sunken, earthen enclosure. Blowing the storage tanks would ignite an incredible fire, but the Israeli commandos were there to destroy the refinery, not simply to torch fuel tanks. Migdol and his men used these massive foxholes as cover, scrambling up and down the sloped sides as they made their way to the center of the refinery, where the cracking ovens were located—also where most of the refinery's workforce concentrated.

The demolitions experts in Migdol's squad worked deftly. The explosive devices were contained in metal tubes that looked like, and were painted the same color as, the piping system running through the refinery. Moving through the labyrinth of pipes, the bombers would stop at a selected location, twist off the top of the device, and trigger a cellular receiver. Replacing the top, they attached the devices in a way that looked perfectly at home in the refinery's maze.

With precision, the squad moved laterally, section by section, toward the western edge of the refinery and the gulf, snipers in advance on point and trailing behind to watch their backs. The heavy guns, with Migdol in the middle, were ready to unleash a lethal downpour on any Iranian who ventured near. The refinery crew was skeleton at best. No one noticed their passage.

Migdol caught a faint wisp of seawater through the pervasive oil smell as he stopped his team's progress. The first squad, their explosives set, should be in the section to his west, some guarding the perimeter, some releasing the inflatables they hoped would take them to rendezvous with the still-submerged submarine lurking in the shallows of the Strait of Hormuz, far off the shipping lanes. Migdol clicked the small, square microphone attached to his shoulder. One click came back, a pause, then another click. His men stood as a unit and moved rapidly through the shadows, joining the first squad just short of the ring road that surrounded the refinery.

All fourteen men were pressed down against an embankment, some looking forward, some looking back for the third and last squad—and any unwelcome intruders. Colonel Migdol trained his eyes on the light-and-shadow maze of pipes and catwalks, willing his mind to wait patiently for the click from the mic on his left shoulder.

Gunfire erupted at almost the same instant as floodlights sprang to life throughout the refinery, bathing the facility in a garish, faux daylight. Migdol heard the keystroke rattle of the Uzis and the deeper thump of the .30-caliber Dror machine guns, but the sound of his squad's defense was nearly obliterated by a growing crescendo of automatic weapons, the sound of battle rolling through the metal thicket—and coming closer.

"Boats." The first team scrambled up the embankment toward the shore while Migdol's team ran toward the refinery compound, ten meters to a ditch and a berm, where they spread out and lay in the dark. Migdol stole a glance at his watch and then looked back into the tangle of pipes. Fewer bursts came from the Uzis. The fighting distant enough that Migdol could not see the gunfire flashes through the brightness of the light flooding the refinery. The sounds seemed to be fading.

He's leading them away. Good man. Good men.

Migdol looked to the soldier on his right, held up his right fist with his thumb sticking up, and then pushed his thumb down as if pressing on a button. Or a trigger. For a long moment, the soldier held Migdol's gaze, then turned to the touch pad in his hand. He tapped the screen. Tapped once again. Looked up at his colonel. Migdol nodded. The soldier tapped the screen for the third time, and the first of the explosions sent a ball of fire into the sky. Like an insatiable beast gathering strength and size, an all-engulfing tide of riotous flames and blinding, white light began flowing in Migdol's direction. "Out. Now."

The colonel lingered a moment, looking into the growing conflagration, turned to follow his men, and saw the demo expert to his right with his head down, the touch pad still in his hand. Migdol scrambled to his right, grabbed the soldier's shirt, and pulled him off the ground. "Out!"

There was no more gunfire. Only the birth of a second sun, this one on earth, and coming closer. Migdol and the soldier ran hard, crossed the ring road, and sidled through the cuts in the perimeter fence. They sprinted across a gravel flat and each rolled over the gunwale into one of the waiting inflatables, which immediately pushed out into the dark waters of the Persian Gulf.

Seated in the back of the inflatable, his legs up on the gunwale, Colonel Avi Migdol could feel the heat on his cheeks as the enormous fireball spread across the refinery and consumed everything in its path. Like his own, the eyes of any defender would be riveted to the conflagration. But Migdol didn't see the flames, only the faces of the seven soldiers being incinerated.

11:10 p.m., Iran Central Bank, Tehran

They didn't know each other. Once a month they were on the same shift. Different parts of the Central Bank of Iran complex, but the same late-night shift.

Aheem Tavana got an email the day before from the national library. A book he reserved was available. There was no book. Tavana, a bachelor, didn't sleep that night.

Famid Hussein received the coded text message before he left for work that evening. Aliyia and the children were out shopping. There was no one to wish goodbye.

Bezalel Khomeini, of the famous name, was sitting in the Chitgar Forest Park by the Kan River—one of the few places in Tehran where a person could escape some of the city's deadly air pollution—when he was Tweeted. Six words from his fictitious uncle, Rashid. He picked up the towel upon which he rested, rolled it up under his arm, and started walking to the bus stop.

The plan was simple, though none of them knew it. Each individual's responsibilities were segmented, compartmentalized, and independent of the others. There were six in all—three coming in to work for the night shift; three finishing their shifts. Each of the six carried a piece of a device. Tavana, the building's messenger, was the collector. As he made his rounds of the Central Bank—the huge, blue cube in the heart of Tehran—Tavana distributed and gathered up parcels and interoffice messages. Of all the parcels he collected that night, Tavana had four small packages tucked inside a canvas bag on a shelf under his cart. Those packages would not be offered up to the Revolutionary Guard for inspection.

A secret member of the Green Wave party, the rabidly defiant opposition to the mullah's iron-fisted rule of Iran, Tavana came up alongside Famid Hussein's desk in the engraving department, ready to receive the last piece.

Hussein held out a small, padded envelope. "For the finishing department," he said, and turned abruptly back to his work.

⸺∿∾⸺

Only the most observant would notice how Hussein's gaze locked momentarily with Tavana's before the messenger moved on without a word of response. Marwan Alami was that kind of observer. She leaned back from her desk to watch Tavana as he made his way through the engraving department, buried deep in the underground levels of the Central Bank building. Tavana's eyes locked with no others. She picked up her telephone while keeping both Hussein and Tavana in view. "The messenger, Tavana. And the engraver, Famid Hussein. Something is not right there. They look suspicious."

Alami listened for a moment. "Yes, my instincts are usually correct. Watch them."

⸺∿∾⸺

Tavana sorted the messages and parcels and left them on the counter in the mailroom for their regular inspection. Nothing moved through the Central Bank building, even a piece of paper, without members of the Revolutionary Guard conducting a thorough inspection. He picked up his lunch bucket and turned to the door. The way was blocked by two members of the guard.

"Leaving before the inspection, Tavana?" asked the captain.

"I have medicine." Tavana tried to remain calm. "It's time, and I must eat food before taking the medicine. Everything is waiting for you." Tavana turned to the side and gestured to the table.

"Give me your bucket," said the captain.

Tavana forced himself to look at the captain as he handed over the round, metal bucket with the tight-fitting lid.

The captain twisted open the lid and rummaged through the contents of the bucket. He pulled out a round piece of flat bread. "Tear it."

Tavana took the flat piece of bread and tore it in two.

"Again."

The captain held out his hand for the four pieces of bread. He looked at the edges, pulled the bread apart. Then threw the pieces back into the bucket and pushed on the lid.

"Your lunch," said the captain, holding out the bucket toward Tavana. "I should make you stay with us, but go. Get your food. Take your medicine."

Tavana took his lunch bucket, edged past the other guardsman at the door, and turned down the hall toward the lunchroom. The packages, including his, were now taped to his thighs, under his blousy, linen trousers. His knees shook, but only he was aware.

Halfway down the hall, Tavana turned and entered the men's restroom. He went into the very last stall—the one just under the security camera in the corner, the one with the dead spot below—lowered his trousers, and sat on the toilet lid. With the precise gentleness of a surgeon, Tavana removed each of the objects from his thighs. Blocked from the eye of the camera, he assembled two devices from the six pieces. He took his lunch from the bucket, replaced the lunch with the two devices, and then flushed his lunch down the toilet.

Tavana washed his hands, left the men's room, and continued down the hallway to the lunch room. Entering the room, he went to the coffee maker, poured himself a small cup of thick, sweet, strong coffee and retreated to a table in the corner. He sat there, sipping his coffee, until his lunch break concluded, then gathered up his bucket and walked back to the mailroom. The captain and his aide were just leaving.

"Feeling better, Tavana?" The captain's question felt more like an accusation.

"Not yet, sir. But I will."

"Then get on with your work."

He watched the two guardsmen saunter down the hall, and then turned into his mailroom. Loading his cart with the inspected deliveries, Tavana took the two devices out of his lunch bucket and stuffed them into the canvas bag below the shelf. He pushed the cart out of the mailroom, his calm exterior belying the riot of fear and dread that raced through his veins.

Marwan Alami waited patiently for the messenger's return. Famid Hussein worked diligently at his engraving table. He hadn't moved from his space all night. But Tavana was scheduled for his final pickup, and it wouldn't be too long. Alami walked to the water cooler and filled a cup. She turned, with a full view of Hussein's face, as Tavana entered the engraving department. Alami glanced over her shoulder. The two guardsmen stood outside the enclosure to the engraving department. All that was needed was a wave of her hand.

Tavana pushed his cart down the main aisle of the department, scanning out-boxes left and right for any waiting delivery. He passed Hussein's desk without a pause. Hussein never took his eyes off the engraving tool and the design he was cutting into the metal. Alami waited a heartbeat. Nothing changed. She shook her head. Disappointed, but undeterred, she went back to her desk.

❧

Tavana did not have access to the vaults, to the stacked bars of gold stamped with the seal of Iran and piled in pyramids a meter and a half high. But he didn't need to get to the vaults. The anteroom of the guards would suit well enough.

From the neat stacks on top of his cart, Tavana handed the sealed message to the guard at the desk and backed his cart into the anteroom so he could return up the hallway from which he came . . . the same maneuver he made every day. But this time he stopped. He knelt on the floor and bent down to tie the laces on his boots. While on the floor, Tavana took the two assembled devices from the canvas sack. There were two large, heavy, reinforced carts lined up in the anteroom, sitting to Tavana's right. With a minimum of movement, using the powerful magnets on the side of the device, Tavana attached one device under the bottom shelf, into the corner of the heavy frame of one cart. With the guard intently studying his work schedule for the next two weeks, Tavana swiftly deposited the other device in the same location on the second cart— under the shelf, a heavy rim surrounding it, invisible to anyone who didn't look from underneath.

It took less than two breaths, and Tavana was back on his feet. He pushed his delivery cart out into the hallway, past the guard at the desk. "Salaam." Without a reply from the guard, Tavana retraced his steps down the hallway. Before him, the captain of the guard and his aide rounded a corner and walked in his direction.

"Ah, Tavana, we've been looking for you," said the captain. The two guards-men flanked Tavana, standing on either side of his cart. "Come with us." The aide took possession of the cart. "There is someone who wants to speak with you . . . and with a friend of yours, I believe."

Tavana bowed his head as he followed the captain down the hall. But his spirit danced with his ancestors. *You are too late. I have repaid my debt. You took my family from me. Now I take something valuable from you.*

⁓⁓⁓⁓

Like most clandestine Israeli actions against its enemies, this one unfolded meticulously. While the two main Iranian refineries were melting into puddles from the searing heat of the phosphorous bombs, the explosions began echoing through Fordow. Up and down the corridors on three levels, light fixtures were exploding and spewing a radioactive cloud that would condemn the facility to a toxic future for the next thousand years. A radioactive poison that sentenced more than half of Iran's nuclear scientists and technicians—along with a large number of North Koreans—to a lingering, excruciating death.

Meanwhile, 130 kilometers to the north, in the capital of Tehran, a squad of six heavily armed Revolutionary Guards—the vault's doors closed and locked—escorted four white-gloved soldiers as they loaded gold bars onto two reinforced carts. The pyramids of gold were dwindling, tangible evidence of the efficacy of the Western world's economic stranglehold against Iran. The crew took the last few bars from a now nonexistent pyramid and had to move on to another to fulfill their quota.

"Let's move, Achmed," said the squad leader. "Hurry, or my dinner will be cold, my wife will be angry, and my mistress will be bored."

"These are the last ones," said Achmed. "And we're ten minutes ahead of schedule."

Ten minutes was enough to change everything—to ruin Mossad's meticu-lous planning. The explosive devices that Tavana had secured to the underbel-lies of the reinforced carts were timed to go off in the middle of the regular pickup, while they were still loading the gold and the vault was sealed shut. But these men were early. And now they were leaving the vault.

The two Revolutionary Guard soldiers in front of Achmed had just opened the outer vault door and the second cart was being pushed through the open inner vault door when the twin explosions ripped through the vault's entrance. The explosive force, though powerful, was not designed to damage the massive, hardened steel doors. Rather, the devices were shaped, the explosives arranged to forcibly disseminate their contaminating payloads.

Achmed, five of the soldiers, and the other cart pusher lay in mounds of shredded flesh, bleeding and stone dead. The sixth soldier, blown back behind one of the vault doors, watched as silvery clouds of glittering dust jetted across the expanse of the gold depository, colliding with the far-opposite wall and spreading in all directions. Like lethal snow, the glittering dust slowly turned yellow as it settled to the floor, coating the pyramids of gold bars and everything else inside the vault. Including the soldier.

It was an unfortunate circumstance for the Israelis, as well as the Iranians, that both vault doors were open when the explosions occurred. Because the second shaped charge blasted another silvery cloud of glittering dust in the opposite direction—out the door of the vault, into the guard rooms and the staging area. The silver comet crashed into the far wall and was fractured in a thousand directions. The particles, yellowing in the atmosphere, wormed through any opening. Large clouds of them were sucked into the Central Bank's ventilation system. Within seconds, the dust was spreading throughout the complex. Worse for nearby residents of Tehran, the building's venting spewed a continuous stream of yellowing dust into the atmosphere, a lethal combination of strontium-90, cesium-137 and carbon-14: a "bone seeker" that would quickly claim the life of any human who inhaled it or upon whom it fell. Dust that would entomb Iran's gold reserves for two hundred lifetimes. Dust that was, at that moment, raining radioactive devastation over several kilometers of the heavily populated, congested, and smog-choked streets of central Tehran.

Ten minutes too early. And ten thousand would die.

7

3:14 p.m., New York City

The metal-on-metal screech set Connor Bohannon's teeth on edge, matching his nerves. He stood in the sprawling NYPD evidence warehouse in the Hell's Kitchen neighborhood of midtown Manhattan, watching two officers maneuver the Jaws of Life—used for prying open the crushed metal of crashed automobiles—into place again. Slowly they forced apart the heavy doors of the antique metal safe that had once resided in the hidden office of Lewis Klopsch, the first president of the Bowery Mission in New York City.

This safe, damaged when agents of the Prophet's Guard hijacked it in transit nearly three weeks earlier, had been the hiding place for hundreds of ancient books, pamphlets, and documents collected by Klopsch during his years leading the Bowery Mission, the third-oldest rescue mission in the United States. Through benefactors like the Reverend Charles Spurgeon and his world-traveling colleagues, Klopsch had amassed a treasure of ancient documents. When Klopsch's office was discovered, hidden for over one hundred years behind the organ pipes of the Bowery Mission chapel, and its massive safe opened, Connor's dad, Tom Bohannon, found an artifact that changed many lives—and altered the course of history.

An etched brass mezuzah sealed with wax was pulled from one of three small drawers in the middle of the safe. It was this mezuzah and the scroll it contained, written in the extinct language of Demotic—the third language on the Rosetta Stone—that sent Tom and his companions on two deadly quests.

First, the team decoded the intricate cipher on the scroll. The message was a letter, which claimed that one thousand years earlier, the Jewish community of

Jerusalem, led by the priest Abiathar, had built and hidden the Third Temple of God under Jerusalem's Temple Mount. As the team searched for clues, agents of the Prophet's Guard—protectors of the scroll and its secrets for nearly eight hundred years—stalked the group's members, attempting to regain possession of the mezuzah and its scroll at any cost.

Over the next several months, the scroll and mezuzah divulged not only the message of the Temple's existence but also clues that led to the unearthing of the biblical Tent of Meeting, Abiathar's plan B to restore ritual sacrifice to Temple Mount. Each driven by their own motivation and coerced into action by the US government, the team eventually recovered the Tent of Meeting. But not without cost. Three friends had given their lives. And ultimately, both the hidden Temple—by earthquake—and the Tent of Meeting—by heavenly fire—were engulfed during the partial destruction of Temple Mount itself.

But one thing was never discovered.

What was in the two locked drawers of Klopsch's safe that flanked the one which once held the mezuzah and scroll that began their saga?

With New York City Police Commissioner Rory O'Neill on his left, Bowery Mission CFO Stew Manthey on his right, and a pencil-thin locksmith with fidgety hands standing to the side, Connor watched as the two police officers pulled the doors farther askew, providing the group with their first look at the insides of the massive safe built by Diebold Safe & Lock in 1896—eight feet wide, five feet high, and three feet deep.

"There's nothing left inside, as far as we know," said Manthey. Closing fast on retirement, his bushy, gray-flecked beard making him look more like Grizzly Adams than a buttoned-down CFO, Manthey was more than Tom Bohannon's co-worker. Through the ten years they had worked closely together, Manthey had become Tom's mentor and friend. "We sold a lot of the books and documents at auction and used the money to renovate the Bowery Mission Women's Center. But we could never figure out the secret to the two drawers—forgot about them, actually, once all the excitement started."

"I'm glad you asked me to come," Connor said to Stew.

"I can't take credit for that. It was the commissioner's idea. He figured one of the Bohannon's should be here when we tried to get those drawers open."

"Helping out like this is the least I can do," said Connor. "I'm just glad Dad's all right." He cast a sideways glance toward the CFO. "Stew . . . do you have any idea how Mr. Rizzo is doing?"

Manthey put his hand on Connor's shoulder. "I don't know. But I'm sure they're fine. And, who knows? This could be another windfall for the mission."

Connor stepped closer to the safe, listing to the right after the hijacked truck carrying it crashed on the FDR Parkway. "Or it could be more trouble."

The locksmith looked over in the commissioner's direction, and O'Neill gave the man a nod. As the locksmith stepped inside the open doors, he set the satchel on the floor and ran his fingers over the two locked drawers.

Manthey leaned in toward Connor. "You needn't worry, Connor. Your mom and dad are in good hands. God hasn't taken them this far to abandon them now."

An image flashed through Connor's mind: the last time he and his dad had a serious conversation. He winced at the memory of the bitter words that flowed out of his frustration and toward his father. Caught up in the current rush of excitement and apprehension, he understood more . . . empathized more. And he hoped for the opportunity to apologize to the man he respected so much.

Connor was twenty-two, two years younger than his sister, Caitlin, and recently graduated from Penn State with a teaching degree, though uncertain if that was the right course for his life. In many ways—good and bad—much like his father, Connor had the same long and lean physique, the same copper-colored hair and beard, the same blue eyes and welcoming smile as Tom. Though five inches taller than Tom and his hair and beard significantly longer than his dad's, both Connor and his father had the same innate curiosity, attention to detail, and easy-going personality that won friends and earned respect throughout their lives. Everybody liked Connor Bohannon.

But today he wasn't too happy with himself. One of the last times he spoke with his dad before the team's second trip to the Middle East, Connor had unleashed sharp words for his father, challenging Tom for getting involved once again in the danger and intrigue of the mezuzah and scroll.

Now with his mother and father in Israel and both Doc and Kallie dead, Connor regretted his anger and the words that caused his dad unnecessary anguish.

And . . . who knew what was coming?

"Whoa, baby . . ."

The words and low whistle that came from inside the safe broke into Connor's thoughts.

The locksmith, keys and pins and other gadgets sprouting from between the fingers of each hand, stepped back a pace from the three drawers—the one in the middle about twice the width of those flanking it. He cocked his head to the side, as if examining the drawers from a different angle would make them open magically. Then he threw all the keys and pins into a bin by his feet and started rummaging through the satchel.

"Somebody's been pretty serious here, bub," the locksmith said in the general vicinity of Commissioner O'Neill, his accent betraying his Brooklyn heritage. "The old locks, you know, like this baby in the middle . . . those suckers were pulled out of these side drawers and replaced with random-width lever locks." He turned toward O'Neill. "You got me?" He returned to his intense dig into the satchel. "You guys could have been working on these monsters for a year and gotten zippo! Ah . . . that's what I need."

The locksmith stood up, his knees cracking in the process, and he scratched the top of his head with a long, stiletto-thin metal rod with nubs in an irregular pattern around its miniscule circumference. He approached the drawers again, holding the metal rod with the deftness of a surgeon about to invade a body.

"The English dreamed up this nightmare—crazy Brits—and, when it was perfected, it drove every locksmith bonkers. But that was over a hundred years ago." He spoke as he inserted the rod into the lock with purpose and care. "The gizmo's got six spring-loaded levers, each a random width to give you an even bigger headache. Try to pick it or use the wrong key, and it triggers a jamming mechanism. Then your goose is really cooked . . . oh, that's one. It's like looking for your socks in the dark, trying to find a pair that . . . oh, that's another."

The locksmith probed and twisted. "Hey, Mack, you want I should open 'em both at the same time?"

Connor looked at Manthey, who shrugged his shoulders.

"Don't wait," said Connor. "Get one open. I want to see what's inside."

"You got it."

One more twist of the rod and Connor could hear the snap.

"Holy cow. We got a winner." The locksmith withdrew the rod and stepped away. "Okay, gents. Who wants to do the honors?"

Manthey gave Connor's elbow a little nudge. "Go on, this has more meaning for you and your family than anyone."

Drawing in a deep breath, Connor stepped in beside the locksmith, placed his fingers around the brass knob at the center of the drawer front . . . and pulled. Like a whisper carried on a breeze, the drawer slid open. Connor looked down and saw a round, metal container, about four inches across.

He picked it up. The metal was a dull gray, heavy, thick, and smooth but soft—malleable—to the touch. The container was about two inches deep, and clearly came apart in the middle, a top and bottom half. Connor put one hand on top and the other on the bottom and flexed his arms to . . .

"You might want to think about that for a minute."

Rory O'Neill was close behind, looking over Connor's shoulder. "Just test it, gently, to see if it's loose or sealed."

Connor relaxed his hands, then tried to twist the top and bottom halves. Nothing. The pieces didn't budge.

"Okay . . . they're either stuck because the container is so old," said the commissioner, "or they're stuck because somebody wanted to keep them sealed. And there could be some risk in getting them open."

"Look. It's your nickel," offered the locksmith. "But let me open the other drawer and see what's waiting for you behind door number two. Maybe it will help you to decide what to do with this thing."

The three men stepped aside so the locksmith could get to his work. Connor handed the metal case to the commissioner.

"Looks like pewter to me," said O'Neill. "Heavy, but soft. You can bend pewter out of shape pretty easily."

Manthey held out his hand, took the container from O'Neill, held it in front of his face, and shook it back and forth. "Something inside," he said. "Almost as big as the container, seems like. There's not much movement."

"There must be some significance to what's in this container," said Connor, taking it from Manthey and hefting it in his hand. "It was in the drawer right next to the mezuzah, so you'd think . . ."

"Well, that's a jab in the eye with a stick."

They turned from the metal container and looked toward the safe. The locksmith held up a brittle-looking, yellowed envelope in front of him, pinching a small spot on a corner between his thumb and forefinger. "I don't think this is gonna rock your socks unless it's how-to instructions for your hermetically sealed container."

Connor felt a quickening in his heart, a heightening of awareness . . . an adrenaline rush moving up from his chest into his head.

He took the envelope from the locksmith—it was square, about four inches on a side. There was no address or any other writing. On the back, over the flap, was a dollop of red wax, stamped in the middle with a stylized K.

Connor accepted the offered penknife from the locksmith, slit through the wax seal, and turned up the flap. He pulled two pages of heavy, beige-colored paper from the envelope. The rush in his veins increasing, Connor scanned the two handwritten pages as fast as his eyes could move and his brain could work.

"Oh . . . this is not good."

Connor began to read:

> *My dear Louis,*
>
> *I dare not send this package to you with the same courier. The contents of this package and the one brought to you earlier by Captain Paradis must never be joined again. I have dispatched this parcel to you via Newfoundland, a longer voyage, in the most sincere hope that both time and distance will confound the intentions of those adversaries who would spare no level of violence to secure these artifacts once more.*
>
> *What you have in your hands today portends the existence of the greatest biblical treasure ever unearthed—a claim of such stunning magnitude that it strains credulity. Yet if true and wielded by those with a thirst for conquest—and my friend, the explorer Sir Charles Warren, assures me he has seen evidence of its veracity—it also presents the greatest possible threat to our civilization and our future.*
>
> *Were it not for the persistence and skill of Edward Elgar, the astounding claims contained on the mezuzah's scroll would remain irrevocably hidden and the full scope of Abiathar's secret message would be lost forever. Perhaps that result would have been preferable. But now that these secret ciphers are revealed, one day someone may have the courage, or the urgency, to determine their accuracy. As for now, I must enlist your faithful assistance once more. Hide these discs where they cannot be found and where their secret cannot be revealed. I earnestly pray that no harm befall you or your family in this sacred duty.*
>
> *Though loath to engage in speculative hyperbole, I bequeath to*

you this most solemn warning. Hide these sprockets well. Within
them resides the key to a destructive power not witnessed on this
earth for nearly three thousand years.

   If Armageddon is to come in our lifetime, Louis, then let it
not be by our hands, but by God's.

   May the peace and protection of our Lord and Savior be
always with you,

   Charles

"We better call Dad," said Connor.

8

11:35 p.m., Jerusalem

"Who should we call first—the cops, Reynolds, or Connor?" asked Rizzo.

They were back in the relative safety of Kallie Nolan's apartment, the story of their pursuit by the Prophet's Guard still hanging in the air. Annie sat on the sofa between Deidre and Rizzo.

Connor's voicemail message on Kallie's phone sounded urgent. Tom ran his left hand through his hair, trying once again to navigate toward the right decision.

He didn't need to.

"Call Sam Reynolds . . . let him know what happened." Annie's voice was firm, calm, determined. "Then we can talk to Connor while Reynolds figures out what he should do."

It hadn't taken them long to cover the half-mile distance from the northern edge of the Me'a She'arim to Kallie's apartment near Ammunition Hill, off the Bar Lev Road. Tom, Annie, and Joe were physically and emotionally exhausted—but surprisingly alert—following the attack of the Prophet's Guard on their walk from Rabbi Fineman's home. They had quickly filled in the details for Rizzo, Deidre, and McDonough.

Tom picked up the phone and called Reynolds. He told Reynolds of their race through the empty streets of Jerusalem, the Prophet's Guard assassins at their heels, then listened for a few minutes. "Twenty minutes? Make it thirty. We may need a few minutes here to get our heads screwed on straight. Thanks."

He replaced the receiver and stood next to the table. "He wants us to meet him at the National Police headquarters. It's just across the Bar Lev Road on

72

Clermont, near the Regency Hotel. It'll only take a few minutes to walk there. Let's call Connor."

"That letter sounds a lot like the first one we found, the one that was with the mezuzah," said his father's voice, coming through the speaker of the telephone. "There's no date or anything on it?"

Connor Bohannon sat in the commander's office inside the evidence warehouse in New York City, with Police Commissioner O'Neill and Stew Manthey listening in. "No, Dad . . . nothing on the envelope, either, except for a wax seal stamped with Klopsch's *K*. Mr. Manthey says the handwriting looks the same as the handwriting in the first letter. But there was a notation at the bottom of the letter, in pencil and clearly added later. The words were printed, but old fashioned, like calligraphy. Somebody took some time with that notation. It said, 'Protected by the Prodigal Son's father.'"

"Well, the letter's gotta be from Spurgeon, I don't have any doubt about that," said Tom. "He sent Klopsch another package and another warning."

"But, Dad, what could . . . I mean, this sounds worse than the first one." Connor looked over at Rory O'Neill.

"Tom," said O'Neill, "I remember saying this to you once before, but this thing isn't over yet. You've wondered why the Prophet's Guard was still making your life a nightmare. There's still more unfolding here."

"You don't know the half of it," said Bohannon. "And Spurgeon's letter just confirms what we've concluded . . . that we never really understood what we were drawn into. Rory, the clues, the threats, the deaths, this whole thing hasn't been simply about a Temple or about the Tent. All the signs we have here lead us to believe—as far as the Prophet's Guard is concerned—they've been chasing something they believe was the most powerful weapon on earth. If they find it, they hope it will be the most powerful weapon again. This isn't about the past, Rory, it's about the future."

Annie jumped in as his dad took a breath. "A future that's getting real short," she said, her voice coming closer to the phone's microphone. "The clock started ticking in 1948 when Israel was created as a state, but it started running a lot faster when the priests held ritual sacrifice in the hidden Temple four months ago, before the earthquake. I don't want to come off sounding like a whacko, but we seem to be living out the final acts of some end-time prophecy movie."

"And now Spurgeon's newest letter seems to confirm what we've feared," said Tom. "Armageddon . . . he really wrote *Armageddon*?"

Silence came across the telephone from Jerusalem. Stew Manthey reached across and put his hand on Connor's arm, giving it a squeeze. "It's okay," he whispered.

"Hey, Connor, tell us about the discs you found." Connor could barely hear the other voices in the background as they talked among themselves, but his uncle Joe's voice was loud and clear.

"Well, that's just it," said Connor, "there was only one disc in the container. And I don't think there was room for another. The disc was wrapped tightly in a well-oiled rag, even after all this time. The container was sealed with what looked like wax, but it was a firm seal, no gaps. And with the rag and the disc, it pretty much filled the whole container. I don't see how two could fit—"

"Connor"—Tom's voice interrupted with both the command of a leader and the demand of a father—"tell me. What does this disc look like?"

Connor Bohannon hefted the leather disc in his hand and then held it up. "Well, it's strange looking," he said. "It's got symbols on it, cut into the surface. And there are . . ."

"Eight arms and eight slots," said Tom, half the world away. "Four of the arms have tabs on the end and four have grooves. And the symbols are on both sides of the disc."

Connor looked at the disc in his hand, exactly as his dad described it. "How did you know that?"

"Because I know where the other disc is," said Bohannon. "Inside the drawer in my desk in the Bowery Mission."

11:55 p.m., Jerusalem

For a few moments, the group continued to sit around the dining-room table, staring at the telephone perched in the middle. Rizzo broke the thoughtful silence.

"So what is this disc you so conveniently have stashed in your office?" he asked Tom. "What are the symbols that are marked on it?"

"I don't know," said Bohannon, scratching his head. "To be honest, I can't remember what's on it. We found it while we were involved in the historic renovations we did at the Mission. Hey"—a light went off in Bohannon's head like a candle in a cave—"the Prodigal Son." He turned and pointed at Rizzo. "That's where it was . . . under the Prodigal Son's father."

Rizzo patted Tom's right forearm, again held tight by the sling. "That's okay, Tom. We know how tired you must be. But I think all this excitement has turned your brain to oatmeal cookies. What are you talking about?"

"I like oatmeal cookies . . . with raisins." In spite of the circumstances, his weariness, and the pain in his shoulder, Bohannon could not resist a big smile at the inquisitor to his left. "Listen, when we were doing the renovations, we wanted to clean and repair the huge Tiffany window at the front of the Mission. So we had specialists come in and take the window apart, piece by piece. The window must be twelve, fifteen feet wide and eight, ten feet high. The only way they could move it was in sections. See, the window is a progression of scenes from the Prodigal Son story in the Bible. After they got the sections out, the workers were cleaning up the window frame. Right under the section that contained the Prodigal Son's father, they found an old, round, pewter container and inside, wrapped in an oiled cloth, was this leather disc with arms and notches. We didn't know what it was, but Tim Maybry, the construction manager, convinced me to keep it. He said it looked like it belonged to something. So I threw it into the drawer in my desk—and haven't thought about it since."

"I wouldn't be surprised if the symbols on the discs were Demotic, same as the scroll," Annie said from across the table. "Did they look like Demotic?"

"Honestly, I can't remember, except that they looked strange at the time. But this is amazing," Tom said. "We just keep finding more and more pieces of this puzzle. Where's it going to end?"

6:03 p.m., New York City

Manthey unlocked the door to Tom Bohannon's office in the Bowery Mission and led Tom's son to the far side of the well-used wooden desk.

"He said bottom left drawer—in a box in the back."

Halfway out, the drawer stuck, then gave way to a greater tug. Manthey reached inside and pulled out a gray metal box and put it on the desktop. Inside was a gray, pewter container like the one they retrieved from Klopsch's safe. "Here, you open it."

Connor gripped the container with both hands and twisted—but this one opened easily. The wax seal was already broken. Inside, wrapped in a well-oiled cloth, sat another of the strangely shaped leather discs with the symbols worked into the surface. Connor Bohannon held the leather disc in front of him. Though similar, this disc varied from the first disc they found in one significant aspect: this one had holes in it, four holes spaced evenly in the sections formed between the arms.

Connor pulled the other container from his backpack and laid both discs on top of Bohannon's desk. He took his fingers and ran them over the arms of the second disc. "They have the same arms, the same tabs and grooves," said Connor, "but they're different."

"Opposite," said Manthey. He reached down, took the two discs, and joined them together. The arms fit perfectly together, tabs on one slipping into the grooves on the other.

Stew Manthey sat in Tom's guest chair and regarded the joined discs. "Do you ever work on Sudoku puzzles?" he asked. "Different numbers going together in different ways on different lines." He separated the two discs and turned one in his hand so that the opposite side was facing the other disc. "Sudoku is the first thing I thought of when I looked at these two discs side by side." He brought the two opposite sides together and, once again, they fit perfectly.

"Wait," said Connor, "how did you do that?"

Manthey took the two discs apart again and turned them over in his hands. "You see how the tabs and the grooves are arranged? It's designed so that whatever way you put them together, a tab lines up with a groove. Here, look at this."

The two discs lay flat in his palms. "The right disc has side *A* facing us, and on its opposite side is side *B*. The one on the left, the one with the holes, has side *C* facing us, and the opposite side is side *D*. You can join *A* to *C*," he said, putting the two discs together, "or"—he turned the one in his right palm over—"you can join *B* to *C*. The same is true for the other side. You can join *A* to *D* or *B* to *D*, and they all fit together perfectly."

Taking the joined discs from Manthey, Connor hefted them in his hand. "Okay, that's cool. But there's got to be a point. Everything we've learned about this mezuzah and scroll is that very little, or nothing, is there by chance. The symbols on the outside of these things—*sprockets* Spurgeon called them—must have some meaning. So when you fit the discs together and the symbols read in order, there must be a reason . . . And what are the holes for?" asked Connor.

Reaching over, Manthey took back the joined disc and separated it once more. "Look at it this way. These sprockets fit together perfectly to form one unit, and they fit together perfectly in four different combinations. But take this solid one," he said, holding it up. "If both discs were solid, the same, then even when you joined the sprockets together, you would be looking at the same symbols you were looking at when they were separated. See what I mean." Manthey joined the leather discs together, showed Connor the sides facing out, then joined them together again, changing sides. "See, you're just looking at the face of each sprocket. You could do that whether they were joined together or apart."

"So if these sprockets have some message to deliver, what would be the point of having such a unique method for joining them together in four different combinations if all you come up with is the same thing you were looking at when they were separate? I think the holes don't determine what symbols we look at, but how we look at them—the sequence."

"Wouldn't there be an almost endless number of combinations?" Connor asked.

"A lot, but not endless," said Manthey. "You can only join tab to groove, not tab to tab, so that limits the number of sequences. So this one with the holes, let's call it the *guide*, reveals four symbols on one side of the solid sprocket. But if you rotate the guide sprocket like this"—Manthey detached the discs and rotated the guide ninety degrees—"then the holes reveal four different symbols."

Connor leaned back in his father's chair, entwined his fingers behind his head, and searched the ceiling for inspiration. "Yeah, but when you rotate the guide sprocket," he said, "then the holes end up displaying all eight of the symbols on that one face—four the first way and then the other four when you rotate the guide ninety degrees. What good does that do?"

"Because depending where you start, you get different sequences. Here, look."

Manthey held up the solid sprocket in front of Connor. "See this symbol"—he rotated the sprocket—"and this one? Those two symbols both appear twice on this side. And look. The same thing is true on the other side. The same two symbols repeated the same way on the other side."

"Okay . . . so?"

"Why was it so important for Charles Spurgeon and Louis Klopsch to separate these sprockets, to keep them apart from the mezuzah and scroll? Why did Klopsch find it necessary to hide the sprockets separately? One he hid inside the window frame during the construction of the Bowery Mission.

Spurgeon warned Klopsch the message on these sprockets could be the cause of Armageddon. So there is a message here. And if there is a message, then the message has to begin somewhere and end somewhere. And if there is a message, then the message is meant to be read. So we have two problems—"

"Only two?"

"Okay, two for now. Here's what I think. If we're going to decipher this message, we need to understand how the message is sequenced—where do we start? Is it one message, four messages, or some different combination? Once we figure out the sequence, the second problem is to decipher what the symbols are telling us."

"How do we find out?"

"I don't know," said Manthey, sitting back away from the wooden desk. "But my gut tells me that finding an answer will be even more complex than you can imagine."

6:55 p.m., Washington, DC

"Baruk won't pick up," said Cartwright, as he cradled the phone. "Either he has his hands full over there, or he can't bear having to face you . . . or both."

President Whitestone paced in front of the *Resolute* desk in the Oval Office. Normally photogenic, his face was drawn and tight this evening and testified to the long, sleepless night he had endured in the residence, waiting for word from his national security advisor.

"We should be celebrating today," Whitestone mumbled as he crossed the presidential seal in the blue carpet. "Whatever nuclear threat the Iranians embodied yesterday has vanished. Their government is impoverished and impotent. With the evidence of Iran's complicity in the assassination attempts, we had the world behind us, cooperating, when we froze their foreign assets. Now . . ."

Whitestone stopped in midcourse and turned to his right, lifting his open palms in a gesture of helplessness.

Cartwright put down the phone. "The reports are only getting worse." Cartwright hated delivering more bad news to the president. He'd known Whitestone long enough, had been his accountability partner for so many years, that he could see the toll the office and now this disaster were taking on the president's health.

"The Israeli scientists are very clever," said Cartwright, perching himself on the arm of one of the twin sofas. "The radioactive gas released into the Central Bank's gold depository was a combination of strontium-90, cesium-137, and carbon-14."

"That's a strange combination," said the president, turning in Cartwright's direction. "Strontium-90 and cesium-137 are two of the main components of nuclear fallout. They would quickly contaminate the gold on their own. Why the carbon?"

"To make it last longer," Cartwright replied. "Strontium and cesium have half-lives of about thirty years, which would have ruined that gold for a generation. But the carbon-14 has a half-life of over five thousand years. The Israelis wanted to be sure that gold was never used again. But it also made the radioactive cloud far more lethal.

"For those who are close to the Central Bank building—which is located in the middle of downtown Tehran—the strontium will penetrate their bodies. It's called a 'bone seeker,' like calcium. The cesium will burn the skin and eyes. Their bodies will suffer from radiation sickness both inside and out. Death will come quickly. But for those farther away . . . well this gas is very light, so it spreads far. Once inhaled, the carbon settles in the body and stays there. You've been given a death sentence and don't even know it. This cloud has been dispersed over a large area. The numbers of dead are multiplying every minute—those who will die this week and those who carry death and will never see another birthday."

Whitestone seemed to falter, a slight waver through his shoulders. He took his right hand and ran it through his graying hair. "God help us . . . God help them."

"But we have other problems," said Cartwright. "There is no actionable evidence as to who was behind the attacks on Fordow and Natanz, the oil complexes, or the Central Bank. Yet, as expected, both the Arab world and the rest of the world community are heaping scalding criticism on the Israeli government . . . on Baruk in particular. Consensus is no other nation has the motive or the means to carry out a raid like this. Hezbollah rockets are falling on northern Israeli villages as we speak. Palestinian leaders are calling for another intifada. The only break we have is that Syria is incapacitated and Egypt remains politically impotent, or there might already be tanks rolling across Israeli borders."

"Our turn comes next," said Whitestone, a somber resolution in his voice. "Perhaps we would have avoided the outcry had it just been the raids. But this nuclear contamination changes everything. We won't escape being tarred with the same brush."

Compassion and concern guiding his actions, Cartwright eased over to the president, took his arm, and led him to one of the sofas in the middle of the room. He captured Whitestone's gaze and held it.

"Jon, your statement this afternoon was perfect. Your rationale for freezing Iranian assets resonated, at least for the moment. And your criticism of the recklessness of the raid on the Central Bank building and the tragedy of its outcome hit the right chord. But you're right; we're most likely going to take some kind of hit. The repercussions from this radioactive disaster are going to last a long time. And if our complicity with Baruk ever comes to light—well, I don't want to think about what that will mean to our position in the world, or the ability of this administration to function. We would face Congressional hearings that would tie us up for years. This is why I think you need to get on TV and make another statement."

Whitestone's face registered the question he asked. "And say what?"

"I think we've got to condemn the Israelis . . . throw them under the bus."

"What? Baruk would be apoplectic. He would probably leak evidence that we were involved. And we were involved, Bill. How can we jump on the Israelis now?"

Seated beside the president, Cartwright sorted through the options once again and came back to the same conclusion.

"We knew these days would come, Jon . . . and we decided to pay the price to occupy this office. Days when our decisions would be politically correct, but perhaps not morally palatable—days when we would make choices that were expedient, self-serving. I thank God those days have been few. But you didn't win all those elections by being mister nice-guy. And you didn't keep your seat in the Senate by being soft or politically naïve.

"If we don't condemn Baruk and his government, we'll be standing alone," said Cartwright. "And the rest of the world will wonder why we've remained silent while thousands of innocent people die excruciating deaths. But if we condemn the use of nuclear weapons as irresponsible, while empathizing with Israel's valid fear of a nuclear Iran, I think we'll be seen as reasonable and moderate. If I know Baruk, he would do the same thing if the roles were reversed."

Jonathan Whitestone settled back into the folds of the sofa. His eyes were shut, his head shaking back and forth. Cartwright witnessed the inner struggle, but there was little more he could do. This was the president's decision.

"Nine tonight?" asked the president.

"Eight thirty. Viewership will be higher."

9

594 BC

Jeremiah stood before the king, Zedekiah, in the Great Hall of the Sanhedrin. King in name only. Zedekiah was a puppet, with the Babylonian emperor Nebuchadnezzar pulling the strings. Though a reluctant and rebellious puppet, Zedekiah still retained the power of Nebuchadnezzar's support and a small troop of Chaldean soldiers to add authority to his words.

"Because the emperor—our great king Nebuchadnezzar, may Baal exalt his name—requests your presence," said Zedekiah, his whispered homage dripping with sarcasm. "That is reason enough. Your caravan will be escorted for safety. The emperor has ordered that you travel in every possible comfort. A wagon is being readied for you, covered to keep out the sun, cushioned to protect your bones. And your servant, Baruch, may accompany you, of course."

After the eleven-year reign of his persecutor Jehoiakim, who regularly had Jeremiah beaten and restrained in the stocks at the Gate of Benjamin because of the prophet's words of rebuke and coming judgment, Jeremiah's health, in his body and his spirit, had been gradually restored over the last two years. Zedekiah was a weak and vacillating ruler, but his periods of support, though unpredictable, afforded Jeremiah the freedom to worship the one, true God of Israel and the time to regain his health as a free man. So he knew what he risked.

"And what if I don't wish to embark on this journey? If I refuse?"

Zedekiah rose from the throne that was much too big for him and came to the edge of the steps that led up to his raised platform. He carried his weakness in every bone and sinew of his body, in every reflection of his mind. Sickly thin, a head shorter than Jeremiah, Zedekiah looked even smaller because he was incapable of standing straight. He moved with the slither of decay, not actually walking, but dragging himself along the floor. His black hair was long, oiled, and as rank as his breath. Zedekiah appeared to be rotting away from within, the victim of his own excess. Even his voice left a veneer of mold on the air carrying his words.

"You will go because the emperor decrees it," Zedekiah whispered. "Or you will go because, if you don't, I will take Baruch's head, boil it in a pot, and feed the broth to your sister's children."

———～～～———

Baruch paced manically through the small room. "But we must remove the Ark and the Tent while there is still time, before Zedekiah rebels openly against Babylon," he pleaded. "Now, with only a few soldiers defending him and his mind as weak as his body."

"Where would we go? Where would we hide something as precious as the Ark and as huge as the Tent?" Jeremiah sipped the water in his cup. It was sweet, recently drawn from the pool at Siloam. "We can't carry the Ark across the desert to Babylon, or to Egypt. The Tent is safe. The Ark is where it should be, resting near the Holy of Holies. It is in God's hands and will remain safe. But the power . . . the power we must protect."

Baruch dropped onto a sack of lentils as if he'd been felled by a blow to the head. The storeroom was small. Dust rose and mingled with the smell of cinnamon and rosemary. They were hidden in the inner confines of the house Jeremiah was given when he was in the king's good graces. A comfortable house, but too close to the palace, too close to the puppet and his spies. Only in this small, windowless room did Jeremiah and Baruch speak of the things that were most precious to them.

"Listen to me, my son," said Jeremiah, taking Baruch's hand in his. "Our choices are very limited and our time is very short. We must decide what is the most important thing to protect, the most important thing to save—because we certainly cannot protect or save all that is our responsibility."

Baruch's eyes filled with tears, and his mouth opened in protest, but no sound emerged.

"Can you and I carry the Tent?" asked Jeremiah. "Even with those who would be willing to help, how much could we carry? How far could we go?

"No, my son, we must save the one thing that could unleash evil on the world. Imagine the disaster that would befall our people if the staff of God ever got into hands of those who work evil."

Baruch jumped to his feet. "But how can you believe that taking the staff to Babylon is safer than leaving it here, buried deep under Mount Zion?" he cried. "We must keep the staff out of the hands of Nebuchadnezzar. Why carry it into his lap?"

"Because in his lap is where it belongs," said Jeremiah. "Come here, my son. Listen to what I must tell you."

Like a man on his way to prison, Baruch dragged himself to Jeremiah's side and sat on his right, on the same, small, wooden bench.

"It is not at the command of Nebuchadnezzar that we will make this journey," he said, "but at the request of Daniel, the prophet of God and favored of Nebuchadnezzar. Years ago, when I prophesied that Nebuchadnezzar would vanquish both the Assyrians and the Egyptians and rule as emperor of the East, it gained me great favor with the king, just as Daniel now has great favor. We must use that favor to our advantage.

"Do you know that Babylon was the first city built by men after the great flood of Noah? The city was founded over fifty-five hundred years ago by Nimrod, grandson of Noah and son of Ham. In the Assyrian way of speech, Babylon means 'Gate of God.' It was Daniel, who in his studies of the ancient Assyrian documents discovered that just as Jerusalem is built on holy ground, Babylon was also built on holy ground.

"Noah shared the great secret with his son Ham, who entrusted it to Nimrod, a mighty warrior. That under the sand, dirt, and silt piled into the region by the great flood was the birthplace of man. Nimrod built the first city of man over the birthplace of man, the site of the garden of Eden."

Baruch put his hands on his head as if to hold his skull together. His eyes were almost as wide as his mouth. "No, father . . . I can hear no more," Baruch pleaded. "I am a weak man. Please, do not leave such a great secret in my keeping."

Jeremiah nodded his wrinkled head. "Yes, it has been a great secret. But now that secret is at risk. Yet it is a risk that gives us opportunity.

"A great tower has been a significant part of Babylon from its earliest days. But just any tower is not good enough for Nebuchadnezzar, emperor of the

East. He has decreed a tower be built that would reach the heavens, so high that he can commune with his god, Marduk.

"Daniel, his chancellor, has been placed in charge of constructing this tower," said Jeremiah. "But to build the tower, the Babylonians need also to dig a foundation—a foundation almost as deep as the tower is tall. And Nebuchadnezzar has ordered that his tower be built over what he believes is the exact location of the garden. For Nimrod, building his city on that spot was an act of worship. For the Babylonians, building the tower over that spot is intended to keep the garden hidden.

"There is only one place in this world where Aaron's staff will be safe," said Jeremiah. "Only one place where it will truly be hidden. And that is returning the staff to its home, allowing God to restore the staff to the Tree of the Knowledge of Good and Evil from where it came. Once the staff becomes part of the tree, who can tell where one begins and the other ends? And what better guardians than the warrior angels of God?

"But you are right, Baruch. We cannot allow the Ark and the Tent to remain here, under the Temple. This fool of a king will one day soon defy Nebuchadnezzar, and the emperor will come. And when he comes again, Nebuchadnezzar will destroy everything—even what we believe is forever hidden beneath the Temple. When we return, we will move the Ark. And over time, piece by piece, we will move the Tent. But my son, the staff comes with us. The Ark is only a box without the staff."

He rose from the bench and crossed the room to a small, dust-covered table, two chairs flanking its sides. "Have you been to the tanner?"

Baruch reached into the cloth bag he had flung onto a bin of barley flour and pulled out a round piece of leather, about two centimeters thick, with a hole in the middle. "It took him quite some time to design the pieces." The leather disc was about ten centimeters across. Baruch separated it into two parts. "He is very ingenious. See, the sides go together the same, no matter how you turn them, and they fit together tightly." He handed the disc to Jeremiah.

"Well done," said Jeremiah. "Now we must prepare."

Babylon

"You honor me with your presence."

Jeremiah continued to bow from his shoulders—the best his aging bones would allow after such a long journey—and spoke to the glittering mosaic floor. "How could my presence honor the emperor of the world?"

"Stand. Bring him a chair," Nebuchadnezzar ordered.

Jeremiah straightened and sat when the chair was placed behind him. He looked up at the throne platform. Nebuchadnezzar was a bear of a man. Taller and broader than any in the royal court, he looked more like a warrior than a king. He wore a long, sleeveless, embroidered tunic, the fringe along its hem brushing across the floor. His arms bore the muscles of a blacksmith—hard, thick, and massive. Wide, gold bands were wrapped around his biceps and forearms, as if trying to constrain his strength. His hair was dark and braided, laddered down his back to his waist. His beard, full, dark, and dense, was braided and oiled so that it jutted out from his chin like a massive spearhead.

For all Nebuchadnezzar's imposing stature and royal bearing, what struck Jeremiah as most surprising was the gentleness of the emperor's face. Jeremiah had expected a hardened, scarred countenance, the face of a ruthless conqueror, an executioner of men, women, and children. But this face revealed no murderer, no butcher. His eyes were gentle and bright, a warm smile lifting his cheeks. There was exuberance, an overflowing of goodwill toward Jeremiah that stunned the prophet.

"You look at me as if I were some apparition of the gods," said Nebuchadnezzar, his voice as smooth and polished as his throne. "What did you expect to see, my friend?"

Jeremiah looked steadily into Nebuchadnezzar's eyes. "My enemy," he said.

The laugh that erupted from the king rocked his shoulders and threw back his head. "Your enemy? How could that be possible?" he asked. "You yourself prophesied about my conquests, about my kingdom, about my power. You are my prophet, my herald to your God who gives me favor. How could I ever have anything but gratitude toward you, my friend? I brought you here to honor you, not to harm you."

Jeremiah was about to chastise this king for his irreverence toward the Almighty when bells chimed from his left. He and others in the throne room turned toward the sound.

He came into the royal courts with the bearing, the raiment, and the attendants of a prince. But unlike the king, Daniel's hair was golden and long, a single braid resting between his shoulder blades. He walked strong and straight, a man of power and influence without fear or deference in the king's presence.

THE ALEPPO CODE   87

Daniel was shorter than Jeremiah anticipated, but he carried his body erect and the glow that shone from his face was supernatural.

"Welcome, Counselor," said Nebuchadnezzar. Daniel bowed at the waist and held his open palms extended at his sides—the Eastern custom that paid homage to the ruler, offered the back of the neck as a symbol of fealty and surrender, and showed that a man's hands were empty of any weapon. "Here," Nebuchadnezzar said, pointing in Jeremiah's direction "is your countryman, Jeremiah the prophet. Take him into your home and care for his needs. He is my guest so that I may thank him for the honor he prophesied over me."

Nebuchadnezzar turned to Jeremiah. "Rest, my friend. It's been a long journey. Tomorrow, if you feel refreshed, perhaps then we can speak of your God and his vision for Babylon."

Jeremiah, still dizzied by the genuine warmth of the king's words and drained of strength by the arduous journey through the Persian desert, inclined his aged head toward the king and turned toward the man whose invitation was the true reason he had spent the last several weeks in such unbearable heat. It was Daniel who begged Jeremiah to make the trip to Babylon—and to bring with him his most precious cargo. "Counselor, I am in your hands."

⸺∿⤳⸺

They sat under a sycamore tree, on a platform raised over the Euphrates River, Baruch at his left side. The combination of shade from the tree and the breeze that flowed as languidly as the river itself brought comfort, rejuvenating Jeremiah just as much as his conversation with these two men so close to his heart.

"I've been here since Nebuchadnezzar's first conquest of Israel, eleven years ago." Daniel held a small, horsehair fan in his left hand, absently brushing the flies from his head as he spoke of his experience as an exile from Jerusalem. "But it's only by the power of God that I've survived this long, and by his grace that I've achieved such favor in the eyes of the king. Both my years and my position have been used by God to bring about his plan."

Daniel was a young man compared to Jeremiah, nearly thirty years his junior. And even though Daniel showed deference to his guest, there was a relaxed, unaffected manner with which Daniel accepted authority and command.

"Once I rose in rank among the wise men of the king, one of the elders told me the story of the city, and I realized that Babylon was built on holy ground. For the Babylonians, it was a secret they wanted to bury. When the emperor selected me to oversee construction of the great tower, I knew this was our chance to protect the power of the staff forever.

"The king was not satisfied with the six towers that currently exist. Nebuchadnezzar wanted a monument to his power, to his empire. He wanted a tower that would reach to the heavens. Now it is almost finished, and the king shall have his moment with God. But he is not aware that the God he will meet is not the God he expects . . . the Holy One of Israel who had his hand on this project from the beginning. Nebuchadnezzar called upon me when his architects and builders claimed the tower he envisioned could not be built. I told him he needed a foundation dug deeply into the ground, on the same scale as the tower above. So he set me to the task.

"In the middle of the month of Nissan, my workers reached the planned depth of the foundation and finished its walls. But while the work began on the tower above, my helpers cut a door in the side of the foundation at its base, and my diggers kept digging. As Nebuchadnezzar built his stairway up to heaven, we dug a shaft deeper and deeper, extending the stairway far into the bowels of the earth.

"We had thousands of Israelites as slave labor. While many workers were forced to build the tower above, just as many continued to dig the foundation below. It was a simple task to divert hundreds of men into the enormous foundation pit each day. A stone stairway was built into the side of the foundation, leading down into the depths. Few of the Babylonian guards ventured into the pit. They were afraid. Those of our captors who did enter, spoke in hushed tones about the very real presence they felt the deeper they went under the surface."

Jeremiah's head was bobbing in agreement. "Just as the presence dwells under Mount Zion. Do you believe the king is aware of where he is building?"

Daniel's fan swished away the flies that gathered unnoticed in Jeremiah's beard. "Nebuchadnezzar never does anything without being fully aware. Nebuchadnezzar's library has several histories that recount the story of Noah and Nimrod—and the garden. For Nebuchadnezzar, building his tower over the location where his wise men believe the garden rests is an act of defiance. His intention is to bury the garden even farther, not only under thousands of years of dirt, but under his great tower, as well."

"But why did you send for me?" asked Jeremiah. "My bones ache when I remain still. Baruch could have carried the staff to you."

Daniel stopped waving the fan and turned to face Jeremiah directly. "Because to enter the garden, we must deal with the angelic ones. And they have called for you, specifically."

"You've been there?" Jeremiah was astonished—and frightened.

"Only once," said Daniel. "And that was enough."

10

ONE YEAR EARLIER

Daniel came out of the sunshine and into the great hall at the base of the tower, his eyes momentarily blinded by the darkness within. But he didn't slow his pace. He walked swiftly across the floor still covered with construction dust to the far side, his eyes picking out the door as they adjusted to the deep shade inside the hall. Several hundred meters above him, the king's masons were still laying stone as the tower inched ever skyward. But Daniel's destination was down, not up.

"They discovered the cavern this morning and sent me to find you," said the foreman, a small, burly man who scrambled in Daniel's wake. "As soon as the first shovel broke through, I ordered the men to stop."

The stone steps were slick as Daniel hurried deeper into the foundation's depths. "Any sense of how large the cavern may be?"

Ezekiel struggled to keep up behind him, but Daniel was fully focused on the stairs as they materialized in the torchlight.

"No, but it must be very large," said the foreman. "A wind blew through the hole when it was first opened, and it was still blowing when I came to fetch you."

They reached the base of the foundation and turned back, into the space under the stairs. Hidden by the near-complete darkness under the stairs, Daniel's fingers felt for the edge of a second door, ran down its length, and found the handle. The moist air inside the door brought a chill to Daniel's skin. Ezekiel lit a second torch just inside the door, and they pushed on.

Here, there were no stairs, only a narrow shaft with a rugged floor the width of two men's shoulders and a roof arched just above their heads. Not for the first time, Daniel thanked his God for the thick clay of the Euphrates flood plain. Hard to dig, heavy to carry, but solid and nearly as safe as stone. Moisture formed on the sides of the shaft, reminding them of the great river nearby but, thus far, the clay held itself in place.

Mindful of the slick surface beneath his feet, Daniel hurried nonetheless. Each of his workers brought sand into the shaft each day, covering the floor, but it was seldom enough.

The shaft was not long, but it curved to the east, away from the river. He could see the faint flicker of light reflected off the walls and, as they moved closer, could hear the sound of muted voices. The last piles of clay dug by the workers had been carried up the shaft, giving Daniel a clear path.

The three teams—one to dig, one to rest, and one to carry the debris up the shaft to the great foundation room—lined up along the walls. Their leader stood at the end of the shaft. His shirt was off, and his left hand held in place some cloth stuffed into a hole about shoulder high.

"What have you found?"

"We are not certain, Chancellor, but there is something beyond here that gives the feeling of being vast and empty. Perhaps the cavern we seek?"

Daniel planted his feet firmly on the base of the shaft and faced the foreman. "Break it down."

———❧———

Daniel lifted the hem of his richly embroidered robe and, leaning on the arm of the foreman, climbed over the pile of clay blocking the hole they had broken through to gain access to the chamber.

The light of his torch was swallowed up by darkness.

"Bring more torches," shouted the foreman. The workers passed burning torches in through the opening to Daniel and the foreman, and then followed, one by one, each carrying a torch in his hand and the fear of God on his face.

With each additional torch that entered, the twilight at the edge of their vision expanded a little farther. Thirty men were now inside. Daniel could see that the space had a vaulted ceiling, but he could determine neither the top of the ceiling nor the far side of the cavern.

To the right and the left, the walls arced away into the distance, the opening crescent of what promised to be a mammoth expanse.

Ezekiel was at Daniel's side. "Can you feel the presence?"

Daniel glanced up. "Do you hear the voice?"

"What?"

"Spread out," said Daniel, sweeping his hand toward the darkness. "Spread out around the edges. Perhaps we can determine its shape, its size."

As if each step would be their last, reciting the Shema Yisrael as they inched along, the three dozen workers gradually brought more light into the space. Now Daniel could see that the cave was not man-made at all. Its sides were rough, irregular, laced with cracks and fissures where clay had broken away, some significant flows of clay, now hardened, that invaded the underground hall in long, ragged fingers. But the farther his men ventured, the larger the space appeared.

Daniel and Ezekiel moved down the center of the void as the diggers searched the depths of its sides.

"Halt!"

Daniel turned quickly at the sound of the command, looking for the foreman to find out why he had ordered a halt. But the foreman was frozen in place—like a graven image, caught in mid-step, his mouth wide, his eyes alive with fear. Daniel strained his gaze in both directions. For as far as he could see, the workers were immobilized.

Ezekiel was just to his right, close to his side. "Can you move?"

Daniel's response was stifled as a shimmering, silver light filled the chamber, which stretched off into a distance that could not be seen, only imagined. What could be seen was both incredible and frightening.

The light revealed a huge, verdant forest, green and lush and alive. Trees and shrubs of all kinds stretched in dense thickets and bordered wide, green meadows. Birds sang in the air, and, from somewhere in the distance, they could hear the sound of falling water. Daniel's heart was thumping in his chest, his mind spinning. *How can it be so green?*

"Come no closer, man of God."

"What was that voice?" Ezekiel whispered.

"Only the called one, the Ordained One, can approach the garden of God."

Daniel watched in awe, and Ezekiel grasped the sleeve of his tunic, as before them materialized an angelic presence. Taller than the tallest trees behind him, the vision was transformed from voice, to vapor, to shadow, to what appeared as a being of substance. He was dressed as a warrior. A glistening golden helmet covered his head, but long, dark, flowing hair cascaded over his shoulders. A golden breastplate, shining like the sun, ended at a sash of spun gold that cinched a silver girdle around his waist. Golden boots covered his feet, ankles, and calves. All this Daniel took in with one swift glance. But his attention continued to be drawn to two things: the furled wings that rounded on either side of his head and tucked behind broad shoulders, and the flaming sword that hung loosely from his right hand.

The angel raised the tip of the sword, the muscles of his forearm flexing, and pointed it at the two prophets.

"You are welcome here, prophets of God. You have been called to fulfill a purpose. It is time to restore the staff to the tree from which it came, until its time will come again."

Daniel was entranced by the beauty of the angelic being. He had the appearance of a young man. His skin was alabaster, with the incandescent glow of old pearls, and flawless. His lips were full and red, his nose long and aquiline. His hair was shiny and black, a mass of waves that tumbled around his face, framing crystal green eyes. He moved with a fluid grace that failed to mask formidable strength.

"You have been called here to complete two tasks. The first is to summon your brother Jeremiah and his servant to join you here, and to bring Aaron's staff with them. The second, once Aaron's staff is restored to its source, is to construct a great wall across this line"—a line of flame crossed the cavern in front of the angel—"that will enclose the garden. In the wall you will construct seven gates."

The angel's words resonated like cymbals and spun in the air like an invitation to a dance, light and melodic. His voice was clear and firm, softly modulated. But in its words, in its breaths and pauses, it seemed like bells chimed in a far distance.

"When Jeremiah comes, bring the staff of God here to be returned to the Tree the Knowledge of Good and Evil. When that task is fulfilled, then you will build the wall, close up the gate, and seal it, never to be opened until the stars of Hope rise once more in the sky. Once the staff of God is returned and the gate is sealed, you will never return here, nor will you remember your calling here. Only Jeremiah will retain the secret of the gate."

Surrounded by the melodious voice of the apparition, entranced by the vision of his beauty, Daniel felt no fear. His heart and his soul were at peace. Then the angel lifted his sword, sweeping it back and forth, its flames scorching the air before him, leaving a comet-like tail in its wake. Daniel shuddered. Thunder erupted in the cavern, hammering at Daniel's eardrums and driving him to his knees.

"I am Gabriel," the angel called, his voice now the sound of a thousand waterfalls, "Messenger of God, Governor of Eden, Guardian of the Gate. This is Michael, Mighty Warrior."

A second angel, as beautiful and massive as the first, materialized by Gabriel's right side.

"Seal the gate and never return"—a great lightning storm erupted around the angels, ricocheting off the walls and ceiling of the chamber—"or you will forfeit your lives and endanger your souls."

The line of fire that stretched before Gabriel and Michael exploded into a conflagration of flame and heat, a thousand times more intense than any furnace.

Gabriel's voice increased in power.

"Only he who is anointed by God shall ever approach the gate. Physical and spiritual death awaits all others. These are the words of the Lord of Hosts."

On his knees, Daniel was terrified by Gabriel's power, oddly comforted by his goodness, and unable to tear his eyes from the angelic being's face. In a heartbeat, everything changed. Gabriel and Michael vanished, the chamber was plunged back into darkness except for the torches still held in the hands of the paralyzed workers, and life instantly came back to their limbs. Some fell; some stumbled as if on a rocking ship; some wept in wonder. Three stepped forward, their torches held aloft, their left hands reaching out as if to touch something in the blackness. They took a step, and another. Lightning flashed and fire erupted from the floor, leaving behind only three, small clumps of ash on the floor, the torches, still burning, lying by their sides.

594 BC

Babylon

Daniel led the way into the chamber, holding his torch aloft. Jeremiah followed, a long, thin object covered in cloth held against his chest with both hands. One end was just above the floor, the other extended above Jeremiah's left shoulder. Ezekiel and Baruch were in the rear.

Other than the light from the torches, the chamber was covered with black velvet darkness, soft to the touch and rich in its thickness, as though it caressed the skin and warmed their bodies as it parted before them and closed in behind them. To Jeremiah, he could have been in the womb or in the grave and the feeling of tender isolation would have been the same.

He wondered how far it was, how long before they would see something, hear something. His heart pounded against the package held fast to his chest. *Lord of Hosts, why do I fear?*

"Reverent awe . . . Humble before His Majesty."

"What? Baruch, what do you speak?"

When Baruch looked over his shoulder toward Jeremiah, his eyes bulged with stark terror, but no words escaped from his mouth.

"Welcome, man of God. Come and enter the Glory of your Creator."

Jeremiah stopped. *Adonai, I am unworthy to be here.*

The three men and their torches continued into the chamber, but Jeremiah waited and allowed the darkness to envelop him. It covered him like the blackest of winter nights. He lost consciousness of everything but the ebony void he could not see, but could only imagine. He was lost. More than lost. He had almost ceased to exist. Jeremiah's equilibrium vanished in the dark, his sense of spatial balance, his presence in the world. He was about to tumble through space, out of control, when a hand rested upon his shoulder.

"Fear not. Do not be anxious for anything. But in everything, by prayer and petition, make your requests known to God."

Jeremiah raised his eyes. Whether he looked up or down, he did not know. But he looked afar. And as he looked, a glow materialized, then pulsed, then grew like the stone ripples in a pond, expanding out in waves of light and dark, light and dark, the light growing and building on each wave. At the center of the pulse stood the trees off in the distance, the light confined to a small circle around them. But the pulsing dance of the waves of light called him to the trees, coaxed his feet, beckoned his spirit.

The light around the trees thrummed—the audible sound of pulsing light. From white to silver. Jeremiah watched in fascination as leaves sprouted on the branches of the trees—the two, side-by-side, their branches expanding—and the color sang from silver to gray . . . from gray to green. And then the choir of the forest joined in, its massed music rising and falling like flood waters over boulders.

He walked out of the blackness, guided by the hand on his shoulder. The music grew louder and more beautiful with the light as he closed the distance to the trees.

The hand on his shoulder stopped his forward movement.

"Your faithfulness is blessed. You stood when your people bowed to false gods of their own making. Now stand in the garden of God, the birthplace of man, from which will come the herald of the last days, the Scepter of the King. Only you, man of God, can return the scepter to its home."

Jeremiah stumbled back as light erupted around him—and the light joined the song. In a flash of brilliance, the garden came alive, more lush and green than anything he could have imagined. A lifelong citizen of the Judean desert, Jeremiah was overwhelmed by the variety and volume of growing things. Yet above it all, at the heart of it all, the trees stood apart. Like the core of the sun, the intense light that beat forth from the trees was blinding and spellbinding.

An implacable invitation pulled Jeremiah forward, even as the fear of God— reverent awe—restrained his muscles and wrestled with his will. A path opened before him, and the song of the garden welcomed him. He came closer to the trees, approached a clearing—and the song stopped. The thrumming of light ceased. Silence so deafening Jeremiah heard his breath.

And a rustling in the verdant growth to his left. To his right, the soft sweep of a cloak as it caressed the grass. Behind him the swish of sandals through the undergrowth. Standing motionless, it was as if the blood had stopped flowing through Jeremiah's veins. The words of Moses, which his father taught him, echoed in his ears. *"The sound of God walking in the cool of the day . . ."*

"Come, man of God. Return the power to the tree."

Jeremiah swallowed, but no moisture coated his mouth. He looked in front of him, partly because he was terrified to look anywhere else. And he had an awful thought. Which tree?

There appeared to be no way to distinguish one from the other. Both stood mighty, their thick trunks rooted deeply, their branches unfurled in long, majestic arms covered in the same, deep green leaf. Jeremiah swung his head back and forth, looking for some marking, something distinctive to separate the Tree of Life from the Tree of the Knowledge of Good and Evil. What would happen if he approached the wrong tree?

"Even now you doubt? You wonder and question my purpose? Have I brought you this far to forsake you now?"

O Lord of Hosts, forgive my weakness.

"No . . . I celebrate your courage. Look, and see."

How anything could surprise him at this point, he didn't know. But Jeremiah nearly fell to the ground as four angelic beings materialized around the tree on his left, flaming swords pointed to the ground, their amazing, glorious wings unfurled from behind their shoulders. Their wings overlapping, the angels blocked all access to the tree on the left.

The Tree of Life.

"None may approach the Tree of Life. But you, man of God, have been fore-ordained to restore what is missing from the Tree of the Knowledge of Good and Evil. Your calling awaits."

The light appeared to dim around the Tree of Life, and grow more dazzling around the Tree of the Knowledge of Good and Evil, mesmerizing Jeremiah and drawing him close. As he moved through the clearing, he was amazed to find the package in his hands growing warmer, stirring as if it were awakening. He held the package out, away from his body and the covering fell to the ground without a touch.

Aaron's staff grew warmer. A glow began to emanate from it, envelop it. And Jeremiah saw a similar glow emerge from the Tree of the Knowledge of Good and Evil, surrounding an opening in the trunk that hadn't been there a heart-beat earlier. Jeremiah's arms began to shake in time with the vibration in the staff, and they were pulled, stretched out toward the light on the tree.

Frightened to hold on to the staff but terrified to let it go, Jeremiah was dragged forward one step, the muscles in his arms wailing in protest.

Then the staff leaped from his hands, flew across the clearing, and folded itself into the opening in the tree.

And Jeremiah fell to the ground as if dead.

⸺⌁⌁⸺

"What happened? We came back for you when we realized you were missing. Did you fall?"

The ground in the cavern was rough and uneven. Jeremiah lay on the ground and looked into the face of Daniel. Nothing in his old body hurt from hitting the ground. Then he thought of the tree and the staff.

"Did you see it? The trees and the garden?"

Baruch knelt down alongside Jeremiah and took his hand to help him up. "How could we see anything in the blackness? Come, master. Can you rise?"

Jeremiah rose to his feet, surprised at how good his body felt, not like the old, frail bones he endured when he entered the chamber. "Did you hear the music, the voices of the angels?"

"We heard nothing," said Baruch. "Sir, where is the staff?"

He gazed into the darkness. "It's home."

Reaching out to take his arm, Daniel drew close to Jeremiah.

"Then we have a wall to build."

※

The sun was lowering across the western desert, the shadows extending down the wide streets of Babylon. Their rooms on an upper floor, Jeremiah could see the great tower rising in the distance, so visible to the world, so important to Nebuchadnezzar. Only a precious few in Babylon knew a far more important construction had only recently been completed deep in the earth under the tower.

It was time to go home. One more task and they could gather the caravan for their return to Jerusalem.

"Open the mezuzah and bring the discs," said Jeremiah, sitting at a small table by the window. "We need to grab the light while we can."

He took a small knife and rubbed it against the flat surface of a whetstone, sharpening its edge, while Baruch removed the end caps from the brass mezuzah and withdrew the leather sprockets.

"What shall we inscribe on the discs?" Baruch asked.

"Directions," said Jeremiah, "for the one who will come later, at the appointed time. The one for whom the staff waits."

Baruch sat opposite Jeremiah, laid the discs with the strange arms on the table—the one with the holes to his right—and accepted the knife from his master. "But if we carve directions into the discs, what if the wrong person finds the mezuzah? They will know the secrets. They will know how to find the staff. If we inscribe the directions in our language, even in the Akkadian of the Babylonians, won't the chance of discovery be too dangerous?"

There was a sheet of parchment on the table, to Jeremiah's right. He pulled the parchment in front of him, close to his eyes, then looked up at Baruch.

THE ALEPPO CODE   99

"This mezuzah, and others like it, have carried many messages back and forth to Egypt. Only we will know which of these scroll holders is the most important. We will pass this knowledge on to the high priest and use the language and the code of the high priests, brought from Egypt. The rest is in the hands of God. We have done what we can, what we've been called to do. Here."

Baruch took the parchment and scanned its surface. Jeremiah had drawn copies of the four sprocket sides. In the solid sections between each arm was one of the symbols of the Egyptian language.

"Inscribe the symbols as I've drawn them. And carve them deep. They will need to last a long time before they are used once more. And, my son . . ."

The knife poised above one half of the disc, Baruch looked up at his master. "We will pray to El Shaddai, for the one who is anointed to uncover these secrets. He will carry the plan of God, and the future of this world, in his hands."

11

SATURDAY, AUGUST 29

8:00 a.m., Jerusalem

Tom trailed as Rabbi Fineman led the team away from his home on Tavon Street and turned left on Shiloh Street, away from the Machane Yehuda market area. The Nahla'ot neighborhood was the earliest Jewish neighborhood established outside the Old City of Jerusalem, in the latter half of the nineteenth century. Tom was impressed with the gentrification that had turned the old buildings into quaint homes full of character. "My wife and I have lived in this neighborhood ever since we immigrated to Israel," said Fineman. "The house belonged to my grandfather . . . our family has lived here a long time. My grandfather and my father were members of this synagogue. We worshiped here on Sabbath. That is how I came to know many of the elders."

Rizzo was right on Fineman's heels, his legs pumping furiously to keep up with the long-striding rabbi. "Hey . . . I didn't think you were Jewish anymore."

Fineman crossed Rama Street and continued the short block to Be'er Sheva. "I may believe in Yeshua, who is our Messiah, and that may make me a Messianic Jew . . . a completed Jew, some might say . . . but a Jew nonetheless. It's like saying if you switched churches you would no longer be Italian."

"I gotcha, Padre. I wouldn't stop being Italian if they named me O'Reilly. But I don't expect these guys in the synagogue would like you too much, since you switched sides and all."

Reaching the corner of Shiloh and Be'er Sheva, Fineman slowed to a halt. Across the street was a squat, nondescript, ochre, cinder-block building, with a brown terra cotta roof. A four-foot-high wall of the same common block—not the glorious and ubiquitous Jerusalem Stone that gave the city much of its radiance—protruded from the front of the building well out into the sidewalk and was crowned by a stout, wrought-iron railing that rose another four feet.

His head cocked to one side, Fineman turned away from the building to peer at Rizzo. "My wife and I have invested a good bit of our time and resources into helping the children and youth of this neighborhood. We're welcome here, regardless of our beliefs. In fact, I think the elders enjoy our regular theology arguments." He looked up, lifting his hand toward the building on the far side of the narrow street.

"The Great Synagogue Ades of the Glorious Aleppo Community . . . Addis—like Addis Ababa," Fineman explained. "Quite a name they have given themselves. But this truly is one of the greatest synagogues in Jerusalem. It was founded in 1901 by two cousins from Aleppo, Syria, who came here with an immigrant contingent of Syrian Jews. This synagogue has continued to be primarily the worship center for Syrian Jews over the last 110 years and is known as a center for Syrian *hazzanut*, a type of Jewish liturgical singing. Today it maintains the rare tradition of *bakashot*, a set cycle of kabbalistic poetry sung in the early hours of Shabbat during the winter months. Although you can't tell from the outside, the interior of the Ades Synagogue is one of the most beautiful in Jerusalem. Come, let me show you."

Tom joined the group crossing the street to the large, metal gate, but he wanted to keep their minds on the task at hand. "So what does all this have to do with the book?"

"Be patient," Fineman said as he pushed open the gate. "All in good time."

⁓⌇⌇⁓

Fineman wasn't exaggerating about the interior of the Ades Synagogue—it was sumptuous in its furnishings and striking in its decoration. Tom was intently staring at the colorful mural that ran around the top of all four walls when he felt a tap on his elbow. He turned to find a young, bearded man, achingly slim, standing beside Fineman. He looked as if he had just come off the kibbutz, tanned, dressed in faded jeans and a soiled work shirt, battered boots long past their prime.

"Tom . . . this is Rabbi Asher," said Fineman, who completed the introductions to the other members of the team.

"Please, call me Benjamin." His smile was wide and welcoming.

"The rabbi has agreed to allow us into the *gniza* . . . the room where old Torah scrolls are kept until they can be properly disposed," said Fineman, a sparkle lighting his eyes.

Benjamin leaned closer to Tom and put his hand on Tom's arm as if they were involved in some conspiracy. "It's where the book is . . . that's what you want to see, right? C'mon, you're going to like this."

Benjamin reversed toward the entrance, turned to the left just before the doors, and ducked under a low portal to a flight of descending stone stairs. "I'm from New York, too," said Asher, his voice trailing behind his body as he disappeared into a below-ground twilight. "But you can't escape your roots." Reaching the basement floor, Benjamin stood before a large, solid timber door, fumbled for a moment with a huge ring of keys, freed the lock, and swung the door out of the way.

"Ronald, you know the drill," said Benjamin, who reached into the back pocket of his jeans and pulled out two keys fastened to a gold star-of-David key fob. "You know what these are for. My grandfather will be down shortly to answer any questions, but I'm sure you can keep these folks occupied until then. Mr. Bohannon . . . enjoy."

The interior of the room was longer than Bohannon expected, running about the full length of the building. It was full of wooden shelves—like bookshelves, but deeper—that gave it a library feel, although the documents on the shelves were scrolls rather than books. Thousands of them. The scrolls were piled high and packed tightly, filling almost every space and blocking almost any light from penetrating into the room. To the right, a small alcove was protected by a wrought-iron fence. Fineman walked up to the fence, unlocked its gate, and turned on a low, diffused light. In the middle of the alcove was a large, wood table, surrounded by heavy chairs. On the table was a large, padlocked metal chest. Fineman unlocked the chest and opened the lid. He pointed to a stack of thin, white cotton gloves. He put on a pair, then lifted the book out of the chest and rested it on the table.

This book looked similar to many other large, ancient books Bohannon had seen in the past—thick leather cover on both sides, embossed and carved in swirling designs, a metal hasp attached to the front and back covers, its hinged end sliding into a metal lock on the front cover. Fineman took a key from inside the metal chest, unlocked the hasp, and carefully opened its pages, one after another.

The Aleppo codex copy in front of them had three vertical columns of Hebrew letters on each page. Each line in the column contained about a dozen or more symbols, about two dozen lines in each column. At the top and bottom of each column, and in the margins between them, were additional Hebrew symbols. While the marks inserted between the columns of the Scripture were generally one, two, or three symbols, the notations at the top and the bottom of each column were generally more extensive, sometimes running several lines, and were written in a smaller size than the characters in the Scripture verses themselves.

"The original codex, held in the Shrine of the Book in the Israel Museum, is missing nearly half its original pages," said Fineman. "The first page in the original comes in the middle of Deuteronomy—the first four books are missing altogether. But this copy—this one is complete."

"How is that possible?"

"It was copied long before the original was destroyed," said Fineman.

Bohannon stood on the left side of the table, Joe Rodriguez on the right, watching as Fineman gently turned each page. Rizzo stood on one of the wooden chairs, Annie by his side.

"How old is this book?" asked Rodriguez. "The original is over one thousand years old, correct? This one looks pretty ancient, itself."

A new voice came from behind them all, near the gate into the alcove. It was soft, but pregnant with authority. "We believe our codex is over six hundred years old."

Tom and the others turned at the sound of the voice. Standing at the gate was a tall, thin, elderly man, dressed entirely in black: suit jacket, shirt, pants, and shoes. His flat-topped black hat was in his hands; white hair tumbled from under his black yarmulke and curled at his temples, dangling just above a thick, wild, white beard. His eyes were dark and questioning, empty of welcome.

The elderly man had not moved a muscle. Tom wondered if he would. Then Fineman stepped forward.

"Rabbi Asher, these are the people I spoke to you about. Those who are—"

"Afforded an incredible honor by my grandson, something I'm not sure was so wise," said the old man, shaking Fineman's hand. "You are welcome to study our codex anytime, Ronald. But you"—he pointed to Tom and his friends around the table—"I'm not so sure about you. You seem to have been involved in a great deal of destruction since you arrived in Israel. I hope you do not bring destruction to our synagogue. What is it you want with our book?"

Tom stepped forward. "Rabbi, we have, all of us, lost a great deal lately. I don't—we don't—comprehend the why of it all. But one thing is clear to us." He stepped closer and offered his right hand toward the elderly rabbi, who studied Bohannon for a long moment, as if he were a new book of the Torah—curious, but skeptical. Then the elderly rabbi reached out and accepted Tom's hand. "Whatever has happened to us, whatever we've been involved in, God's hand has been on it, and his call is on it. We're just trying to determine our next step. And knowing what's in this codex appears to be the next step. We've been following clues to Jeremiah and the shepherd's staff from New York to Egypt to Ireland to this room today. I'm just trying to understand what God wants us to do. And I think—Rabbi Fineman thinks—it's possible we may find some answers, some truth, in this codex."

Rabbi Asher removed his hand from Bohannon's grasp. Measuring his step like a toddler on ice, he moved to the side of the table and sat in one of the stout, wooden chairs. He closed his eyes; his chin fell to his chest. After a deep breath, he looked up again. "So, I shall tell you a story."

⌇⌇⌇

"Nebuchadnezzar, king of Babylon, laid siege to Jerusalem and captured the city on three different occasions," said Rabbi Asher, his arthritic hand laid on the cover of the book. "As a result of the first siege, Nebuchadnezzar took thousands of captives back to Babylon, including the prophets Daniel and Ezekiel. After the second siege, Jeremiah gained Nebuchadnezzar's favor with his prophecies of the king's victorious future. But before Nebuchadnezzar destroyed Jerusalem following the third siege, God directed Jeremiah to hide the Jews' most sacred objects—the Tent, the Ark and its contents, as well as the sacred vessels.

"Many scholars believe, and Jewish tradition holds, that the report in Maccabees—that Jeremiah buried the Ark and the Tent of Meeting on Mount Nebo in Jordan—was actually a diversion created by his servant Baruch."

Rabbi Asher used both hands to open the book. He appeared to measure the number of pages and then pried the book apart. He drew his finger, right to left, across the small notes at the top of the page, from the book of Jeremiah in the Codex, and read:

> "For this is what the Lord Almighty says about the pillars, the bronze Sea, the movable stands and the other furnishings that are left in this city . . .
>
> "They will be taken to Babylon and there they will remain until the day I come for them," declared the Lord. "Then I will bring them back and restore them to this place."

"The notes of the Masoretes here, at the top of the column, tell us that Jeremiah, knowing of the coming destruction to be wrought by the armies of Nebuchadnezzar, removed what the notes call 'the sacred vessels' from their hiding place in the caves under Temple Mount." Rabbi Asher moved his finger to the top of the middle column. "Jeremiah's scribe, Baruch, altered the records to protect the truth. The scholars who created the notes in the codex claim Jeremiah hid the Ark, the Tent of Presence, and the golden vessels of the Temple in a place known only by the Aaronite high priest and passed down verbally through each generation of high priest that followed. But Aaron's staff—the instrument of God's power—Jeremiah returned to its home. These Masoretic notes tell us Jeremiah traveled to Babylon. While there, the prophet Daniel revealed a great secret. This note, here, says, 'And the staff of G-d was returned to its rightful place.' That is all the book tells us."

Rabbi Asher bowed his head, spoke in a barely audible voice, and closed the codex. He turned to face the group.

"But that is not all we know," he said. "Many believe the staff, perhaps reunited with the Ark, will be the weapon of Armageddon—the weapon God will use to destroy the armies of the world who mass on the plain of Megiddo.

"From our tradition and what the book tells us, I believe Jeremiah braved the eight-week, thousand-kilometer journey to Babylon where he met with Ezekiel and Daniel, who was the king's chancellor and ran the government. Because ancient Babylon was built on the same spot that contained the garden of Eden before Noah's flood, I believe Jeremiah's intention was to restore Aaron's staff to its place of origin . . . to the Tree of the Knowledge of Good and Evil."

Rabbi Asher spread his hands and looked around the table. "So now you know what our fathers wrote in the most accurate recording of Scripture in history. Tell me. What does it mean to you? What is this next step you must take?"

"To be honest, at this moment I don't know," Bohannon admitted. "But tell me—how is it you have a complete copy of the codex when most people believe the only extant version of the codex is incomplete, housed in the Israel Museum? It could be dangerous for you to have it."

Rabbi Asher motioned for Fineman to return the codex to its secure home. "This synagogue was established in 1901 by a group of Syrian immigrant Jews— led by the cousins Ovadiah Josiah Ades and Yosef Isaac Ades. That was more than four decades before Israel was declared a state and the central synagogue of Aleppo was sacked. Sometime in the early days of the codex's residence in Aleppo, the rabbi of the synagogue, an ancestor of the Ades cousins, executed a complete copy of the book, including the Masoretic notes. The rabbi's family kept it hidden—insurance, as it were, for the original."

His fingers touched the cover like a lover.

"This is a beautiful book," said Rizzo. "Priceless. But if it's the only complete copy of the codex, why keep it hidden? Why isn't this one in the Israel Museum?"

"It is safer here." Rabbi Asher waved his hand above the book. "Credible witnesses insisted the codex was complete when it was rescued from the synagogue in Syria, complete when it was delivered into the care of an Israeli government official. There is strong suspicion the pages of the codex were deliberately ripped out. Perhaps for money. Perhaps for a more sinister reason. That I don't know."

The rabbi turned and leaned his back against the table. "What I do know is that as long as this synagogue stands, we will protect this book with our lives. Until Messiah comes."

12

Oliver Stanley's name was barely out of the presidential secretary's mouth before he was through the door to the Oval Office, his florid face redder than normal, his jaw set and hard.

"Do you know what you have done to Baruk? He's finished. His government coalition won't survive—"

"Good morning, Ollie," said the president. His jacket was off, draped over the back of his chair, and he was reviewing reports from the Office of Management and Budget, never a pleasant experience. "Why don't you sit down?" Whitestone pointed to one of the straight-backed chairs in front of his desk.

The secretary of state stood behind the chair, his hands gripping the wooden back. "Why wasn't I consulted? How can you make such a radical shift in our support of Israel without discussing its repercussions with me, with State?"

Whitestone looked up from the distressing budget reports. He lifted his right hand, pointing, and nodded his head at the chair. "Sit down, Ollie."

Some of the bluster slipped from Stanley's voice as he stepped around the chair and followed the president's directions. "You've kept me in the dark about too much, Mr. President. You and Cartwright."

Jonathan Whitestone knew this moment was on the horizon. Stanley had served his purpose. Now he stood in the way. Whitestone no longer trusted Stanley's advice and didn't seek his counsel about his dealings with Israel's prime minister. The secretary was dead meat and didn't know how far outside of the inner circle he actually was. This would not be pleasant. But it was necessary.

Whitestone already knew who Oliver Stanley's replacement would be—should the secretary resign.

"There is no way we could remain silent on the tragic consequences of Israel's raid against Iran's Central Bank." Whitestone said the words with a straight face and firm conviction. Lies came easier the longer you sat in this chair.

Stanley stared hard at the president. "You know very well there is more than one way to make a statement like that."

Whitestone didn't intend to give in to Stanley's anger one inch. He caught the secretary's stare and returned it a hundredfold.

"Baruk would never have taken an action like that on his own," said Stanley. "We both know you could just have easily confessed our own complicity in the attack on Iran. But that wouldn't have played so well on the world stage, would it? You are taking a huge risk here, Mr. President. Cartwright is not your foreign policy advisor. I am. Or I should be. But Cartwright has your ear, and unfortunately, you've got a mall cop for your advisor."

Whitestone had run through tougher bullies than the secretary on his journey to the White House, and he wasn't about to cower in front of Ollie Stanley.

He lowered his head and looked over the top of his reading glasses. "Don't push your luck, Senator. You wouldn't be in that nice office of yours if it weren't for the fifty-five electoral votes I needed from California. Cartwright has more geopolitical savvy in his eyebrow than you have in your whole department. And, Ollie—I would keep your personal thoughts about Iran to yourself. It would help your job security."

The secretary of state's back stiffened, and his shoulders rolled back, helping him sit more erect in the chair. His eyes narrowed, and a hardness Whitestone had dealt with in Congress once again returned to his patrician features. Oliver Stanley looked like a stern schoolmaster about to issue a severe punishment. "If it's my resignation you seek, Mr. President, you may have it. I no longer have your confidence—that has been clear for some time. And you no longer have any need for my state's electoral votes. I'll have the letter to you in twenty minutes." He stood to his feet. "You value your reputation as a man of faith, a man of integrity. But I tell you the truth. No one can hide their true character in this office. What you do will find you out."

Stanley extended his right hand. Whitestone ignored it.

"I don't envy you that day. Godspeed, Mr. President." Whitestone wasn't sure if the words were a blessing, or a curse.

8:00 a.m., New York City

On a weekday, it was a terrorist's dream—thousands of tightly packed bodies inching along the platforms in the depths of Grand Central Terminal at very predictable times. Each arriving train added to the masses snaking along the platforms, climbing the steps in patient rank-and-file. Over 750 thousand people passed through the ornate terminal each weekday, most in those few hours in the morning and evening when the metropolis filled and emptied with commuting workers.

The platform of track 29 was much less crowded this early on a Saturday, but Connor couldn't help but wonder what he would do if people started dropping like flies in front of him, some poisonous gas sweeping along the platform in his direction. An attack wasn't as impossible as he'd once believed. His entire family had endured the threat of the Prophet's Guard. He still had to purposefully stop himself from shying away from every Middle Eastern–looking man he saw. A shiver ran across his shoulders, and he shook his head. *Get a grip.*

He walked up a ramp, through one of a rank of gates, and found himself in the exquisite expanse of the majestic train terminal celebrating its centenary. In the middle of the Tennessee-granite main hall was an octagonal information booth with "the clock" at its apex—the iconic symbol of Grand Central, now worth ten million dollars—and the place where thousands went to meet. Connor crossed the hall with its vaulted, zodiac-designed ceiling, Michael Jordan's Steakhouse at one end of the concourse and a new Apple store at the other. He made his way through Vanderbilt Hall and out onto 42nd Street. And into the teeth of Manhattan's frenetic pulse—even on a Saturday.

On his way to meet Stew Manthey at the Collector's Club on East 35th Street, Connor quick-stepped past the Pershing Square Grille, keeping pace with the human flow, and set off up the hill on Park Avenue. The Collector's Club, under the direction of Dr. Richard Johnson Sr. until his murder just days earlier, was one of the nation's most influential stamp-collecting societies. After retiring from the chair of the Antiquities College at Columbia University, Dr. Johnson pursued his second passion. And it was in the vault at the Collector's Club, secure and climate-controlled, that Abiathar's scroll rested, along with the mezuzah, which had carried the scroll for over one thousand years.

Connor found Manthey waiting on the steps of the stunning Baroque-style townhouse, a straw fedora on his head to ward off the August sun. Ringing the bell, Manthey greeted the matronly woman, dressed in black, who answered.

"Hi, I'm Stewart Manthey, CFO of the Bowery Mission. I called earlier?"

"Yes." She looked like a schoolteacher, but her eyes were hard, unwelcoming. Over her shoulder, she glanced into the building's lobby. A uniformed guard emerged from within. "Do you have some identification?"

Stew and Connor offered their driver's licenses.

"Oh . . . you are Mr. Bohannon's son?" she said to Connor, a faint remnant of English accent moderating the rebuke in her words. "The man who began our misery." She handed Connor his driver's license as if it carried typhus. "I'm sorry. You of all people would understand that, after all that has occurred, we must be more vigilant. Come in if you must."

They crossed the small lobby. The guard unlocked a heavy, but clearly new, wrought-iron gate, and they entered the rear room—the heart of the club's philatelic collection. But the ranks of wooden file cabinets and packed bookcases attracted no notice. They turned right, stepped behind some heavy, velvet curtains, and faced the gleaming steel door of a massive vault.

"Please turn around. Security, you know."

Backs to the vault door, Bohannon and Manthey both heard and felt the *whoosh* of air escaping from the sealed vault.

"Come along."

In the dim, filtered light, they followed the woman to a metal bank of drawers. "It's the mezuzah you wish to see . . . not the scroll itself?"

She opened a large, square drawer, removed a leather shoulder bag, and laid it on a metal table in the middle of the vault. "If you push this button, it will put more light on the part of the table where you are working. Try not to destroy anything else while you're here."

Manthey opened the leather bag and pulled out a cloth-wrapped cylinder. "They've been through a lot here." Connor felt like Manthey was reading his thoughts. "Seems like a lifetime ago, but it's only been a few months since Winthrop Larsen was murdered right outside." He unwrapped the etched, bronze mezuzah. "That blast nearly wrecked this building. Then there was the break-in. Now Doc's dead. No wonder we're not very welcome. Here, why not test your theory."

Connor took the mezuzah in his left hand. With his right, he examined one of the end caps. About the girth of a mid-sized telescope, the mezuzah was an engraved metal cylinder, about four inches in diameter and about eight inches long. Along two-thirds of its length was a U-shaped metal bar, the open end snug against the outside of the container. When a scroll occupied the inside of the mezuzah, pulling on the metal bar would begin unrolling it.

With a look toward Manthey, Connor applied some pressure to the end cap—first pushing up, to see if the end cap would separate from the rest of the cylinder; then gently twisting to see if it might unscrew. It didn't budge. He looked down the length of the cylinder, trying to get a vantage point that might reveal evidence of a seal between the cylinder and the flange of the end cap that extended over the end of the cylinder.

"It doesn't look rusted," said Manthey. Connor could feel him at his back, looking over his shoulder. "And I doubt it's welded shut. How would anyone get a scroll inside?"

Connor moved the mezuzah away from his body and held it at arm's length.

He put one hand on each end of the mezuzah, covering both end caps. Then he pushed the two ends toward each other. As he pushed, he applied pressure to twist the caps in opposite directions . . . clockwise with his right hand. When nothing happened, he changed direction, counterclockwise with his right hand.

That's when he felt the snap.

Soft, subtle, but there nonetheless. With the snap, both end caps were released from their restraints and could spin freely on the shaft. But they didn't come off. The knurled knobs on the ends of the center shaft prevented the end caps from moving completely away from the cylinder.

"Halfway home," Connor said, his voice low enough the conversation could have been with himself. He tried unsuccessfully to unscrew first one, then the other of the knobbed ends. He pushed on the knobs, trying to force them toward the center of the shaft. Nothing.

"Not the same, eh? Good try," said Manthey.

Connor held the partially dismembered mezuzah in his hands and wondered what to do next. What was left? The knobs had to come off. He closed his eyes and tried to visualize the knobs from all angles. Light emerged. He picked up a thin-bladed letter opener from the shelf behind him and inserted the blade into the narrow space between the shaft and the knob. When he felt resistance Connor stopped, then applied steady, growing pressure. And the knob separated from the shaft.

"Good thinking," said Manthey, raising his bushy eyebrows.

The two end caps free from the shaft, Connor laid them down on the table's surface, the inside, cup-like surfaces pointing up. From his backpack, he took one of the leather sprockets, unwrapped it, and placed it in the receptacle.

"Perfect," he said and turned his head toward Manthey. "Now what?"

Manthey scratched at the bristly beard on his chin. "Well, let's compare the symbols on the sprockets with the ones on the scroll. Even though the scroll is written as a substitution cipher, we may learn something. There was a guy over at the Met who your dad talked to early on about the Demotic symbols. Let's see if we can get ahold of him."

13

3:00 p.m., Jerusalem

On Eliazar Baruk's desk sat the day's editions of *Yedioth Ahronoth*, the Tel Aviv tabloid that was the largest circulation newspaper in Israel; the English dailies *Jerusalem Post* and the left-leaning *Harretz*; along with the Hebrew daily newspapers *Maariv* and the right-leaning, free *Israel Today*. "When was the last time you saw the same lead story in all these newspapers?" asked Baruk.

"Not often." Levi Sharp, director of Mossad, Israel's international spy apparatus, sat across the desk from the prime minister. "War probably. Today they have it all."

Israel was in a near-chaotic uproar. And Baruk and his government were tottering in the midst of the outcry.

The spreading radioactive cloud raining death on a sizeable segment of Tehran's population, caused by the botched action against the Iranian Central Bank, was enough to shake confidence in any government. But Baruk's chances of survival had already been damaged by the shocking Muslim attack on Temple Mount only days prior and reports of a government insider turned traitor who assisted Hezbollah in its deadly attack. He was already crippled by the ongoing investigation into campaign financial fraud. Now blared from the front page of each newspaper was the realized fear of retaliation from Iran's militant Islamic allies. Hezbollah rockets were flying into Israel's northern settlements and creeping farther into the country.

"How many have fallen so far?"

Sharp glanced at the briefing paper in his lap, but the numbers had not changed since he first saw them thirty minutes earlier. "Three hundred forty into Kiryat Shmona alone. It's a wasteland. Over one hundred into Haifa, and Hezbollah appears to be determined to move its shelling down the coast."

"Where's Orhlon?"

"Readying the IDF for a strike into Lebanon. Our planes are in the air, waiting for your order."

"It will look like desperation, trying to save my neck."

"Yes, it will. But we have no choice."

"No word on Shomsky?"

"No, sir."

"We could use his conniving mind right now," said Baruk. He ran his hand through the gray curls at the back of his neck. "Do we have enough votes?"

"Not my expertise," Sharp said of the pending no-confidence vote scheduled in the Knesset for the next hour. "But I doubt it. The US State Department has urged all American nationals to leave Israel at once. And the American president's press conference was a killer."

The prime minister of Israel picked up the phone on his desk. It was answered immediately. "Send in the air force . . . you have my approval." He hung up.

"We'll hold on the ground forces, for now. We'll leave that decision to my successor. Let's go."

9:30 a.m., New York City

Despite the heat and humidity, even at an early hour Central Park pulsed with activity. Riders on racing bikes, dressed in a bright rainbow of team colors, flashed past serious runners, earnest joggers, and resolute walkers along the macadam roadways that were now rescued from automobile traffic. But the automobiles were still very much in evidence, the steady throb and occasional honk of snaking traffic on Fifth Avenue and cutting across the park on the 81st Street viaduct created an inescapable backdrop to life in Manhattan. But Connor's mind was in another world.

Rising above him was Cleopatra's Needle, a seventy-foot red granite obelisk removed from the Egyptian port city of Alexandria by nineteenth-century explorer archaeologists who believed plunder was honorable. A resident of Central Park's eastern fringe since 1880, when it took 112 days to move the obelisk from the Hudson River dock, Cleopatra's Needle was the oldest man-made object in the park. Just steps north of the Metropolitan Museum of Art, this obelisk was one of three that were removed from Egypt—the others in Paris in the middle of the Place de la Concorde, and in London on the Victoria Embankment.

"At least we paid for ours," said Bob Ford, guardian of the Ancient Near Eastern collection at the Met, as he led Manthey and Connor Bohannon to the knoll upon which the Needle looked out over Central Park. "The Khedive of Egypt, Mehmet Ali Pasha, was more than happy to swap the obelisk for the money he needed to keep his government afloat. William H. Vanderbilt donated $100,000 to secure the obelisk and transport it to New York."

"Dr. Johnson and your father . . . ah . . . contacted me a few months ago with . . . um . . . some questions about the Needle," said Ford, stumbling with both his words and his footing on the steep hill upon which Cleopatra's Needle perched. "I wasn't able to help them much then, and I'm not sure how much help I can be now. But let me show you this."

Ford walked around the base of the obelisk to the west side—the side that was least weathered, where the markings were more distinct. He pointed to the base of the obelisk. "Those symbols look like yours."

Connor pulled a piece of paper from the back pocket of his jeans, a copy of the symbols he and Manthey had found on the sprockets. He held it up against the symbols at the base of the obelisk. "Look at that . . . look at the way they repeat. Almost identical to what's on the sprockets." He turned to Ford. "But what does it mean?"

Ford leaned back against the obelisk, ancient Egyptian hieroglyphs framing his head. "I wish I knew. We have a lot of items at the Met with Demotic characters. But almost all of our samples are on shards of pottery or small swatches of parchment or papyrus. Nothing large enough to help break the Demotic puzzle. A group at the Oriental Institute has worked on a Demotic dictionary project for over forty years. The team has been led for decades by Dr. Roberta Smith. We send them images of all our stuff. So does almost every other museum in the world.

"Earlier this year, the institute team announced it finally completed its task—cataloguing all the various meanings of all known Demotic symbols. The dictionary they completed is almost two thousand pages long. One letter has, I think, eight hundred different meanings.

"I talked with Dr. Smith a few weeks ago, and she and her team were as excited as kids at Christmas. They were stunned when somebody sent them a copy of the scroll your dad discovered—it's the largest single example of

Demotic writing ever unearthed. If there is anybody who can help you figure out what you've got in your hands, it will be Dr. Smith and her team at the University of Chicago."

Connor's hopes disappeared. "Chicago?"

~~~

He had been sitting in the taxicab for more than an hour, and his nerves were ready to snap. The cab was against the curb on the southwest corner of the intersection at Fifth Avenue and 84th Street in Manhattan, its flashers on. It was in a no-parking zone, blocking a lane that should have been open to traffic, and naturally incurring the wrath, curses, and gestures of nearly every driver who had to swing back into traffic to get around the stationary cab.

But posing as a taxi driver had worked once before, and Tarik Ben Ali, their leader, thought it worth the chance. But Tarik didn't have to sit here behind the wheel, scanning forward and backward for New York City police, his heart jumping every time a delivery truck nearly ripped off the rear quarter panel of the mustard-yellow Ford. Mustafa clutched his chest in alarm as the driver of a rumbling cement mixer laid heavily on his air horn. The massive vehicle swerved, like a two-ton python, back into the main lane of Fifth Avenue and careened across 84th Street.

Mustafa had the keys in his hand to turn on the ignition, determined to find a safer place to wait, when they came out of the building three-quarters of the way down the block.

~~~

"We could walk down to Lexington and get the Six train," said Connor as he and Stew exited the Metropolitan Museum opposite 83rd Street.

Manthey looked uptown on Fifth and raised his right arm. "Let's take a cab instead."

Its flashers still blinking, the taxi slowed to a halt as Connor jumped in and Stew followed. "Bowery at Prince," he told the driver. "Better to go down the FDR and cut across Houston than try to go through the city."

~~~

The FDR . . . it brought back unpleasant memories for Mustafa, who nearly three weeks ago had been a passenger in a truck that crashed on the 59th Street exit ramp of the FDR as it tried to escape the police. Mustafa still carried the bruises and sore right shoulder from that crash as a memory.

Mustafa turned off the flashers, checked his rearview mirror, and was about to pull away.

"Don't go straight," said the older man in the back. "Go left on 82nd and cross town. There will be less traffic that way. Then you can get on the FDR at 79th Street."

You give orders like Tarik Ben Ali.

Mustafa edged his cab across two lanes of congested traffic on Fifth and managed to turn left on 82nd. He knew it didn't matter what route they took: the destination was the same. Only these two would not reach the Bowery Mission. At least not in their current state.

"Hey, you forgot to turn on the meter."

Mustafa pushed the button to start the fare calculator. "Thank you, sir." *Just wait.*

There was little traffic on the FDR along the East River. But as Mustafa drove his taxi off the ramp onto Houston Street, even on this end of Houston, in Alphabet City, amid the largest public housing project in New York, the street was clogged with vehicles and streaming with people. As Mustafa guided the cab farther west along the wide, four-lane avenue, the traffic and the flow of pedestrians grew heavier. On an August Saturday, with tourists swelling the ranks, it was near pandemonium. Mustafa didn't care. This was familiar turf to Mustafa and his Prophet's Guard brothers. And he trusted the crowds would help hide their intent.

The taxi inched to a stop at the traffic light on the corner of Avenue A.

"It might be faster if we walked," said the older man. Mustafa began to panic. *It's too soon. They can't get out now.*

"Wait, sir. There must be another way."

—⁓⁓—

Manthey's eyes were on the driver, and he was about to suggest they bear right on the other side of the intersection and make the angled turn to drive up First Street, when the back doors on both sides of the taxi opened at the same time.

Stew felt somebody push hard against his back, shoving him into the middle of the seat where he collided with Connor's right shoulder.

—⁓⁓⁓—

Sitting on the driver's side, Connor's first thought when the door opened was annoyance that somebody was trying to hop into their cab while they were still using it. That thought lasted about a millisecond as the intruder threw the weight of his body at Bohannon and drove him into the middle of the back seat. It took no great flash of understanding for Connor to know what was happening. He knew his assailants. He didn't know their intention. But he wasn't going to wait to find out.

Connor yielded to the driving force against his left shoulder, allowing his right hip to pivot off the seat. His head and right shoulder slammed into Manthey's chest. Connor quickly pulled his knees to his chest and—with his hands pushing against the seat—kicked out with both feet, hitting one of the intruders in the chest with his heavy Timberland boots, driving the man up and back, half out of the driver-side door.

"Drive!" hissed the man hanging out the door as he reached wildly for something to save him.

—⁓⁓⁓—

As the vehicle sprang to action, Manthey's body jolted toward Connor. A searing pain punctured Manthey's right side as the right shoulder strap to his backpack—holding the sprockets—was cut away. His left hand grabbed for the strap over his left shoulder as the pack was pulled away from his back.

—⁓⁓⁓—

Mustafa angled to the right to race up First Street . . . except the traffic light was still red. He missed the three young men who were halfway across Houston Street, but the *Daily News* delivery truck didn't miss him. As the taxi bolted into the intersection, the truck slammed into its right front fender, throwing the taxi into a spin and turning the occupants into projectiles.

〜〜〜

Hurled back to his right, against his attacker, Manthey heard a sickening crack as the rear passenger-side door of the taxi slammed shut. There was a cry of pain, and the sudden release of pressure against his shoulder.

〜〜〜

Connor tried to lift himself off the floor of the cab, but his hand slipped on something wet and he dropped back onto the floor. Connor looked up to see Stew staring at him, his right hand dripping with blood.

"I've been stabbed."

Stew's eyes shone with the wild fury of a predator about to defend itself, but the backpack was held tightly in his left hand.

Connor quickly scanned the cab. They were alone.

"You'll be okay, Stew. We can—"

The sirens were already getting closer, the Good Samaritans lining up at both doors.

"I'm a doctor. Please, just stay where you are."

14

6:00 p.m., Jerusalem

A sweet aroma of cooking tomatoes, heavy with garlic, drifted into every corner of Kallie's apartment. The air-conditioning was cranked up, doing battle with the August heat that sucked dry every drop of moisture and shortened every reservoir of patience. Sammy Rizzo was in the kitchen making "gravy," what non-Italians call spaghetti sauce. Two hours ago, Rizzo stood up, said, "Cooking is therapy," and walked out the front door. An hour later he was back, a bag-toting taxi driver in his wake. Rizzo retired to the kitchen with his supplies, and the only evidence of his presence was the pungent aroma and a few scattered snippets of Puccini's *La Bohème* sliced to silence in mid-sentence as if Rizzo's joy collided with the raw memory of his grief.

Annie was intoxicated by the familiar smell of cooking gravy, visions of her Grandmother Loscalzo's house on a Sunday afternoon, all eleven sons and daughters and their families arranged around a motley collection of tables as her grandma carried platter after platter of homemade pasta and meatballs into the dining room. It was a struggle for her to remain focused on the conversation . . . except the conversation was outrageously impossible.

"Look, it's time for a reality check here," said Deirdre. She was standing in the alcove, a stack of dishes in her hands as she prepared to set the table for dinner. "You guys are tossing around the Ark of the Covenant, Aaron's staff, and the garden of Eden like you're putting together a shopping list for the grocery store. Don't you realize how crazy this all sounds? And even if the most bizarre story in the history of the world happened to be true, then what? What are you going to do? Take out a map and measure out the distance to the garden . . . check out the road conditions? Come on . . . so what if the Prophet's Guard is looking for Aaron's staff, even if we assume you're right and this staff was Moses's H-bomb. What are they going to do? Where are they going to find it? How could it make any difference at all?"

Annie sat in an uncomfortable Danish chair that was all angles and hardwood. Tom and Joe were across the room on the sofa. She was so conflicted, she remained stuck in this ungodly chair, unsure whether to join in the conjecture or join in something more real, like cooking gravy or setting the table.

"It makes a difference to them," Annie said, peeling herself from the vinyl and walking over to the sideboard to grab a handful of forks and napkins. "They want something desperately, the secret of which they protected for nearly one thousand years. They think we are the key, or the roadblock, to them finding what it is they seek: the power to conquer, the power to rule, the power to enshrine Allah as master of this world." Placing the last fork, she moved alongside Deirdre and took her hand. "No matter how crazy these theories may seem . . . and this *is* dime-novel stuff, the one reality we can't escape is that the Prophet's Guard will not stop, will not allow one of us to stand in their way, until we are all dead, they are all dead—or they have Aaron's staff in their hands."

"I understand all that." Deirdre shook her massive copper curls. "If, in fact, Jeremiah intended to return the staff to the Tree of Good and Evil in the garden of Eden, the garden was engulfed by the flood of Noah. Then there were thousands of years between the flood and when Jeremiah went to Babylon. How did he know where to look? And there's another twenty-five hundred years between Jeremiah and today. How could anyone ever expect to find the garden after all these years? I wasn't totally asleep during my Catholic education, so if anyone *could* find the garden, what about the angels with the flaming swords?"

Deirdre's logic was persuasive, but Annie knew there was another element to consider. "If it couldn't be found, why was Spurgeon so fearful about anyone discovering the sprockets? Why did he say the sprockets were more dangerous than anything discovered before? Look, I don't think there's any getting out of this for us. I can't speak for the rest of you, but if finding this staff is the thing that finally sets us free, then I'm finding that staff."

Deirdre shook her head, her blue eyes flashing like drawn sabers. "So now what?"

Rizzo emerged from the kitchen, balancing a large bowl of red gravy in his arms. Alarmed, flashing back to Grandma's dining room at the same time,

Annie reached down and took the heavy bowl. She turned to the rest. "Let's eat while everything is hot. We can save the world after we're fed."

⌁⌁⌁

Absently tapping his fork against his empty plate, Joe wondered again about his reason for being here on this quest, with these people. Was he really considering the garden of Eden a real place? After all that had happened, what did he really believe? A lapsed Catholic, the object of Deirdre's constant prayers, Joe never felt out of place in the "born-again" Bohannon family he married into. They loved him for who he was—not the guy who walked away from his faith and the Catholic Church when he went off to college, but a devoted husband and father, a man of character and integrity.

He inspected the back of his fork as his mind slipped back to the dawn of August 25—four days and a world ago. What had he witnessed that morning, other than a desperate and bloody battle on Temple Mount? How could he explain what he felt in his heart—above the fear—when the pillar of fire turned into a pillar of cloud as dawn broke over the smoldering canyon that was once the Mount? How could he reconcile the answers to Tom's prayers, what seemed like one miracle after another, with the deaths of so many? What was happening? What did it mean? And, why him? Why was he here? He felt a stirring in a place he hadn't scratched in an age. What if there was more behind Tom's faith than Joe was willing to accept? What if . . .

An Irish brogue brought him back to the present.

"These have all been interesting discussions, I must say." Brandon McDonough looked down the table, past the gravy-splattered plates and the now-empty bowls. "I've been both exhilarated and appalled at the glib way in which we have considered marching off to the garden of Eden. It's an alluring fairy tale, but . . ."

Rizzo twiddled with a chunk of rigatoni on his otherwise vacant plate. "Putting it that way makes it sound like we'd have a better chance swiping a leprechaun's gold than finding the staff."

His head nodding agreement, McDonough pointed his fork at Rizzo. "For once I agree with you, Samuel. But beyond the unlikely nature of success in this endeavor, there is at least one other question that we have failed to consider."

"Will global warming cook my eggs in the morning? Does a stitch in time really save nine?" Rizzo's cherubic countenance was trumped by the mischief in his eyes.

"Ummm . . . excuse me . . ." McDonough stammered. "What?"

"Skip it, Paddy-boy. What was your question?"

"Well, Samuel, assuming it can be found," said McDonough, "why take the staff from the garden? If Eden is where it came from, and if it's been safe there for the last twenty-five hundred years, why move it? Why remove it and bring it . . . where? Where would it be safe? Jerusalem? London? In a vault somewhere? If Aaron's staff is, in fact, the most powerful weapon in the history of the world, why bring it out of hiding, from a place no one can find—perhaps no one can enter? It just doesn't make sense, eh?"

Deirdre got up and started clearing the plates. Annie picked up a bowl and then turned to McDonough.

"I've wondered the same thing a couple of times myself," said Annie, "and I keep coming back to what's probably the most important point for me. Don't you think this is the completion of the task . . . the final step of the calling God's put on our lives? Finding Aaron's staff is apparently the root of all that has gone before. Charles Spurgeon finds this mezuzah and sends it to the Bowery Mission, where it sits in a safe for over a hundred years gathering dust and it just happens to be found now?"

That's what I'm saying, thought Joe. *Why now? Why us?* A thought helped him find his voice.

"There's one other consideration." Joe looked down the table at McDonough. He pulled his hands through his unruly salt-and-pepper hair. "The Temple Guard and Prophet's Guard have been fighting over this mezuzah for more than a thousand years, trying to complete their understanding of the riddles and clues on the mezuzah and scroll . . . trying to track down this staff of power. Well, we've figured it out—almost, I guess. But let's assume all this conjecture we're tossing around is true—that Jeremiah took the staff back to Babylon, looking for the garden. If we can figure it out, why can't somebody else figure it out? What if the Prophet's Guard were to find out what we know? What would they do with it . . . the Muslim Brotherhood? They haven't given up. Don't you think it would be a risk if we just gave up?"

Bohannon joined his wife in clearing the table. "Annie's right about one thing. The Prophet's Guard isn't going to let us just walk away from this. I'm beginning to think that, whether we like it or not, we're involved, and they are going to force us to finish it. I'd rather it be on my terms than theirs." He looked around the table. "I think we need to go back to the synagogue. We only looked at a small section of the book of Jeremiah this morning. There could be other clues in other parts of the book, in other notations. But remember what the rabbi said to us as we were leaving? Aaron's staff, with the Ark, could be the weapon of Armageddon, the weapon God uses to destroy all the armies that come to attack Israel. Can we afford to take a chance that weapon falls into the wrong hands? What if the Prophet's Guard could harness and use the power of Aaron's staff?"

Tom walked down the table and put his hand on McDonough's shoulder. "And there's another thing to consider. What would Doc do? If he were here right now, what would Doc Johnson be telling us we should do? Give up? Go home? Or continue to seek what might be the most amazing archaeological discovery of history?"

11:26 a.m., New York City

"You know, I'm not as much of a Neanderthal as you think," said Manthey. "I know about Skype."

Connor Bohannon was adjusting the screen of the laptop to give as wide an angle as possible. "That's great. How many times have you used it?" He turned away from the screen to glance at Manthey, who stood to his right. The Mission's CFO held a hand against the bandage on his right side where the Urgent Care doctor had sewn a dozen stitches to close the knife wound he'd received in the taxi. The cut was painful, but no longer threatening.

"Use it?" he mumbled. "But I know about it."

Connor shook his head. "How's that cut? Can you sit?"

"I may not Skype, but I can sit."

"Okay . . . here, sit. Left click on that icon."

⟿⟿⟿

Roberta Smith was at her desk early that morning, waiting for the connection to open. She would have stayed up all night if necessary.

For forty years, Smith had been the driving force behind the Demotic Dictionary Project at the University of Chicago's Oriental Institute. Over those years, many team members had toiled, tarried, and then moved on. But Roberta Smith stayed. This was her passion. This was her baby. And six months ago, she gave birth.

After decades working mostly in relative obscurity, the University of Chicago announced that the Oriental Institute's Demotic Dictionary Project was complete. Smith's team had researched each of the twenty-three core Demotic symbols and recorded every one of the possible definitions of each symbol. Their dictionary was massive, over two thousand pages in length.

Because Demotic was a spoken language in Egypt long before anyone ever wrote it down, not only had various dialects developed over the one thousand years it was spoken, but the symbols had also taken on a wide range of disparate definitions depending on the populations speaking it.

So the Demotic symbol that was identified by the letter *H*—and there were four of them—had over seven hundred pages of symbol variations and explanations, and more than eight thousand different definitions. The least complex symbol, the symbol for *F*, was recorded with *only* one hundred definitions over ten pages. By adding the nuances of meaning that emerged from combining two Demotic symbols, it was easy to see a very simple truth.

Even at the Oriental Institute, where they knew more about ancient languages than anywhere else in the world, the team *may have* deciphered the various definitions of the symbols. They *may have* even gotten to the point where—they believed—they could make informed assessments of the general meaning or purpose of certain documents. But they still couldn't claim to know what any of the thousands of Demotic examples currently known to be in existence really meant.

Now, after all that immersion in Demotic, after all her years of research and nearly four decades of shepherding the dictionary to completion, Roberta Smith sat in front of her computer with the excitement of a first visit to the circus.

Several months ago she had been introduced by a colleague to Dr. Richard Johnson Sr., former chair of the Antiquities College at Columbia University and, now retired from academia, director of the Collector's Club in New York City. Johnson had come to her with the most remarkable document she had seen in her entire professional life. It was a complete, intact scroll containing a lengthy message in Demotic symbols. The message was written in a code that Johnson and his colleagues had broken, allowing them to decipher the message. Not by translating from the Demotic, which would have been a miracle, but by deciphering the code and then comparing the code symbols to the Rosetta Stone—inscribed with three languages: Greek, Demotic, and hieroglyphics— converting the Demotic symbols into Greek symbols and thereby breaking the secret of the scroll.

Johnson not only shared images of the scroll and the message it contained, but he also told her some of the details of the harrowing experience he and his comrades endured in the bowels of Jerusalem's Temple Mount.

Now Dr. Johnson was dead, murdered by the relentless agents of the Prophet's Guard, and Tom Bohannon's son, Connor, had called, desperate for an immediate conversation on Skype. The screen on her computer cleared . . .

⌇⌇⌇

"Dr. Smith? Hi . . . I'm Connor Bohannon and this is my dad's close friend Stew Manthey. Thanks for taking the time to meet with us."

At first glance, Dr. Roberta Smith looked exactly as Connor had imagined. Well past middle age, dark but graying hair pulled back in a bun, black-framed glasses sliding down the bridge of her nose. But that's where the caricature stopped. Dr. Smith wore a smart, black business suit with a crisp white shirt and a string of pearls at her neck. Her cheekbones high like a model's, the sparkle in her dark eyes belied the gray in her hair.

If she were thirty years younger, thought Connor.

"I don't intend to be rude, but I'm afraid we don't have much time," said Connor. "I believe Doc Johnson talked to you about the safe my dad found in the Bowery Mission. There were three drawers in that safe, two of which they couldn't open. With the help of the NYPD, we got those drawers open yesterday. You know my mom and dad and the rest of the team are still in Jerusalem. Mr. Manthey and I found something we believe will be very important to them, and we're hoping you might be able to help us figure out what it means."

Connor slipped the two sprockets out of their protective containers . . .

⌇⌇⌇

Roberta Smith didn't know what she was looking at.

"What is that?"

Connor Bohannon picked up a thick disc that looked like leather and pulled it apart into two thinner discs.

"These are the sprockets that were originally inside the mezuzah that held the scroll," he said. "They held the center spindle in place. Each side is separated like slices in a pie. These raised arms have nubs; they divide some sections. And the arms alternate with these grooves that divide other sections. When you put them back together again, the arms with the nubs fit into the grooves with these slots in them."

Bohannon held up the separated discs in front of the camera for her to see. One of them was solid; the other had four holes evenly spaced around the disc within the eight spaces between the arms and the grooves.

On the face of each of the discs, Roberta saw some very familiar symbols. Her old friends, Demotic. "It's more of your code?" Her low, modulated voice sounded far away, even to her.

"That's what we were hoping *you* could tell *us*," said Manthey.

He took the two discs from Bohannon and joined them, fitting the arms into the grooves. "I noticed something odd when we first took them apart and put them back together." He separated the discs again, held up the one in his right hand and pointed it toward the camera. "Side A," said Manthey. Then he flipped over the one in his right hand and once again fit it into the half in his left hand. "See, side A fits into this one, and side B also fits into this one. You can flip over the other disc, also, and those sides also fit together . . . they all fit the same—A to C . . . A to D or B to C . . . B to D."

Ingenious, thought Roberta as Manthey continued to join the discs together in different combinations. "There must be a reason—"

"Yes . . . the symbols," Manthey said.

He pulled the discs apart and held the solid one up for her inspection.

"One symbol that appears to be in the same pattern appears on both discs, no matter what way you combine the halves. Do you see that little snake squiggle?"

"Yes. In the Demotic language, for the purpose of identification, we refer to that symbol as the letter *D*," said Roberta.

"Well, it appears every fourth symbol on both sides of both discs. There are eighteen other symbols on the discs. Although some appear more than once, there is no pattern like the snake squiggle. But look at this."

Manthey held the disc with the holes in his right hand and combined it with the solid disc. He held it to the camera. "See . . . Mr. Squiggle appears every fourth symbol. And if you turn one disc ninety degrees, they fit together perfectly again, and Mr. Squiggle is still every fourth symbol. It's the same no matter how you put the sides of the sprockets together or how you rotate the discs. Mr. Squiggle shows up as every fourth symbol."

He took the two discs apart again and held them in opposite hands. "There are four ways to view the symbols each time you combine a side to a side—the first way, a ninety-degree turn, one-eighty degrees, and two-seventy degrees. Four views on each combination of sides—sixteen views overall. Each of those views reveals eight symbols—three symbols and Mr. Squiggle; three symbols and Mr. Squiggle. See?"

Roberta had drawn four large circles on two pieces of paper in front of her and was scribbling down the symbols as Manthey rotated the discs. "Yes . . . I'm following you." To the right of the circles she had a pad of paper where she had inscribed sets of the symbols from the sides she had seen thus far. "If you assume each four symbols is a set either starting with or ending with the symbol *D*—Mr. Squiggle as you call it—then there are thirty-two sets of four, correct?" Roberta looked down at the sets on her piece of paper. "Mr. Manthey, are all the sets unique? None of them are the same?"

"That's correct," said Manthey, who combined the two discs again and held the resulting object up to the screen. "The sequence of the symbols that you can see through the holes is the same no matter how you combine them—three symbols and then Mr. Squiggle; three symbols and then Mr. Squiggle. The symbols, or the order of the symbols, change each time. But each time you switch the sides or rotate the guide disc, the one with the holes, the pattern remains the same—three symbols and Mr. Squiggle." Manthey looked up at the camera. "Don't you find that odd?"

Roberta laughed in spite of herself and clearly her laugh startled both men.

"Are you kidding? Everything you gentlemen have come up with so far has been a little odd, don't you think? The largest existing sample of Demotic in history—in perfect condition. A temple under a mountain in Jerusalem. Moses's Tent of Meeting in a cave in the Negev. And now a one-thousand-year-old Rubik's cube of a message in an extinct language. Yes, Mr. Manthey, I do think it a bit odd, but not for the same reason you do. And here's another question, no offense—but how did the two of you figure all this out?"

"Sudoku," said Bohannon.

"What?"

"Sudoku . . . Mr. Manthey likes puzzles."

Unbelievable. All of this is unbelievable.

Roberta took a moment to marvel at her incredible fortune. In the course of a few months, these amateurs had introduced her to the two most fascinating examples of Demotic in recent history. She shook her head, picked up her pencil, and continued inscribing on the pad of paper to her right. "This is an exceptionally complex puzzle you've discovered." She looked up at the camera. "The question I keep asking myself is why . . . why would someone go to such Byzantine lengths to hide something that, ultimately, is meant to be shared with someone else?

"Mr. Squiggle has about one thousand meanings listed in our dictionary." She held up the paper upon which she was writing. "But look at this: these other symbols change position relative to Mr. Squiggle as you rotate the discs, and as you assemble and disassemble the sides, correct?" She didn't wait for an answer. "But the symbols are not all completely random. Look—you have nineteen distinct symbols. Mr. Squiggle shows up in all thirty-two combinations. But the other eighteen symbols also recur . . . six of them eight times, the other twelve, four times."

Roberta pulled the paper back to glance down at it and get oriented, then took her pencil and pointed at the symbols in two circles on her paper. "Normally with just a few symbols and those changing positions, it would be very difficult to venture a guess at which direction to take . . . hmmm . . . no pun intended."

Bohannon looked perplexed. "Excuse me?"

"Mr. Squiggle may have a thousand meanings, but those meanings become dramatically limited when it is used in conjunction with numbers. And these symbols"—she pointed—"these symbols, these symbols, are all numbers."

She looked up to see if reality had dawned on either Bohannon or Manthey, but their faces were as blank as an unplugged computer terminal.

"These are numbers . . . sequences of numbers."

Roberta Smith turned away from the sheet of paper and stared into the camera. "Mr. Bohannon . . . what are you looking for?"

"Well, we're just trying to figure out—"

"No. I don't mean this puzzle. I mean, what is your father looking for? This crew has unearthed a thousand-year-old temple and a two-thousand-year-old sanctuary tent. What are you looking for now? What are you searching for that this message could help you discover?"

Manthey returned her stare with a growing intensity. "You know, don't you. You know what it says?"

"No," said Roberta. "But I know what it is. We have papyrus documents that are lists of numbers. Often, when the numbers are combined with other symbols, we get a pretty good idea what it means."

She lowered the piece of paper. "In this context, with these accompanying symbols, I am as confident as I can be that Mr. Squiggle means 'paces.' There are numbers ahead of the symbol for paces. What we have here," she said with a depth of importance and awe, "are directions."

15

One stalk of celery in one fist and another sticking out of the pocket of his shirt—a nondescript, pale khaki work shirt—Rizzo came out of the kitchen to find Joe staring out the window.

"Deirdre's mom still with Gracie and Paul?"

"Yeah," said Joe, turning away from the window, "and all three of them are getting a little edgy. Deirdre checked this morning when we were over at the synagogue. Gracie thinks, because she's nineteen, we should have left her in charge—which is why we didn't. Paul just got his driver's license and feels like a prisoner. And Mary is unhappy with the role of warden, not to mention her fear for all of us over here. Not a very happy bunch. Deirdre's in the back room with her Bible. She always finds peace when she reads her Bible. She and Tom are alike in that—things get tough, and they lean on their faith."

Biting off a huge chunk of celery to keep his mouth busy, Rizzo evaluated the twinge of jealousy that shot through his heart. What did he have to lean on other than regret? If only Kallie . . .

Rizzo crossed the room, reached in past the celery stalk, and pulled two pieces of paper from his shirt pocket. "I was looking at these on the flight from Egypt after Doc died, but then I forgot about them with all that happened."

Tom and Annie were on their way back to the Ades Synagogue to look at the replica codex more closely, and McDonough's snores were probably knocking plaster from the ceiling of the bedroom. Rizzo unfolded the two sheets of paper. He handed the first one to Joe. "These are some of the notations I wrote down from the margins of the Aleppo Codex pages the Temple Guard possessed. I didn't know then if we'd have any use for them, but it seemed important." He handed over the second sheet. "And you're familiar with these guys." Three lines of *C* characters, the Dorabella Cipher.

"You know, there are still a lot of questions about this whole mystery that we haven't really resolved. It's like that line in Abiathar's scroll message to Meborak that said, 'Look to the Prophets for your direction,' which eventually led us to Jeremiah and the Tent of Meeting."

"Missing that little gem cost us dearly," said Joe.

"But this one," Rizzo said, pointing to the Dorabella Cipher, Sir Edward Elgar's birthday gift to Dora Penny, a simple cipher of eighty-seven characters, still unbroken after 150 years, "is the one that's bugged me the most. What does this thing mean—and what part does it really play?"

"It gave us the sequence of the scroll . . . it's how we broke the code."

"Yeah, but look . . . what if there is more to it? This cipher"—Rizzo started pacing around the apartment, his arms orchestrating punctuation as his mind raced with ideas—"has stumped the best minds and the fastest computers. I mean—jeepers—the scroll itself was already written in a code, in the symbols of an extinct language where the letter *T* has what? Like eight hundred thousand meanings?"

Joe shook his head. "When I was growing up in Washington Heights, the Dominican kids on the corner would call you *jablador*."

"Ha . . . blah . . . door? Does that mean handsome?" Rizzo was still pacing, headed across the living room.

"Not quite. To be kind, let's just say it means somebody who stretches the truth, just a little."

"Yeah, okay." Rizzo spun on his heel to face Joe. "But how much more obtuse does Elgar's secret code need to be? Elgar didn't write this cipher just because he didn't have the *New York Times* crossword to keep him busy."

He started pacing the room again, his hands twirling like a windmill. "Would Elgar spend so much time perfecting a code so intricate, clever, and impenetrable that it's never been broken and then simply put it in a birthday card to the schoolgirl daughter of a preacher in the English countryside? No. The Dorabella Cipher must be hiding something—something that Elgar and Spurgeon knew they wanted to keep secret, and a secret that was *not* the existence of a Temple under Temple Mount."

Counterbalancing Rizzo's animated gyrations, Joe sprawled out on the sofa, lifting his long legs onto the cushions. "Okay. Let's say the cipher does have a role to play. But what is it? And how would we know? Just like you said, people have been trying to crack the Dorabella Cipher for over a hundred years with no success. What are we going to learn from it? What does it matter?"

"Look, dragon breath, what if it does matter—what if it matters in some way we don't understand yet?"

"Like what?"

"I don't know. The codex spent time in Alexandria, the same place Spurgeon picked up the mezuzah and scroll. Could it be possible that Spurgeon had a chance to see the codex while they were in Egypt?"

"No, the codex was in Aleppo by then, long gone from Egypt. You think Elgar and Spurgeon went looking for the staff?"

"I don't know what I think."

"I'll say *amen* to that."

Rizzo stopped his pacing, walked over to the sofa, and stood eye-to-eye with Rodriguez. "What I was going to say is I don't know what I think about Spurgeon and Elgar looking for the staff. But what I do think is that Elgar and Spurgeon figured it out—the whole shooting match. They discovered Abiathar's scroll. They realized the power of Aaron's staff, and I think they probably discovered the location of the garden."

Rodriguez pushed himself up into a sitting position, his face a puzzle. "But how could a couple of old guys like Spurgeon and Elgar travel from Egypt to Babylon? Alexandria, they take a ship. Babylon, they've gotta cross over six hundred miles of desert?"

"They wouldn't have had to. Maybe they talked to somebody who did."

"Like who?"

"Sir Charles Warren." Rizzo felt the wicked smile rise on his cheeks as he watched the thoughts and emotions move like flashcards across Rodriguez's face. "You're not the only nerd who knows how to use the library."

7:00 p.m.

Joining the people entering the Ades Synagogue, Bohannon took one of the yarmulkes from the basket by the door as Annie covered her head with the shawl she had brought. It was just before sunset, when the synagogue began its Sabbath-ending evening service of Syrian Hazzanut, the Middle Eastern–style Jewish liturgical singing that was one of the unique features of Ades services.

Entering the vestibule, Tom and Annie turned to the right. Bohannon was concerned to see the elder Rabbi Asher waiting by the stairs to the lower level.

"You have come just in time," said Rabbi Asher. "Once the service begins, the doors are closed and entrance is denied. Come. Let me get you established before the service begins. I need to be in place."

They descended the stairs with alacrity and entered the *gniza* that Rabbi Asher unlocked for them. He moved to the table in the front section, ignoring the long rows of wooden shelves containing the collected Torah scrolls of the synagogue that stretched away for thirty yards in the building's basement. They joined the rabbi in donning the white cotton gloves resting on the table and watched as Asher unlocked the metal box containing the synagogue's copy of the Aleppo Codex, lowered it like fragile treasure, and opened to the book of Jeremiah.

"I must go to the service, so please keep notes. If you have questions, my nephew will come to help you read the notations and answer your questions. I don't know what secret you are hoping to discover, but I wish you good fortune."

With that the rabbi pivoted and exited as quickly as he had entered. When he was gone, Tom turned to Annie.

"Now what? Where do we start? Where do we look for Jeremiah's secret—the entrance to the garden?"

A cold current of air passed across the back of Tom's neck, causing a chill to run down his spine. The room filled with the intoxicating smell of exotic spices, accompanied by the distant sound of bells and trumpets, which segued into a voice.

"Perhaps I can assist you with your search?"

To Tom's right, an audible *ooohhh* drifted from Annie's mouth. He could see why. From between the stacks emerged a young man of such extraordinary beauty Bohannon had to look closely to make sure it wasn't a woman. The young man's skin was unusually pale, and his bright green eyes were surrounded by waves of black curls. He moved with the grace of a dancer, but the muscles under his shirt belonged to a wrestler.

"I've been sent to help you," the young man said.

The rabbi's nephew looked nothing like him.

Annie turned toward the book and caressed the page with her gloved hand, running her finger over the beautifully wrought Hebrew letters. "We're trying to understand more about the notations around the book of Jeremiah."

"Ah, yes," said the young man, his words reverberating under the low ceiling, "but I don't think we start with Jeremiah. I think we start with Daniel."

Bohannon was surprised, and showed it by the quick snap of his head in the young man's direction. "But Jeremiah—"

"Yes. Jeremiah is important. But what you may not know is that when Jeremiah arrived in Babylon, about 594 BC, Daniel and the prophet Ezekiel were already in the city, having been taken captive earlier by the Babylonians. Nebuchadnezzar laid siege to Jerusalem three times; the final time, in 587 BC, he was so enraged by Zedekiah's rebellion that he decreed the city be completely destroyed. Daniel was one of the Hebrew hostages deported to Babylon the first time in 605.

"Daniel rose in rank and stature while in captivity and served three Babylonian kings—Nebuchadnezzar, Darius, and Cyrus. He was known by the name Belshazzar and was highly exalted and very powerful in spite of his Hebrew heritage. He rose to the position of chancellor under Nebuchadnezzar, second in power only to the emperor. He knew everything the king knew."

The young man's voice was clear and firm, softly modulated. *He could have a career in public speaking.*

"Daniel interpreted dreams for Nebuchadnezzar, which helped him rise in the king's court, but he also had visions himself, three of which were interpreted for Daniel by a man dressed in linen, with a belt of finest gold around his waist—a man identified as the angel Gabriel, who stands in God's presence. Two points you should know—first, in the first year of Darius, Daniel received a vision of Israel's deliverance from Babylonian captivity by 'reading the word of the Lord given to Jeremiah the prophet,' a vision that was interpreted for Daniel by Gabriel. And, second, in the book of Enoch, also in Jewish mythology, even in John Milton's *Paradise Lost*, Gabriel is identified as the ruler, or governor, over both the garden of Eden and the cherubim who guard its gates.

"I believe," said the young man, moving to the table and putting on a pair of gloves, "if you wish to find the entrance to the garden of Eden, you should look first at the Masoretic notes surrounding the book of Daniel."

As he turned the pages from Jeremiah, past Lamentations and Ezekiel, Annie came to his side. "How do you know what we're looking for?" she asked, her eyes narrowed and her voice on edge.

"I was told. Here, this is what I sought."

Tom watched as the young man looked at Annie, so close to his side, with a tenderness that made Tom blush and envious at the same time.

"May I read to you?" The young man's voice spun in the air like an invitation to a dance, light and melodic.

Annie's eyes questioned, but softened.

"Here," said the young man, "in the book of Daniel, is the third time the angel visited with the prophet. Prior to explaining to Daniel what will happen to the Jewish captives in the future—'a time yet to come'—the man identified as the angel Gabriel says that he was dispatched to Daniel on the first day of Daniel's prayers, but that he was resisted by the prince of the Persian kingdom for twenty-one days. 'Then Michael, one of the chief princes, came to help me because I was detained there with the king of Persia.'"

The young man moved his gloved hand to the top of the page and the notations at the top of the column of letters. "Our learned scholars wrote this as explanation, here at the top of the page and continuing at the bottom:

> The Prince of Persia, and his demonic hordes, resisted Gabriel at the gate of the garden, preventing him from entering the Persian kingdom from the kingdom of G-d. The Prince of Persia stood above the gate of the garden and held the gate for three times seven, until Michael, the chief of G-d's warriors, joined Gabriel to overcome his power.
>
> In a "time yet to come," the man of G-d will answer G-d's call and stand in the gate of G-d. The way to the garden will be open to him, and he will fulfill the prophecy written here, "But at that time your people—everyone whose name is found written in the book—will be delivered."

Bohannon's head was spinning, entranced by the young man's voice and confounded by the words he read. "What does it mean?"

The young man stepped away from the book and walked to the other side of the table, facing Tom and Annie.

"In the book of Jeremiah he writes about the things in the Temple of God, 'For this is what the Lord Almighty says about the pillars, the bronze Sea, the movable stands and the other articles that are left in this city . . . "They will be taken to Babylon and there they will remain until the day I come for them," declares the Lord. "Then I will bring them back and restore them to this place."'

"You are concerned," he said, "about why God would want to bring Aaron's staff from the garden, where it has been safeguarded for nearly three thousand years. You are anxious that those who seek its power could capture it."

Annie gestured toward the young man. "How do you know these things?"

The young man placed both hands on the table. "What do you think this has been about from the beginning? If God wants to protect the staff of Aaron for another three thousand years by leaving it in the garden, don't you think he can do that? Even if men like the Prophet's Guard or the Muslim Brotherhood think they can find it and use it, is it too much for God to put a stop to their plans? Is his arm too short? And if you bring it out, do you think he is incapable of protecting it in the very world he himself created?"

The young man turned his attention to Tom and leaned into the table. "But you, man of God, have been called to a task. You don't understand why. People called by God seldom understand why. But clearly God knows why. And there is a purpose here. Think of all the wisdom, hidden wisdom, that has been imparted to you in the last several months, the codes and secret messages that unfolded before your eyes: Abiathar's scroll and that journey under Temple Mount to the Third Temple of God; Jeremiah's long path of clues to the place where he had hidden the Tent of Meeting; discerning the hidden mysteries of the Aleppo Codex and its message about Aaron's staff. And you found the two, interlocking sprockets with a message that could not have been translated until recently when the University of Chicago's Oriental Institute completed its forty-year project to create a Demotic dictionary."

Annie continued to shake her head. "But, wait. Where have you gotten this information?"

The young man did not slow down.

"Think of the opposition you have encountered and overcome: ancient, secret societies searching for the same information; incredibly powerful men, organizations, and governments who wanted to stop you; murderous attempts on your lives and the lives of your families."

He moved from the far side of the table and approached Tom and Annie. He placed a hand on each of their shoulders and sent a current of warmth along the ridge of Tom's shoulders. His eyes seemed to refract light from some internal source—peaceful and calming in one respect but bursting with life and promise in another.

"You, Tom, and your team have traveled over three continents and transcended each of these obstacles. And now you find yourselves in an old Syrian synagogue, in the spiritual center of the world, searching for the staff of power from the hand of God. And after all that has gone before—after all of this— you still wonder if searching for Aaron's staff is the right thing to do?

"Then allow me to tell you a story. The Creator of all things placed the stars in the sky before the beginning of time. The planets, the solar systems, the billions of galaxies all move as a perfect celestial clock—you can precisely chart their movements back in time or forward into the future. We look to Daniel, not Jeremiah, because Daniel was a wise man who became a teacher of wise men in Babylon, where a wise man was called a magus. Daniel was the teacher of the magi. It was Daniel who taught the magi to watch for the sign in the sky, the confluence of Jupiter and Venus that formed the brightest *star* the heavens had ever produced. And it was Daniel who plotted the sky of the Bethlehem Star five hundred years before that night occurred, and used that celestial structure to protect the staff of God until the day God called it forth once more."

The young man removed his hand from Annie and put both hands on Tom's shoulders. The room began to darken at its edges and close in on Tom. He was compelled to keep his gaze locked on the hypnotic green eyes. "Those God calls, Tom, he always equips and enables. God has equipped you to uncover all these secrets and enabled you to understand their meaning. You are, actually, on a mission *for* God, not from God.

"God wants the staff found," he said. "That I know. The staff is a symbol to this world, a reminder of God's power and his justice. Perhaps Aaron's staff will turn the people of this world away from those things that glorify man and insult the God who created man."

Bohannon felt the chill run down his spine once more, and a sepulchral silence entered the *gniza*. "I tell you the truth. If that staff still has life, I would fear greatly for this world." The young man's words had lost their melody, but developed a razor's edge. He seemed to have grown in stature. "Pharaoh hardened his heart toward God so many times that God finally hardened Pharaoh's heart permanently, and look what happened to Egypt: the plagues. What would happen to this world if God turned his patience to wrath? Would he use the same instrument to unleash that wrath? Would he release the same plagues?"

A shadow crossed Bohannon's eyes. A dusky haze filled the room as it darkened even more.

"Why does God want the staff found?" The young man's voice was a whisper, retreating from Bohannon's ears. "Is Aaron's staff to tap into the rock once

THE ALEPPO CODE   139

more and bring forth the spiritual water of revival so that nations will be saved? Or is it to open God's justice and bring cleansing on the world? Regardless of God's plan," he whispered, "this is your task. This is what God has created you to do. And you should allow nothing to stop you."

Bohannon fought for clarity of mind and vision.

"How do you know all this? Who are you?"

As he removed his hands from Tom's shoulders, a broad smile crossed the young man's face and warmed Tom's soul. "My father calls me Gabriel. My brothers also."

"I don't—"

Steps fell heavy on the stone stairway leading from the upper floor. Annie and Tom turned for a heartbeat to see Rabbi Asher at the bottom of the steps. "Mr. Bohannon, I promised you—"

"Rabbi, your nephew Gabriel here . . ." Tom turned, his left arm swinging in an arc toward the young man.

But no one was there.

Bohannon looked down the empty length of the stacked shelves and then at his wife, whose face glowed like the sky before a rising sun. They turned to the rabbi.

"No, Mr. Bohannon, this is my nephew Gabriel here," said Rabbi Asher, his hand on the shoulder of a teenager in an ill-fitting black suit. "I told you that I would bring him to you. Now I must get upstairs before the service begins. Gabriel," he said to the teenager, "please help Mr. and Mrs. Bohannon read the notations in the codex."

16

11:15 p.m., Tehran, Iran

His private jet landed at Tehran's Mehrabad Airport, well out of the fallout zone, in the middle of the night and was unobstructed as it taxied to the far end of the tarmac, turning into a huge, darkened hangar in the corner farthest from the main terminal. The hangar doors moved with quiet dispatch, closing off all visual access in less than a minute. A phalanx of black, stretch limos with darkened windows were parked in a chevron formation to the left of the now-stationary jet.

When King Abbudin of Saudi Arabia descended the stairs, the Iranian security agents had no idea which vehicle the king would select. There were seven limos and, before the front door of the airplane swung open, dozens of Saudi guards poured out the back door and surrounded—and searched—each of the vehicles.

Abbudin was dressed plainly this night, the king wearing a simple white kaftan under an open, dark green robe, a black-checked keffiyeh on his head. His heavy face was dominated by the many-layered, sagging bags under his eyes, the small, pointed beard isolated to the apex of his chin.

Without hesitation, King Abbudin stepped into the third limo on the right wing of the chevron. Bodyguards and aides scrambled into the other three vehicles on the same wing. Two Cadillac Escalade SUVs stood sentinel at the point of the chevron and began to pull away, gaining speed as they burst from the hangar and crossed the tarmac to a heavily guarded, open gate. As the chevron of limos exited the gate, it split in two, and the wings drove off in opposite directions.

Tehran's congested and logic-defying traffic problems were avoided because of the late hour. The convoy raced down the Lashkari Expressway and, instead

140

of turning north to the president's official residence in the Sa'dabad Palace in Shemiran, turned south toward Shahr Park. Following the Cadillac SUV, the motorcade whizzed past the British and German embassies and turned right onto a small street that backed the Iran National Museum. Turning into a thin driveway flanked by the Islamic Era Museum, the vehicles skirted the fountain in the midst of the formal gardens and pulled up—hidden by trees—at the back of the Ministry of Foreign Affairs.

Abbudin's bodyguards formed a human shield around their king as he stepped from the limo. This tight knot of security moved silently to the rear entrance of the ministry building, but turned left, down a short flight of steps to an underground level. Once through a heavy, vault-like door, most of the security squad pulled away to man surveillance locations while two of his most trusted guardians accompanied the king down a long, sloping hallway, deeper into the bowels of the building. At the far end, two French doors opened. Standing in the doorway was the supreme leader.

"As-salaam alaikum," said Abbudin, a nod of his head acknowledging his host, "and Allah's mercy and blessings."

"Wa-alaikum salaam, my brother, the same to you. It is an honor to have you under our roof." Imam Ayatollah Ali Ghorbani, the second supreme leader of the Islamic Republic of Iran since the Islamic Revolution overthrew the shah in 1979, looked much like his predecessor—old, bespectacled, a full, long white beard covering a third of his face, a large black sarband on his head. Like his mentor Ayatollah Ruhollah Khomeini before him, Ali Ghorbani was one of the Shi'a clerics who helped design the Iranian theocracy, a fundamentalist Islamic state effectively ruled by the self-appointed Assembly of Experts, which selected the supreme leader. "I apologize for the clandestine nature of your arrival, but even here in Tehran, we have become victims of traitors and Zionist aggression. Let me assure you, we are safe here. We are upwind of the radiation, and this bunker is secure. Come, let us rest."

His right arm nearly destroyed by an assassination attempt in 1981, when a bomb concealed in a tape recorder at a press conference exploded beside him, Ghorbani extended his left hand and escorted King Abbudin farther into the depths of the foreign ministry building.

"It is good of you to come to Tehran," Ghorbani said as they walked along the corridor and turned into a comfortable sitting room. "I must admit I was a bit surprised when I received your request."

Ghorbani led Abbudin toward two facing, upholstered chairs flanking a small, round table. Above them hung a life-size portrait of the late supreme leader, Ruhollah Khomeini. The portrait was their only companion as their aides and bodyguards wasted no time leaving the room.

Abbudin, understanding the risk he took by asking for this meeting, didn't waste any time, either.

"Your Excellency, I come to you tonight as a tangible assertion of my solidarity with you and your countrymen at this time and to offer you the support of the Saudi people. I only ask that you and I put aside for the moment the many things that divide us and allow me to speak of the more important things that unite us."

Ghorbani sat back into the softness of the chair, his eyes never leaving Abbudin's face. The Saudi king knew this was the pivotal moment.

The supreme leader's voice was welcoming, his Arabic—in place of his native Farsi—was perfect, but his words carried the sting of truth. "By those things that divide us, do you mean the funds and arms you are currently supplying to the Sunni terrorists who are trying to overthrow the legitimate government of my Shi'a brother Baqir Al-Musawi in Syria? Or do you mean the American warplanes you permit to be based on the Saudi peninsula? Or do you mean the recent assassination of the Imam Moussa al-Sadr, father of Hezbollah, at the hands of one of your sons?"

King Abbudin was fully aware of the extensive intelligence apparatus the Iranians maintained throughout the world, but even he was surprised by Ghorbani's last comment. "Yes, those things and many others I'm sure you and I could articulate," said Abbudin, wrapping his robe more tightly around him in the subterranean chill. "And those are the things I am asking us to put aside for the moment—to put aside in pursuit of a higher goal than the Sunni-Shi'a enmity that saps our strength and blinds our intentions."

Ali Ghorbani's face was expressionless. "Tell me, then, why are you here?"

"I'm here," said King Abbudin, moving up to the edge of his chair, "because you and I seek the same thing, what is sought by all true followers of Islam: annihilation of Israel, destruction of Western civilization, and reestablishment of the Caliphate."

"And you have the means to make these things a reality?"

Abbudin could feel the hook setting.

"With your help."

"Tell me how."

"I once again control the Muslim Brotherhood. Al-Sadr lost control in Egypt, and Hosani's foolish ego and inept leadership was a setback for the movement. The Brotherhood has returned to the shadows, where it flourished for eighty years, building schools and bakeries, making disciples, and baking bread for the poor and leaderless. The generals think that cutting off the head will kill the body. The body grows stronger and will sprout new heads. But the Brotherhood remains committed to its ultimate goal—jihad and the overthrow of Western culture—and will continue to undermine pro-Western governments. Jordan will soon feel the hot breath of the Arab Spring.

"During the economic crisis in the West, particularly in the midst of this credit crisis in the European Union, a consortium of Saudi banks has worked through a series of fronts and dummy companies to purchase euro debt in staggering amounts. When the time is right, these Saudi banks—which I control—will call in this debt for immediate payment, bankrupting the governments of Europe.

"The time will be right," Abbudin continued, "when several things happen at once: when Saudi oil will stop flowing so freely because, we will claim, Brotherhood terrorists have sabotaged our pumping capacity; when the Islamic Republic of Iran shuts down the Strait of Hormuz to protect itself from additional aggression by the Zionists; when Western military bases are closed across the Islamic world; and when both you and I come to the aid of our brother Baqir, sending him tanks and troops, putting an end to this civil war in Syria so that Hezbollah is free to concentrate once more on Israel. Then these tanks and troops will be available, and in place, to roll up to the gates of Jerusalem."

Pushing up with his left hand, Ghorbani rose from his chair and walked to a sideboard against the wall. He poured a glass of water and brought it back, handing it to Abbudin. "A fine plan. But what will you do when America launches her cruise missiles, when her B-2 bombers begin targeting our tanks and our troops?" Ghorbani returned to the sideboard and came back with water for himself.

Abbudin raised his glass to the supreme leader, as if offering a toast. "America will be isolated, impotent," he claimed. "All of her allies will be silenced, economically emasculated as they have tried to do to Iran. We will bankrupt their economies. And crush them if they try to intervene. The financially desperate governments of Europe will confound the Americans for us, by calling for restraint while we push forward with our objectives—a political and economic coup to secretly exercise almost total control over German, French, Italian, Greek, and Spanish banks and governments."

Ghorbani nodded his head, his beard bobbing across the top of his water glass. "And what of us, my brother? Our nation sits on the edge of a much more imminent economic collapse: our gold reserve unapproachable, our oil production cut by more than half, American warships clogging our lifeline at Hormuz. How do I pay my soldiers? How do we keep food in the markets?"

The king of the Saud rested his glass on the small table by his side. Gathering up his kaftan and robe, he rose from the chair and bowed low from the waist. "Your Excellency," he said as he straightened, "the days of Sunni-Shi'a enmity are over. We are Muslim brothers; we are united in the call of the Prophet to jihad against the West. You have the promise of the House of Saud, the promise of the Muslim Brotherhood. Our banks are as open to you as our hearts. Come, we will supply all you need, a gift from one brother to another."

Ghorbani studied King Abbudin with the calculated assessment of a jewelry vendor in the market square. "And in return?"

Abbudin smiled. "Airlift your army and your tanks into the plain of Marj al-Saffar in Syria to support Al-Musawi, but ready to turn west into Israel. I will supply the cargo planes. The Brotherhood and my banks will withdraw support from the rebels. Send your warships into the Persian Gulf and attack the Americans. We are with you, esteemed brother. The might of Islam stands behind our brothers in Persia. Our time is here. Our destiny is now."

"Very well. But do not allow the arrogance of advantage to cloud discretion," said Ghorbani. "Once again I ask you about the long arm of the American military. Their weapons are not to be underestimated."

Not for the first time, Abbudin held his anger in check. *Your day will also come—you and all who malign the House of Saud.*

"You knew of the old man of the desert?"

"Ah, yes," said Ghorbani, "another brother who fell beneath the sharp blade of Saudi revenge. What of him and his assassins?"

Abbudin refused to rise to the bait. "For centuries the Prophet's Guard has sought the most powerful weapon in the history of the world—the staff of Aaron which imparted power to the Jews' Ark of the Covenant. Today, the Brotherhood has breathed new life into the Prophet's Guard and joined in that search. I believe the successful completion of that search is closer than ever. No military force will be able to stand against us."

Laughter burst from Ayatollah Ali Ghorbani like a backhanded slap. "Hah! You put your faith, and your hope for world domination in a fanciful story told by old women to infants? And where will you find this magic stick?"

His fingers felt for the dagger that was concealed under his robes. *Soon . . . one day soon.* But Abbudin kept his response to words.

"More than a stick, my brother. It destroyed all of Israel's enemies. Only fair that, now, this weapon be used against the Jews. And a devastating weapon it is. We believe we know where it is and the way for us to get that staff into our possession."

"And where is it?"

"Inside the gate to Adam's garden."

"And why is this stick not already in your possession?"

Yes . . . why? "It will be. And soon. Al-Sadr's hate was too small," said Abbudin. "The Caliphate will become the third world superpower. The West will be in the death grip of economic and political anarchy. We don't need occupying armies; we will occupy their banks and tie their hands.

"And while the West is handcuffed and impotent, we will deal ultimately, and finally, with Israel. We will wipe it from the map of the Middle East—and perhaps use its own weapon, a supernatural weapon of mass destruction, against it."

17

"I thought it would be quick once she figured it out," said Connor, "but it took us hours to come up with this, going back and forth, testing out each theory to see if it held up against all the possible combinations of the discs."

Tom looked at the screen and the chaotic schematic that Connor held in front of him, fifty-six hundred miles away in New York where it was early evening. Rizzo was sitting on Tom's right, the rest crowded behind them trying to see the screen of the secure laptop Sam Reynolds had given him.

"Buster," said Rizzo, "I've had Picasso dreams that looked better than that scribble. It looks like the universe in the midst of the Big Bang gone bust."

Connor lowered the sheet of paper. "Glad to see you're back to form, Mr. Rizzo. Here. Let me make it simple."

"Wait a minute, Connor." Annie pressed in from Bohannon's left to get in the camera's frame. "Are you okay? You look . . . different. Stressed? Is there something wrong? Where's Caitlin?"

"You don't need to worry, Mom. I'm fine. I'm a big boy, and Caitlin and I are staying at Uncle Dan's, like you wanted. Don't worry—we're as safe as we can be."

"I'm glad you're both safe," said Tom as he rubbed Annie's hand.

"Yeah. I wish you and Mom were here, too, but I know this is . . . bigger . . . than you just wanting an adventure. I'm sorry about—"

"I understand, Connor. You were right. There's nothing to apologize for. We'll be fine. God is directing our steps."

"Eeeeewwwww—goo patrol." Rizzo pushed his way in front of the camera. "Come on. Let's get back to that work of art—what did you guys find out?"

Holding the paper in front of him so the camera could still record the image, Connor slid over to the right. "Dad, what are carved into the sprockets are directions."

The silence of a church service filled the apartment.

"Directions? Directions from Spurgeon?" Tom asked.

"No, Dad. Dr. Smith believes the sprockets are just as old as the mezuzah—probably twenty-five hundred years old, give or take. And since they're in Demotic and the scroll was written in Demotic, there's obviously some kind of connection. But there was something else that Stew discovered."

"As soon as she said we were looking at directions, I started working the probabilities," Stew said. "Dr. Smith began by adding possible solutions in a random fashion—'if this one means north then this one might mean south'—but that was just taking us down a lot of blind alleys. I figured if the sequences were in fact directions, they must include two basic elements—both how far and which way—distance in numbers and direction in letters. We knew Mr. Squiggle was highly likely to mean paces, so the numbers would be before the paces and the way to go would come after.

"The first challenge was to decipher the number, or numbers, before the word *paces* and the direction after—was it a one-letter or two-letter direction? It took us awhile, but I think we finally got that right. What really had us stumped was where to start. Where did the directions start? That's what all those circles and symbols on the drawing are—the discs and different combinations. That's when Dr. Smith realized that some of the set sequences were actually different, in a different pattern."

He took apart the discs, checked out the faces, then attached them again in a different combination. "See, this is an odd one," he said, holding the face of the disc to the camera. "You can see there are three symbols and then Mr. Squiggle. But Dr. Smith figured out they were in a different order. Mr. Squiggle was out of sequence. We soon realized there were actually two things going on with these discs. Half of the ways we could view the symbols were exactly the same pattern: two numbers, paces, and a direction letter. In the other half of the views, Mr. Squiggle came after the direction instead of before it. Every ninety-degree twist on the guide disc alternated the relative position of Mr. Squiggle and the direction symbol."

"Whoa, Hiawatha," said Rizzo, throwing up his hand. "My brain just blew a gasket. Sets and patterns and paces and directions. I don't know if we're going to the market or we're going to Mars. Can you make it all a little more complicated? And then I can just check out completely."

"I'm with Rizzo on this one," said Joe, from over Tom's shoulder. "I lost you back at Mr. Squiggle Part Two. What does it all mean?"

Stew put down the pieces of paper. "In a nutshell, we've got sixteen sets that tell us to go this many paces in this direction. Simple. But the other sixteen sets are not so simple."

"Swell. Shoot me now." Rizzo dropped his head into his hands.

Stew scratched his beard. "Well, with the symbols changing position relative to each other, Dr. Smith couldn't be sure. She thought one group said something about *choosing one* and *follow by hand*, and the rest looked like some sort of astrology. She said it looked like stars and planets, a sequence of stars and planets. Then it hit her that they were astrological directions. She said the Chaldeans numbered the constellations and some of the major planets—what they thought were big stars. After doing some research, she determined that the second sixteen sets of symbols looked more like a combination than directions. You know, like a combination to open something. And she thought it might be saying something about the Roman god Jupiter and—"

"No. Not the Roman Jupiter, but the planet Jupiter," Tom interrupted. "And I bet there's a symbol for Venus."

"How do you know that?" Manthey asked.

"This sequence of stars and planets is not astrology," said Tom. "I'm confident this sequence is intended to represent the sky on the night Christ was born, the Incarnation. And I believe that sequence—starting with the confluence of Jupiter and Venus, which became known as the Star of Bethlehem—is the pattern that will need to be touched by hand to gain entrance. I don't think the correct interpretation is about choosing one, like choosing a place to start. I believe it says *the chosen one* is to follow this pattern by hand."

Bohannon looked sideways to Joe and opened both hands, palms up, in an unspoken question. He turned back to the computer screen.

"Stew, do you know where we're going?" Tom tried to will himself through the computer and into Manthey's understanding.

Manthey raised his gaze from the diagram. "Not really, but maybe," he said. "I like puzzles. I think I'm starting to put some of the pieces together. But, no, I don't know for sure."

"But you think you may have a combination for us?"

"Maybe—at least part of one."

Tom stood and turned away from the computer, motioning Annie and Joe to join him a few feet away. "How much do you think we should tell them?"

Joe stretched his neck as he shook his head. But Annie was more direct.

"Nothing—and that's not negotiable." Her voice had the force of a slamming door. "The more they know, the more of a threat they are to our friends with the amulet. We're not putting Connor or Stew in any more danger than they already are."

Joe looked like a recently captured jungle cat in his first cage. He couldn't remain still. His shoulders rippled forward and backward. He shifted from one foot to the other, and his hands wrestled with the air. But his words were calm, confident. "Really doesn't matter. If the Prophet's Guard still has guys in New York, then your kids, our kids, Stew Manthey, they all are probably already in their sights. What we tell them or don't tell them today won't change that."

Annie's eyes were pleading. Joe's eyes were closed as he pulled in a deep breath. Tom felt alone, again. It was up to him to make a decision: the loneliest place in the world.

"Then," said Tom, "we tell them what we're looking for."

"Tom!" Annie's fingers balled into fists.

He took her hands and pried her fingers open. "Listen, Annie, they're already in the middle of this thing. They're thousands of miles away, and they've got the clues. We're going to need all the help we can get to make sure we go in the right direction. What if they have information that we need, that is critical for us, but they don't know to share it because they don't understand what we're trying to do? They have what may be the last piece to the puzzle. They need to have some understanding of what the puzzle looks like so they can assess the piece in their hands." Annie's eyes still pleaded, less intensely, as Tom turned back to the computer, his heart racing and his soul praying that he was doing the right thing. *God, protect my boy.*

"Stew, it's a long story, and we've got very little time. We've discovered a connection from Abiathar to Jeremiah that led us to an ancient book. In that book was a coded message that revealed to us what this whole ordeal has really been about. The Prophet's Guard has been after the mezuzah not because of the message on the scroll, but because of the story that all the messages tell us. A story combined with this book we've studied, which tells us Jeremiah carried Aaron's staff to Babylon to return it to its source—the Tree of the Knowledge of Good and Evil in the garden of Eden."

Connor motionless to his right, Stew didn't bat an eyelash. "Someday I've got to process why what you've just said doesn't make me believe you should be committed to an asylum. But it doesn't. What does this have to do with Aaron's staff?"

"That's the key to the whole thing. Aaron's staff was the true power of the Ark of the Covenant. It was the staff that brought down the plagues of Egypt, that split the Red Sea, that knocked down the walls of Jericho. When the staff was removed from the Ark, the Ark had no power. The staff is the most powerful weapon in the history of the world. And the Guard—we think the Muslim Brotherhood is behind it all—they want the staff. They want it to help usher in Islamic rule over the entire earth."

"Okay, now I get it," said Stew. "And you believe these directions will help you—"

"Yeah . . . to open the gate of the garden of Eden. When we get there, I expect there will be some combination or code needed to get in."

"And there's also that little item of the angels with the flaming swords guarding the place so Adam could never come back."

"Yes," said Bohannon. "There's that, too. But one hurdle at a time. I'll worry about them if and when we ever get there. But for now, give us what you've got . . . the directions and the combination. We'll—"

"Dad, wait." Connor pushed his head on-screen. "How do you know where to start to find the garden of Eden?"

"Ha!" blurted Rizzo. "This I want to see. If you guys think we're crazy now, wait till you hear this cockamamie yarn. Go ahead, Moses. Tell them about the burning bush."

Bohannon looked over to his wife. The team had listened to their story of the Gabriel encounter with the same level of disbelief and wonder that Tom and Annie felt in telling the tale. But there it was. Tom heard stories of other people with "angel encounters." He was always skeptical. But how else to explain that extraordinary conversation in the basement of the Ades Synagogue?

"Well," said Bohannon, "I, ummm . . . we, ummm . . . I mean, I guess . . ."

"Great start," laughed Rizzo. "Next thing you'll be telling Connor that you met an angel."

18

SUNDAY, AUGUST 30

5:13 a.m., Doha, Qatar

Only three months earlier, his father, Sheik Achmed, announced he was transferring power as the Emir of Qatar to his thirty-three-year-old third son, Khaliffa. Now, Sheik Khaliffa bin Nasser al-Bruni faced an unexpected crisis.

Normally, one couldn't find a sleepier little Persian Gulf country than Qatar. The richest nation in the world, with a per capita income of $109,000, Qatar provided its citizens—two hundred fifty thousand of the two million inhabitants of the Qatar Peninsula—with free housing, free medical care, free education, and low-interest loans for anything else they needed.

An absolute and hereditary emirate under control of the al-Bruni family since the middle of the nineteenth century, Qatar held to a precarious balancing act.

On the one hand, Khaliffa's father spent more than $1.5 billion to build the Al Uedid air base, now the comfortable home for American F-15 fighters, B-1 stealth bombers, and Patriot antiballistic missile batteries of the 379th Air Expeditionary Wing of the United States Air Force, and the USAF Central Command for the Middle East.

On the other hand, the Sunni al-Bruni family of Qatar was one of the main supporters of the Muslim Brotherhood in Egypt and its deposed president, Mohammed Ayet. During the one year Ayet and the Brotherhood were in power, Qatar lent, or gave, Egypt $7.5 billion. The Qatari government also was one of the first to recognize the Libyan opposition's National Transitional Council as the legitimate government of Libya amidst the 2011 Libyan civil war, was a major power broker in crafting the peace agreement for Darfur, and was now a prime advocate of Palestinian rights in Jerusalem.

Sheik Khaliffa fully expected to continue walking the tightrope his father had stretched over the tiny country's international presence. But now, his visitor threatened all Khaliffa had come to expect was not only his present reality, but his future, as well.

"You no longer have any need of the Americans," said King Abbudin. The sun was just rising over the Persian Gulf with the promise of withering heat as the Saudi king rested comfortably in the corner of a cushioned divan in the midst of Khaliffa's Doha palace. In spite of an all-night round-trip journey to Tehran, the elderly king still looked fresh and alert. "The value of your oil fields and the lake of natural gas that extends along the borders of both our nations will rise rapidly now that Saudi oil production has been crippled."

"Better to have the Americans as tenants than as enemies," said Khaliffa. There were no servants present, so Khaliffa poured coffee for both the king and himself as he frantically tried to find a safe way out of the disaster King Abbudin requested. "You ask me not only to allow social unrest, but to create it in order to establish a basis for expelling ten thousand American military? Forgive me, Your Excellency, but what you request appears neither wise nor prudent. How does Qatar benefit by bringing mass demonstrations to the streets of Doha?"

He was young, perhaps, but the new sheik was no fool. King Abbudin was asking him to arrange for a popular revolt in the capital with thousands of Qataris protesting an elaborate fabrication, the destruction and defilement of Qurans at a local mosque by drunken members of the American Air Force, an affront to Islam he could stage with complete credibility. But at what cost to his peaceful, wealthy nation?

"The time is coming quickly, my young king, when all of us must choose our friends carefully. With whom would you prefer to be allied: the Americans or the Brotherhood? The military coup in Egypt that overthrew Ayet will crumble. Tourism, Egypt's greatest source of hard-currency income, is vanishing. Hotel occupancy in Luxor and Aswan is at four percent. One hundred hotels have closed, and those that remain have cut employees' salaries by seventy-five percent. In a choice between the military and bread, which will the Egyptians select?

"Do you believe the Brotherhood is now impotent because it is once again outlawed in Egypt?" asked Abbudin. "For eighty years the Brotherhood flourished in the shadows, growing strong among the people, spreading throughout

THE ALEPPO CODE   153

the world beneath the unsuspecting eyes of the West. Recently the Brotherhood forced a vote in the Jordanian parliament to expel the Israeli ambassador as a show of support for the Palestinians losing their homes in Jerusalem. The Muslim Brotherhood is more than Egypt, and its power and influence stretch around the world.

"Ever since your father and I signed the defense cooperation agreement three years ago, the safety and security of Qatar has been as important to the family Saud as our own. We have much that binds us together, Your Excellency. Better to have you and me control any street demonstrations than a criminal group like Al Qaeda."

Khaliffa felt the veiled threat. He knew how much money the Saudi king funneled into the Wahhabi clerics who steered the efforts of Al Qaeda. If both the Brotherhood and Al Qaeda were now under the control of King Abbudin, and if Abbudin's plan to bankrupt Europe bore fruit, what hope did he—did Qatar—have of surviving on its own?

"Tell me. How would we convince the Americans this uprising was their fault?"

8:14 a.m., Tel Aviv

Yhanni Goldsmith was lining up the tables at the Zuni restaurant along the esplanade near the beach road. The sun was shining and the sky was so blue it almost hurt his eyes. Crisp white linen tablecloths rippled in the breeze off the Mediterranean, each table shaded by a large, forest-green umbrella. He was on his way to get the silverware tray, already estimating the tips that brunch would bring, when he saw the first flash of light, then more flashes walking down the esplanade, each followed by a thunderous explosion and a roiling plume of smoke, dirt, and debris.

It was the second explosion, closer than the first, that triggered Yhanni's response—that and his regular IDF reserve training—even before he heard the whine of the rockets or the wail of the warning sirens. He raced into the restaurant, ripping off his long apron, tore through the kitchen to the waitstaff lockers. He pulled his Uzi submachine gun out of his locker and slung it over his shoulder, grabbed his uniform helmet and flak jacket, and raced out the back door, determined to reach his unit's rallying point.

The jacket, had he been wearing it, would have saved his life. The Zuni restaurant disappeared in a roaring fireball, a shard of metal shelving piercing Yhanni's back and driving him, lifeless, to the sand.

—◊◊◊—

She left home before the sun came up. The roads were awful, the checkpoints so frequent that, had she left any later, it would be afternoon before she reached the outskirts of Kiryat Shmona. But it was her mother's birthday. The old woman refused to move from her family home in the village of Kfar Giladi, north of Kiryat Shmona, regardless of—or in spite of—the Jewish settlements that surrounded her and the potential danger of living so close to the Lebanese border. Her mother was steadfast. She would not become just one of thousands of other Palestinians, herded into overcrowded, hopeless refugee camps by the occupying Israeli forces. She had a home where her mother and her mother's mother had been born before her. She was not leaving.

Petra evaded the ever-growing potholes on the road from Route 90 to Kfar Giladi and tried to dismiss the devastation she had witnessed in Kiryat, where Hezbollah rockets were pounding the inhabitants. Coming around the turn near the military cemetery was when she first saw the smoke. It was rising from the southern part of the village.

Ignoring the ruts, Petra pushed on the gas pedal, urging the aged, yellow Volkswagen into a mad rush toward the village while holding both her breath and her fear.

She turned onto a dirt road, the madrassa school to her left in flames. When she came to the street of her mother's house, she skidded to a halt. A crater blocked the middle of the dirt street, smoke rising from its pit. Down each side of the street, debris marked the location of what once were houses. Staggering from the car, she ran in a stumbling panic to the first house on the left, now a pile of broken stone and crushed mud brick. Petra sat down in the sandy grit of the road and stared at a thin, wrinkled arm pointing to the sky. It was sticking out from the bottom of a pile of rubble, her mother's rings on its fingers.

10:02 a.m., Strait of Hormuz, Iran

Rear Admiral Chauncey "Chipper" Woods was six-four, just tall enough that he had to duck each time he passed through a door on the USS *Ingraham*. At

278 pounds, he no longer fit comfortably in the captain's chair on the bridge of the Perry-class missile frigate. Chipper had long ago conceded he was well past his physical prime.

Too tall, too big, and too old, Chipper Woods was much like the ship he skippered. The last of fifty-three Perry-class missile frigates built by the US Navy, the USS *Ingraham* was one of the few still serving on active duty. Like most of Chipper's old buddies, the majority of the frigates had been decommissioned. But after twenty-five years, the *Big I* still protected shipping lanes as effectively as Chipper Woods stalked the narrow passageways of this aging warship.

His rank was too senior to be piloting an old tug like the *Ingraham*, but Admiral Woods had two things he cherished: the 230 officers and crew of the *Ham*, with whom he'd served for nearly two decades, and the close friendships that come with forty years in the navy—many of those friends now top brass in US Navy Command, the men who kept Woods on the bridge of this ship—*his* ship.

Chipper stood on the forecastle of the *Ingraham*, just outside the bridge, praising his God for the smell of the sea, the warmth of the sun on his face, and the blessing of having any ship under his feet at this point in his career. These days would be few in number, so Chipper Woods celebrated every one of them.

The *Ingraham* was part of the US Navy's Fifth Fleet aircraft carrier battle group surrounding and supporting the USS *Nimitz* nuclear-powered aircraft carrier, a floating city manned by over five thousand sailors, fliers, and fighters. The ships of the Fifth Fleet were making life unpleasant for the Iranian Navy and keeping open the Persian Gulf shipping lanes, especially those running through the tactically critical Strait of Hormuz. Today, the *Big I* was sailing point, turning fifteen knots under half power and running well in advance of the main battle group as it crested the Qatar Peninsula and turned west into the heart of the gulf.

"Got some chatter," said his XO, standing in the doorway to the bridge. "You'll want to hear this."

Commander Jeff Griggs was career navy, just like Woods, but didn't have the same kind of connections. He didn't have an ego problem, either. So even though in other circumstances Commander Griggs would have by now skippered the *Ingraham*, he was satisfied, until his time came, to be serving with his friend. They made a good team.

"What's cooking?" asked Woods as he turned away from the railing and his reverie.

"The airwaves just exploded with Farsi, like everybody in Iran is talking at the same time. Lieutenant Morgan is sorting it out, but this is not normal."

Commander Griggs stepped aside as the admiral entered the bridge, but he seized the moment. "I don't like this, Chipper," he whispered.

Woods stopped in his tracks and cast a sidelong glance at his executive officer. Griggs was never wrong. "Sound General Quarters," snapped Woods. "Get the birds warmed up and call—"

"Incoming!" shouted the weapons officer, and every head turned to the bank of radar and sonar monitors. "Three . . . six . . . incoming missiles, very fast, skimming the waves. I'm picking up multiple screws behind them. Thirty seconds to impact."

Commander Griggs was on the squawk box. "We are under attack. Evasive maneuvers. Engage all defenses. Prepare for impact."

Admiral Woods looked over the shoulder of the weapons officer. "Unlock the Phalanx system and set free the fiftys." Then he picked up the radio to the Flag.

"We see 'em, Chipper," said Admiral Hayes. "Maybe Phalanx . . ."

"Get the birds off the deck, Jeff!" called Woods.

"Twenty seconds."

"No, Charlie, not six. Some, not all. They're coming in low. We've got a ch—"

Thunder erupted from amidships as the radar-guided, .20-millimeter Gatling gun of the Vulcan Phalanx system started firing forty-five hundred rounds per minute of armor-piercing tungsten shells from its six parabolic barrels. Then everything happened too fast.

The Ingraham's two Sikorsky Seahawk helicopters lifted off almost simultaneously, the roar of their rotors added to the pounding fire of the Phalanx and the two massive explosions that sent up pillars of seawater far off the Ingraham's starboard side.

"Ten seconds, sir. I've got multiple small craft closing fast. Some corvettes on their heels, and a Kirov-class cruiser turning heavy screws."

The Ingraham's .50-caliber machine guns joined the fight, adding their jack-hammer thumping to the growing roar of battle. One, then another, massive explosion—closer now—off the starboard side. Admiral Chipper Woods moved to the starboard side of the bridge. "They're gonna be dropping mines all across the strait, Charlie. Be careful."

Woods dropped the radio in his right hand and grabbed the railing with both hands. He could see the rooster-tails of sea spray racing toward his ship. "Hold on!"

The Perry-class had proven itself a tough ship in past engagements. Probably the other thing that saved her was that Phalanx took out the closest missile not a hundred yards from impact. The shock wave was so intense, it rocked the frigate to port. As she settled in her roll back to starboard, the last missile hit, but above her waterline. That knowledge gave Rear Admiral Chipper Woods a final moment of comfort as the missile collided with the *Ingraham*'s superstructure, just below the bridge.

2:46 a.m., Washington, DC

"How many casualties?" President Jonathan Whitestone's long strides were quick-stepping toward the Situation Room, Bill Cartwright, his national security advisor, close on his heels. Despite the early hour, Whitestone's mind was as sharp as his temper.

"We don't know yet. The *Ingraham* is holding its own right now. Fires aren't out but under control, and the magazine isn't in danger. Looks like she'll stay afloat."

"Where's the *Nimitz*?"

The doors to the Situation Room flew open at the president's approach, and he asked the question of the massed joint chiefs. "Where's the *Nimitz*?"

"The Nimitz Battle Group is on the other side of the peninsula, still in the Gulf of Oman, coming up from the south," said Admiral Boyd, secretary of the navy. "Ten, twelve hours away. Too far for its planes. *Ingraham* was running point."

"What about the *Truman*?"

"Just cleared the Suez Canal," the secretary said of the newly deployed aircraft carrier group. "Won't be much help."

Whitestone reached his chair at the head of the table. "What's happening in the strait?"

"CentCom tells us the Iranians have sent two battle groups into the strait," said Admiral Boyd. "Probably subs out there, too, but we don't know how many—not yet. One of the groups came out of the naval base at Jask, and they've been laying down mines—eight ships. The other group came out of Bandar e-Abbas. The missile attack was to cover that group, to take out the *Ingraham* so that group could lay mines north of the Oman Peninsula."

Whitestone had swung his chair around to look at the map on the wall behind him. "What are we doing?"

It was the silence that quickened his pulse. Not the aggression of the Iranians—that was expected after the "Israeli" sabotage at the Iranian oil refineries and the US freezing of Iranian assets—but the silence of the men who controlled the most powerful military force in the history of the world. Whitestone turned back to the table. The defense secretary was standing at the other end.

"That's what we were discussing when you came in, Mr. President. To be honest, sir, we're not sure what we're doing—or what we should do next."

Robert Calvin, the defense secretary, was a decorated military veteran of Desert Storm and became a no-nonsense CEO of General Dynamics, the fourth-largest US defense contractor. He had business and military contacts around the world at the highest levels. And he never hesitated on making a decision. Until now.

"Mr. President," asked Calvin, "where is the secretary of state?"

"He resigned—yesterday. Why?"

"We're going to need him."

Whitestone felt a sudden calm. He cast a glance at Cartwright, to his left, then back at the secretary of defense. "Tell me."

An aide came into the room and handed the secretary one page of paper. As he read the report, Calvin looked over toward Cartwright. "Sorry, Bill," he said, holding up the sheet. "These are coming in as we speak. Mr. President, an hour ago the emir of Qatar closed the Al-Uedid Air Base. It was reported this morning that a bunch of drunken US airmen broke into two mosques last night in Doha, burned all the Qurans they could find, and defiled the mosques in ways the news sources said they could not repeat. Thousands of Qataris took to the streets in protest. About twenty thousand massed in front of the emir's residence, demanding prosecution of the offenders and expulsion of American forces from Qatar." Secretary Calvin looked up. "The emir caved—he's not like his father. The base and all operations at the base are shut down until further notice. All military personnel are confined to the base. Our stealth fighters are on the ground.

"Just before you walked in, we received a cable from Manama naval base in Bahrain. The French have declined to move their ships out of port with the rest of Combined Task Force 150. This"—he held up the sheet of paper in his hand—"is a report that the Spanish government has also ordered its ships to stand down."

"What's happening, Bob?"

"Mr. President, the Iranians are deploying the asymmetric attack strategy we've anticipated. I suspect this is the first of a series of 'swarming attacks' on our ships. The Islamic Revolutionary Guard Corps will launch its fleet of small, fast-attack craft—armed with torpedoes, rocket launchers, and other anti-ship weaponry—at the Nimitz Battle Group as soon as it's in range. They will position these small craft at the hundreds of launching points that surround the gulf, including small islands and coves, providing cover that would enable surprise attacks.

"At the same time they will use the narrow width of the strait to launch the same kind of attack as they did at the *Ingraham* . . . Russian-made Sunburn missiles fly at three times the speed of sound. At its narrowest, the strait is only twenty-one miles wide. Those missiles would close on any ship in less than thirty seconds."

"But we have—what—three hundred ships in and around the Persian Gulf? Superior fire power, superior weapons systems. What's stopping us from just going in there and wiping out the Iranian navy?"

The secretary of defense sat down as if an incredible weight had been added to his shoulders.

"In 2002, we spent over 250 million dollars to stage a massive war game in the Persian Gulf. It was called Millennium Challenge. The exercise is the exact one we face today in which small, agile speedboats swarmed a naval convoy to inflict devastating damage on more powerful ships. According to reports on the war game, the exercise concluded in less than ten minutes, after which forces 'modeled after a Persian Gulf state' had succeeded in sinking sixteen US ships, including an aircraft carrier. That was only the first day. The next day, the sheer number and speed of the swarming attacks from rocket-equipped speedboats and land-based cruise missiles overwhelmed the vastly superior US ships. It was a crushing, total defeat.

"Mr. President, without air power, our ships are sitting ducks. We not only don't have air power with Al-Uedid shuttered, we also don't have allies. Italy just told its captains to stand down."

19

Orhlon was prepared for the vote. He was prepared for that morning's vote and its anticipated result. He didn't expect Eliazar Baruk to survive the firestorm engulfing both his government and the man himself. But this? He had failed to see this coming.

Meir Kandel was so far to the right in his political philosophy, he made Orhlon feel like a liberal. "Ultra" was to downplay his radical positions. How Meir Kandel, head of the conservative Jewish Home Party, had wrangled his appointment as interim prime minister of Israel until elections could be held in four months, was a mystery to Orhlon. A mystery, but—with Hezbollah rocket attacks increasing in volume and accuracy—it was also a reality that General Moishe Orhlon, defense minister for the State of Israel, needed to deal with immediately.

Orhlon preferred driving himself, but in these times, he relented to having an armed driver and escort. If Baruk could be attacked in his own home . . .

The nondescript military vehicle raced up behind the nondescript government office building on Kaplan Street in Qiryat Ben-Gurion, between the Bank of Israel and the Ministry of the Interior. Orhlon's bodyguards were flanking the back door of the car before the general could get it fully open. Well known to the guards, all three nonetheless presented their biometric ID cards and submitted to the iris scanner before gaining access to the building.

Kandel was waiting in Baruk's office . . . *no, the prime minister's office*, thought Orhlon. Unlike Baruk's fashionable and regal bearing, Kandel looked like he had just emerged from the banana fields in a kibbutz—his khaki work shirt sweat-stained at the armpits, his khaki pants in need of a good cleaning. A head shorter than Orhlon, Kandel was round in shape, but hard in body and disposition. He wore the same grizzled, gray stubble on his chin as he did on his head. Welcome and warmth were as foreign to Kandel as Palestinian rights.

There was no preamble, no pleasantries.

"When can the IDF move?"

"Move where, Mr. Prime Minister?"

"Lebanon . . . and down from the Golan."

Calculations flooded Orhlon's mind, stalling his response. Readiness reports and threat assessments were fresh, digested less than an hour ago. He traversed the terrain in his mind, reconnoitered the disaster of Israel's last incursion into Lebanon when Hezbollah shredded the IDF.

"We can bring reserves to the front today. The Golani Brigade armor and artillery will be at strength and can move tomorrow."

Kandel looked at the watch on his muscled, tanned arm. "Tell Brigadier Bertz that I want the Thirty-Sixth Armor Division moving in twenty minutes. The Seventh Brigade is to leave Mas'ada, cross the border at Quazzani, and swing west, to the coast, just north of Tyre."

"That's thirty kilometers!"

"Yes," said Kandel, stepping to a map pinned to the office wall. "I want to cut Lebanon in half and then squeeze the Hezbollah rocket encampments from both sides. Where is the 188th?"

"Rihaniya."

"Close enough. Send them across the border to destroy the rocket launchers at Yaroun and Rmaich."

Orhlon knew where this was going . . . another war with Lebanon. So be it. But, for the moment, he must protect his soldiers. "Mr. Prime Minister, without support the tanks will be blind, they will be vulnerable—they will be decimated. We should—"

"You need your armor, your ground troops, yes?"

"Yes, Mr. Prime Minister."

"Then I suggest you get your armor started and your ground troops moving, General. Let the air force loose once more and pound Hezbollah's strong points. But the tanks move in twenty minutes. Is that clear?"

Orhlon needed to be on the phone—now. "Yes, Mr. Prime Minister."

"Good. Then ready the heavy bombers. We strike Iran tonight . . . Natanz. The Iranians are focused on the American warships in the Strait of Hormuz and the radiation poisoning in its air. And Syria is in no condition to oppose us or offer retaliation. This is the time to strike. The world will have its eyes on Lebanon. So we go after Natanz tonight, with everything we have. Understood?"

Orhlon was already at the door. "Yes, sir." He hesitated, turned, and faced Kandel. "You are taking quite a risk."

Kandel turned away from the map to look at Orhlon as if he were an alien. "No risk," he said, his voice devoid of emotion. "Destiny. And opportunity. An opportunity which may not come our way again. This time, you are to crush Hezbollah. See to it."

Orhlon was out the door, already on the phone to his commanders. It was time for war.

10:04 a.m., Ghajar, Israel

It was a line on a map, the border between Ghajar, Israel, and Quazzani, Lebanon. This invisible but very real border sliced through the midst of four buildings in the middle of the community, cutting as cleanly as the loyalties in each home. On one side, Israel. One step away, Lebanon. And no fence to separate the two.

Colonel Isadore Stanfill struck the obligatory image of a tank commander. The colonel stood in the open hatch at the top of the turret in his Israeli-designed Merkava Mark 2 battle tank. The field glasses held to his eyes scanned the buildings on the Lebanese side. He was waiting for half his brigade to form up behind him on the road from Ma'sada. The other fifty were split on his flanks.

Stanfill was grateful his tanks didn't need to run the gauntlet between the buildings of Ghajar and Quazzani. This mission was insane enough without having to maneuver through tight streets looking for Arabs with rocket launchers. Cross the border, turn left, and run for the coast. Whose idea was this, anyway? Thirty kilometers on a straight line. Stanfill's Mark 2s could cover that thirty kilometers in an hour at full speed. But there was no straight line between Quazzani and Tyre, just a series of deteriorating, twisting roads in a maze of dead ends. Either his tanks would risk a run down the Latani River valley, an undulating series of meanders and switchbacks that would take forever and leave him vulnerable. Or, as General Orhlon had ordered, he would lead his column along the road to Qantara, smash the Hezbollah rocket batteries that were raining death into Kiryat Shmona, and join up with the flanking column to the east that had attacked Osair, and the one to the west, turning south at Ghandourive and pushing hard to join up with the 188th Brigade on its way north from Rmaich.

With two hundred Israeli tanks massed to the north of the border, Israeli ground troops, armor, and artillery could push up from the south and catch Hezbollah in a vise. At least, that was the plan. In 2006 that plan hadn't worked very well. Hezbollah was ready then, and countered every Israeli move, driving the IDF from Lebanon. Stanfill thought this new plan a fool's errand. He was old-school. He believed in the tactic of overwhelming force massed into one decisive blow.

But that wasn't the strategy for today.

"Start up the engines," he said into the radio mike on his lapel. "It's time to move."

10:08 a.m., Jerusalem

Annie was getting frustrated. It seemed like every step forward was a fight. All she wanted was some real end to this nightmare. Why was Tom so resistant? Sure, Tom was emotionally and physically exhausted from the desperate and ill-fated race to save her and Kallie. His damaged shoulder was in a sling, and his body one, huge bruise. But this was no time to wait, to rest.

"These thugs and murderers are a threat to us and to our children. They've torn our lives apart."

Tom and Annie sat on a wood-slat bench in the shade of a large cypress tree near the memorial at the top of Ammunition Hill—the site of a bloody battle during the Six-Day War, not far from the apartment. Annie wanted a place where she could speak to Tom privately. The apartment was getting too crowded.

"Don't you think I know that?"

She could feel his Irish getting up.

"But we don't know anything. At best," said Tom, shaking his head and gesturing with his left hand, "we have half the story."

She spoke as softly as her mangled nerves would allow. "Tom, what's wrong with you? Some days you're positive, some days you're negative—let's keep going . . . no, let's stop. I don't know what's going on. And I don't know what to expect, but we've clearly been given a mission from God. Remember Gabriel?"

Twice he opened his mouth to speak, the second time turning to face Annie. But the words were having a hard time finding their way to his lips. He shook his head.

"I'm tired. I'm tired of making all the decisions. I make a decision, and we take a six-hundred-mile excursion into the desert of Iraq because we think these directions on the sprockets will lead us to the garden of Eden? Well, how do we get into that country, eh? More important, how do we get out? And what do we do when we get there? Just wander around in the streets of Saddam's Babylon until the spirit strikes?"

"Why not? It worked for you before," said Annie, the snap of her words carrying more of an edge than she intended.

She took Tom's hand. "I'm sorry. That wasn't fair. But we keep thinking this nightmare is over, and it continues to pull us back in—because the Prophet's Guard hasn't stopped and we are in their way. But it hasn't stopped for me, either."

In the distance, a string of vehicles with flashing lights were followed by what looked like a convoy of military vehicles, all racing west on Highway One toward Tel Aviv. But Annie's mind was focused on one burning thought—all those she loved were being threatened or killed, and she was ready to do anything to have it end.

"I still see her face in my dreams," said Annie. "I watched helplessly as those murderers sliced open Kallie's throat. You weren't there. You didn't see the look in her eyes. But I can't forget it. Tom . . . I'm going. I'm going to finish this, even if I'm the only one who wants to continue. And the people who are out there who want to do us harm? I'm just as determined to do them harm. Not revenge, but justice. Tom, we are called to this task, remember? I don't think there's any getting out of this for us. I can't speak for the rest, but if finding this staff is the thing that finally sets us free, then I'm finding that staff."

"What happens if we *do* find it? What will we do with it?"

"I don't—"

The ring made both of them jump. Tom looked at his wrist, at the light flashing on the improbable wristwatch he had been given by Sam Reynolds—the one that doubled as a satellite phone. This couldn't be good news. Tom raised his wrist, pressed on the watch face. "Yes?"

"You weren't at the apartment," said Reynolds.

"We went for a walk."

"Well, you're going for more than a walk. Get packed. You're leaving. All of you. I can't get you on a plane until tomorrow morning, but you're going out on the first one in the morning. Make sure—"

"Wait. What's going on?"

"You'll find out soon enough. Nothing good. I've got to go. Just be ready early tomorrow. You're leaving, Tom. Like it or not, you're all going home. And there's no discussion about this. You're going to be on that plane in the morning, even if I have to tie you into the seat."

Reynolds disconnected with a finality that was disconcerting.

Tom met Annie's inquiring gaze. "C'mon. We have a decision to make."

10:18 a.m., Saudi Arabia

Colonel Farouk, one of the king's myriad cousins, set the last of the charges against the rear wall of the vacant metal building. He looked down the lane of sand, through the compound of pipes, huts, and small empty buildings that were not in existence a week ago. A few trucks were scattered along the lane in front of the buildings. Two large tankers were stationed alongside the two-foot-wide pipes that emerged from the Saudi sand but didn't exist under it, and ran through a series of valves, completing the charade.

His aide drove into the lane in a Jeep and stopped by his side.

"Our pumping station is secure. It looks like a mound of sand, like the thousand mounds of sand that stretch away on either side of it. We're ready."

The colonel flipped the switch on the last of the charges and climbed in alongside his aide. "Drive east one hundred meters."

The Jeep raced along the surface of the sand, kicking up a tail of grit in its wake. His aide pulled the vehicle into a tight turn so the colonel could survey his handiwork. Within moments, a series of explosions leap-frogged through the compound, creating enough damage to make the site look devastated, but not enough to reveal its bogus reality.

Once they drove back, the colonel walked through the wreckage, taking time to inspect the result. He engaged the underground devices that would pour thick, black smoke into the atmosphere.

"Good. Let's go to the next location."

———∿∾———

"You set off the explosions yourself?"

"Yes, Your Excellency."

"And the result?"

"Just as you requested, Your Excellency. From the air or a satellite, the pumping stations will appear as if they have been totally destroyed. Fires are burning at each location and will continue to burn with heavy, black smoke until your command to extinguish them. The pumping equipment is effectively camouflaged. Our planes flew over the sites this morning and could see nothing of the intact units."

Saudi King Abbudin smiled. "Thank you, Colonel. You have done well. You will receive my appreciation."

20

They were all in the living room, except Rizzo. The television was on. It didn't matter what channel because all channels were broadcasting the same thing— images of explosions, smoke, and fire as Hezbollah rockets dropped death into Israeli cities. Even Tel Aviv was hit this time. Ben Gurion Airport had been spared, but only a limited number of flights were getting through Israel's tightened air defenses.

The banners across the bottom of the screen, one in Hebrew and one in English, reported the news that Iran had just attacked American warships and blockaded the Strait of Hormuz.

"'Tis no surprise, now is it?" said McDonough. "After those raids on Iran, with all those poor people dying, 'tis no surprise there's been some retaliation. As me sainted mother used to say, 'Everyone feels his own wound first.'"

Deirdre was scrunched into a straight-backed chair next to the television, her legs crossed tightly and her hands wound as tight as a mother's fear. "Do you think this will mean a war?"

"It already is a war," said her husband, standing by her side.

"I want to go home, Joe. The kids are there. They'll need us." She looked up into his eyes. "Can you find out when we can get a flight?"

Tom stood in the doorway with Annie. None of those in front of the TV had noticed their return.

"We've got a flight," Tom said into the room, startling Deirdre. "We've been ordered to leave tomorrow morning, first thing. Sam Reynolds called, and it's all arranged. We all go home tomorrow."

He and Annie walked across the living room and joined the group in front of the TV. "Reynolds told us we'd soon find out why."

But before Tom could settle in front of the scenes of rocket warfare, his brother-in-law grasped his left arm and steered him away from the TV. "You're just giving up?"

Tom shook his head. "What are we going to do, Joe? I mean, ignoring all the logistical obstacles in our way for the moment, there's a war starting out there. How could we . . . I mean, how do we get around a war? And what do we do even if we get into Iraq, if we got to Babylon? The stuff that Stew and Connor got off the sprockets would probably help us if we ever got to stand before the gate to the garden of Eden—that still sounds weird saying it. But where do we look? How do we get to wherever the garden is located, which is probably underground after twenty-five hundred years?"

"But, Tom, if it couldn't be found," asked Annie, coming to his side, "why was Spurgeon so fearful about anyone discovering the sprockets? Why did he say the sprockets were more dangerous than anything he had discovered before?"

Bohannon ran his hand through his hair—seemed to be less of it now than just a few months ago. "I don't know. The directions from the sprockets cover a short distance—some paces this way, some paces that way. You're not going to cover a lot of ground doing that. Maybe they'll help if we find the garden. But how *do* we find it?"

"Road signs."

Tom turned to see Rizzo walk into the room, some papers in his hand.

"Look, Sam. Right now we don't need your wisecracks." Joe wasn't attempting to keep the frustration from his voice. "Reynolds is determined we're leaving tomorrow morning, one way or another. Unless we can come up with some ideas, we're all heading home."

"I'm serious," said Rizzo. He walked over and put three sheets of paper into Tom's hand. "The Dorabella will lead us to the garden."

"Are you kidding?" snapped Joe. "How would you know that? How are we going to decipher something people smarter than us have been trying to break for the last 150 years?"

"Well, you don't have to worry about that," said Rizzo, gesturing toward the paper in Bohannon's hands. "I've already figured it out."

The news report continued to flow from the television, but for Tom, the room suddenly became silent. He looked at the sheets of paper in his hand, covered with columns of symbols. When he looked up, he joined the rest of the group in staring at Rizzo, dumbfounded and mute.

It was McDonough who broke the spell. "You solved the Dorabella?"

"It's really pretty simple," said Rizzo. "Any one of you could have figured it out, too. Look. Come over here."

Holding out his hand, Rizzo retrieved the papers from Tom and walked into the dining area, the others close behind. He climbed up on a chair and laid out the three pieces of paper on the table. Each one was about eight inches on a side, marked with a large red letter at the upper right corner—*A, B, C* from left to right. Down the length of each sheet were three vertical lines of symbols. Rizzo pointed to the sheet of paper on the left.

"These are the relevant Demotic symbols from Abiathar's scroll," he said, pointing to the sheet marked with an *A*. "When we considered the possibility that Elgar used the code pattern on the scroll to help create the code pattern for the Dorabella Cipher, that opened the door—testing out the pattern on the Dorabella with the pattern on the Rosetta Stone. It didn't matter that we couldn't translate the Demotic symbols. We simply followed the pattern of the Demotic symbols to the corresponding Greek, translated the Greek letters to English and came up with Abiathar's message.

"So," said Rizzo, pointing to the sheet on the left, "these Demotic symbols over here correspond to—are the same as—these Greek letters on sheet B over here. *A* equals *B*, right?"

A smile began to spread over Tom's face as comprehension dawned.

"Elgar wrote the Dorabella Cipher over there"—he pointed to the third sheet of paper, with the red *C* in its upper corner—"in the same pattern as the Demotic symbols he found on the scroll. Which means that *A* on the left also corresponds to, is the same as *C* on the right. Correct?"

"Simple algebra," said Annie. "A substitution code."

"Bingo, boys and girls!" Rizzo nodded his head as if it were the clapper on a bell. "If *A* equals *B*, and *C* equals *A*, then *B* must equal *C*. Which means that in the Dorabella Cipher, these little C-shaped squiggles must correspond to, match up to, these Greek letters that are the same as these relevant Demotic symbols from the scroll. Write down the Greek symbols in the order of the Dorabella, translate to English, and—voilà!" Rizzo raised his fists in a Rocky pose. "We've got a winner."

"Simple . . . but amazing," whispered Tom.

Joe put a hand on Rizzo's shoulder. "You are an evil genius, Sammy."

"Thank you. I accept the compliment."

"An astoundingly fine piece of work, Samuel." Brandon McDonough rounded the far side of the table. "But what does it say?"

"I'll tell you what it says, but first"—Rizzo leaned back in the chair and smiled—"let me tell you what I think it means.

"I told Joe the other day that I was sure the Dorabella had some further role to play in this drama. So I went to work on Kallie's computer—didn't take long to break the password. I discovered that Charles Spurgeon developed a long relationship with Sir Charles Warren when both lived in London."

"The guy who tunneled under the Temple Mount?" asked Joe.

"The one and only. Warren was also, at one time, the chief of police in London and returned to London after several of his military assignments overseas. On one of his trips back to London, after being in command of the British garrison in Singapore, Warren took a long detour. Instead of returning all the way to England by ship, he sailed up the Persian Gulf and took the land route to the Mediterranean. On the way, he joined up with a British Museum archaeological expedition with which he spent more than a month. Want to guess where they were?" Rizzo paused and glanced at the blank expressions around him before he dropped the bomb.

"Babylon. The leader of this expedition was an Assyrian Christian named Hormuzd Rassam. He spent four years digging in and around Babylon. Found a lot of famous stuff. But what's interesting to us is that his mother was born in Aleppo, Syria. Her father was Ishaak Halabee—that's like Isaac. He was the chief rabbi of the Aleppo Synagogue."

By this time, Tom and Annie, Joe, Deirdre, and McDonough had all pulled up chairs to the table and were passing around the three sheets of Rizzo's paper.

"Well, I'll be . . ." Tom sat across the table from Rizzo, just shaking his head.

"Yes, you will," said Rizzo. "Warren found it. I don't know how, but Warren found the way to the garden."

Rizzo pulled another, smaller piece of paper from his pocket. "Listen, this is what the Dorabella says:

> lion of babylon through ishtar gate
> seven stadia to embrace daniel face
> portal of brick. steps are beyond

"Holy Mother . . . if it weren't me own ears," said McDonough, "I wouldn't believe what I'm hearing. 'Tis really the gate to the garden?"

Rizzo handed the sheet of paper to Tom, who looked at it as if he held the words of God in his hand. "We won't know for sure," said Rizzo, "until we go and knock on that gate."

"More likely until we knock through some brick." Joe came up to Tom's side as if only looking at the message made it real. "I doubt there would be any door left in Babylon that somebody hasn't gotten through in the last two thousand years."

Tom passed the paper to Annie, who looked at it for a split second. "What do you think 'Lion of Babylon' means?"

"Already looked it up," said Rizzo, turning to Annie. "There's no stone out that way. Almost all of Babylon was constructed of bricks made from clay dug from the banks of the Euphrates River, which ran right through the middle of the city. Plentiful supply, but the bricks don't last forever. The bricks deteriorated in the heat, crumbled if there was any rain. So the Babylonians took to glazing the bricks. That helped, but not over thousands of years. That's why much of Babylon was just a mound of decaying clay until Saddam started rebuilding the city on the ancient foundations.

"But there is one thing in Babylon made of granite . . . and after twenty-six hundred years, it's still standing. It's a statue of a lion standing over the body of a man. The lion is the symbol of the goddess Ishtar. It was one of the main symbols used in the decoration of Babylon. There are lions all over the walls of Babylon. At least there were until Europeans began plundering Babylon to fill their museums. This granite lion, specifically, is called the Lion of Babylon.

"The statue is located at the end of a long, wide avenue called the Street of Processions, north of the main wall. The Street of Processions continues through what was Babylon's most famous and beautiful gate—the Ishtar Gate—and then continues south through the city, past Nebuchadnezzar's palace and the great tower, then turns right and crosses a bridge that spans the Euphrates. The street is still there. But the Ishtar Gate isn't."

At that, everybody in the room looked at Rizzo.

"During the first fifteen years of the twentieth century, the German Oriental Institute conducted a dig at Babylon. The Ishtar Gate, the eighth gate in the walls of Babylon, was a double gate—a smaller one in the front with a more massive one of the same design behind it. Both were constructed from blue-glazed bricks adorned with reliefs of lions, aurochs, or bulls and dragons. The smaller one was fifty feet high, the larger one probably twice that, and thirty feet wide. The Germans took them home—or as much of them as they could find. The smaller one is reconstructed in the Berlin Museum. The bigger one? Well, they couldn't fit that one in the museum, so they've got it in storage, in pieces."

"So what's that do to our directions?" asked Rodriguez.

Logical question, and he knew it was coming. Rizzo turned over one of the larger pieces of paper to show a rough map he had drawn earlier.

"We have the Lion of Babylon, here"—he pointed at his map—"and the Street of Processions running south. Most representations of Babylon put the Ishtar Gate about here." He pointed to a rectangular box spanning the street. "Seven stadia are about one thousand feet shy of a mile. I figure that ends up about here . . . right near Nebuchadnezzar's palace and the great tower. It would be a good spot to begin searching for 'Daniel's face'—whatever that means."

Rizzo looked up from the map and stared straight at Bohannon. Tom's stomach began to turn. Right back in his lap again.

"Well, boss, whatta we do now?"

21

12:06 p.m., Persian Gulf, near Larak Island, Iran

It was slippery on the metal grating along the catwalk, but that didn't stop Lieutenant Andrew Stone from running flat out down the starboard side of the ship's platform. The claxon horns were still wailing the call to general quarters, and Stone was late. He knew he was late. But he didn't want to be left behind.

The USS *Ponce* was an ugly ship. Some people say a camel is a horse designed by a committee. Those people would think the USS *Ponce* was designed by a committee under the influence of some banned substance. *Ponce* looked like someone had sawn off the back half of the ship, twenty feet above the water-line, slapped a wide, flat deck on what was left, and sliced off the stern into a squat, abrupt ending. Commissioned in 1971 as an Austin-class Amphibious Transport Dock, *Ponce* was on its way to retirement at the Philadelphia Naval Shipyard when, eighteen months earlier, it escaped the floating scrap heap. Its rusted carcass underwent a rush retrofit that turned the forty-year-old relic into the navy's newest weapon. It was the navy's first Afloat Forward Staging Base, an old ship recreated for a new type of warfare. She was essentially a floating military base that could land attack helicopters on the rear deck, launch an amphibious marine battalion for incursion, sweep mines out of the water, or act as a forward command post or hospital. Lieutenant Stone's navy was more flexible, more adaptable, and more lethal than two decades earlier.

The Persian Gulf wasn't very rough this day, but the *Ponce* was running at flank speed, and spray was a constant companion, coating every surface on the aft deck and below. Lieutenant Stone held firmly to the lifelines as he raced along the catwalk at the side of the ship. He was fresh out of Annapolis.

Warm-hearted, genuine, and prone to clumsiness, he was still finding his sea legs. But he wasn't going to get left behind.

The nine thousand-ton *Ponce* carried a fairly common array of armaments, including eight .50-caliber heavy machine guns, a pair of .20-millimeter Phalanx radar-guided, rapid-fire Gatling guns that could pump out over eighteen hundred rounds a minute, along with the Typhoon Weapon System: two .25-millimeter Mk 38 Mod 2 chain-fed auto cannons with laser range-finders, big-punch guns that could deliver armor-piercing or high-explosive rounds at 180 per minute.

But it was the "Death Star" that made *Ponce* unique.

The long-awaited Laser Weapon System—shortened to LaWS—was successfully mounted and tested late in 2013, and the USS *Ponce* became the first US Navy ship to deploy what the sailors and civilian mariners aboard the ship lovingly called "Death Star."

The navy's newest marvel, LaWS was so fast in its targeting ability and so lethal in its accuracy that it was a deadly foe of SWARM—the favorite tactic of Iran's navy, which involved sending dozens of small, heavily armed attack boats the size of pleasure craft against a destroyer or aircraft carrier, inflicting catastrophic damage simply because there were so many of them it was impossible to destroy them all in time.

But not, the navy hoped, with Death Star.

Lieutenant Stone's assignment wasn't the remote monitoring of the LaWS or any of the *Ponce*'s other fixed-weapons systems. Stone was assigned as junior officer on an inflatable amphibious assault vessel, along with a senior officer, petty officer, and a dozen marines. Amid the three hundred military and civilian mariners scrambling to their battle stations on the *Ponce*, three amphibs were trying to launch from the ship as it cut through the Persian Gulf at full power, their mission to bring wasting destruction to the Iranian small-craft naval base at Larak Island.

It was a mission they could fulfill—if they could fight their way through SWARM . . . and if Death Star didn't mistake them for hostiles.

Lieutenant Stone didn't care about the danger or uncertainty of their mission. He was going to war. This is what he trained for. This was what he secretly longed for. Fourth-generation navy, grandson of the admiral who was commander of naval forces, Far East, during the Korean War, son of a decorated

Navy SEAL commander in Vietnam, this was his opportunity to walk in his ancestors' footsteps, to prove his mettle.

His men immediately recognized his nautical skill, his unfeigned candor, and his commitment to working shoulder-to-shoulder with them in any task, at any risk. They nurtured a protective affinity for their new JG. They called him "Stoner." He loved it, and he wasn't going to miss this opportunity because he wasted precious moments searching for his battle helmet.

Armed with a bow-mounted light machine gun and the weapons cradled in the arms of the marines, the amphibious craft were straining at their tethers in the lee of the racing *Ponce*, away from the flotilla of attacking boats approaching on the far side of the ship. A sailor threw off the bowline just as Lieutenant Stone leaped into the stern of the *Lucky Dog*. The Typhoon system cannons thudded round after round at the attackers, and distant explosions recorded both the effectiveness of the gunners and the Death Star's accuracy.

Stone's boat, *Lucky Dog*, circled for a moment at full power as the other two boats were released from their moorings. They formed up into a chevron formation and threw their engines into full speed as they emerged from the protection of the *Ponce's* stern and into the battle. Rather than try to pierce through the heart of the swarming attackers—a suicide mission at best—with Lieutenant Stone's inflatable at point, the assault force was to flank the attackers, try to avoid direct engagement, and make, at all haste, for the short cliffs on the south shore of the naval base at Larak Island.

It took less than thirty seconds for that plan to get thrown to the wind.

———⁓⁓———

With the first lieutenant at the helm and the petty officer manning the machine gun at the bow, *Lucky Dog* bounced through the wake of the *Ponce* at full speed, the marines holding fast to lifelines rigged amidships. Plowing into the *Ponce's* last trough, Stone could see across the bow, and what he saw knocked the starch out of his socks.

Hundreds of small craft were swirling across the surface of the sea in a discordant, ever-changing dance that inexorably pressed closer and closer to the massive bulk of the aircraft carrier USS *Nimitz* and the flotilla that accompanied her. Worse for *Lucky Dog* were the four boats that were bearing down on this trio of attack boats, less than one hundred yards distant. Before Stone could shout a warning—one that would have been unheard in the maelstrom of noise that echoed across the water—the Iranian vessels opened fire with rocket launchers, machine guns, and small arms.

The first rocket hit *Lucky Dog* in the bow, at the waterline, just below the machine gun. As if the officer at the helm had slammed on the brakes, *Lucky Dog* drove her broken snout into the sea and heaved the aft up at a steep angle. Trying to make his way to the arms locker forward, Lieutenant Stone was thrown into the air and was falling back into the boat when the second rocket hit, slicing *Lucky Dog* in two. Breaking into pieces, half of the red-hot rocket skimmed the top of the boat and severed Stone's left leg at the knee. Before he could feel any pain, Stone could see the blood, the bodies of the dead marines, and the Persian Gulf coming to embrace him.

10:40 a.m., Saudi Arabia

"I'm sorry, Mr. President. I understand what a blow this will be to your economy . . . the economies of other countries . . . but these criminals who call themselves terrorists drove into the compounds in stolen military vehicles, in full military uniforms. Our garrisons were taken completely by surprise. They attacked both pumping stations at the same time."

King Abbudin held his son's gaze while he listened to President Whitestone's shocked response on the other end of the phone call.

"No, I am certain. Those two pumping stations control two-thirds of the oil that we deliver to the tanker fleet waiting in the gulf."

Crown Prince Faisal sliced an apple with the razor-edged, curved dagger, barely concealing a smug smile. King Abbudin could not afford to be overconfident.

"We have full teams on the way to each station as we speak. But again, I don't know how long it will take to restore full capacity. The repairs necessary will be determined by the extent of the damage and the time to complete those repairs could be hindered by any number of circumstances. But believe me, Mr. President, we will do all in our power to have those pumping stations back online as soon as possible."

The Saudi king listened carefully to Whitestone's response, weighing the president's words and his tone.

"No . . . I did not know about this attack in the gulf. Be assured of one thing: we will take no pity on anyone who threatens the security of our nation. Yes, Mr. President, I will keep you informed as to our progress. Goodbye."

Abbudin replaced the receiver and turned to face his son. "Well, Faisal, it appears Al Qaeda in Yemen has already claimed responsibility for the destruction of the two pumping stations. Our subterfuge appears to be working."

8:42 a.m., London

"Nigel . . . have a look at this, will you?"

Quinn Barclay handed his boss, and doubles partner on the squash court, the transaction log he had just run on his computer. "What's happening in Ireland?"

It had been a long night for Nigel Hunter, careening from club to club with Maureen, and the cobwebs clogging his brain had not yet succumbed to the massive amounts of Starbucks caffeine he was pouring into his body. At this point of the morning, he would have trouble understanding a comic book.

"It appears as if someone is settling quite a large debt," said Hunter, holding a report in Barclay's general direction. Barclay made no move to retrieve it.

"An incredibly large debt, Nigel. UniCredit of Ireland had a call this morning on a one hundred million euro note—that's sovereign debt, Nigel. Who calls in sovereign debt on a Sunday, without notice? The Irish bank had to tap into its parent, UniCredit of Italy. We should—"

Hunter put his hand on Barclay's arm. "Hold on, Quinn. It's early. The transactions will begin to even out. Give it some time. I've got to get some coffee."

Nigel Hunter got up from his walnut desk in the HSBC tower in London and walked to the door of his office, looking in vain for his secretary. "You would think the second-largest bank in the world could afford to hire enough help, even on the weekend," he mumbled. Reena was nowhere to be seen. He stopped the first girl who passed his door. "Clarice, I need more caffeine. Toddle down to the Starbucks and get me a refill, please."

When he turned back into his office, Hunter saw Quinn Barclay still standing by his desk, the transaction report still in his hand. It was Nigel Hunter's job to keep track of the monetary transactions of the largest banks in the eighty-eight countries where HSBC did business. It was a task he generally assigned to his staff—like Quinn. And it was a task he did not want to tackle this morning.

"You're still here?"

"Nigel, I think this is something—"

Peter Carruthers, always polite and deferential, stopped and knocked on the open door. A small stack of paper was bunched up in his right fist. "Have a moment?"

This time, without waiting for an answer, Carruthers quick-stepped across the carpet, side-stepped Quinn Barclay, and shoved the stack of papers in Hunter's direction. "Banco Santander and EFG in Greece just received calls on sovereign debt that neither bank can cover. The Bank of Spain and the National Bank of Greece have stepped in, but . . . well, I don't think they're liquid enough."

The cobwebs were replaced by a headache, but the headache was trumped by a fear growing in Hunter's chest. "How much?"

"Two hundred million in Spain, one hundred million in Greece."

"Dollars?"

"Euros," said Carruthers.

Nigel Hunter looked at the other two men in his office and all three understood the magnitude of the disaster they were witnessing. "Who could be doing this?" he mumbled to himself. Hunter swept up his jacket from the back of his chair and was moving as he stuffed his arms in the sleeves. "Follow me."

22

12:17 p.m., Persian Gulf, near Larak Island, Iran

The blood pumping from his left stump, sheared below the knee by the rocket, mingled with the seawater dripping off his body as Lieutenant Andrew Stone pulled himself into what was left of the stern of the *Lucky Dog*. How this hunk of inflatable was still afloat—and whether it would stay afloat—was a problem for later. How to keep from bleeding to death was Stone's immediate concern. He pulled the belt from his uniform khakis, wrapped it around the stump, just above the knee so it wouldn't slip off, held his breath, closed his eyes, said a prayer, and pulled.

Stone knew he screamed from the pain. He just couldn't hear it. Phalanx and the .50-cals were still banging away at the swarming Iranian boats, explosions rocked both the air and the sea, and the air smelled like bad meat at a cookout. But when the blinding bolts cleared from his eyes and the pain subsided from unbearable to withering, Stone quickly looked around to assess his situation.

He had managed to pull his body over an inflated cross member, used as a seat, and into a shallow well between the seat and the boat's stern. Precarious, but afloat, Stone rested his back against the gunwale. The tourniquet had staunched the flow of blood considerably. All around him the mayhem of battle continued unabated. The Iranian small boats were pressing closer to the *Ponce*, their zig-zagging wakes tossing around what was left of *Lucky Dog* like laundry flapping in a stiff breeze. But they were ignoring the shattered body of Lieutenant Stone and the shattered remains of *Lucky Dog*. There were bigger fish in the sea—like the *Ponce*. Or the *Nimitz*.

Stone found the first-aid kit strapped under the gunwale where it was supposed to be. He poured saline solution over his stump, covered it with a quick-clot packet and an Israeli pressure dressing and drove a hypodermic of painkiller into his thigh. There was another container secured to his right, stenciled "EXPLOSIVES." Stone looked at the waterproof box and wondered what he could do with some explosives in the middle of this battle.

And he *was* in the middle of it.

Ordnance was flying over his head—which he kept down, close to the gunwale—from almost every direction. The Iranian boats—some well-armed, small coastal attack boats, others hastily reconfigured pleasure craft with mounted machine guns and RPG launchers—were swirling in random arcs that often passed on either side of the mangled inflatable, drawing fire from the ships and aircraft of the Fifth Fleet. Attention seemed to be everywhere except on the useless hunk of Neoprene tossing aimlessly on the waters of the Persian Gulf. Stone thought of his father. What would *he* do in this situation? *Would he ever know?* For the first time Stone regretted the decision he made before entering the academy. *Shake it off. You're not helpless. What can you do?*

His eyes fell once more on the box to his right. The explosives in the box were miniature limpet mines, smaller versions of the magnetic mines placed against the hulls of ships for over one hundred years. These limpets were designed specifically for use against smaller craft and were to be used in the attack on the Iranian naval facilities.

With the morphine doing its job, Lieutenant Stone felt little discomfort as he reached to his right, unfastened the securing ropes from the explosives box, and pulled it to him. He released the latches and opened the box. Inside were two dozen miniature limpets—two levels of twelve—each secured in foam rubber cushion. The mines were small enough to fit in the palm of a hand, a rounded oval—like a football—but flat on one side where the magnet was located. Because of the strong magnet, that side was heavier than the rest of the mine, assuring that the limpet would fasten properly to the hull of any metal ship.

Stone looked at the mines. They reminded him of the footballs he and his brothers used to sling around the back yard of their home in Dallas, each one claiming to be the next Troy Aikman. And that fleeting vision of flying balls filled his mind with purpose.

Lieutenant Stone kept his head down at the level of the gunwale behind him, but he could look out the shattered front of the boat and see the swirling vessels of the enemy. He ignored the fiberglass-hulled pleasure craft. But the open-water ships, metal hulled, those he tracked. He hefted one of the deadly mini-mines, feeling its weight, its balance, his eyes never leaving the swarm of boats. And he tried to assess just how much time he might have left. And how many touchdowns he could score.

<center>~~~</center>

While the wild dance of a hundred zigzagging boats was enough to generate vertigo in any observer, Stone discerned a more predictable pattern in the naval boats steered by more veteran hands. They moved more slowly, purposefully picking their way through the rollicking wakes and avoiding the paths of the more frantic vessels. Swarming, yes. Moving quickly, abruptly changing direction. But the maneuvers of these skippers were measured, not manic. And that deadly ballet often came in close proximity of the maimed hulk of *Lucky Dog*.

Stone steadied his right leg against the inflated crossbeam, got his hands under his left thigh, lifted the stump, and pushed with his right leg, forcing his lower back against the hard rubber gunwale—and driving an excruciating dagger of pain through his left thigh and hip. He fought to retain consciousness and then pulled the munitions box closer to his right side.

Gasping down two, quick, deep-cleansing breaths, Stone placed his left hand on the deck of the inflatable and held the first of the limpets loosely at his right side. The first one would be interesting. How far could he throw? What could he hit? Would it stick? Would it go off? *Off!* Stone looked down at the mine in his hand and realized he needed to set the timer. But for how long? How long would it take for the right boat to get close enough? How long would it take for him to set the timer and get the mine ready to launch? How . . .

There was only one way to answer all of those questions. Stone flipped up the cap on the end of the limpet mine. The timer could be set in minutes, not seconds. He pushed the up-arrow to 1, then pressed the red button—and began to count.

Fifty-nine. Fifty-eight.

How long to throw, hit, and clamp on? Five seconds?

Fifty. Forty-nine. Forty-eight. Forty—

Cushion. He needed a little cushion, some wiggle-room . . . just in case.

Forty-three. Forty-two. Forty-one.

Now he needed a target. *Lord, give me favor.*

Twenty-three. Twenty-two.

A gray coastal patrol boat was moving through the mayhem, edging its way closer. Stone gauged the speed and the distance of the boat, the weight of the mine, the strength of his arm. And he waited.

Nineteen. Eighteen. Seventeen.

The coastal boat was too far. But a small cutter sliced in his direction. He wondered how long he could wait.

Thirteen. Twelve. Eleven. Ten.

Seven. Six.

He couldn't wait any longer. Any port in a storm.

Four. Three.

A fairly large, heavily armed fishing boat, in a wide, fast turn, cut a heavy wake near the *Lucky Dog*. Probably fiberglass hull. But a massive, metal winch affixed to its stern. *Don't throw a baseball. Throw like Troy Aikman.*

Stone pulled his right hand up and threw the mine with all the strength left in his body. It soared as if it were designed for the NFL, cutting through the air in a perfect spiral. And missed horribly. Horribly for the fishing boat. The mine arced high over Stone's target, the metal winch, as the fishing boat completed its turn away from *Lucky Dog* and would have continued for quite some distance had not it run smack into the back of the boat's bridge, falling through a gangway to the deck. Where it exploded in a giant orange-yellow fireball, obliterating the bridge and splitting the fishing boat amidships.

Smoke pouring out, its hull careening as its split was forced farther apart by the rush of seawater. Stone watched in awe as the fishing boat listed to starboard and slipped beneath the churning waves.

Stone yanked a second limpet from the munitions box, hastily punched in the numbers, and looked for his next target.

—⁓⁓—

Two missed completely, the explosions unnoticed in the chaos of battle, but three others had found their mark. Shattered, smoking pieces of two smaller boats floated on the surface not far from *Lucky Dog*, and an Iranian patrol boat was listing heavily, limping east toward Iran's coast, a hole in its side, just above the waterline.

Stone was encouraged, not just from his improving marksmanship but also from the clearly diminished number of attacking boats. Phalanx, Death Star, and quarterback Stone were harvesting destruction throughout the swarm. But time was running out. Particularly for Stone. His shattered leg continued to bleed, and its stump was turning a sickening color. He didn't think there were many more throws left in this body.

He held a mine in each hand—each armed and counting down—and prayed for something big to come within range.

Twenty-five. Twenty-four. Twenty-three.

Running at flank speed, nimbly and randomly swerving to evade the destructive bursts from Phalanx, an Iranian patrol boat was driven in Stone's direction by withering fire from the American flotilla. The timing would be tight, but if he kept coming closer . . .

Sixteen. Fifteen. Fourteen. He's in range . . .

Some heavy ordnance exploded in the sea, just to the port side of the patrol boat, and it heaved heavily to starboard. Racing directly toward *Lucky Dog.*

Eleven. Ten. Nine.

Stone cocked his right arm. *It's too close! I'm not . . .*

The limpet mine flashed through the air. Stone switched the second mine from his left to his right hand as the first one clanged hard against the hull of the patrol boat.

Five.

He lifted the second mine just as the bow of the patrol boat's hull sliced alongside *Lucky Dog.* What remained of the inflatable bounded away from the charging ship, spinning in circles accelerated by the boat's wake. Stone steadied himself and tried to focus on the ship as it flashed in and out of his frame of vision. It was on the second circuit that Stone noticed the Iranian gunner staring down into the careening inflatable.

One.

Like a quarterback under a blitz, Stone slung the limpet side-armed in the general direction of the patrol boat.

Zero.

The first explosion coincided with the gunner triggering his machine gun in *Lucky Dog's* direction. The second explosion swallowed up the sound of the first, but not the sight of the bullets ripping across the surface of the sea . . . until Stone was blinded by the light . . . and the Persian Gulf finally claimed the rest of *Lucky Dog.*

23

Interim Prime Minister Meir Kandel sat across the table in Central Command's conference room with the smug nonchalance of a man in control of power. It was not an attitude that General Moishe Orhlon was accustomed to seeing in his prime minister, and one he disliked even more coming from Kandel—a right-wing zealot determined for all-out war with the Arabs. Israeli citizens were dying, his troops were engaged in a foolhardy, impulsive invasion of southern Lebanon, and Israeli warplanes were massing for a strike against Iran. And Kandel sat here as if he were playing some parlor game, unconscious of the real cost of his decisions.

Orhlon, Israel's defense minister, had a massive, interactive smart screen behind his chair, with maps, grainy video, and troop movements displayed across its face. But it was Kandel's face that Orhlon was forced to study. The prime minister demanded his attention.

"This is a great day, General. History will mark this day as the beginning of Israel's ultimate victory for the security of our people." Kandel reclined in his chair, a thick cigar between his right thumb and forefinger. "The fools on the left are screaming, begging for restraint. Can you imagine? Restraint. And you, Moishe, you will be famous."

Two weeks from his last cigarette, Orhlon's stomach turned, and his head spun from the thick cigar smoke. "Famous, I don't care. What I do care about is that our tanks and armor are exposed if they are attacked without support. Hamas fighters are pouring into the streets of Gaza, attacking Israeli troops, and Iran is threatening to launch a dozen long-range missiles that will destroy large sections of Tel Aviv. Mr. Prime Minister, this action could be a disaster. We need more time; we need better planning before we—"

The phone to Orhlon's left began to buzz, one of its buttons lighting up. The general reached for the phone, knowing the call came neither from the Operations Complex on the lower level nor from his adjutant. Not many others had this number.

"Yes?" Orhlon recognized the voice at once, but for a moment failed to realize its significance. He looked over at Prime Minister Kandel, whose eyes were closed, the smile still painted on his face. "It's for you. It's the chief justice."

Passing the phone to Kandel, the gears in Orhlon's mind were spinning. If he was correct about the meaning of this call, Orhlon's next decision would be which of his commanders to call first.

"Yes?" Kandel sat up in his chair.

"When?" The smile came off his face.

The cigar whizzed past Orhlon's ear. "They can't do that."

Orhlon watched as Kandel's face tightened, his eyes narrowed like a prize-fighter about to launch a counterattack. "What War Powers Act?" Kandel was on his feet, one hand clutching the telephone, the other hand leaning on the table for support. "This is legal?"

Slowly, Kandel's eyes came off the floor and settled on Orhlon. Hate boiled in those eyes. "Yes."

Kandel handed the telephone back to Orhlon. "It's really for you." He turned and, without another word, stalked out of the Command Center.

Orhlon put the phone to his ear. "Yes?"

"General, this is Supreme Court Chief Justice Abraham. You recognize my voice?"

"Yes, Your Honor."

"Good. The cabinet, joined by the court, recalled the Knesset into an emergency session under the War Powers Act. A vote of no-confidence was called. Labor, Yesh Atid, Palestinians, even Likud and the Jewish Home from the right, all voted to disband Kandel's government. The anger at his arrogance—the vote was overwhelming."

Perhaps there is time.

"Who is the new interim prime minister?"

"Who? They all wanted the same man," said Chief Justice Abraham. "They want you, Moishe."

This he didn't expect.

"They want you to end this madness. We're not ready for a ground war. It's you, Moishe. They all trust you. And Likud has formed a National Unity Coalition to give you their support—three-fourths of the Knesset signed up."

Orhlon was shaking his big, shaggy head. "But I'm not a politician."

"No, Moishe—and that's a blessing. You are a man of character and integrity who is trusted on both sides of the Knesset. Lead us, Moishe, just like you lead your men. Go, do it now. Israel needs a man like you."

He held the phone in his hand for a long moment after the chief justice hung up. Unexpectedly, Orhlon now found himself commander of a nation, and not only of its military. He searched his mind for the right plan. Orhlon pushed the 0 button. He was talking before the voice on the other end could speak.

"Open up a secure line to the White House. I want to speak with President Whitestone."

9:36 a.m., London

Sometimes, paper felt more reassuring, more permanent and reliable. The computers were fast and the screens a technological marvel. But sometimes, you just needed to see it in print.

Nigel Hunter held five pieces of paper in his hands. He would read one, move it from the front of the pack to the back, and read the next. He had completed this ritual three times and begun a fourth when the chairman spoke.

"This is the end of the world."

Hunter tore his eyes from the ensnaring pages and transferred his attention to Lord Albert Alderson, chairman of HSBC Europe and board chair of the European Central Bank, the most polished gentleman Hunter had ever known. Not only did Lord Alderson dress as if he set the standards for *GQ*, but he also physically looked the part of a gracefully maturing man of means—tall, athletic, chiseled good looks, graying at the temples, always a smile, and never a hair, a button, or an emotion out of place.

Now Nigel Hunter was really scared. Disheveled, in his wrinkled corduroy pants, Lord Alderson looked like a man hijacked from his breakfast. The chairman's face was as ashen as the gray in his hair. And fear found a home in eyes that previously had never once doubted themselves.

"Sir, what can we do?" he asked.

Lord Alderson took the pages in his hands and crumpled them up into a large ball, pressed them together, and flipped them, underhanded, into a dustbin alongside his desk. "Nothing. There is nothing we can do. Greece will declare bankruptcy by this afternoon. Spain and Italy won't be far behind. Those countries can't print their own euros. The debt call is over a half-billion euro so far, it continues to rise, and there is not enough liquid cash in the entire EU to satisfy these debts. Not immediately, as is required. So the dominoes will begin to fall—Italy, Portugal—even France and Belgium are at risk. Once sovereign nations begin to collapse, there may be no end to it."

"But the EU won't allow a continent to fall into bankruptcy, will it?"

The touch screen on the chairman's desk lit up with an incoming call. His eyes were on the photo of his family strategically located on a corner of his desk, the sunlit windows behind it to avoid glare. "There is no EU. Not after today." He touched the screen, turning on the speaker. "Yes?"

"Lord Alderson, it's the Saudis."

Hunter recognized the voice on the other end of the conversation as that of the bank's president. And it sounded panicked. "Abbudin must be responsible. The National Bank of Saudi Arabia somehow gained control of billions in euro debt. They're calling it all. I've had two bank presidents text me already to say their banks were taken over by the Saudis this morning."

Lord Alderson picked up the pen lying on top of his desk and absently began tapping on the back of his hand. Then he spoke into the touch screen.

"Transfer as much as you possibly can into our American accounts. But move quickly. We have less than an hour. See if you can salvage one to two hundred million."

Alderson's voice was strong, but his finger quavered as he tapped the surface of the touch screen to end the call. Nigel Hunter's hero stared at the top of his desk for a long, silent moment.

"We are being conquered . . . invaded," he whispered. "The Arabs will own Europe by the end of the week." He tapped the touch screen once more. "Get me the prime minister."

4:49 a.m., Washington, DC

Momentarily back in the Oval Office to complete some critical phone calls, Whitestone was surprised with how remarkably calm he felt. He stood leaning against the edge of the *Resolute* desk, while Bill Cartwright sat closer to the speaker phone on one of the sofas.

"General, I join in celebrating this change in government, particularly with you at the helm," said the president. "And I'm hopeful the Arab states will welcome your earnest and sincere promise to withdraw your troops from Lebanon. You are an implacable foe, Moishe, but a man everyone in the region trusts."

"Thank you, Mr. President. But Hezbollah must stop the rocket attacks—today. Our nation and our leaders did not support what one misguided man tried to accomplish. And I'm ready to order our troops back across the border, but not until the rockets stop."

Whitestone looked across the short distance to Cartwright, his eyes asking an unspoken question. Cartwright nodded in assent.

"There is, though, Mr. Prime Minister, the residual international outrage regarding the attack on the Iranian Central Bank. Radiation is still drifting down on parts of Tehran. And now we're in a shooting war with Iran in the Strait of Hormuz. None of that is going to disappear with the Knesset's moves, no matter how welcome."

The silence stretched for more heartbeats than Whitestone was comfortable with. He opened his mouth to make another argument—

"Mr. President, you and I have known each other a long time," said Orhlon, who first connected with Whitestone more than a decade earlier when the general addressed the megachurch Trinity Baptist near Dallas on the state of Israel's security and his country's gratitude to evangelical Christians who offered Israel their unwavering support. Whitestone was a deacon at Trinity who guided Orhlon during his visit and offered the hospitality of his Texas home. "So, Jon, this is not the time for veiled truths. You and I both know how deeply you and your military were involved in the attacks on Iran. I need your support, Jon, and Israel needs your support—publically."

Whitestone pushed himself off the desk, crossed the room, and sat on the sofa opposite Cartwright. "You have my promise, Moishe. We'll stand by you. And the world will know it."

"Thank you, Jon. Now I've got to try to stop a war."

Cartwright, Whitestone's newly appointed secretary of state, leaned back into the softness of the sofa. "Well, that's a surprising change. Welcome . . . but unexpected. What about Abbudin?"

Whitestone steepled his hands together and pushed his fingertips against each other. "I think our conversation with the king just took on a different flavor. We can get tougher, but we need Abbudin to exert some influence. If we're going toe-to-toe with the Iranian military, then we need the Al-Uedid air base in Qatar reopened. And we need it now."

—~~~~—

"I cannot answer for the sheikh." Abbudin's voice, coming from the speaker-phone, sounded as slippery as oil. "His nation is in turmoil, as are so many others as a result of the misnamed Arab Spring. This spring has been nothing but disaster for the Arab people and our countries. All of us must be very careful."

Whitestone pushed the mute button.

"Something's wrong here," he whispered, even though the microphone on this end was turned off. "This isn't the same guy we've dealt with before."

Whitestone pushed the button again.

"Your Excellency, the United States, Saudi Arabia, and Qatar have been steadfast allies for decades, helping to bring security and stability to all of our nations. Allies stand together, even when faced with opposition."

"Yes . . . well . . . times change," Abbudin purred.

Whitestone went rigid, like a hunting dog on the scent. His prey was coming into clearer focus.

"Times change?" he repeated. "Is it possible, perhaps, that because times have changed that two pumping stations are destroyed on the same day, sending global oil prices to crippling levels . . . our military air base in Qatar is closed on the same day . . . and the Fifth Fleet is attacked in the Strait of Hormuz—all on the same day? Is that coincidence, or is more than the time changing?"

No sound came through the speaker.

Whitestone attempted to keep the power of this room from changing his nature. Really, he did. But at times . . .

A man who ruled a nation of sand with the lowest literacy rate in the world was trying to *play* the president of the most powerful nation on earth. This president didn't like being played. And the stock market would fall off the edge of a cliff tomorrow.

An aide came silently into the room and handed an envelope to Cartwright as the president weighed his next words. He was about to speak when Cartwright raised a hand.

"A moment, Your Excellency," said Cartwright, handing a sheet of paper to Whitestone.

The president scanned the sheet, glanced across the table at Cartwright, who was visibly agitated, and read once more, letting the implications sink in.

"Your Excellency, in the last few hours the euro has become a worthless currency. Europe is essentially bankrupt. And the finance ministers of Spain, Greece, and Italy all agreed to the financial takeover of their economies by Saudi banks."

"I do not know, Mr. President. My cousin is in charge of the bank."

"Well, it might be wise to ask your cousin what he's up to," said Whitestone, trying to keep his anger in check. "Your cousin's bank just called in over five hundred million dollars of sovereign debt. You are igniting a financial Armageddon that could destroy the economies of Europe. Abbudin, you can't allow this to happen."

Whitestone immediately regretted using the king's given name. It was an affront to the House of Saud to use a ruler's given name without being given permission.

"Mr. President." The king's voice had a new edge to it, sharper, dripping sarcasm. "Your nation and the nations of Europe have long relied on the largesse of other people's money to support a lifestyle you could not afford. You are correct. Much is happening at the same time, including the aggression of your Fifth Fleet in the Strait of Hormuz, an Israeli invasion of Lebanon, and the massing of its warplanes to strike—again—our Iranian brothers. Apparently, this time, without your help."

Whitestone winced. He had hoped his complicity in the attacks on Iran's oil, gold, and nuclear facilities would remain a secret, at least longer than this.

"So do not lecture me about what *I* must do for *you*. Do not imagine you can demand me into obedience. I am not a puppet who dances at the end of your strings. In fact, I have that position reserved for someone else."

The atmosphere in the Oval Office crackled with tension, like heat lightning on a summer night. The king's voice—softer, calmer—failed to break tension's grip.

"In such an uncertain world," said King Abbudin, "it is the prudent and the wise who prepare for the unknown. My cousin, our nation, are simply preparing for the unknown. We have pumping stations to repair. More alarming is the fate of the Saudi economy if war closes the strait, if our pipelines are attacked, if

THE ALEPPO CODE   191

our products cannot get to market. Laying aside a significant reserve of cash is the prudent thing to do to ensure the continued well-being of the Saudi people. And I answer to the Saudi people, Mr. President, not to you."

It was a coup. Whitestone knew that now—a worldwide economic and fiscal coup. And Whitestone finally knew his ultimate enemy. Without firing a gun, dropping a bomb, or invading a nation, the Arab world was about to crush Western civilization.

A chill ran through the marrow of Whitestone's bones, so deeply rooted only a walk on the sun would have warmed his soul.

"You will find that we do not surrender," said the president, taking off the gloves of protocol and pretense. "We drove you back into the desert once, and we will do it again."

A laugh from the pit rattled out of the phone.

"When you have no heat in the winter, when your lights no longer work, when your silos lie barren and empty, when you have no fuel for your vehicles, what will you drive us with then? When your world reverts to the Dark Ages, you will come crawling, begging for bread. And we will watch you die, infidel. *Allahu Akbar* . . . Allah is greatest."

24

The hospital was . . . well . . . not what Tom Bohannon expected, especially for the military. No drab, concrete slab exterior or mustard brown walls on the inside. The Augusta Victoria Hospital, on the southern side of Mount Scopus near the Mount of Olives, looked like a hotel from the outside because that had been its original purpose. The ubiquitous Jerusalem stone walls glittered in the late afternoon sun, set off by large windows looking out over the Kidron Valley to the Old City, but the hospital also benefitted from beautiful landscaping with hibiscus trees, running wisteria, and rosemary hedges flanking every walkway.

Once inside, Bohannon wondered if he should be looking for a concierge desk. Tall, Herodian columns flanked the front door. Black granite floors and smoked-glass walls angling in toward the rear of the lobby framed the huge entryway. And off to the right, a massive atrium looked like a tropical forest with songbirds fluttering among the trees. Bohannon was startled when he heard a soft voice to his left.

"Can I help you?"

Turning to the sound, Bohannon was again surprised to find a young female Israeli soldier standing by his side, an iPad resting on her left forearm. Her standard fatigues fit like a designer suit; her hair was jet black and pulled into a bun at the back of her head. Though Bohannon wouldn't describe her as beautiful, she had an arresting look—small and thin, high cheekbones, and mesmerizing brown eyes. He was still staring when she spoke again.

"Are you here to visit someone? I'm Corporal Heim. Perhaps I can help you."

"Oh, yes . . . well," Bohannon stammered, "I'm here to see a friend . . . Sergeant Fischoff. I'm sorry; I don't know his first name."

The soldier gave Bohannon an appraising once over, turned to the iPad, and tapped the screen a few times. She turned back to Bohannon. "Your friend, but you don't know his first name?"

Regaining his composure, Bohannon could sense the wariness of the corporal.

"We met under very unusual circumstances," he said. "The sergeant and his squad were dispatched to find my wife and her friend. They were kidnapped. I happened to be in the Hummer when the orders came through. I know—it's a strange story. But I was there when the sergeant was injured in the wreck. I helped pull him out. I just wanted to see how he was doing."

The corporal weighed Bohannon's story. "Come with me, please." She walked deeper into the lobby and around a reflective glass wall. As he followed to the other side, Bohannon was stunned to see a military outpost—a dozen fully armed Israeli soldiers in flak jackets, on their feet and constantly moving along the length of the wall. Others monitoring a bank of closed-circuit television monitors with an array of electronic equipment outside of Bohannon's experience.

"This hospital is a ripe target for attack at any time," said Corporal Heim, answering Bohannon's unspoken question. "Even more so today. Nearly one thousand Israeli soldiers are in this hospital, a significant number of them field officers, most of them unable to defend themselves. So there are two first-line goals for this hospital: one, protect it against any kind of terrorist attack and, two, give our wounded soldiers a special place that tells them how much we honor their service to the nation. One way we do that is to give them the best medical care possible. Another way is to have the most effective security possible. We want our patients to relax and recover. So we're always on alert but seldom in sight.

"For instance," she pointed over her shoulder, "you underwent a full body scan as you walked between those columns, and what's under the black granite floor will react if the weight on it exceeds 275 kilos within ten meters—the running weight of three men with weapons.

"Please, wait in here."

"But how do—"

Corporal Heim opened the door to a well-appointed but sterile office. Behind the desk sat an Israeli captain. "Please, sit down." He motioned to a chair in front of the desk. Bohannon's anxiety meter clicked up a notch as he sat before the captain.

"Do you have your passport?"

Bohannon pulled the small blue booklet from his back pocket and handed it to the officer.

"Thomas Bohannon." The captain looked up from the passport. "And you would like to see Sergeant Fischoff. But you don't know his name. Is that correct?"

Bohannon was about to answer when Corporal Heim entered the office and handed some papers to the officer. The captain scanned the pages, stopped, and read one section a second time. He looked up at Bohannon with a different expression on his face.

"You appear to be quite a unique tourist." The captain rose from behind the desk and came around to stand before Bohannon. "Thank you," he said, extending his left hand to Bohannon. "Sergeant Fischoff would probably not be alive if not for you and his corporal."

Bohannon's hand was crushed, but his anxiety had tanked.

"Come. Let me take you to see the sergeant."

The interior of the hospital rivaled the entryway in richness of detail, and the number of nurses and doctors testified to Israel's commitment to its military. The captain stopped at a large wooden door. "I'll leave you to your reunion," said the captain. "Please, stay as long as you like."

Bohannon pushed open the heavy door with his left shoulder and entered a bright room, muted by a curtain over a large window. There was only one bed—more comfortable looking than any hospital bed Bohannon had ever seen. He stood, uncertain, in the doorway until Fischoff turned in his direction. The effort that took was etched across his brow and reflected in his eyes, a slow, stuttering process that demanded all his concentration. But Fischoff offered a smile of welcome that warmed Tom's heart.

"Mr. Bohannon." Fischoff's voice was raspy and low, sounding as if it came from the bottom of a pool. But his eyes were bright as Bohannon came to his side. "Good to see you're still in one piece." Fischoff's face clouded. "I was very sorry to hear about the young woman's death. I wish we had been on time."

Bohannon felt the stab of guilt and regret. Annie lived. But Kallie . . . "I know you and your men all risked your lives to save theirs," he said. He looked at the thick square of bandages taped to Fischoff's neck. "How are *you* doing?"

Fischoff's left hand went up to the bandage, a snow cone of cotton gauze stuck to the side of his neck. "I'm a lot better than I have a right to be," said

Fischoff. The sergeant grimaced as he shifted his body weight to the left to get a better look at Bohannon. "If it wasn't for you—"

"And the corporal," Bohannon interjected.

"Yes, and Corporal Feldstein. The two of you saved my life that night." A flicker of fight crossed Fischoff's face. It was the same look Bohannon had seen on top of the crusader tower in Jerusalem's Citadel, just before Fischoff flung himself off the tower's platform and crashed onto the deck of the muezzin's minaret. "And we got the bad guys. I'm happy, for you, that it's over. Go home and have a life, Mr. Bohannon."

"Please, call me Tom." He rested his sling against the railing alongside the hospital bed and leaned closer to the sergeant. "I once asked your first name, remember? And you told me *Sergeant*. Sergeant Fischoff."

Fischoff nodded. "Yeah, I was just acting tough."

"Well, I need to know your first name, now," said Bohannon. "We should be on a first-name basis for me to have the courage to ask what I want to ask."

The sergeant leaned back against his pillows, rays of the late afternoon sun coming through a crack in the curtain and falling across his bed. Half his face was lit by the sun, half in deep shadow. Bohannon searched for clues. He waited, his heartbeat counting the seconds.

"Perhaps . . ." Fischoff shifted in the bed. "My alert system is telling me I should hear your request first, before we get too friendly." Dust floated in the sunbeams. Bohannon prepared himself for a disappointment. Fischoff pushed himself up, full into the light.

"Jeremiah," he said. "My parents were religious."

"Of course . . . it would be Jeremiah."

Again Bohannon shook Fischoff's hand, and this time the grip was firmer, tighter, an exchange of promise, of bonds, of trust.

"What can I do for you?" asked Fischoff.

Bohannon pulled up a straight-backed chair and sat with his legs straddling the chair and his good arm resting on the top rail of the chair's back.

"I don't know how much you've learned about how this all started," said Bohannon.

"All I know is that you have been a thorn in Shin Bet's side for quite some time and that you were in some way involved with the events that led up to the earthquake and the first destruction of the Temple Mount."

Running his hand over his mouth and chin, smoothing down his reddish-gold beard, Bohannon tried to stifle a grimace. "Well, it's a bit more than that, I'm afraid." Bohannon described how he and his librarian and academic friends found the scroll and mezuzah, broke the codes, and found the hidden Temple and the Tent of Meeting—all while under attack from the Prophet's Guard.

Before Tom could finish, Fischoff raised his hand, palm out.

"Wait a minute," he said. "You make that sound as easy as reading the newspaper. You're telling me you and a librarian figured all that out and then survived the aftermath?"

Bohannon shook his head. "Let's just say there was a lot of divine intervention involved, some dumb luck, and a team of people who came together who are a lot smarter than me and who helped figure it all out."

Fischoff's eyes examined Bohannon with a new level of interest. And respect. "The divine, huh? I'm a Sabra," he said, "born here in Israel on a secular Jewish kibbutz. I've seen a lot done in the name of religion, and not all of it was good. I understand, to an extent. I've spent my life caught in a dichotomy of what I want to believe, because it justifies my life and my decisions, and what I saw in the way my father's faith guided his life and his decisions. When I compare the two, my father's life was more peaceful . . . no, more confident than mine. There was something there. Do you understand? He knew what he believed, why he believed it, and it guided him in all he did. Me . . . I'm not so sure. But I think I've seen what belief in God can do, and I believe God is with you. So tell me why you're here. I'm not promising anything, but I am listening."

"From what we discovered, we believed Abiathar's plan was to restore ritual sacrifice for the Jewish people—whether in the rebuilt Temple or, if the Temple was destroyed, in the resurrected Tent of Meeting. Abiathar removed the Tent, maybe the Ark of the Covenant, from Mount Nebo, where Jeremiah hid them, and moved it to a cave along Scorpion Pass in the Negev, just prior to the Crusader's rape of Jerusalem."

"There wasn't a very good result from your participation in that series of events," said Fischoff. "The Tent was incinerated, the concrete platform of the Temple Mount imploded from the heat, and . . ."

"And a lot of people died—again," said Bohannon, "including some of my friends, and a whole lot of Israeli soldiers . . . your friends."

"So why are you still here?" asked Fischoff. "Why don't you just go home and get back to your normal lives?"

Bohannon stood, stretched, and walked to the window. "That question has haunted me from the moment I saw Kallie Nolan's lifeless body," he said as he looked out the window. "I'm tired of making decisions that cost people their lives. I didn't think I could handle the burden anymore . . . didn't want to."

"It's the curse of being in command," he heard from behind him. "That weight can destroy a man. What changed?"

"Two things," said Bohannon, the sun warming his back as he turned to face Fischoff. "Two nights ago, very late, we were walking back to Kallie's apartment. Three black-clad men chased Joe, Annie, and me through the streets of Jerusalem. We still have something other people want and that they think is worth killing for. And our lives won't be worth living until we finish this thing and get these guys—the Prophet's Guard—off our backs.

"The second thing is, finally, we think we understand what's been at the core of this escapade from the beginning. There was more to the mezuzah than just Abiathar's messages to his counterpart in Egypt, more than the Temple or the Tent.

"There's a book called the Aleppo Codex," Bohannon continued, warming to his subject as the sun warmed his bones. "It's in the Israel Museum. The codex is a Masoretic text of the Tanakh, the first five books of your testament, which was created by a rabbinical committee that convened in Tiberius on the Sea of Galilee about a thousand years ago. We've seen the original book in the museum, but we've also been able to search through the only full and complete replica of the codex, in the Ades Synagogue in the Nahla'ot section of Jerusalem."

"I know it," said Fischoff. "My father was not a rabbi, but he was a learned and devout believer in the Law and the Prophets. And he imbued all of us with the same zeal. I've seen that book. What does the codex have to do with this mezuzah of yours?"

"We believe Abiathar was a key member of this rabbinical convention in Tiberius, one of the primary authors of the Masoretic notations in the codex. His hallmark is at the edge of the final notation. You know, we always wondered why Abiathar went to Tripoli in Lebanon the second time he was exiled from Jerusalem instead of heading back to Tyre. But now we believe that Abiathar's first stop in exile was in Tiberius, where he participated in the creation of the codex, and then he continued on to Tripoli, where he may have hidden a copy of the codex in the Dar al-Ilm, the great library of ancient Tripoli.

"But we found something else in the pages of the codex, an almost unbelievable story but a story that is supported by almost everything else we've learned from and about this Abiathar. What is described in the Masoretic notations is not Abiathar's personal story, but the story of his ancestor, Jeremiah, and a journey that strains the bounds of our faith."

Bohannon felt the presence again; that almost indefinable sense of reverent awe and personal experience that signaled the proximity of the divine. He shook his head in disbelief as he crossed the floor once again to the straight-backed chair and sat down.

"When Abiathar removed the Tent of Meeting from its burial place on Mount Nebo, where it was hidden by the prophet Jeremiah, we're pretty confident he also found the other things Jeremiah supposedly buried, including the Ark of the Covenant."

Fischoff did a double take at Bohannon's last words. He reached toward Bohannon with his left hand. "You're serious, aren't you? Up until now I figured you and your friends were just normal folks who got pulled into something much bigger than they ever imagined. But this . . . you're going to pull a Spielberg on me? You mean this is all about a search for the Ark?"

Tom found himself shaking his head, more in wonder and surprise at what he was to say next than in contradiction of Fischoff's conclusion.

"Sergeant . . . it's even weirder than that. We're not after the Ark," said Bohannon. "From everything we've seen and been instructed about the Masoretic text in the margins of the Aleppo Codex, we believe what Abiathar unearthed on Mount Nebo was the true power of the Ark . . . and in that cave on Mount Nebo he also discovered what Jeremiah did with that power."

"What do you mean, the power of the Ark?"

"Think back on the story of the plagues of Egypt. What brought down the plagues on Pharaoh and his people? Think about the parting of the Red Sea. What power was exercised to divide the water from the land? Not the Ark. The Ark didn't exist then."

Bohannon watched the expression on Fischoff's face as the wheels of his memory and imagination began to spin and search and finally light on something.

"You're talking about Aaron's staff, aren't you? You think Aaron's staff was the true power of the Ark?"

"No," said Bohannon. "We know it was.

"The Masoretic notations in the Aleppo Codex are clear about this. From the time of the Prophets—probably before—the learned councils of Torah scholars harbored a closely held secret. They were confident beyond words that power resided in Aaron's staff. And only when the staff was in the Ark did the Ark have any power.

"Think about it," said Bohannon. "You're a learned man about your Torah. You—"

"Yes," Fischoff interrupted, "I know Scripture. I know what it says in Exodus. 'Then the cloud covered the Tent of Meeting, and the glory of the Lord filled the tabernacle. Moses could not enter the Tent of Meeting because the cloud had settled on it, and the glory of the Lord filled the tabernacle.' The Ark had power because it was the mercy seat, the dwelling place of God's presence. Any power in the Ark, any power in the staff all came from the same source."

Bohannon was nodding his head. "Yeah, we've had the same discussions. The staff is just a stick of wood. It *is* God's power at work. But what is God's plan? How does he intend to manifest his power? We know that God infused Aaron's staff with power in the past. We believe there is a plan for the staff in the future. And I believe David's priests believed the same thing.

"Think back on the history of the Ark. When it was brought to Jerusalem from Obed-Edom's house—the place where David left it after one of his guys was killed for touching it—Scripture tells us it contained only the stone tablets of Moses. David sent his priests, Zadok and Abiathar—ancestor of Jeremiah and ancestor of our guy—to bring the Ark back to Jerusalem. The Ark left Obed-Edom's house in Nacon, but the most learned men of your faith believe Aaron's staff didn't leave with it. And why is that? Because the Aaronic priesthood knew that Aaron's staff was the instrument of power in the Ark. And that power needed to be protected. And it needed to be hidden.

"The Israelites nearly lost Aaron's staff once—when the Philistines captured the Ark and paraded it all around their country. Bad idea for them, since everywhere they took the Ark a plague broke out that was so deadly the Philistines begged the Israelites to take the Ark back. That's when Zadok, Abiathar, and their Aaronic priesthood decided they needed to do something to keep Aaron's staff from falling into the wrong hands."

Fischoff was shaking his head, a weary smile turning up the corners of his mouth. "This is quite a fable you're spinning here, Mr. Bohannon, but—"

"Look, will you please call me Tom?"

"Okay, whatever I call you you're still off your rocker with this story. Sure, there are lots of circumstantial situations that fit your bizarre theory. You could spin a fantastic yarn out of almost any one of a dozen well-known scriptural stories. But that doesn't make them real. I mean, tell me . . . where does a stick get that kind of power? God . . . yeah, I could see God wielding that kind of power. And maybe God works through people and things. But a stick?"

"Remember, that stick was dead and then came to life, a dry stick budding into a blossoming almond tree right in front of Pharaoh," said Bohannon. "That was after the stick became a snake, ate up all the sorcerers' snakes and then became a stick again. Pretty cool stick if you ask me."

"All right," said Fischoff. "Let's make an assumption that Aaron's staff has power and Jeremiah buried the Ark and the Tent on Mount Nebo. What happened then? You found the Tent in a cave in Scorpion Pass in the midst of the Negev Desert, hundreds of kilometers from Mount Nebo. So where's the Ark? Where's the staff?"

"Those are good questions," said Bohannon. "When my brother-in-law broke through the wall in that cave and discovered the hiding place of the Tent of Meeting, the Tent wasn't the only thing hidden behind the wall. But he didn't get the chance to discover the rest. Some of your soldiers were right on his heels and took control of the cave before Joe could get through the wall. And right now, the Israeli army and the Israeli government aren't telling us much about what else was in that cave. But one thing we do know pretty confidently . . . Aaron's staff wasn't there. Even if the Ark of the Covenant was in that cave, Aaron's staff wasn't anywhere close."

"Yes, but—"

"Sergeant, there's one other thing that maybe your father didn't know: the key element, the most essential part of this great conspiracy," said Bohannon. "In the Hebrew Midrash it was written, thousands of years ago, that Aaron's staff had been handed down through the ages. Noah had the staff on the first ark, Abraham had the staff in his migration from Ur of the Chaldeans, Joseph had the staff in Egypt, and we know Moses had it."

Fischoff scratched his head, his fingers running through the iron-gray stubble. "So where did it come from? And I think you're just dying to tell me."

"The rabbi at the Ades Synagogue brought out some other books while we were there that confirmed what Rabbi Fineman told us—that Aaron's staff was severed from the Tree of the Knowledge of Good and Evil in the garden of Eden when Adam and Eve were thrown out of Paradise."

The steel-blue eyes were fixed on Bohannon like radar beacons tracking an invader. "And this legend has what to do with you?"

Bohannon got up from the chair again and began pacing back and forth across the floor at the base of Fischoff's hospital bed. His left arm started punctuating his sentences.

"The Prophet's Guard, the guys with the lightning-bolt amulet, have been opposed for over a thousand years by another group, the Temple Guard, who were the first group to gain control of the mezuzah after Abiathar sent it to Egypt. The Temple Guard hid the mezuzah and its message at St. Antony's Monastery in the Red Sea desert. Over six hundred years ago, one of the monks deciphered the message on the scroll about the Temple being buried under Temple Mount. So a group of warrior monks formed to protect the hidden mezuzah. The Prophet's Guard and the Temple Guard have been fighting ever since for control of the mezuzah and scroll, but not because of the buried Temple.

"Both of these groups had access in St. Antony's vast library to a partial copy of the Aleppo Codex. The notations told them part of the story about the power of the staff. For the Prophet's Guard, their entire focus is not on the Temple, but on Aaron's staff. They want to find Aaron's staff. They want the greatest weapon in the history of the world to help them wage jihad."

"And to help them wipe Israel off the face of the earth," said Fischoff.

Bohannon turned from the curtained window. "Honestly, I don't know. God used his power against the people of Israel when they disobeyed him—a plague of snakes in the desert that wiped out thousands. And God has allowed others to inflict their power against God's people—like the conquest of Nebuchadnezzar or the destruction of Jerusalem by the armies of Rome. But if the Prophet's Guard and the people behind them, probably the Muslim Brotherhood, can get their hands on Aaron's staff and wield its power, you can stop worrying about Iran's nukes. We're all in trouble."

"So your government is asking you to track down Aaron's staff?"

"Not at all," said Bohannon. "As far as I know, neither the president nor the CIA have grasped the real meaning of what's going on here. If they did, they'd probably be crawling all over us right now.

"No . . . nobody's pushing us to do this. We need to do this for ourselves, to finally get the Prophet's Guard killers off our backs and out of our lives," he said. "We need to get the staff before the Prophet's Guard does."

"How are you going to do that?"

"Because we know where to look."

Fischoff's left hand was toying with the huge bandage on his neck, his eyes on some distant thought. He turned back to Bohannon. "Where are you going?"

In spite of the incredible nature of his story thus far, Bohannon knew the next few moments would be the most difficult, and the most critical.

"Iraq."

Fischoff opened his mouth and raised his hand, but stopped. "No, I don't think I want to know. You've got a way in, don't you?"

"Yes."

"And you don't want to tell the government—yours or mine—or ask for their help, because . . ."

"Because I don't want any interference, and I don't want any leaks," said Bohannon. "The Prophet's Guard has been one step ahead of us, like they know what we're going to do before we do it. The news reports are saying there was a mole in the Israeli government. We don't want the Guard waiting for us when we get there. Sergeant, you are one of the few people in this country I can trust."

The sergeant grimaced and shook his head. "What do you need?"

As Bohannon laid out his request, Fischoff's expression never changed, never wavered. "I think if we're successful in this quest, we're not going to have the luxury of taking a leisurely stroll back to Jerusalem."

"So, if necessary, you want me to get you out of Iraq and across the Hashemite Kingdom of Jordan illegally. You want me to help you select the best way to cross Jordan, and you want me to lay out a way for you to get back into Israel without going through one of the border crossings. That's it?"

Bohannon felt a bit foolish as he heard Fischoff recite back his request. But, in for a penny, in for a pound. "Well, not just me," he said. "Me and the team—Joe, Sammy, and my wife, Annie."

The sergeant threw up his hands and laughed out loud. "Are you kidding me? Your wife? Didn't she just suffer enough? You want to take her across a thousand kilometers of desert populated only with bandits and snakes?"

"No," said Tom. "I'd never do that to my wife. No . . . Annie is the one demanding that we go. In fact, she's pretty critical to what we're hoping to do. I don't want to tell you too much, but Annie's got the contacts we'll need once we get inside Iraq and the justification for why we're there. And she's more determined than any of us to see this crazy episode of our lives come to an end.

Between you and me, I also think she's hoping to find a way to deliver some payback for Kallie Nolan's death."

Silence filled the room. Fischoff glared at Bohannon with a fiery intensity, and Tom wondered if he'd just committed his greatest blunder. The silence stretched to the point where Bohannon was ready to walk out.

"Get me the pen and paper on that table," said Fischoff. "I like you, Bohannon. And I think you're on a mission that is way beyond your ability. I like that, too. You remind me of my father." He started writing on the tablet. "Call this number. Ask for Ithzak. Take what he gives you. Then leave the rest to me."

"But . . . how . . ."

"You saved my life, Tom. I owe you. Don't worry. Listen to Ithzak. Do what he says, and we'll get you home."

25

"You've been busy, Mr. Prime Minister."

Whitestone sat at the head of the large table in the Situation Room, bunkered deep under the White House, Cartwright to his right, cabinet members and the Joint Chiefs spread around the cluttered table's circumference, Israel's Moishe Orhlon on the phone. The aides tried, but they couldn't keep up with the accumulated coffee cups and discarded briefing papers that grew in piles on the table's interior. Smoking had been banished from this room many disasters before, but the stale cigarette smell lingered in spite of the strong coffee and high anxiety.

"There was no time to waste, Mr. President."

"Hezbollah appears to be holding to its word. The rockets have stopped?"

"Yes, Mr. President. It seems as if Nazrullah and his thugs were stunned by their government's overthrow in Lebanon," said Orhlon. "Where were they to turn? The Syrian army is an empty shell. President Al-Musawi hangs by a thread. And with the Iranians so focused on their own myriad crises, who would have suspected the sudden eruption of the Arab Spring in Tehran? It appears that massive popular demonstrations against Ghorbani and the Ayatollahs are filling the streets of Tehran and other Iranian cities. The pillars of Hezbollah's power have crumbled. The threat to our north is silent—for now."

Cartwright fussed with an empty coffee cup. "Mossad has been very successful, Moishe. My congratulations on moving so swiftly and effectively."

Whitestone pointed to the flat screens on the wall opposite him and gave a thumbs-up signal.

"Not possible without the help of your operatives recently creating an opposition party in Lebanon, Mr. Secretary."

"And a lot of money."

"It comes in handy at times, yes."

Whitestone leaned in and propped his elbows on the table. "Are we ready for the final step, Moishe?"

"The final, and the most satisfying, yes. Mossad's agents have invested years preparing for this day. I wasn't sure it would ever come. Abbudin will regret his deception about the destruction of Saudi oil production."

"We have the map up on the screens now," said the president. "Where will your men hit them?"

"Ras Tanura refinery—their largest," said Orhlon. "I thought it only fair that we also hold the king to his word and make sure the pumping stations at Al Jalamid and Ash Shu'bah were destroyed. I wouldn't want anyone to think that King Abbudin was less than truthful. In an hour, those pumping stations will actually cease to exist."

"Good," said Whitestone. "Admiral Marrin? Are we prepared?"

A white-haired sailor with perfect posture, Admiral Robert Marrin, chief of staff of the US Navy, sat at the middle of the table, wearing his full dress blues. The left side of his uniform jacket was fully armored with ribbons and medals. "The Fifth Fleet has effectively destroyed the Iranian navy. All of its major ships are either crippled or at the bottom of the Persian Gulf. Our new weapon systems performed exceedingly well. We've inflicted devastating losses on the small SWARM attack boats. Any remaining have fled back into Iranian bases or hideouts of their own. And we're hunting those down. But we've suffered staggering losses, sir. The results of our war games were accurate to that point. We've suffered significant losses from both Iran's new, low-flying, ground-to-sea missiles and the sheer number of the small attack boats."

Admiral Marrin picked up a sheet of paper in front of him, but he didn't need to read it. The facts were sewn into his soul. "Carrier Strike Group Eleven was hammered. The *Nimitz* suffered heavy damage from missile strikes. The destroyer *Warren P. Lawrence* and the frigate *Vandergrift* both sunk. The *Higgins* and the *Ponce*"—he glanced at the president—"taking water, status uncertain. The British destroyer *Dragon* so badly damaged she may not make it back to port. Over three thousand casualties, nearly twelve hundred sailors dead or missing. And some incredible acts of heroism. But we're still in fighting shape, sir, and more than capable of fulfilling our next mission. Our battle groups have formed around Carrier Strike Group Ten and have made way for the Saudi coast. Nothing will leave Saudi ports without our permission. Particularly their tankers. And no help is getting in."

"Very well. Bill, are we ready on the ground?"

"Yes, sir. Our men are operating with the local Mossad agents and the three most influential opposition groups in Saudi Arabia. Today those groups will join together for a massive rally. Our people will make sure the rally quickly becomes a people's revolution that will sweep through Saudi Arabia—an uprising of impoverished Saudis that effectively threatens the reign of the family Saud. It will start in the coastal cities and then move inland to Riyadh. We figure three to five days before Abbudin will be forced to abdicate. We'll be there to help set up a provisional government—we've already selected the cabinet. Then we hit the Salafist clerics and the Al Qaeda cells."

Silent during the discussion, Prime Minister Orhlon cleared his throat. "Ah, no offense, Mr. Secretary, but is there any fear that Al Qaeda could move into—"

A naval aide ran into the Situation Room, commanding everyone's attention, leaned over Admiral Marrin's left shoulder, a yellow sheet in his hand, and whispered into the admiral's ear.

Marrin closed his eyes and nodded his head. He looked up the table, and his gaze locked directly on the president. Whitestone felt his blood freeze.

Andy.

"Mr. President, I regret to inform you that your son has been missing in action for the past several hours. We've hoped for a more definitive report." He raised the yellow sheet from the table. "Lieutenant Andrew Stone's body was recovered from the Persian Gulf twenty minutes ago. I'm sorry, sir."

No privilege. He didn't even want to use his real name.

The world twisted. An unrealized pain rose from some dark place deep in his being. His vision blurred, and the sound of an avalanche echoed in his ears.

Orhlon's voice rose from the speaker, breaking the reverent silence that shrouded the room.

"Jon . . . I am so deeply sorry. He was a wonderful young man."

The president of the United States returned to the present, to the men sitting around the table, to the duty his countrymen had entrusted to him. Thousands of other sons and daughters had died that day. Thousands more might die if their commander in chief was distracted by his personal emotions. He needed to ignore the pain in his chest and focus. And he needed to call his wife. The pain ticked up a notch.

"Jon . . ." It was Orhlon again. "I swore I would get revenge for Lukas Painter's murder. Abbudin has been at the root of it all. Now we can both take the steps necessary to fully bury our dead."

26

In 1988, Annie Bohannon was a promising photographer for *National Geographic* when she took one of the most iconic cover photographs in the history of the illustrious magazine. *The Kurdish Rebel* was the image of a young woman of the *peshmerga* guerrillas—rebels under attack by the government forces of both Turkey and Iraq—her baby boy perched on one hip, her Kalashnikov automatic weapon perched on the other. The young woman looked boldly into Annie's camera with world-weary, piercing emerald eyes and the riveting cover image catapulted Annie's career.

A year later, when she learned that the young woman had been executed by an Iraqi general—primarily because of the notoriety of the *NG* cover—Annie had laid down her cameras and walked away from her career. Just three weeks ago, determined not to be left behind when the team returned to Jerusalem, she reached out to her former photo chief and asked for a new assignment. Annie promised her former boss another blockbuster cover image, this time from the refugee camps outside the Old City, where thousands of Jews and Palestinians lived side by side in a tent city as a result of the destruction caused by the earthquake that split the Temple Mount in two. It was an assignment she had failed to complete.

She was staying with Kallie Nolan in her Jerusalem apartment when they both were kidnapped by agents of the Prophet's Guard. Ultimately, Kallie was murdered and Annie was rescued. Now, two days after Kallie's memorial service, Annie was on the phone once more with Vince Kasper at *National Geographic*. She knew there was an *NG* crew already in Iraq, documenting the pillaging of Iraq's museums and ancient sites in the chaos following Saddam.

If she could persuade Vince . . . this could be the perfect cover for their entry into Iraq.

"Do you think he'll go for it?" asked Deirdre as Annie held the phone in her hand, digging up the courage to make the call.

"I hope so. Tom barely had to get the words out before Alex Krupp offered one of his corporate jets to get us there. And Latiffa Naouri is already working on our documents from the Baghdad end through the Iraqi Antiquities Commission. If the sergeant will help us figure out a way to get home, that leaves Vince. If Vince doesn't come through, I don't—"

"If Vince doesn't come through we can always try Larry, Moe, and Curly." Rizzo was building a tower out of playing cards. "Otherwise, we're gonna be out of ideas when Tom gets back. There, the Tower of Babel—Rizzo-style."

Annie took a deep breath and punched in the familiar numbers, the connection almost instantaneous.

"Hi, Vince . . . it's Annie. Listen . . . yes, thank you, it was very frightening. I know you did, and I appreciate it. But listen, I've got a favor to ask. It's a big one, and I can't tell you why, but I'm sure it will be worth—

"No, we're not coming home—at least not yet," said Annie. "We've uncovered some information that explains why people are still trying to get their hands on what we have or force us to tell them what we know, information that changes everything, including our plans. But we need your help."

"Sure, Annie," said the voice on the other end of the line. "Just tell me what you need and, if it's possible, it's yours."

"Thanks. Do you still have that crew recording the decay of Saddam's rebuilt Babylon?"

"Yeah, they've got about another week's work before they wrap up."

"I need that crew, Vince."

There was a pause at the other end of the line. Vince was a friend, but he wasn't a fool, and operating the crew in Iraq was costing *National Geographic* thousands every day. Annie could almost see Vince mentally calculating both the fiscal impact and the risk he was taking with his position.

"It will be worth every minute of their time," Annie said. "Listen, I can't tell you exactly what we're after. If we're right and find what we're looking for, it's going to make for an incredible story that will capture headlines all around the world. And it will be exclusively yours."

"Now you're talking. I trust you . . . and your instincts. You haven't steered me wrong yet. Tell me. What do you need?"

〰〰〰

"The crew will be waiting at the Baghdad airport," said Annie. "We'll set up camp near Hillah, sixty miles south of Baghdad, about five miles south of the ruins of ancient Babylon. But we've got them for no more than a week, that's all Vince can cover—unless we find something more concrete."

"Do you really think we can look like a documentary television crew?" asked Rizzo. "I don't know anything about television except for *Amazing Race*."

"And *Barney*," said Joe.

Rizzo waved the back of his hand toward where Rodriguez was sitting with his wife. "Funny man. If you took the time, you'd realize there's a lot you can learn from *Barney*."

"Like how to dress?" Joe needled.

"Like how to count to ten, Brillo-head." Rizzo got up from the table and walked into the kitchen as his tower of cards collapsed.

Annie felt a pang of compassion for Rizzo. She saw Joe steal a quick glance in Deirdre's direction.

"I think we've got the old Sammy back with us again," he said in a low voice.

Annie's compassion turned red. "I think you better be careful," she snapped. "He's still the old Sammy, but he's a wounded and damaged Sammy who's trying to show us a brave face. He's emotionally brittle, and he could shatter at any moment."

Joe turned to face Annie head-on. "Sure, he's hurting," he said. "But I don't think applying kid gloves is the best way to treat Sammy right now. He's tough—tougher than you may realize. And the way to help him through this— I think—is to help him be the tough Rizzo that he is at heart. Needle him and let him needle you right back. Get his combative juices flowing again. Sure, his heart is broken. He's grieving. But he'll stay broken and grieving if we don't challenge him. He can go through the eight phases of grief when we get home, but right now we need Sammy ready to fight."

"You'll all need to be ready to fight, I'm afraid." Rabbi Fineman was picking up the playing cards, trying to rebuild Sammy's tower.

Annie could see the concern on his face. "We know it will be dangerous," she said.

The rabbi slowly shook his head. "No, I don't think you do," he said. "You are venturing into the most unstable geography on earth, and probably the most deadly. Syria is in the throes of implosion—there is no government control in half the nation, and Al-Musawi thinks pouring poisonous gas on his own citizens is the way to maintain the legitimacy of his rule. Lebanon is still in the grip of a terrorist organization with scores of rockets pointed at Israel. Hundreds of thousands of refugees are fleeing over every border to the point that national boundaries are obscured. And there's a naval battle going on in the Persian Gulf that might already be a third Mideast war.

"Westerners are not only viewed with suspicion in Arab nations, but they are often harassed and threatened by mobs of Islamists. Saddam may be gone, that war may be over, but ISIS has overrun nearly one-third of the country and they are cutting off the heads of people they don't like. You won't be that far from the fighting. It may be a simple thing to get into Iraq, but with what you're seeking, it will be much more difficult to get out."

8:12 p.m., New York City

Secretary of the Treasury Robert Gephart walked down Maiden Lane with the confidence and aplomb of a man who used to own the real estate upon which his soft, Italian calfskin loafers walked—which he did. Once. Once, the movers of Wall Street shook at the mention of his name. Now, operating in service to the president he admired and supported, Gephart no longer owned, officially, the power he once held at Lehman and Bear Stearns. Not legally, anyway.

At the tiny dot of a park called Nevidon Plaza, Gephart turned left on William Street and stopped in front of an ornately carved wooden door. There was no number at the entrance, no name on the three-hundred-year-old Federal-style building.

Sunday nights in the Financial District of Manhattan were as quiet as Coney Island in January. Gephart knocked once, looked over his shoulder at the empty street, and entered the darkened building as soon as the door was opened.

"Robert, I believe you know Finance Minister Lin."

"Yes, thank you, Abraham. The minister and I were undergrads at Stanford together. Minister Lin, I am blessed to see you again, and grateful for your support."

Lin Hu Na was CEO of the Industrial and Commercial Bank of China. With three trillion dollars of assets, ICBC was the largest bank in the world. He was also the most powerful financial official in the government of the People's Republic of China.

His host, Abraham Rothschild, was chairman and owner of the Rothschild Group and Rothschild AG Bank in Switzerland, but more importantly was also the controlling force behind what was called the Bern Consortium, the shadow cabinet of the Swiss private banking system. These two men controlled more of the world's wealth than even the Arab conspiracy trying to conquer Europe. Lin stepped toward Gephart, his hand outstretched. "No need to thank me, Mr. Secretary. We're all here with one purpose, to save the world we know from the world we fear. Let us get to work."

Gephart's heart warmed. After all these years, the most important thing in finance was still true. Life was all about relationships. Sure, nations and agendas were important. But when push came to shove, who you knew was so much more important than where you lived or who you served.

Rothschild put a snifter of brandy on the table next to Gephart and returned to his chair on the far side of the empty fireplace. "As the euro continues to devalue, Abbudin has ordered Saudi banks to demand immediate repayment of loans they made to eurozone countries. The European Union is facing bankruptcy. Economically speaking, Spain, Greece, and Italy have ceased to exist."

Gephart picked up the snifter and swirled the golden liquid around its crystal sides as he calculated why these men were here . . . and what the next few moments might cost.

"Mr. Secretary," said Rothschild, "the Saudi banks, the Arab world, have eaten us for dinner. They own everything . . . everything that matters. If something dramatic doesn't happen in the next twelve hours, the Western world will cease to exist and the Second Caliphate will extend from Germany to India and beyond for as long as any of us will live. Minister Han and I don't intend to allow that to happen. You need to know what we intend to do."

PART TWO

אֵת

GARDEN OF
GOD

27

MONDAY, AUGUST 31

"Do you have the water bottles, Sammy?"

"Sure. Same as the last time you—"

"How many?" Annie didn't stop as she crossed the living room of the apartment, just turned her head in Rizzo's direction.

"Six, just as many—"

"Good. Fold them tight."

Annie heard Rizzo's grumbles as she looked out the window. But she had more on her mind than Sammy's gripes. She looked across the parking lot, down the Bar Lev Road. *Is there enough time?*

She turned away from the window and passed close to Rizzo, who was still wrestling the five-gallon, collapsible plastic water jugs into the bottom of a knapsack. "Cushion them so they don't squeak," said Annie, her voice low and soothing as she laid her hand on Rizzo's shoulder. "We'll need every one of them where we're going."

Annie walked down the hall and past the bathroom, headed for the kitchen. The bathroom door was open. "Got the first-aid kit?"

Joe looked up, a brush in his hand and his mouth full of toothpaste. "Yessh," he spluttered.

"Make sure there's extra antibiotic and extra bandages." She left a gurgle in her wake.

Tom was in the kitchen, carefully packing boxes of dried food, cushioned by his surrounding clothes, into a large duffel bag.

"Is the satellite phone turned off?"

"I've got the battery in my pocket. Reynolds won't be able to track our position."

"Sugar and salt?"

"Yes, I told—"

"Spoons, knives, forks . . . cups?"

"Yes," said Tom, turning to his wife. Annie could see objection in his face, then it changed. "Oh . . . forgot the cups. But you're marching through here every ten minutes like a general getting his army ready for a long march. You're giving everybody the willies."

Annie opened her mouth, but took a deep breath instead of snapping at Tom. "I know. I'm sorry. There's just so much to remember. The *NG* crew has enough supplies for themselves, but not for the four of us. And we have so little time. Sam Reynolds could be here any minute, and I don't think we're ready."

"I'll be ready," said Tom. Annie could feel the comfort of his hand on her cheek. "We'll be as ready as we can be. I just hope this plan works."

Annie placed her hand on his. "It has to. It's the only one we have." She swept her gaze across the kitchen once more. "Bring some bleach—we'll need to keep things clean, or we'll all end up with—well, we don't want it. Let's huddle in five minutes."

Without a glance back, Annie turned on her heel, exited the kitchen, and entered the small dining alcove. Deirdre and McDonough leaned over, looking down at a map spread across the table.

"Aye . . . it's a trip I wouldn't wish on me uncle Seamus, and I wasn't too fond of him to begin with," said McDonough, shaking his head. "That's a long way. Too much for me, even if I wasn't required back at Trinity. 'Tis a marvel the old gent, Jeremiah, could make it to Babylon and back."

"Over six hundred miles," said Annie as she came up behind them. "Desert all the way, very little water, and too many bandits just waiting for people foolish enough to wander off the main highway."

Deirdre looked up from the map and caught Annie's gaze. "Are you sure you need to go . . . not get home to your kids? Are you sure this is the best way back?"

"Sure? I'm not sure of anything," said Annie. "It's my idea. I'm the cover. But first we need to get there, and then we can hopefully maneuver around Iraq with some level of freedom. I don't know if it's going to work, but it's the best

I could think of. At least we have a legitimate reason for being in Iraq. After that—well, who knows what we'll find."

"Or how you'll get home," said McDonough.

Annie put her hands on her hips and let out a sigh. "Fly out, I hope. Krupp's going to leave his plane there for us. And if we can't fly out, we rely on Fischoff. If absolutely necessary, we come back across the desert."

"Where do you meet the *National Geographic* crew?" asked Deirdre.

"They'll meet us at the airport in Baghdad. So once we hook up with them, our cover should be pretty solid." Annie had pulled in some pretty heavy favors, and she would be in their debt a long time. She, Tom, Joe, and Rizzo now carried official *National Geographic* IDs and work documents connecting them to the photo team already in Iraq.

Annie looked down at the faint line crossing the al-Anbar Desert, and her hopes felt almost as faint. If it came to a race across the desert wastes, her final phone call last night, after Tom had fallen asleep, might be the one that saved their lives. Tom wouldn't be happy about this one, but it was Annie's ace. And she was pretty sure they would need to play it at some point.

"What about Reynolds?" asked Deirdre. "He's the first big hurdle. He's smart, he's cagey, and he's experienced. I think it's going to be pretty difficult to pull off the sleight of hand you've got planned."

Annie turned to fully face her sister-in-law. Deirdre had recently turned forty-five, but time failed to diminish any of her stunning beauty—flawless skin, flaming red curls, and blue eyes bristling with mischief. "Honey, that's where you come in. We need you to flash those big blue eyes so that Sam Reynolds will forget what country's he's in. You've got to keep his attention, and his mind off us. You just get between Reynolds and the van, and lead him on. Make sure he's not looking at anything but you."

Annie glanced once more at the map. She was about to call across the room to Rizzo when the front door buzzer cut short her thoughts.

"Showtime," whispered McDonough.

6:24 a.m., London

"A long, sad day, Mr. President. I am so sorry to hear about your son." The United Kingdom's prime minister, Michael J. O'Neill, stood in front of a bank of computer screens in a fortified room under 10 Downing Street, the

Admiralty's three senior officers in an arc around him, all studying the deployment of ships in the Persian Gulf.

"Thank you, Michael. What will Parliament decide?"

Whitestone was to the point. This was no time for personal sentiments.

"I think both Houses are more incensed than I am," said O'Neill. "I've never seen Lords and Commons so single-minded. It may be foolhardy to stand against the Saudis—they seem to have all the cards—but we're a determined bunch when someone attacks this country. The rest of the EU may crumble, Jon, but Britain stands with you. Our ships are not turning back."

Admiral Slater pointed to a screen on the right and the prime minister nodded acknowledgment.

"HMS *Valiant* and HMS *Nelson*," said O'Neill, "are turning away from the flotilla now, Jon, but they are not returning to port. Our boys have put on a little visit to Bandar-e Abbas. Your lot can leave that naval base to us. *Valiant*'s crew specifically asked for this assignment—they have a history, you know."

Forty-seven sailors from HMS *Valiant* were killed in a 1998 explosion when an Iranian mine detonated against the ship during war games in the gulf. The mines had been laid by Iranian ships from the Bandar-e Abbas naval yard, in anticipation of the war games. Sailors had a long memory.

"I only wish we could bomb Riyadh back to the dust of the desert." But O'Neill knew his government would never survive military action against an "ally" because of a banking decision. And Saudi Arabia was so overrun with foreign nationals that collateral damage would be catastrophic.

"What else do you hear, Michael?"

The prime minister shook his head in disgust. "Our chaps at the Exchequer never saw this coming . . . don't believe any of us could. The Saudis control the national banks of Italy, Portugal, Greece, and Spain, and have ordered the military of all four nations to stand down until further orders. We are keeping the Bank of Ireland afloat, and we will not allow this contagion to go any further in the United Kingdom. I can't be sure of France. The French banks have taken a massive hit. But, Jon, the worst of it is Germany. I think the Germans may cave. Turns out their hard cash reserves were not as extensive as they led the rest of the world to believe."

"We're on our own?"

"That's what it looks like, Jon."

Michael O'Neill cursed his luck. Three months in office and now this.

"Well, Mr. Prime Minister, if we can't bomb the Saudis, we can sure as blazes bomb the Iranians. And we can open the strait again. The *Truman* is close enough to launch air strikes against southern Iran; the Fifth Fleet has been given orders to sink every Iranian vessel afloat in the gulf; and . . . well . . . as soon as the strait is open, let's just say we have joined with an old friend, newly appointed Prime Minister Orhlon, and have a special gift we're going to deliver to King Abbudin."

"But what about the banks, Jon? Abbudin is strangling the banking system of the entire EU. We can hit Iran, but the EU is in economic freefall. Abbudin is going to own the entire continent if something isn't done to stop him. I can keep Britain afloat, but the rest of the EU is sinking fast."

7:12 a.m., London

Lord Alderson walked into the boardroom in the HSBC Tower in a panic—panic for his nation, his fortune, and his family—perhaps not in that order. These next ten minutes, he believed, would lead to the extinction of all three.

The boardroom could have been lifted out of any number of castles in Europe. In fact, this one had been dismantled and shipped from Bavaria, reconstructed to its former glory, including the paintings of the Bavarian family that once owned such opulence. Its richly ornamented and superbly polished mahogany walls reflected off a shimmering, golden oak floor. At its inlaid teak conference table, large enough to accommodate two dozen, only two men occupied the room—both of them flanking the chair at the head of the table.

Alderson ignored the head chair and stood next to his old friend, Abraham Rothschild. Across the table was Lin Hu Na. They were two of the most powerful financiers in the world.

Why these two men should arrive unannounced—today—was a mystery that only added to Lord Alderson's growing certainty of disaster. Vultures, ready to strip the bones of the once-powerful EU? Alderson was unsure . . . even of Rothschild.

Bowing deeply from his waist, Lord Alderson paid homage to the man across the table. "Minister Lin, it is an honor. Your presence is most welcome." He straightened and turned to Rothschild. "Abraham, you have selected an interesting day for a visit."

As Lord Alderson eased into the chair next to Rothschild, the old man reached out his left hand and placed it on Alderson's arm.

"We're not here for a visit," said Rothschild. "Last night we met with Secretary of the Treasury Gephart in New York City to whom we suggested a course of action. We told Secretary Gephart, and we are here to commit to you, to the banking industry of the European Union, all the resources of the banking industry of China and the banking industry of Switzerland. You have available all the resources that we have at our disposal."

Lord Alderson waited for the next sentence. It didn't come.

"Forgive me, Abraham, but I must ask. For what purpose?"

Rothschild looked stunned. "We are not here for plunder, Albert. We are here to help. No strings. Abbudin has overplayed his hand if he thinks he can bring Europe to its knees under the dominion of the crescent moon. Minister Lin and I had a conversation. It is not in the best interests of the Republic of China to see Islam rise up a new Caliphate. It is certainly not in the best interests of the House of Rothschild. At this moment, Minister Lin and his government have joined with Bern Consortium to make one billion euros available for immediate deposit into the European Central Bank. We wanted to meet with you face-to-face to assure you—so that you may assure your colleagues—that this loan carries no interest, no demands, no time limit. Settle your debts with the Arabs. Let us know if you will need more. Then, together, we will see what needs to be done to permanently secure the future stability of the European Union and to defeat this economic jihad."

9:22 a.m., Jerusalem

Placing a firm clamp on Joe's left arm, Deirdre looked up into her husband's eyes. They only had a moment—Tom and Annie were talking to Reynolds by the door.

"Be careful, Joe . . . please. I don't want to have to tell the kids that . . ."

His fingers brushed her red curls away and settled on her cheek.

"I'll be back," he said softly. "I don't know how, but I just feel . . . confident. God's been with Tom through this whole thing. We'll be okay."

"Just with Tom?"

Deirdre saw a flash of understanding cross Joe's face. "What do you mean?"

"You've been different. Ever since I got here for Kallie's service, I could see it, feel it, hear it in your voice. You've experienced a lot, but something has changed you on the inside." She waited for his response.

Rodriguez took a deep breath, expanding his chest and throwing back his shoulders. He looked at Deirdre as if he would tell her the secrets of the universe. "I—"

"Let's go," said Reynolds. "C'mon. We gotta go if we're going to catch that plane."

Rodriguez moved his fingers under Deirdre's chin. "I'll tell you all about it when I get back. Maybe then it will make more sense to me. I love you and tell the kids—"

"Let's go!"

───※〜〜───

Oskar Tell had one foot on the running board of the weather-beaten nine-passenger van, its factory-applied paint scoured clean from too many excursions through the desert, and the other foot planted firmly on the ground, his left arm held stiff and straight, his hand leaning on the roofline. To any observer, it would appear Tell was the *only* thing keeping the van upright.

The visual was intentional, drawing stark contrast to the gleaming new Dodge Caravan that rested a few feet away in the hands of his cousin Tobias.

Oskar had chosen well from the fleet of vehicles parked outside the commercial hangar where the planes of Krupp Industries emptied their crews and cargo. As the entourage left the apartment house on the Bar Lev Road, the old man had turned left, making a beeline for the spotless new Dodge. Behind him, the beautiful, red-haired woman had stumbled over the threshold coming out of the apartment building, and was leaning heavily on the man in the suit to get her balance, both her weight and her momentum moving them toward the new van on the left.

Tell's cousin moved quickly to the building doorway, grabbing the two bags the man dropped as he tried to keep the woman upright.

"Those two . . . that's right," she said, looking over her shoulder, her lips close to his ear. When she turned back, the man's eyes were as bright as a July afternoon in the kibbutz. "Thanks, Sam," she said. "Without you I would have ended up in the dust."

They came to the side of the van, and it was clear the man in the suit wanted to help, but wasn't sure how to . . . where to . . .

"Why don't you get inside," she said, "and just give me your hand so I can climb in?"

Oskar Tell enjoyed working for Mr. Krupp. The ongoing repairs to Temple Mount—now suspended because of the pillars of fire and smoke that still alternated over the blackened hole that once held the Dome of the Rock—were more interesting than growing bananas on the kibbutz. And now this. A secret mission to outwit the American. Oskar had no idea why he was being asked to help with this subterfuge. But the money in his pocket was more than he made in two months on the kibbutz. Perhaps he could buy that ring for Josephina.

⌇⌇⌇

Annie stood in the doorway of the apartment building and watched with growing appreciation as Deirdre skillfully guided Reynolds's every move. *Joe, you're lucky the girl loves you so much.*

Joe, Tom, and Rizzo left the building and turned toward Tell and the ramshackle van on the right. Annie hefted the duffel bag in her right hand and moved to the right, following the three men. Tell had thrown open the back hatch and was stuffing their bags into the storage space. Annie handed her bag to Tell, waiting for some word or protest from Reynolds. But the challenge never came.

⌇⌇⌇

Traveling west on the Ben Gurion Highway, the two vans remained fairly close together for the first ten minutes, driving in the right lane at the same excessive speed as all the other vehicles on the road.

"Where will we separate?" asked Tom.

He was sitting in the front passenger seat—Joe, Rizzo, and Annie in the back. Tell, the driver, pointed into the distance.

"A farther bit, I think, and then I slow a little," Oskar Tell's accent was a heavy German-Israeli guttural, "then a little more. Soon, you see, we will have good separation, yah? The closer we get, the cars will all come," his left arm waved to the right, "and we be lost, fast.

"Don't be to worry," said Tell, "when we reach exit, other van will be disappear. Then I call Tobias and tell him I must need petrol. We be fine. No one see."

Tell turned his full attention to the growing traffic as he guided the van onto the ramp. Rounding the banked curve at speed, the aged van swayed on its creaking springs and seemed ready to lose its adhesion to the concrete roadway. Tell held tightly to the steering wheel until the curve flattened and the van settled back into a more upright posture.

Tom peeled his fingers off the dashboard handle he held in a stranglehold and looked left at the driver. "Handles like a sports car, eh?"

⸺⧫⧫⸺

Sam Reynolds looked in the right side mirror, then swiveled in his seat to look out the back window. "I don't see them behind us."

"No problem," said the driver, his heavy accent rolling his consonants. "Lots of traffic. And Oskar is slow driver. Don't worry. He's slow, but here he'll get."

⸺⧫⧫⸺

The first van had just pulled up in front of the international terminal when the radio crackled.

"Tobias?"

"What do you want? I need these passengers to unload."

"Is my tank is empty. There is no petrol out of airport. I stop now and fill."

Tobias shook his head and looked at the man on his right. "Needs petrol." He pulled the radio mike off the dashboard hook and pulled it close to his face. "You be better get them here on time or Abner will have your head with schnitzel. Lose this job you can't afford."

"Is okay, Tobias. I be there. Don't be to worry."

Tobias switched to Yiddish. *"It is working."* Then switched back to English. "Not to foul this up, okay?"

Tobias hooked the microphone back on the dashboard. "My cousin is good man," he said, looking at Reynolds. "But sometimes"—he shook his fist—"is not so smart."

※

Oskar Tell navigated the ramshackle van past the entrance to the International Departures terminal and continued along the loop that circled the Ben Gurion Airport complex. At the end of the main terminal building, a service road ran alongside a large, gray metal warehouse. Reaching the end of the service road, the van turned right and pulled alongside the commercial aviation terminal . . . the place where high rollers parked their private and executive jets. Waiting in the crowded parking lot on the side of the commercial terminal was a white panel truck, Excelsior Aircraft Catering lettered on its sides.

Tell steered his vehicle perpendicular, stopping as his van came abreast of the truck, obscuring it from the view of anyone in the commercial terminal. "Quickly . . . out." Tom jumped out of the front seat, sliding open the side door, as a tall, thin man came around the white truck and pulled open its rear doors. With the precision of circus acrobats, Joe, Rizzo, Tom, and Annie grabbed their gear from the van and jumped into the back of the catering truck. The doors slammed shut just as Tom remembered he failed to thank their driver.

※

Reynolds paced back and forth in the exit lounge, looking at his watch with every passing loop. "Never should have let that driver out of my sight without getting his phone number, or his cousin's." He held an iPhone to his right ear, waiting for a response from the van rental company. Reynolds stopped. "What do you mean you can't give me his phone number? I don't care if it is company policy. You're the company. Change the policy. This is an emergency. I—"

※

Deirdre felt badly for Reynolds. He was a nice guy. He was a huge help to Joe and Tom. Almost lost his job. Now he was going to get in trouble again. Too bad. She leaned over and caught Reynolds's elbow as he passed by on another circuit of the seating area around Gate 21A in the international terminal. He almost lost his balance turning to look in her direction, a question crossing his fretful face.

"They called the flight," said Deirdre. "Boarding has started."

Tall, self-assured, calm in crisis, the State Department veteran looked at Deirdre as if she had popcorn blowing out her ears.

"What are we going to do?" asked Deirdre, pointing in the direction of the gate. "Where are they? Could something have happened to them just coming to the airport? In a few minutes, we've got to go. Or miss the flight. What do we do?"

Reynolds stood there, iPhone in one hand, watch raised on the other, shaking his head back and forth. "You've got to go. I've got to find out where they are." He lifted the mobile phone to his ear once more when Deirdre reached out and held his arm in place.

"You're not coming with me?" she asked, her eyes opening wide. "Brandon's on a flight to Ireland. I'm going to be on my own, have no protection, all the way back to New York?"

Reynolds gave Deirdre a look that swung between fury and frustration. "I'm sure you can take care of yourself on an airplane," he said, "just like you've been taking care of me for the last hour, right?"

Reynolds bent over and jerked Deirdre's carry-on up to his shoulder. "Look, my job is to get you on that plane. So you're getting on, and then I'm going to find the rest of them and get them on the next plane to New York. And I'm not going anywhere until I get my job completed. So you're getting on the plane." Reynolds spun on his heel and marched toward the boarding gate.

A smile on her face, Deirdre followed in Reynolds's wake as his mutterings drifted back to her. "You'll be perfectly safe, and all of you will be home soon. Or I'm going to get assigned to a one-man office in Tajikistan."

***

It was cold and dark in the back of the refrigerated catering truck and the four of them were perched on the edge of some low shelves that offered minimal comfort. Joe was about to ask a question when the unseen driver slid open a vent and answered it for him.

"We're crossing the runways, and we'll be there in thirty seconds. Get your gear ready. I'll back up to the jet and open the rear doors so we're close to the fuselage. I'll come around and grab a case of food and carry it to the open galley door. Don't do anything until I can look around and make sure it's safe. Then move quickly and hoist yourselves into the galley."

⧁∿∿⧁

The leather seats were soft enough to sleep in, the sound-proofing perfect so the whine of the engines stayed outside. Tom was thinking about a nap when the door to the cockpit opened and Alex Krupp walked down the aisle, his wild red hair a counterpoint to the impeccable gray, pinstriped suit that hung perfectly from his tall frame.

Krupp was a billionaire industrialist, CEO, and heir to the vast Bavarian conglomerate. But he was also Tom Bohannon's fraternity brother and room-mate at Penn State where they formed a lasting bond. And it was Krupp who helped rescue them from under Temple Mount months ago and whose estate in Bavaria was their refuge when they broadcast to the world the existence of the Third Temple of God, hidden for a thousand years.

A broad smile on his face, Krupp stopped in the aisle separating Tom's and Annie's seats.

"Yo, Mr. Krupp." Rizzo hopped off his seat and walked up to Krupp with his hand outstretched. "Thanks for rescuing our sorry butts again but, hey, where's the beer and the *Fräuleins*?"

Krupp sat on the armrest of a seat and grasped Sammy's hand in both of his. "Good to see you, too."

"Alex, what are you doing here?" said Tom.

"What, you think I'm going to let you have all the fun?"

⧁∿∿⧁

They were gathered around a small conference table in the aft section of the cabin. "So there's nothing else I can do to help?" asked Krupp.

"You could give us a ride back to Jerusalem," said Rizzo. "It's a long walk from here."

Tom was surprised when Krupp hesitated.

"I can try," said the industrialist. "It's getting very dangerous, very quickly out there. I need to get back to Jerusalem to make sure our interests—our men and our equipment—are protected as much as possible. But I'll send the plane back once I reach Jerusalem, if I can. The Israelis could shut down their airspace at any time. What do you plan to do when we land?"

Annie Bohannon started to open her map case, but thought better of it. "The *National Geographic* crew will be there, but our arrival has been managed by Latiffa Naouri, the chief historian of the Iraqi Antiquities Commission. We worked together the last time I did a shoot in Egypt, and she's arranged for our entry visas. We'll be in good hands."

28

Four dusty and battered Land Rovers that appeared to be on their last legs pulled up beside the black Lincoln and out poured eight men—as grimy and dusty as the Land Rovers—who had just spent the better part of a month living in the desert. In their well-worn and varied work clothes, these men had the appearance of commandos more than photographers on a remote shoot.

They joined the woman standing next to the Lincoln, all eyes staring down the runway.

Inside the commercial aviation terminal, in a small maintenance room at the corner of the building, a tall, thin, dark-skinned man in the blue coveralls of the airport maintenance team gazed intently out a dust-encrusted window. The sun was on the far side of the building, so his vantage point gave him a clear view of the Gulfstream as it pulled alongside the knot of waiting people. Even though he had been called and told to be watchful, he doubted he could ever be of use to the leader. It was only when the little man bounded down the stairs to the tarmac that he realized these were the ones who were sought.

With the Lincoln Town Car in the lead, the four battered Land Rovers followed one behind another, made a U-turn and headed toward the south gate of the commercial aviation complex.

Only when the convoy left the airport compound, on the road south, did the man pull his mobile phone from the pocket of his coveralls and—his heart beating faster than a spinning propeller blade—punch in the number he was given should this very circumstance become a reality.

"Hello? Yes, this is Taurog. I work at the Baghdad airport. I was told to call you if—"

"You have seen them?"

"Yes. A Gulfstream landed not long ago. It was met by four Land Rovers . . . a group of photographers and film makers from *National Geographic* who arrived last month."

"How do you know it was the ones we seek?"

Taurog wiped the sleeve of his shirt over his perspiring brow and tried to slow his heartbeat. "Two men and a woman, but it was the little one who convinced me. He came out last. Black hair, thick glasses, about 120 centimeters tall."

There was the sound of muted conversation in the background. "You have done well. You and your family will be rewarded. Thank yo—"

"Wait!" Fear and excitement roiled around in his stomach as Taurog realized he was almost yelling. So close to reward, he would not fail now. "Naouri was with them, the chief historian of the Iraqi Antiquities Commission."

"How do you know this?"

"She is very popular. Her photo is often in the newspaper or on television. Everyone in Baghdad knows Naouri and what she's doing." Taurog took a breath to slow his racing heart.

"And what *is* she doing?" The voice was growing more agitated.

"Babylon . . . she is trying to save Babylon. Since the fall of Saddam, the Babylon he built on the ruins has been ravaged by the poor, looting the city for its bricks. Naouri is trying to save what's left of the ancient bricks from the looters. She wages a losing campaign. But," said Taurog, "what is most important is that Naouri greeted the American woman as if they were old friends or sisters. Perhaps you should consider Babylon?"

<hr>

It looked like any other tobacco shop on the outskirts of Baghdad, not very prosperous and covered by desert dust and ancient smoke. The old man standing by the door folded up the cell phone as he leaned against the wall. Leader of the Iraqi division of the Muslim Brotherhood's clandestine enforcers, the Special Apparatus, the old man had been told of the change in leadership but, still, was surprised when the call came from Saudi Arabia. Now it was his job to find the American team and stop them—at all costs.

The four-vehicle convoy kicked up rooster tails as it sped down a highway covered with dry, tawny sand. Annie was in the front passenger seat of the leading Rover, trying to see out a front windshield that was half covered by a spider web of fractures.

"You guys must be on a pretty tight budget, Mike," she said to the driver. "Couldn't the magazine afford to get you a few more respectable vehicles?"

"Part of the plan," said Mike Whalen. "These beat-up old Rovers are as important to us as our equipment. We don't want new vehicles. We don't want to look too prosperous. It's like the Wild West out here. There's no government, virtually no police. With four vehicles, we are noticeable, but we also appear formidable with the crew we've got. And for all the natives know, we could be a rogue military unit. Low profile is our middle name."

Whalen and his photo-video crew were a hand-picked bunch with a unique combination of skill sets.

Whalen was an ex–Navy SEAL, a head short of six feet tall with a wild shock of curly, white-blond hair that seemed to be permanently windblown from the Harley in his garage at home. He had the compact build and fluid motion of a man who understood and was comfortable with his own strength. Whalen converted his military specialty, underwater photography of targets and defenses, into a keen eye for the drama of light and contrast. His crew of eight did include an Emmy-winning filmmaker and photographer, Leo Matkins, who couldn't fight his way out of a paper bag, but who could conjure up unforgettable broadcast images that stayed with viewers long after the TV was quieted for the night.

But Matkins was an acceptable exemption because his two equipment handlers—Grant Bowman and Michael Papa—were both former Big Ten offensive linemen who ceaselessly argued the relative merits of Michigan and Ohio State. The vehicle wrangler and mechanic, Sal Molluzzo, was a Ranger master sergeant who did two tours in Afghanistan; the sound man was a long, lean Brit, James Leonard, who spent six years running terrorist surveillance for MI5; but Whalen's two go-to guys were both ex-marines and former NYPD Anti-Terrorism Task Force veterans, Fred Atkins and Steve Vordenberg, who had become first-rate lighting techs, but whose main job was often to keep them all alive.

Under the floorboards of the Land Rovers was enough firepower to keep away any roving band of Iraqi marauders, and the team was equipped with the Harris Falcon III handheld, multi-band radios, the AN/PRC-152 in use by most American and NATO armed forces.

"Whalen, your team is about as low profile as a kick in the teeth," said Annie. "But God knows these guys are the only way you could operate here and the other inhospitable places *Geographic* has sent you. I feel a lot more comfortable having them along."

"So who is the woman in the Lincoln?" Whalen asked.

"An old friend," Annie replied. "Latiffa Naouri, the chief historian of the Iraqi Antiquities Commission. We met on my assignment to the Valley of the Kings. We were both early in our careers, and Latiffa was educated in the States. We spent two weeks together and just connected. Latiffa always knew her career in Egypt would be limited because she was a woman. Which is one of the reasons, I believe, that she jumped at the chance when the position here was offered.

"But she had more than a career change reason to leave Egypt. Her father was a prominent Cairo University professor who campaigned openly for a more moderate Islam. But his enemies were powerful.

"Most people don't know that Egypt was the birthplace of Al Qaeda. Ayman al-Zawahiri, the mastermind of 9/11 and Bin Laden's second-in-command, was the founder of Islamic Jihad in Egypt in 1980. In 1981, Islamic Jihad was behind the assassination of Egyptian President Anwar Sadat. Over the years, Islamic Jihad operated in the shadows, but it grew in size and power, finally evolving into Al Qaeda in 1998. At the beginning, al-Zawahiri was a Muslim Brotherhood activist in charge of the Brotherhood's secret squads, the Special Apparatus. Latiffa's father was murdered by the Special Apparatus because of his opposition to Islamic fundamentalism. And she is aware that her position here in Iraq would become tenuous if the power of the Islamic radicals continues to grow. I thought the Brotherhood was dangerous, but they look almost humane when stacked up against groups like ISIS. I didn't have to tell her much before she was anxious to help."

"What kind of help can she give us?" asked Whalen.

"Access to Babylon," she said. "And the freedom to move about. There is some security, trying to keep the site from being looted, but they are not very effective. Naouri will make sure we have plenty of room to operate."

Whalen didn't take his eyes off the thin ribbon of asphalt that was visible in the middle of the road, but Annie Bohannon could tell he was assessing her and the reasons she had arrived in Baghdad.

"I'll tell you about it when we get there," said Annie.

⸻≈∿≈⸻

Following Annie's instructions, the *National Geographic* crew avoided the hotels in Hillah and set up a tent camp out in the desert, in a dry riverbed that was once the Tigris River, ten miles southeast of Babylon. Whalen and his team erected a handful of black tents, two of which housed the resting Land Rovers. From a distance, they might look like a typical Bedouin camp. Except minus the goats and horses, and none of them wore the traditional dress of the desert wanderers. Annie hoped no prying eyes would get too close.

They gathered in the largest tent, Annie's team along with Naouri, Whalen, and the two NYPD veterans.

"Are you going to tell us what we're here to do?" said Whalen.

Annie had a decision to make. She came to Iraq with the rights and responsibilities of a leader. This was her expedition, and she could keep it that way by holding on to control. But she knew, in her mind and her heart, that while she could competently lead a photo team, this quest was not hers to lead. It belonged in Tom's hands.

"That's a long story, Mike, and one in which I've only played a relatively small part." She turned her attention to her husband. "Tom, why don't you and the guys fill in Mike and his crew about how this started, where it's taken you so far, and why we're here today. That will take awhile. I've heard this story before and I'm hungry. So, Tom, you talk, and I'll cook."

⸻≈∿≈⸻

The story told, and everyone fed, the expanding team sat around a camp table, waiting for direction. "So what's the plan?" Whalen was at the end of the camp table with Leo Matkins to his right, Vordenberg and Atkins to his left. Naouri sat beside Annie.

"Well, Vince said we could have you guys work with us for a week," said Annie.

"But I don't think we have a week," Tom interjected. "One of the few constants in this whole crazy escapade is that the bad guys have been one jump ahead of us almost all the way. Every time we think we've gotten away from the Prophet's Guard, somebody with a lightning bolt amulet shows up. Or somebody sent by the Muslim Brotherhood. And here we are now, right in their back yard. If we weren't safe in New York, or in Jerusalem, I think we'd be crazy to think we've got a lot of time here. We should expect to get discovered tomorrow and have to escape immediately."

Silence greeted Tom's warning as all eyes at the table fell on him.

"There is no escaping the *al-nizam al-khas*, the Special Apparatus of the Brotherhood," said Naouri. "They are everywhere. They have eyes everywhere. And they are heartless murderers, Westerner or Muslim doesn't matter. I thought I escaped them when I left Egypt after my father was murdered. But I know they watch me here. So, no, you do not have a week. You may not have a day."

"Then we can't wait," said Annie. "Latiffa, can we get into Babylon today and still have some light so we can set up a shoot?"

"If you leave now."

"Okay, then. We're going on a reconnaissance mission. We follow the directions and we see where that takes us. If we find the portal, we go in tomorrow at sunrise. Mike, bring all the gear we need."

"The Rovers and the cameras are always loaded and ready to go. We'll need to leave two guys here to guard the camp."

"Latiffa, can you get us to the Lion of Babylon?"

"Certainly. That is not difficult."

"Good," said Annie. "Then while Matkins and his crew are shooting the Lion, some of us will go for a walk as if we're looking for locations. All of you, grab a hat and let's go."

Annie was on her way to her tent, passing Whalen and the two NYPD vets, and overheard Whalen's lowered voice. "Fred, unlock the weapons. Offense and defense. You ride with me and we'll split up the civilians."

She stopped, knelt on one knee, and tightened the laces on her boot. "Steve, you take Matkins, Rodriguez, and Rizzo with you. First, go find James and tell him to get his British butt in gear and scout in front of us. Bowman can ride with him, and they should rig some diversion in case it gets hot in Babylon. Make sure everybody has fresh batteries in their radios. Papa and Molluzzo will stay here with one of the Rovers as backup and wire the perimeter for us while we're gone."

Annie got back to her feet and kept moving to get her pack, but now she felt like she was going to war.

Following Naouri's vehicle, the *National Geographic* crew pulled off the rutted and decaying back road and onto a sandy track in the midst of the bleak and barren desert, a small, wooden sign in Arabic the only indication that something other than wasteland was in the vicinity. She waved from the back window of the black Lincoln Town Car, the three Land Rovers fell in behind, and they moved off down the track. Little more than eroded tire indentations, the track wove in and out of the ubiquitous sand dunes toward the west.

Ten minutes later, the Lincoln slowed and came to rest beside a small, brick guardhouse. A red-and-white-striped barrier blocked the desert track. A guard who looked as bleak and weathered as the surrounding landscape ambled absently to the car, barely scanned the credentials handed out the window, and waved the caravan onward as he leaned on the end of the barrier to lift it out of the way.

"Not a lot of security out here," said Tom, watching the limited exchange.

"This is the back door," said Whalen. "The main entrance is west of here, over by the Euphrates River. That's where the Ishtar Gate is, overlooking the river. But there are too many eyes on that side."

"Surprising, though," said Tom. "If this is one of the entrances to the ancient city of Babylon, I would have expected a little more than a senior citizen to be guarding the treasure."

"There's no discipline out here," said Whalen. "No police outside Baghdad, almost no government. One thing Saddam accomplished was discipline. It's almost vanished since our invasion took him out. Not just here, but all over Iraq. A great, untold disaster of the Iraq war is the massive looting and devastation that occurred to museums and schools and historic locations around the country. The destruction of irreplaceable national treasures was wanton and savage. In a way, we're lucky there's even this level of security this far from Baghdad. Otherwise, Babylon might have ceased to exist again."

A gritty dust, thrown up in the Lincoln's wake, peppered the Land Rover's windshield, distracting Tom so that the convoy was turning down a lane of red-brick buildings before he began to register that they had entered the city. Making the turn, Whalen pulled farther to the right, releasing the Land Rover from the Lincoln's wake. A long avenue stretched out in front of them, a seemingly endless monotony of mud-red brick—walls, buildings, towers. Tom could easily see the difference between the ancient, original brick and the newer, more uniform bricks used by Saddam Hussein to rebuild New Babylon upon the Old.

"Impressive, but boring," Annie observed from the back seat. "Saddam needed a decorator."

The black car turned left, the convoy in tow, and emerged from the rebuilt city headed south. The line of vehicles drew abreast of a large crater to their right, and came to a halt.

Naouri got out of the Lincoln and walked back to the first Rover as Tom was checking out the crater. There were actually two gigantic holes in the desert. The first was more irregular in its shape, rusted tools and discarded metal beams strewn about its cusp. The first crater angled down more than fifty feet to a flat space that surrounded the second crater.

Scrub trimmed the rim in washed-out green, and it was easy to make out the edges of the massive, square hole in the ground. But nearly impossible to gauge its depth.

Naouri removed her sunglasses and pointed into the black abyss. "I wanted you to see this before we headed over to the Lion. Saddam Hussein was entranced by many things. One was rebuilding the ancient power of Persia, and her capital of Babylon. Another was to uncover any trace of the Tower of Babel. Years before the first invasion, Saddam somehow diverted one of the Russian surveillance satellites circling the globe and got it to fly over this area. The scans and photos showed this cavernous hole under the surface. Its square shape was so distinct, there was no doubt the crater was man-made.

"It took seven years for the engineers and workers to uncover the crater— the foundation of the tower—in a way that wouldn't result in tons of dirt burying the base of the foundation. They finished the work not long before the Americans came back the second time. Saddam never got to set his eyes on his discovery. And it's sat here, fairly undisturbed, ever since."

Naouri went back to the Lincoln, and they drove farther into the city.

5:01 p.m., Baghdad

Gamal Muhammad entered the tobacconist shop, creating swirling vortexes as he passed through the heavy, blue-gray haze created by the six hookahs being smoked at the perimeter of the outer room. He rounded a small counter manned by an attendant who was as dark and wrinkled as an old cigar, opened a door, and entered a back room where the air was clear. His master had the windows open, the dusty curtains finding intermittent life in the occasional breeze, the pungent smell of auto exhaust and decaying produce from Baghdad's fruit market masking everything else.

Muhammad fell into the upholstered chair facing the desk, the toll of his all-night vigil weighing heavily on his skin and bones. "They arrived in Babylon about an hour ago."

"And from where did they come?"

His master's voice was calm, pleasant, as if they were speaking of a mutual friend. But Muhammad knew the edge that lay just below the surface, an edge he did not wish to approach. "We don't know. We've searched for them from the time we were informed of their arrival. We've been up and down the road from here to Hillah. I personally led a group through the streets, seeking knowledge of their presence. None was to be found. We were looking in the desert when word came that they were already on-site, looking at different locations. They must have come in from the east, through the back gate. There is no communication there."

Muhammad's concentration was on the floorboards, but he could feel the fierceness of his master's displeasure.

"They are strangers here. You were born in this desert. You know it as well as you know your own face." The voice was quiet but powerful. "You know what we've been ordered to accomplish. Go. Now. Follow them. Find out where they are searching and prevent them from finding what they seek—or take it from them. And finally put an end to that Egyptian woman's meddling life. He was very clear about our mission. Complete it and you will be well rewarded. Fail? Well, your family will not like the price of your failure."

29

5:04 p.m., Babylon

Naouri directed her driver to bypass Procession Street, one of the few intact streets in Babylon and one of the few elements of the ancient city protected in any way. Saddam had restored the high walls that flanked the bricked street along its entire length, making it easy to restrict access. But the convoy had little trouble navigating the unpaved, serpentine side streets coming through the city. Rather than drive through the Ishtar Gate, Naouri avoided the most visible landmark of Babylon and skirted its entrance to the north.

She led the vehicles alongside a wide, flat stone plaza covered with the blown grit of the Iraqi desert. The driver brought her Lincoln to a halt at the still-standing corner of a building, its walls about two and a half meters high for about six meters on each side of the corner, then stepping down to the plaza in various stages of decay.

The combined team piled out of the vehicles and joined Naouri at the southern edge of the crumbling western wall. "This is a good place to leave the vehicles. They'll have a little shade, and they are out of the main routes taken by most visitors."

〰〰

Mike Whalen grabbed a duffel of gear, eased toward the MI5 veteran, James Leonard, and lowered his voice. "Once we have the gear unloaded, take one of the SUVs and drive over to that rise there." He pointed to the west. "Get on the high ground and keep an eye out. Watch our backs, okay?"

"It would be my pleasure," said Leonard. "We appear to be dangerously exposed here . . . long sight lines . . . little cover. Perhaps I should enquire of our Italian duo, Mr. Papa and Mr. Molluzzo, and request them to get into position as backup?"

"Good idea," Whalen nodded. "Have them set up a rally point on the far side of the pit where the tower was built. And you, be careful, the sun will be behind you. Stay close to the ground."

"Like a woodchuck, mate. Like an invisible woodchuck."

"Whatever . . ." With a languid ease that belied any concern, Whalen returned to the edge of the main group where Naouri was holding court.

━━∽∿∕∿━━

"Let me orient you a little," she said, facing the group. "Although this is the northern edge of what now remains of the city, in the time of Nebuchadnezzar, Babylon stretched farther north about twenty kilometers to the beginning of the first wall, which was one meter thick and surrounded the entire city, from river bank to river bank, in a long, sweeping arc north to south. About one hundred meters inside the crescent of the first wall was the second wall, even larger and thicker than the first. It was in the second wall that the original Ishtar Gate was constructed, one of eight gates providing access to the city of Babylon. What now represents the Ishtar Gate, Saddam's smaller and less imposing replica, stands over there"—she pointed—"to the west.

"Inside the second wall was the majority of the ancient city, athough even during Nebuchadnezzar's reign, the city spilled over onto the far, western bank of the Euphrates, forcing the construction of a number of bridges.

"Lucky for us, and critical considering your directions, Nebuchadnezzar built his palace, his gardens, near the Ishtar Gate, at the northern rim of the city. The gate and Procession Street were the great triumphal entrances for the king and his armies when they returned from battle with plunder and slaves. So it makes sense that he would not want to cross the entire city to get home after a long campaign.

"Over there," said Naouri, pointing east, "is the tacky Babylon Square that Saddam imagined as the new center of the city: an empty, dusty building that was intended to be a museum, a vacant gift shop, abandoned restaurants, all of it being reclaimed by the desert. But we're going this way."

Naouri rounded the crumbling wall and entered the plaza. In the center, its weathered head pointing south, its rump pointing toward Saddam's much vilified palace on a hill overlooking the ruins, was the gray granite Lion of Babylon, more than twenty-five hundred years old and still distinct and impressive. It stood just under two meters high to the top of its head and about three meters long at the base of the pedestal. The lion was standing, its head up, looking at the great city. Flat on the ground, lying the length of the statue, under the lion's belly, was the figure of what appeared to be the arms and legs of a man.

"The lion was the symbol of Babylon," said Naouri. "It was the form taken by the god Marduk, one of the images for the goddess Ishtar. The body represents all of Babylon's enemies, vanquished and defeated."

"I hope that doesn't represent us," said Rizzo. "I don't feel like being any lion burger."

⌇⌇⌇

Racing down the highway in spite of the lowering sun shining in his eyes, Gamal Muhammad had one hand on the steering wheel and the other wrapped around his radio. The connection was terrible, and he struggled to get himself understood.

"No, no. They are already in Babylon. I don't know how they got there. Naouri must have brought them in the back way. It doesn't matter. Go find them. Find out what they are doing. Don't let them leave, and watch every step they take. I'm on my way."

⌇⌇⌇

Resting her back against the snout of the Lion of Babylon, with a compass in her right hand, Annie turned toward the south. "From the Lion, through the Ishtar Gate, seven stadia . . . Latiffa, how can we follow these directions without . . ."

"Well first, what kind of stadia are you measuring?"

"What?"

"There are many. The Greek stadion was 176 meters, the Babylonian was 196 meters, and the Egyptian 209. According to Herodotus, a stade was equal to six hundred feet of your measure. Which one? It could make a difference of more than two hundred meters over seven stadia."

Annie closed her eyes and took a deep breath. She was frustrated with herself for not knowing this in advance.

"Split the difference: 185 meters—about forty-two hundred feet. But how do we measure it off without being seen?"

Naouri pointed to the east. "Through those ruins, between the walls. We need to avoid Procession Street. If there are tourists, if there are watching eyes, that's where they will be, walking down to see the Ishtar Gate and Nebuchadnezzar's palace. But there is another street on the other side of those ruins that runs parallel to Procession Street. You can measure the distance while you are on that street and then find your way to Procession Street."

⌘⌘⌘

A pair of black SUVs dulled to a tawny gray by the desert drove slowly through the sparsely occupied parking lot on the western fringe of Babylon, rounded the curve in front of Saddam's deserted palace, and approached Hussein's scaled-down version of the Ishtar Gate. Two large Iraqi men rode in each vehicle, their heads shaved clean, Russian-made automatic weapons tucked between their thighs and the doors. Their eyes showed no life but never stopped moving.

⌘⌘⌘

"How do you want to set up the photo teams?" asked Whalen.

Tom almost didn't recognize Annie . . . not the Annie he knew. She was wearing snug blue jeans, a short-sleeve khaki shirt, and a sleeveless safari jacket, its pockets bulging with her "stuff": extra lenses, viewfinders, even a small, collapsible tripod. Two .25-millimeter Nikon digital cameras hung from straps around her neck and a wide-brimmed Tilly Air-Flo was on her head, a blond ponytail dropping down her back. The smile on her face made her look twenty years younger.

It had been an easy decision, asking Annie to take control of the group once they arrived in Babylon. Theoretically, and on the official Iraqi documents, this was her photo shoot. She was the chief photographer, the one with all the experience. It was natural for her to lead, to help this motley group look like a true *NG* photo crew. Tom was fascinated with the transformation in his wife.

Surprised and proud at the same time. Annie slid into leadership as easily as she slid into her old slippers at home.

"Mike, you and Leo and your team should stay here and set up a shoot on the lion. And keep an eye on the equipment," Annie responded, surveying the site and the location of the sun. "The rest of us will take a walk and start counting distance. We've got to clear where we think the Ishtar Gate is located and measure from there."

"Hey, Annie. Take Steve and Fred with you. Just in case."

"C'mon, Mike, we're just going for a walk to look around. We'll be back in a few minutes. Joe, how long is your stride?"

"A shade short of three feet, last time I checked."

"Okay, it's going to be less than a mile. Keep track of distance the best you can. You get near two thousand steps, let us know. Everybody grab your pack. Don't go anywhere in the desert without your pack—without water, without your gear." She walked over to Tom, rested on her haunches, and stored the two cameras and the contents of her safari jacket in her camera bag. "I won't be needing this stuff but, Tom, could you carry this viewfinder for me?" Her voice dropped to a whisper. "Keep an eye out. There are more people wandering around than I expected. You can use that thing to look around . . . watch our backs . . . and it won't look suspicious." Then she was back on her feet.

"Latiffa, can you go with us?"

Naouri looked around her, as if expecting a sudden, unwelcome visit. "I can walk with you to show you the street. After that, I must return to Baghdad, or I will be missed."

"Okay. Let's go."

30

Naouri had returned to her car for the trip back to Baghdad, leaving the Bohannons, Rodriguez, and Rizzo on the ruined streets. But even without Naouri, they could tell when they reached the city wall. Originally twenty-five feet thick and over seventy feet high, the wreckage of the inner wall was still discernable. Bohannon stood in the middle of a long stretch of missing wall, like a rough-surfaced four-lane highway running south. He could see the re-created Ishtar Gate in the distance, much smaller than the hundred-foot original, but still beautiful as the blue-glazed bricks glowed in the late afternoon light.

"Wow, this is beautiful, even if it is only a scale model," he said. Annie and Joe were on the other side of the wall, Joe getting ready to pace off the distance to what they hoped would be the culmination of the Dorabella message. Rizzo was by Tom's side, using the viewfinder—like a small telescope—to get a closer look at the Ishtar Gate.

"Saddam may have been a madman," said Rizzo, "but he wasn't crazy. He sure knew how to get things—

"Yo. Who's that?" Rizzo had the viewfinder up to his eye, scanning the distance. "We've got company."

Tom could see them in the distance. A couple of SUVs had pulled up next to the Ishtar Gate. It only took a moment for them to turn and head directly north.

"They're coming fast," said Rizzo. "Let's vamoose!"

Tom and Rizzo scrambled over the rubble of the ruined wall. Annie and Joe were already ahead of them, running down the street. They cut left through a doorway.

"Come quickly. This way."

Without thinking, Tom reached for Rizzo.

"I can run, you dunce." Rizzo was breathing heavy, and his legs were pumping like a runaway locomotive, his pack slapping against his back, but he was keeping up. "Watch out!"

Tom glanced up just in time to avoid running into a low arch, but his injured right shoulder caromed off the opening. Before he could respond to the pain, two hands grabbed his shirt and pulled him through.

"This way."

Joe and Annie had turned right on the far side of the arch and ducked under a low opening to the interior space of an ancient room. There was no roof, and the ruined walls were irregular in height, but it was enough to hide them for the moment and no SUV would be able to follow them through the small openings in the walls.

They stood close together, listening, trying to watch in all directions at once as light began to fade from the sky and twilight gathered in the corners of the ruined buildings.

"Bad guys?" whispered Joe.

"No. It was a Mr. Softee truck." Rizzo had his hands on his knees, sucking in deep gulps of air. "What do we do?"

"Can't stay here," said Joe.

"They may be looking for us," said Annie, "but they don't know where we are, and they don't know where we're going. Joe, how far have we come? Any idea?"

"I don't know. I've lost count."

"We're not going back?" asked Rizzo.

Tom joined the others in looking over at Annie. In spite of the circumstances, he was proud of their tacit acknowledgment of Annie as leader.

"Okay. Look, whoever they are," said Annie, "they're not here to help us. That means we've been discovered. Somebody knows we're here—Prophet's Guard, Muslim Brotherhood, who cares. And that means our time is short. This may be it—our one chance. I don't know. But I don't think we give it up just yet. Let's keep going, try to stay inside the rooms. At least stay away from the street. And let's see how far we can get. Maybe we can find 'Daniel's face' before they find us."

The four exchanged glances and an all-for-one, one-for-all feeling welled up in Tom's heart. They were in this together. No one wanted to quit. But one thing had to change. Tom allowed his pack to slip off his left shoulder. He reached up with his left hand and removed the sling from around his neck. Sparks darted down his right arm as he stretched it out and put strain on his damaged shoulder.

"Tom!" Annie whispered.

"I'll get it fixed when we get home," he said, glancing in Annie's direction. "Right now I need two arms. I can handle the pain." He tossed the sling into the dust. "Let's go."

Whalen cast one more glance to the east, where Annie and the team had disappeared into the streets of Babylon. The sun was slipping deeper into the west. Their light would soon be gone. Atkins and Vordenberg were at his side, the two NYPD anti-terrorism vets who were his right- and left-hand men. Smart, resourceful, they were hired by *NG* for their experience with sound devices—bugging apartments and warehouses was an art form—they were taught lighting, and they provided oft-needed muscle.

A British accent crackled on the radio. "We've got some visitors, chaps. Two sets. One coming to you. The other apparently looking for our mates."

Whalen glanced over at Vordenberg. "Pack it up, Steve. We're moving. Fast."

Fred Atkins was at Whalen's side. "The civilians."

"Yeah, I know. But we're too exposed . . . we can't get caught here. Steve and Leo can drive these two Rovers, and you and I will try to find Bohannon. We'll meet them on the far side of the tower's foundation"—he glanced at his watch—"in thirty minutes."

Whalen toggled the radio. "James, wait for us at the rally point."

"Roger, that."

Annie led the group between two crumbled buildings and into a narrow alley. Walking quick-step, not running.

"Quiet," whispered Annie. They came to a break in the alley, another street cutting across it. She peeked around the corner. Cruising slowly down

Procession Street, just passing the street that intersected their alley, was one of the gray SUVs. "They're looking for us."

⁓⌇⌇⁓

Whalen fitted the night-vision goggles above the brim of his hat, slung the pack between his shoulder blades, and picked up the Swiss-made SIG Sauer, .30-caliber, short-barrel 751 semiautomatic rifle, set for three-round bursts. He stuffed a half-dozen extra twenty-round magazines into his battle vest.

"Ready." Atkins came up to his side, equally equipped.

Whalen stepped between the two Rovers, where Matkins and Vordenberg were getting the last of the gear back into the vehicles. "Steve, you and Leo take the Rovers to the rally point. James is headed there now. Take different routes and try to avoid our uninvited guests. We will see you in thirty minutes. If we're not there in thirty, well . . . stay together. We'll come to you."

"See you in thirty," said Vordenberg. "And Whale, don't get lost. You still owe me ten bucks."

Atkins and Whalen were running east as the Rovers drove into the gathering dark.

⁓⌇⌇⁓

"I've been running so much lately I should enter a marathon," muttered Rizzo, his legs pumping as he tried to keep up with the three people in front of him. *Don't fall behind . . . don't be a liability.*

He was definitely at a disadvantage. They were hustling along a narrow alley, the partially destroyed mud-brick walls of differing heights. The others could probably venture a glance when the wall was low, but all the walls were over Rizzo's head and he plunged on with no idea what was happening around him.

"Looks like we're moving roughly parallel to Procession Street." Annie's voice was strained, breathless. Whether from exertion or anxiety, Rizzo couldn't tell. "Joe, any idea how far we've come?"

Rizzo ran into Rodriguez as he jolted to a stop behind the other three. "Hey!"

"Quiet!" hissed Rodriguez. "I don't know. I've been trying to figure it out as we ran—how long a stride, how many strides. I can't say for sure, but I think we're close. We need to risk getting up to Procession Street pretty soon."

Perspiration began rolling down Rizzo's back. His shiver was involuntary. "Let *me* go. It's getting dark. I'll be harder to see."

"Not in that shirt," said Rodriguez.

"We're all going . . . through the rooms," said Annie. "C'mon."

———◇◇◇———

Still shaken by the threats from his master, Gamal Muhammad had pushed his Toyota to the breaking point on his fevered drive from Baghdad. He slowed his speed to navigate the long, looping curve around Saddam's palace—but not enough. The road was covered with sand and gravel, except for tire tracks where repeated use kept a path clear. In the turn, Gamal's Toyota drifted out of the track cleared by other cars. The Toyota lost its grip and the back end began driving as if it had a mind of its own.

When Gamal pressed on the brake pedal, the car looped around completely at least twice before leaving the road. Still spinning, it was airborne. But not for long. The right rear dropped into a ditch, and the Toyota whipped around, slamming the driver's side door into a mound of brown gravel. Brute force stopped the car's motion, a shock that Gamal felt throughout his body.

Steam was enveloping the front of the car's body, and pain was taking up residence in Gamal's back. But he remained conscious. And determined. His right hand felt around on the car's seat and found the radio.

"I'm at the Palace curve." His voice sounded like the grit still swirling inside his car. "Crashed. Come get me."

———◇◇◇———

Vordenberg was on foreign territory, and it was getting dark, which gave his pursuer a distinct advantage, but there was nothing else to do. Vordenberg engaged the red, night-vision lights attached to the front bumper so he could at least see some distance ahead. But now he was an illuminated target.

He turned east to avoid a crumbling, brick wall. He knew the yawning chasm that was the Tower's foundation was south . . . a bit west of the old city. Leonard, Matkins, and the rest would be there: reinforcements. But first he had to lose the vehicle that had started following him as soon as he left the plaza surrounding the Lion of Babylon.

He glanced into the rearview mirror once more, expecting to see the gray SUV gaining ground. The SUV's lights bounced crazily as Vordenberg led the chase over ruined walls and through un-reclaimed neighborhoods of ancient Babylon. Suddenly it veered off to the right.

Vordenberg put his hand on the machine pistol in his lap and cast a sideways glance to his right. But the SUV was gone. He could see its lights bouncing in the distance.

Strange . . . but thanks.

He throttled down quickly and doused the lights. It would take longer, but he would find his way to the Tower's foundation in the dark. And hopefully not bring any unwanted guests with him.

———

The large, bald Iraqi man—Achmed—stood beside the second SUV and looked across the roof at his partner. "It's Gamal. He's crashed his car. Ismail's gone to get him. It's up to us."

Son of the tobacco shop owner, Achmed bent over and reached into the SUV. He stood back up with an automatic pistol in one hand and an encrypted, multiband radio in the other. He stuffed the radio into his shirt pocket. "Keep circling on the main streets. I'll go through the alleys, hopefully get behind them. If you see them, call."

———

Whalen led Atkins, double time, north, away from the Ishtar Gate and Procession Street, perpendicular to the direction taken by Bohannon's crew. He planned to loop east, hoping to flank and get in front of both Bohannon and the SUVs that were looking for them. His gamble was no one would be looking for the cavalry coming from the east. He hoped.

———

"Go ahead."

Annie nodded toward the opening. They crouched inside a small room with a narrow, empty doorway that opened onto a wide, open space. Just beyond was

Procession Street. Tom put his hand on his wife's arm, gave it a little squeeze, and scrambled to the edge of the door.

At well-spaced intervals, diffused, indirect light came from behind the walls of Procession Street, keeping the street in twilight, not penetrating far beyond. Staying in the shadows inside the door, Tom had a limited view to the east or west along Procession Street, but he could make out where they were. He had reviewed several photos on the Internet. They were slightly east of Nebuchadnezzar's palace, which was essentially just a huge, flat, empty square with massive ruined walls on three sides. Bohannon leaned into the wall to look farther west and saw something he didn't expect.

He twisted his head and examined the inside of the room he occupied. In a far corner was the remnant of stairs that once led to the roof. Hunched over, he trotted to the stairs, climbed halfway, and poked his head up like a periscope breaking the waves. He looked both ways on Procession Street, validating his observation, and then joined the rest at the bottom of the stairs.

"There are wide openings in the walls along Procession Street, alternating on either side. The openings are shallow, horseshoe-shaped. They look like amphitheaters, with seating levels around the circumference of the arch, as if they were made like stadiums, for watching something—perhaps the parade of triumphant armies returning to the city. But listen. The directions told us to go seven stadia, and we thought it was distance. What if they meant go to the seventh stadium? The seventh area to watch the parade?"

Tom watched a smile rise on Annie's face.

"But," asked Rizzo, "how do we know which one is the seventh?"

Now it was Tom's turn to smile. "Because, if I counted correctly, the seventh stadium is almost next door, directly across from Nebuchadnezzar's palace."

⌁⌁⌁

Achmed's eyes had long ago adjusted to the darkness. Now he saw through every shadow, waiting for any shadow to move. He was a deadly shot. Even in the dark.

Move. He scanned the alley, looked around the corner of a wall. *Come. Move.*

⌁⌁⌁

"Out in the street, back through the alleys, or over the wall?" asked Joe.

"It's too dangerous in the street."

Rizzo took a look up at the ragged top edge of the ruined wall. "You get on top of that wall, and you're probably visible to anybody in the city."

Annie nodded. "Tom, how far to the entrance?"

"Maybe twenty, thirty feet."

"Too far."

"Look," said Tom, "down the other end, where Saddam rebuilt the walls along the street, they are really high. But down this end they're still only eight, ten feet high, depending where you stand. Maybe we can find a way in from behind the stadium."

"Okay . . . we go back through the rooms or find an alley," said Annie. "We need an alternative. The street is too dangerous."

⸺∿〰⸺

Atkins was at his shoulder, but looking back the way they had come. "How far do you think we should go?" he whispered.

"Maybe another half mile, then double back."

"Moon's gonna be up soon."

"Yeah . . . we don't have much time."

One more glance in each direction and Whalen left the shadow of the ruined wall, ran across the open street toward the location of Nebuchadnezzar's palace.

⸺∿〰⸺

In the alley behind Procession Street, Rodriguez stepped off twenty-five feet. The old wall here was uneven in height, a little more than eight feet at its lowest point, but still too high for Joe to reach on his own. He knew Bohannon couldn't very well give him a boost one-handed, so Joe motioned Rizzo over. Together—their fingers interlocked—Bohannon and Rizzo formed a foothold. Rodriguez stepped high and placed his boot in their hands. *One, two, three.* He pushed off with his grounded foot at the same time the two men lifted their hands and propelled him to the top of the wall.

Pressing himself against the uneven bricks as best he could, Rodriguez pulled his legs up so he could lay flat along the top of the wall and check out the other side. The amphitheater looked to be about six or seven feet deep from its apex to the edge of Procession Street. Three levels of seating surface, one higher than the next, hugged the circumference of the semi-circle. But there was an opening at the very center of the arch, creating a section of seating on either side. The opening was just below Joe.

Joe pivoted on his elbows and lowered his body about three feet to the top level of seating. Crouching, watching his step, he moved down the other levels and stood on the ground between the two sections of amphitheater seats in the stadium. Conscious of every sound, he edged toward the only opening, on Procession Street. Nothing stirred. Joe backed away from Procession Street, turned to help the others over the wall, and stood face-to-face with Daniel.

⸺∾∾⸺

The pistol resting gently in his hands, he wasn't sure if the movement was real or imagined. Either way, he would investigate. High up, along the top edge of a damaged wall. He only saw . . . sensed? . . . the movement out of the corner of his eye. But his senses were reliable.

Crouching in a dark corner of a ruined house, Achmed withdrew his multi-band, handheld radio. "Come east. Twenty meters. Watch along the tops of the walls."

⸺∾∾⸺

Hanging from the top of the wall, Rodriguez dropped back into the alley. He motioned to Tom.

"Once you get on top of the wall there's a short drop to the top level of seating on the other side. We'll get you up first, then Annie. After we hand up the packs, Sammy will come up and you can drop one of the pack straps down to give me a hand. Listen"—Rodriguez looked at them all—"get off the top of the wall as soon as you can. It's pretty visible."

⸺∾∾⸺

Babylon turned into freakish, swimming green goo when Whalen powered up his night-vision goggles. He was lying flat on a low rooftop, scanning the streets, alleys, and walls he could see. Solid walls appeared to waver as he moved his head. But nothing else moved. He looked down and gave Atkins a thumbs-down signal, then turned his goggles back to Procession Street. Looking west he noticed the green goo move. A body scrambled on top of, and over, a ragged wall in the distance.

He dropped silently to the ground. "Forty yards west. Looked like Rizzo."

〰〰

"How do you know it's him?" Rizzo whispered.

They stood close together in the space between the two sections of amphitheater seats, Procession Street to their backs. The alcove between the seats was a little less than three feet wide and about four feet deep . . . about half the depth of the amphitheater. Rizzo pressed close to gaze up at the carved image. The face was a silhouette, looking to the right, carved into a square section of stone placed within the clay bricks of the wall between the seating sections. The cameo itself was fashioned within a concave circle inside the square. Rizzo stretched to run his fingers over the stone, similar to the stone of the Lion of Babylon. This image was meant to last. "This could be like Babylonian graffiti. They didn't have any spray paint back then."

"Give it a rest, Rizzo."

"No, really. We don't know what's in the rest of these stadia along Procession Street." He moved out of the way so Annie, then Tom, could get a closer look at the image. "Maybe they've got these cameo appearances all along the way, like a walk of fame. Unless we're sure we traveled the right distance since the Ishtar Gate, how can we be sure whose mug it is looking back at us? Could be Daniel. Could be Mo Linskey for all we know."

"We're directly across the street from the palace," said Annie. "Makes sense a tribute to Daniel would be here. Let's follow the directions and see what happens." She stepped up to the wall and placed her hands on the square of stone cut into the bricks. "What did it say? 'Embrace the face of Daniel'?" As gently as cleaning a baby's cheek Annie began caressing the inanimate stone, running her fingers over the hair, the eyes, the chin of the carved image. Nothing happened.

〰〰

The amphitheater opening wide to Procession Street, Rodriguez felt exposed, which made him nervous. He left the group in the space between the seats and climbed up two levels flanking the street. Crouching down, only his head rose above the top edge. He cupped his hands around his eyes and squinted down the street, into the distance.

"Something is moving out there," he said with muffled voice. "Looks like a vehicle . . . and it's coming this way."

Tom stepped up behind his wife. "You've got to hurry," he whispered.

⸺∿∿⸺

Sliding from shadow to shadow, Achmed moved from room to alley, toward where he saw the movement. He clicked off the safety and fingered the trigger.

⸺∿∿⸺

"What am I supposed to do?" Annie turned to Tom with a frantic look.

"Here . . . let me try."

Tom moved closer to the carved face. He placed his hands, one on each side, against the circular bas-relief that held the image. *Lord, please help us. We're just trying to be obedient. Show us what to do next.* Tom felt the anxiety of those waiting behind him. In the urgency of his prayer, he leaned against the carving. "Please, Lord . . . help us."

Embrace the face of Daniel. Turn his face toward you.

"What?" Tom glanced over his shoulder but was only met with questioning looks. He turned back to the carving. Bohannon took his left hand and placed it upon the ear on the left and took his right hand and wedged it into the indentation that was carved away to create the profile. His fingers searched the edges of the face, looking for something against which he could exert some pressure. Just under the eyebrow, above the bridge of the nose, he felt a very small hole. He tried his index finger, but it was too thick. He hooked his little finger into the depression and pushed it in to get as much leverage as possible. Something clicked.

Immediately, Tom felt slackness in the medallion, a weakening of the resistance. He exerted more pressure on the left of the carving and pulled with his finger. The image budged, but didn't release. His finger objecting to the strain, Tom pushed even harder with his left hand.

Joe loped down the steps and came to his side. "We've got to move!"

⟨≈≈≈⟩

Achmed heard the voices. Just on the other side of this wall. The alley was narrow. He pushed the automatic beneath his belt at the small of his back, wedged his boot into the wall on the right, pressed his hands against the walls on each side, and lifted himself halfway to the top of the wall.

⟨≈≈≈⟩

With a stone-on-stone scraping sound, the medallion broke loose, turned on a pivot, and Tom found himself staring into the face of Daniel. The medallion was carved on both sides and Daniel's eyes stared, unseeing, into Tom's. Bohannon placed his hands on both of Daniel's cheeks and examined the rough surface. The slight pressure moved the medallion back, deeper into the wall. Bohannon continued the pressure and the medallion slid all the way into the wall. As it disappeared . . .

Crack!

⟨≈≈≈⟩

The loud *Crack!* brought Whalen and Atkins to an abrupt halt at an intersection with an alley. Whalen tried to orient himself to the sound when Fred Atkins tapped him on the shoulder and pointed west along the narrow alley. Thirty yards away, Whalen could see a large, body-shaped shadow lifting itself toward the top of the alley wall. Atkins laid his semiautomatic rifle on the ground, slipped a knife out of the sheath on his belt and took quick, purposeful steps.

⟨≈≈≈⟩

The shop-owner's son heard the scraping, then the crack. *It must be the Americans.* Achmed dug his boots into the wall, steadied himself with his left hand against the bricks, and reached behind him for the automatic.

It took a moment for the hand upon his wrist, its grip like a clamp, to register. In that moment, he lost. An excruciating pain erupted in the small of his back where he reached for his gun. In the same moment, the hand upon his wrist violently shoved his right arm up and under his shoulder blades. He came off the wall and slammed into the dusty ground, face first.

The breath was knocked out of his lungs, but already life was pouring out of his body.

⸻

They all flinched. Tom stumbled against the retreating medallion as part of the brick wall to his left dislodged and shifted slightly ajar from the rest. Tom peeked into the cavity. Inside the opening was a small chamber, an ancient wooden door, set in an arched, brick portal, on the far side.

They heard sounds from Procession Street—a car . . . a door closed.

Tom pulled on his pack and was through the opening in a flash, Joe on his heels.

As Annie and Rizzo pressed into the small alcove, Tom grasped the metal ring in the wooden door with his left hand, but Joe was at his shoulder. "Let me."

Joe pulled on the ring with all his weight. Nothing. He planted his boot against the wall beside the door and pulled. Tom thought the world could hear the creaking and cracking as the door inched open. The air escaping from the black void behind the door was cold, and carried the decay of ages.

"We're going in there?" Rizzo peered into the blackness. "Maybe this is something you should pray about."

"Quick . . . before they see us."

Pulling a flashlight from a side pocket of her pack, Annie stepped through the door, followed by a more reluctant Rizzo. Bohannon and Rodriguez left the alcove and moved just inside the door. They turned in the tight space and found another iron ring on the inside of the door. They pulled on the ring until their backs ached. Slowly the door yielded and inched back into place, sealing the entrance. But not before Bohannon noticed the brick wall of the amphitheater close over the outer opening.

"Watch your back." Tom could hear Annie behind him. "There are steps just inside the door."

Annie swung the beam of her flashlight and Tom could see the stairs, leading down, just a few feet inside the wooden door. "Is that the only light we have?"

"I've got a small, battery-powered lantern in my pack and this MagLite," said Rizzo, pulling the short, thin, but dazzling light from the pocket of his photographer's vest. "Here"—he handed it to Tom—"you can get the beam higher."

"Cut the lights." With a whispered urgency, Joe kept his ear pressed against the seam where the door opened. "Quiet."

31

Whalen and Atkins slipped into the amphitheater like a soft breeze on a lace curtain—barely noticeable—and immediately saw it was empty.

"Where did they go?"

Noticing footprints on the sandy floor, Whalen stepped over to the medallion. "This carving got their attention. There are some footprints there, and more over here."

Getting down on his hands and knees, Whalen scraped his knife along the base of the brick wall. "See the sand pushed back?" He laid his hand on the wall, leaned down to where the wall and floor met and raised his voice a few notches above a whisper. "Tom! Annie! It's Mike . . . it's safe. Open up."

They listened, Whalen getting on his stomach to press his ear against the crease at the bottom of the wall.

"Nothing?"

Whalen looked up. "Looks like they found their gate."

"Now what?"

Whalen got up and brushed off the sand. "We wait. As long as we can. C'mon. Let's get to the rally point before the moon comes up."

——⁓⁓⁓——

Tom inched to Joe's side. "Can you hear them?"

"No, not really." Joe glanced back at Bohannon. "Just some scraping sounds. We must have left our tracks in the sand."

"Can they get in?"

THE ALEPPO CODE   257

"Don't think so," said Rodriguez, turning away from the door. "Don't think the wall has budged. But maybe we better get out of here."

"Where is here?" asked Rizzo.

———∽∿∽———

They stood in a tight knot at the top of the stairs, Rizzo holding Annie's flashlight straight down, near the floor, so they had some light to see each other but, Tom hoped, not enough to seep under out the door.

"Look," said Annie, "it doesn't matter where we are, in a sense. What's important is that we found Daniel's face and it got us in here, at the top of these steps. This is it. It's where we're supposed to be. Down there"—she pointed down the steps—"is either nothing, and we've all been scammed, or it's the garden of Eden, and we've been led here by a power that is way beyond us."

"Or we could find the creature from the Black Lagoon," said Rizzo, looking down the steps. "But I don't think so. I think what's down there is something way more scary than anything I've ever imagined. So . . . what are we waiting for?"

Rizzo started to spin around in the direction of the stairs, but Joe put a hand on his shoulder. "Hold on, Sammy. Let's think about this first. Do we have any food, any water?"

"I've got a full water bottle," said Tom. "Annie has one, too."

"And I've got some granola bars," she said.

"Okay," said Joe, "we've got some rope, a compass, but no weapons . . ."

"Hands of steel . . . *hatcha!*" Rizzo swiped the air.

"No weapons," Joe emphasized. "Whalen and his crew know we were headed this direction, but really nobody knows where we are. We don't know how much oxygen is down there, or what danger, and we don't have any first aid. There are a lot of reasons our primary focus should be on trying to get out of here, rather than trying to get farther inside. What if we get lost?"

Tom put a hand on Joe's arm. "Joe—you? You're afraid of getting lost?"

"I'm just saying. Somebody's got to give voice to the obvious. I don't know if my faith stretches as far as yours, Tom."

What did Joe just say? "Your faith is as strong as you want it to be," said Tom.

"Well, I don't know if it's strong enough yet, to go walking down those steps." Joe took a step back, away from the group. "I've been deep underground twice in the last three months, wandering around in the dark and the cold, wondering whether I'd ever see the light of day again. To tell you the truth, I was hoping to never experience it again. I don't like it. Makes me feel closed in . . . jumpy. If we didn't have to go down those stairs, I'd be more than happy. But . . . there's no other way to find out what's down there without going down ourselves." Joe stepped back into the circle. "And it's what we came here for. So Sammy, what *are* we waiting for?"

"That's better. I thought I was going to have to beat you into submission. C'mon, let's get moving."

Annie moved forward and took the flashlight from Rizzo. "Okay, I'll go first with the flashlight. We'll—"

"No . . . I'll go first," said Tom. He came to Annie's side and held out his hand. "We get back on the photo shoot, you can be in charge again. But down here"—Tom looked down at the blackness below—"no disrespect, sweetie, but I'm going down those stairs first. Then Sammy with the MagLite—keep it pointed down so we can all see the stairs—and then you and Joe behind you, okay? We'll save Sammy's lantern for later, if we need it. And don't bunch too close together. I don't want to fall into a pit if these stairs stop all of a sudden."

They lined up behind Tom like three blind mice. "Let's get down there and back up while we still have these lights." He took the first step.

⎯⎯∿∿⎯⎯

The steps were rough, cut out of the same hard clay that made up the walls, and had an indentation in the middle worn down by the feet of the past and a sheen of condensation that made footing tricky. They extended down at a forty-five-degree angle and seemed to keep going. The tunnel was narrow, about three feet wide, and the ceiling—after being vaulted near the door—was low, so that both Joe and Tom were forced to lean over at the waist, throwing off their balance. Tom had the flashlight in one hand, the other pressed against a wall, in case he needed to suddenly put on the brakes.

They descended cautiously, but not slowly. Bohannon felt more and more vulnerable with each passing step.

Joe was right. We're coming down here with nothing. We're just asking for trouble.

After an eternity—about ten minutes—the stairs stopped. The tunnel leveled out, but only so the stairs could switch back. A hairpin turn. The stairs continued down, farther into the darkness.

⌁∿∿⌁

"I feel like I'm wearing this tunnel. If it gets any closer, my left and my right will be on the same side."

Rizzo was right. The farther they descended, the closer the walls became, the closer the ceiling became. The more claustrophobic the feeling became. If it weren't for the roughly hewn steps, clearly man-made, Bohannon would have thought himself in some crack in the earth's crust. The cool, dry air at the top of the shaft had long ago been traded for the damp, rapidly warming air of the tunnel. It, too, was closing in around them.

Tom came to a short, flat space where the steps ceased. No hairpin turn. Nothing.

Tom held the flashlight above him, scanning the walls.

"It doesn't go anywhere."

"What do you mean?" asked Joe. "It's got to go somewhere."

Tom swept the floor with his yellow beam, looking for any crack, anything that looked different. "There's no way out. The stairs stop; there is a short, flat floor. And then nothing."

Rodriguez edged into the tight space, Rizzo and Annie remaining on the steps. The walls were uneven, scraped or dug out of the clay, the ceiling arched. But even in the apex of the arch, both Rodriguez and Bohannon were stooped over at the shoulders.

"No one's going to build stairs down to here and not have a way out," said Joe. "Look for something that's not obvious."

Rizzo, on the final step before the landing, turned his shoulders sideways. "Great. Look for something you don't see."

Tom swept his light around toward Rizzo, and stopped. "Sammy, you are right again. Look under your feet."

Rizzo bent at his waist and looked between his legs. "What am I looking for?"

"Come down off the steps and turn around," said Bohannon. He angled his flashlight to illuminate the ground at Rizzo's feet. "Look at the face of the last step."

Rizzo turned to face the steps.

"There's something different about that step . . . see the section in the middle." Unlike the other steps, which were solid, the bottom step appeared to be in three sections—two larger sections on each side and a smaller section, like the end of a brick, in the middle. "Joe, move back," said Bohannon. "Annie, come down off the steps. Let's all stand on the floor."

The four of them squeezed into the small space.

"Annie, can you push against that section in the middle?"

Bracing herself with her hands out to the side walls, Annie placed the sole of her right boot against the three-inch-square space in the middle of the stair. The hard clay face of the section gave way and was pushed farther under the stair as Annie pressed harder with the front of her boot. They heard a soft, sliding sound as the lower seven steps slid back under the other steps and opened up a passageway.

"Man, I knew this was going to be fun," said Rizzo. He edged past Annie and moved toward the opening. "First disappearing steps and now secret passageways. Jeremiah was a cool dude."

The opening was about five feet high. Tom couldn't tell how deep. He was maneuvering to get on his knees so he could crawl into the opening.

"Hold on, big guy. This is one adventure that has Rizz-Man written all over it. That space is just my size. Let me go check it out, and I'll come back and report to you, *mon capitaine*. Annie, dig that lantern out of my pack, will ya?"

Bohannon didn't like relinquishing responsibility, especially where there could be unknown dangers, but Rizzo was right. The space was just his size. He could walk in standing up and have a lot easier time checking out what was under the steps.

"Okay, but be careful. Take a look around, see what's up ahead. But don't go too far."

Rizzo took the lantern, edged past Annie, and turned his head at the entrance to the opening. "Yes, Dad. And I'll have the car home before dark. Don't worry. I know how to avoid trouble."

"Sure, Sammy," said Joe, "just like the time you—"

"Gotta go. *Hasta la vista*."

Rizzo quick-stepped through the opening. Almost immediately, all Tom could see was Rizzo's shadow being illuminated by the light from the lantern. But it wasn't long before Rizzo and the light turned left. For a few minutes there was a receding glow. Then darkness. And silence. Tom started counting the seconds in his mind.

Rodriguez was trying to find a position that was less excruciating for the aches in his back. "Stop worrying, Tom, he'll be all right. He's made it through more than most. Besides this gives us a chance to rest, and maybe we should pray for him and for us."

Bohannon kept his eyes on where the shaft turned left. It remained dark. "Sure—good idea. But still, I hope he's all right."

―――∿∽∾―――

Turning left, away from the steps, Rizzo held the lantern in front of him, illuminating the shaft. It was similar to the one he had just left—rough walls cut into the hard clay of the Euphrates plain, its roof vaulted just above his head. Despite the number of years these tunnels must have been in existence, they were in remarkably good repair. There were few cracks or gaps in the floor or walls, and the roof appeared to be as solid as the day it was first cut from the clay.

As he walked along the shaft, Rizzo was trying to gauge distance in his mind. His plan was to keep going until something changed, until he had something concrete to report to the others about what was ahead.

He heard the sound—a rolling gurgle—before he saw the source. The tunnel swerved a bit to the right and, as he came around the bend, the light from the lantern glinted off something in the distance, something moving along the floor.

"Yo, baby!" Rizzo snapped, stopping in his tracks and taking a quick step back. *What is that?* His heart was thumping like the drummer for Bruce Springsteen's E-Street Band as he tried to decide whether it was more dangerous to stand his ground or run with headlong abandon back down the shaft. A seismic shiver registered a Richter response along his spine, as he shook from the tips of his toes to the end of his nose.

Rizzo squinted behind his Coke-bottle lenses and held the lantern higher. Something out there was moving. And it was moving along the floor. And it looked big.

Scenes of Jon Voight getting squeezed like a peach in *Anaconda* kept flooding Rizzo's mind, a never-ending loop of reptilian rage, Hollywood-style.

"Yo, who are you?" Rizzo shouted, hoping to scare off, and not attract, whatever it was that was undulating over the floor of the shaft. "Go home and squeeze a grape!"

Nothing happened. The shape kept moving, as if it were on a conveyor belt passing perpendicular to the shaft, and continued to emit that throaty gurgling that sounded to Rizzo as if the unknown beast were swallowing its dinner. Or the appetizer to its dinner.

Rizzo was about to beat a tactical retreat—*no sense getting swallowed by some slithering slime*—when the light went on in his brain, and he felt like a doofus.

He lifted the lantern again and began pacing purposefully toward the moving mass that glinted in the distance—an underground river that no longer looked like Smaug, the Terrible.

The river wasn't as wide as he first thought. As it raced past the openings of the shaft, the water sloshed up into each side of the tunnel making it look wider than it was. But it looked very deep, moving fast, coming out of a well-worn hole in the wall on the left side of the tunnel and rushing into an almost identical hole on the other. Rizzo approached carefully, wondering why the river didn't just veer off into the shaft he occupied, while he looked for slick spots on the clay floor. As the floor got wetter, Rizzo's footing got more precarious, so he stopped and leaned against the side wall, holding out the lantern to better see whether this fast-moving river was passable.

He held the lantern aloft and could just see the outlines on the other side. This was one of those times when his small size was a disadvantage. He flexed up to stand on his toes and stretched out his arm.

32

8:22 p.m., Babylon

Joe was slumped into an awkward and painful-looking semi-sitting position in the opening under the steps, like a hound waiting for his master to come back through a door. Tom could see Joe's lips were moving, but his eyes didn't leave the darkened shaft.

"Are you okay, Joe?"

"No . . . yeah . . . I was just . . ." Rodriguez turned his head to look at Bohannon. "How do you believe?"

"What?"

Joe shifted on his haunches and faced Bohannon.

"Tom, I've got to be honest. When we went to the ballgame, and I said I wished I had the kind of faith you have? Well, honestly, I could feel something then. I don't know when or how—there have been so many unexplainable things that we've experienced—but somewhere along the way, I began to think that all this stuff you've been saying, been living, was real. Not only your faith was real, but your God was real, Deirdre's God, my mom's God. This Jesus I was taught as a kid, somewhere in this adventure, he became real to me, too. And when I was on top of Temple Mount and fire was pouring out of the sky and spreading in my direction, when the platform imploded and started sucking everything into the chasm, including the truck I was hiding in, that was the day I found myself praying and believing that my prayers were being heard."

"But . . . ?"

Joe turned his gaze back to the opening. "But when fear comes, how do you hold on to that faith? When you want to believe, but . . . How long do you think we should give him?"

Tom looked at his watch. "It's only been ten minutes."

"Seems like an hour."

"I know," said Annie. "He'll be okay. Give him time. He's probably being very careful. If I know Sammy, he won't come back until he's got something important to tell us."

<center>~~~~~</center>

The rushing water, surprisingly cold, hit him like a torrent. Rizzo didn't have time to register that his left foot had slipped across the slick floor. His right arm—stretched out and up, holding the lantern—doomed his right shoulder to slide away from the wall. What his mind registered was terror . . . panic . . . that flashing millisecond of realization that this might be the last moment of his life. And then self-preservation kicked in.

Rizzo was jostled back and forth, moving fast with the water, but not tumbling. He kicked toward what he thought was up, his lungs starved for breath, and broke the surface.

Rizzo pumped with his legs, strained for some semblance of stability by frantically waving his left arm through the water, fought a frustrating battle to keep the lantern close to the surface, emitting a deep twilight into the water tunnel, and tried with limited success to keep at least his nose above water without shredding his head against the roof speeding past, so close.

All of this happened within heartbeats, each fact like a photo being developed in front of his face. He realized that, for once, his small size was an advantage. He had more room to maneuver. But then another, more urgent thought hit. *How long can I do this?*

Panic began to rise once more—there, but out of his control. *I gotta get outta here.*

The soles of his boots slammed into the hard surface of a wall, but his leg muscles—tense and alert like the rest of his body—acted like shock absorbers, gathering up the momentum of the rushing water and pushing his body up higher. His shoulders thrust up from the torrent, Rizzo rose to almost a sitting position. The roof of the tunnel had been eroded higher by the pounding water at this junction. In the fleeting moment he was above the water, Rizzo realized that the water, after piling up against the wall, was running off to the right.

Rizzo curled his body as he took a deep breath and pushed against the wall with all his might, forcing his body to the left. For a heartbeat, the current held him, but then he began to sink as he pushed farther into the water, to the left, away from where the torrent now raced into the blackness. Rizzo flailed with his left arm, pulling himself deeper into the backwater, kicking with his legs, until the back of his neck collided with the edge of the wall behind him.

Closing his eyes, relief wrestling with terror—relief that he hadn't drowned and had been able to escape from the rampaging torrent; terror at being lost, alone, and trapped—Rizzo pulled in deep draughts of the dank air and tried to slow his heart, hoping he wouldn't die here from a heart attack after surviving the river. For the moment, he was alive. And alive was better than dead. And he wasn't about to give up.

A ledge?

The lantern was still lit . . . he could tell that from the faint light that illuminated this backwater. He pulled the lantern from the water, steadied it against his chest, and forced his failing body to twist to its left. As he rotated on his shoulder, Rizzo reached out with his left hand to steady himself against the ledge and reached up with his right hand to place the lantern on the edge of wet clay.

And looked into the void of another dark and threatening shaft.

———⌇⌇⌇———

All three of them were now looking into the opening under the stairs, Annie's flashlight illuminating the short shaft between them and the turn left. Tom didn't want to give voice to his feelings, but Rizzo had now been gone almost thirty minutes, and unbidden images flashed into his mind.

"Maybe we should go in and take a look around?" Annie's question sounded more like a plea.

Tom faced another critical decision. Should one go in, or should—

"We're all going," said Annie, bringing her beam back into the landing so Tom could see her face. "If only one of us goes and Sammy needs help, will one be enough to help him? And if you think the two of you are going, you're not leaving me here alone."

Tom read the resolve in his wife's eyes and knew his decision was going to be a hard sell. "I'm sorry, but I think I go in and you and Joe stay here, just in case—"

The sound coming down the stairway from above them stopped Tom's words in his throat. There was the clank of metal against metal. Bohannon looked up the stairs. He thought he saw faint light where once there was pitch black. Then the light moved.

"Inside, quick," he whispered.

Dropping down to their knees, first Annie, then Joe, then Tom crawled into the opening under the stairs. Annie crawled through the opening on the left, and Joe followed, but stopped just inside the junction, twisted around, and stuck his head out as Tom crawled into the shaft. "Turn off—"

Rapid-fire gunshots erupted like a monstrous thunderstorm inside the tight, narrow stairway, ripping up the clay floor and sending ear-ringing echoes into the small shaft. Tom recoiled from the cacophony, his back pressed into the deepest part of the recess under the stairs, his flashlight at a cockeyed angle as its haft hit the floor.

They could hear voices now, hard-soled boots thudding on each stair, and Tom could feel Joe and Annie inching away from the recess, into the shaft that had swallowed Rizzo. But Tom's eyes weren't on his wife, or on the opening of the space under the stairs—the opening through which the hard-soled men with the guns would soon come. No, his eyes were above his head, where the beam of his flashlight illuminated the roof of the recess.

Above him, Tom could see the lowest step, where it and the steps above it had been pulled back into the recess when they released the latch. On the inside of the recessed steps, on the underside of the lowest step and the one above, Bohannon saw once again the small, square, brick-size section in the midst of the stair's riser.

We'll be trapped.

But we'll be dead if I don't. God help us.

Bohannon raised his left hand and, without hesitation, pushed hard against the square section. There was a loud *snap* and the stairs above his head dropped down and slid forward, falling into place with a thud from the weight and with a strange hissing sound that Bohannon surmised somehow sealed the movable stairs to the clay floor and the walls surrounding it.

"Tom!" cried Annie. "What did you do?"

It didn't take Rizzo long to measure his options. He had pulled himself from the water, but he was cold and wet. Stay here and hypothermia would probably kill him before he starved to death. There was no going back the way he came. And jumping once more into the racing water rushing into the black hole on the other side of the ledge he occupied was an invitation to drowning. His body was beginning to shiver. The remaining life span of the lantern was a dread-filled unknown.

He looked into the beckoning darkness. His emotions and his mind were waging a titanic battle. Stay and die. Or go in that hole and risk a panic attack in the bowels of the earth.

Rizzo remembered something from his youth. A prayer his mother would whisper when their situation was most dire. *"Where there is faith, there is hope."*

With the prayer echoing in his mind and the underground river pounding behind him, Samuel Leonard Rizzo took a deep breath, gathered up his courage and the lantern, and nudged it in front of him as he pushed his head and shoulders into the shaft.

———∿∿———

Annie Bohannon's eyes pleaded with her husband.

"We weren't getting out that way—not anymore. And if we left the stairs open, how long do you think we would have survived when whoever is above us came for a visit?"

There was no panic in Annie's voice, only the flint of resolve. "We are not going to die in here. Tom, you will get me home."

Like synchronized swimmers, his wife and Rodriguez both took deep breaths and pushed back their shoulders. "There's only one way to go," said Joe, looking over his shoulder and down the shaft. "Let's move."

"Okay, but we turn off one of the flashlights. From now on, unless it's necessary, only one flashlight on at a time," said Tom. "Joe, you go first . . . slowly. There's a reason Sammy hasn't come back."

Joe twisted around in the tight shaft and squeezed past Annie. As Joe and the light inched along the tunnel ahead of them, Tom came up behind his wife and laid his hand on her shoulder. "'May the Lord bless and keep you. May the Lord make his countenance shine upon you and be gracious to you. May the Lord turn his face toward you and give you peace.'" Tom brushed his fingers across her cheek. "We'll be okay."

Annie swallowed hard and nodded. On her hands and knees, she started following the fading light.

33

9:10 p.m., Babylon

Rizzo shut his eyes for a moment, tried to relax, and then pushed on. His progress was excruciatingly slow. First Rizzo pushed the lantern along the floor of the shaft, as far as his arms would allow, and then crawled after it, trying not to lean upon his scraped and bleeding knees any more than necessary. But the shaft itself, while generally smooth from the water that once ran through it, was an undulating snake, swishing left, then right. He could see differing grades of erosion on the walls, signs that water often moved through these tunnels at changeable depths. The floor lifted in twisted knots of clay, the roof sweeping down to create narrow passages Rizzo needed to squeeze through. Only a supreme assault of his will kept Rizzo from curling up in a fetal ball to escape the walls pressing in on every side and crying himself to death. *How long can I keep this up? Is it really worth the effort to push forward like this? Rizzman . . . who are you trying to kid? You need help.* Rizzo's head dropped to his hands. *Are you up there?*

—⁓⁓⁓—

Joe had scrambled only a few yards when he stopped. "The shaft opens up. It gets higher." Tom could see the light in front of him moving, sweeping around what must be a larger chamber. "I think we can stand."

Tom and Annie pushed through the opening into the expanded shaft and got to their feet. Standing erect felt glorious. Joe picked up the pace. It was frustrating for Tom, who couldn't see anything but the dark backs of Joe and Annie.

He kept straining to see if there was any other light in front of them, but it was nearly impossible. Then Joe stopped again.

"Aawww, man. You're not going to believe this."

Joe looked down at the fast-moving channel of water and wondered what could go wrong next.

"There's a river up here. Fast. Looks deep. And it's in our way."

He turned and looked past Annie to his brother-in-law.

"Unless you've got a bridge stuffed into that backpack, we're in trouble."

———※※———

It took a moment before Rizzo comprehended what he *wasn't* seeing. The shaft came to an opening in the wall, but where he expected to see the shaft continuing off into the distance, there was nothing. The light crossed through the portal and was swallowed up by the dark beyond.

The shaft came to an end.

But where—

Rizzo edged forward slowly, aware of the surface under his hands and the darkness beyond the tunnel. He didn't want to trade the one for the other. Strange, how he had been so frantic to escape this tunnel and now it afforded him a sense of security and protection against the dark void before him.

A steady breeze now moving his thick, dark hair, Rizzo came to the edge of the opening. He was afraid to look over the edge and find a precipitous drop, dooming him to entombment in this tunnel but, as he extended the lantern through the opening, he saw something he didn't expect.

There wasn't much of a drop on the other side of the opening—six to ten feet and the space opened up into an irregular chamber about twenty feet high and just as wide. Its surfaces were smooth grooves carved out by fast-moving channels of water from long ago. And on the far side of the chamber were two tunnels. Two.

Rizzo calculated the distances in his mind. Probably six feet to the floor of the chamber from the lip of the opening. Not wise to try to jump with the lantern in his hands. And he wasn't going to leave the lantern here. He took off his belt, lay on his stomach, and dangled the belt over the edge. Too short. Looping the belt back into his pants, Rizzo looked at his boots.

—⌇⌇⌇—

"Too wide to jump?"

"Yeah, and the current is awfully fast," said Joe.

Annie came to his side. "Sammy wouldn't have gotten over."

"No, not at this depth he wouldn't." Joe's mind flashed to an image of Rizzo being swept away into that deadly, dark tunnel. He shook his shoulders to chase away the dread and gazed into the black hole to his right where the river disappeared into the wall of the shaft. "But we have to."

They were all going to get wet. The only questions were how, and who went first.

"Maybe I could tie a couple of ropes around my waist," said Tom, "and I could ford the river while you and Annie hold on and keep me from getting swept away."

Joe thought about the possibility for a moment. "The only way that can work is if someone was on the other side and could pull you across." He reached up and touched the roof of the shaft. It wasn't that far above his head. He looked across the river. It wasn't that far across. "I've got an idea. Tom, give me three of those pitons."

Based on their earlier adventures underground, Tom and Joe had included a few items in their packs they thought might come in handy. One safety measure—though heavy—was the ropes. Another was the spelunker's gear. Their helmets were still back in the Land Rovers, but the rest of the gear had been packed long ago, just to be ready.

Tom slipped off his pack, sending a shiver of pain through his shoulder, dug into a pocket, and pulled out a handful of hardened steel pitons—sharp-pointed rope hangers that mountain climbers or cave divers drove into stone or wood or clay. Their design locked them in place, and they could support more than five hundred pounds of weight.

Joe stepped back and inspected the tunnel. He needed to get up enough speed, and the fulcrum point needed to be as far out over the water as possible. He stepped up to the edge of the fast-moving water. "Here, hang on to my belt while I lean out over the water."

Both Annie and Bohannon came up behind him and Joe leaned forward, the piton in his left hand, a hammer in his right. But he couldn't get far enough over the water. "Wait, let's try a rope."

He grabbed a coil from the floor. "Let me turn around so I can lean backward. Tie one end around the belt loop on the right side of my pants, and the other end around a belt loop on the left side. Then you and Annie hang on to the ropes and keep me steady while I try to drive this piton into the roof."

Joe leaned against the ropes as he moved close to the edge of the river. The Bohannons played out the ropes, Tom's left arm straining under the pressure, and Joe found himself looking up at the ceiling, the river rushing below his back. He held the piton in his left fist and with short, awkward strokes, drove it into the hardened clay. His body swaying with each swing, Rodriguez fought to keep his feet from slipping on the wet floor. He took a third piece of rope and threaded it through the eye of the piton.

The lantern hanging at the end of his shoelaces, Rizzo lowered it slowly to the floor below. The last thing he needed was to break that light. As it settled on the clay floor, Rizzo dropped the shoelace over the edge, turned his body, and tried to find a firm grasp on the smooth clay at the opening's edge. He pushed his knees out and wiggled to his waist. His legs dropped perpendicular to the wall and, as his fingers grappled for a hold, Rizzo fell.

Standing about twenty feet up the shaft, Joe visualized in his mind the next few moments. Like riding a rope swing out over the water, Rodriguez needed to gain momentum on this side of the underground river, hang on to the rope as it pivoted against the piton and, at just the right moment, release his hands from the rope. He wasn't worried about that part. It was landing on the other side that had him concerned. And the odds of whether he would break a leg.

Rizzo's boots hit the floor with a thud. He thought he was balanced enough for his feet to land flat. But his left ankle buckled, he cried out in pain, and his body crashed to the eroded floor of hardened clay. Rizzo's ankle heralded the promise of swelling to join the pain, but this was no time to lie around waiting for bad things to happen.

He retrieved the lantern and relaced his boots. Picking himself up and standing in front of the tunnel entrances, vainly trying to keep weight off his bruised ankle, Rizzo considered his options. Right or left? Left or right? He hobbled over and looked into both tunnels. Each one showed the smooth-faced erosion of moving water. Which way?

"When you come to a fork in the road, take it," he said into the silence. No coin to flip, Rizzo shrugged his shoulders. "I hope this is the right shaft." And he entered the left.

When Joe landed in water on the other side, he was surprised, for a heartbeat. But then he was too focused on keeping his feet and not falling back into the river. A river that seemed to be growing in size and speed. Waving his arms forward, Joe regained his balance and took two steps out of the water, turning quickly to look at Tom and his wife on the other side. "Hurry up. The river's getting bigger."

"How's it getting bigger?" Tom wondered.

"It's a river. I don't know." Joe's words held an edge of urgency. "Annie, hurry. I'll catch you."

Tom heard sounds behind him as he pulled the rope back and put it in Annie's hands. He looked up the shaft as the darkness behind them grew gray.

"That's voices."

"I know. Get moving. I'll be right behind."

Annie ran faster, and was lighter, and cleared the river easily, landing in Rodriguez's arms.

"They're coming."

"I know. I can hear them." Joe swung the rope back in Tom's direction. He was already up to his ankles, and the swiftly moving river was pulling at his grip on the floor. The rope was still at least a foot away when it changed direction and swung back toward Joe. Tom glanced over his shoulder, then to his left where the river was coming out of a fissure in the wall. The river was growing in volume and speed. And the voices were getting louder.

He grabbed Joe's pack off the floor with his left hand. "Here!" He threw it with all his might into Joe's arms. "Here's Annie's."

"Wait!" Annie's voice was strained. "Grab the rope, Tom."

He looked across the raging water and was forced to take another step back. "I can't reach it. Here, catch this."

Bohannon lofted Annie's pack. As Joe caught it, Tom tied a loop of rope, one end around his waist, the other end to the straps of his backpack. "And this one."

A flashlight beam illuminated the shaft behind him. "Stop!"

34

When he heard voices, Sammy Rizzo started to cry.

He was cold, exhausted—physically and emotionally spent. His stomach felt like the inside of a tornado, and his head pounded with a vicious headache, all the result of wrestling with the claustrophobia that threatened to paralyze his every movement. Fear ceased to be a factor long ago, supplanted by a debilitating dread that he was walking through his tomb, that his desperate effort to find a path of escape was destined to failure.

Rizzo traveled along the left-side tunnel for several hundred yards when he came to a small chamber, and the end of the tunnel. Along the right, up near the roofline, was a large hole, the only exit other than reversing direction and going back to the fork.

He sat on the floor, his head drooping, growing more despondent the more he debated with himself about the viability of his options. Where did the hole go? Was there a way out? But how could he reach it? If he went back to the fork, would the right tunnel provide any better result?

None of the options held much hope.

"Hurry up. The river's getting bigger. Annie, hurry. I'll catch you." Rodriguez! The voices came through the hole at the top of the shaft, amplified like in a megaphone. Distant, but clear.

Before he even thought to react, the tears were running down his face. *They're close!*

Rizzo jumped to his feet. "Hey! Hey, it's me!" he yelled. Only echoes returned. He looked up at the hole just below the roof. He was short, but his legs

were strong. If he could get a running start . . . if his ankle held up . . . maybe
. . . He turned to gauge the distance to the far wall. His lantern dimmed.

⪼⪻

Joe caught the pack and the rope. Without hesitation, Bohannon ran a few steps
back, turned, and then raced toward the growing river. He took two steps into
the water and launched himself at the rope hanging from the piton.

⪼⪻

Spinning round, Rizzo saw the bulb in the lantern pulse, dim to bright, and
then shine brighter than ever before. *Oh, God!*

Which is when he saw the water running down the passage from the direction he'd come.

Rizzo turned and jumped as hard as he could. If he could reach the hole
above, maybe the light would last long enough for him to reach the rest of the
team. His stubby fingers stretched for the lip of the hole, but he was at least two
feet short. He shot a glance back, over his right shoulder. The water was running
faster and beginning to cover the floor in his small chamber.

*Maybe I can tread water and float up to the hole? Doofus! Where's the water
going to go when it gets that high?*

Rizzo looked around frantically. He had only one chance.

He pulled his Swiss Army knife out of his pocket. Pushed the lantern closer
to the wall, under the hole. Took a few steps back until his shoulders were
against the far wall. Then launched himself, ignoring the pain in his ankle,
sloshing through the growing stream.

⪼⪻

The sound of running feet was obliterated by the thunder of an automatic
weapon in an enclosed space. Bohannon could hear the bullets thudding into
the thick clay along the walls. But his focus was on the rope.

⪼⪻

Kicking his knees high to pull his boots out of the water, Rizzo splashed across the tunnel in two giant strides, landed with his right boot on top of the lantern and pushed up with all his strength. Rizzo dug the fingers of his left hand into the wall and, using his left hand as a fulcrum, swung his right arm over his head, stabbing the steel blade of the knife deep into the hard clay.

He almost lost his grip when the echoes of automatic weapons reverberated along the opening.

⸎

Stretching, not thinking, Tom reached for the rope with both hands, but there was very little forward momentum left. As he grasped the rope, his left hand slipped. Tom screamed in protest as all his weight bore down against the damaged joint. His legs splashed into the river, slowing him down even more. Sucking in a huge, great breath, Bohannon's throbbing arm lost contact with the rope and the rushing water started driving him downstream.

⸎

The knife was imbedded only three to four inches inside the lip of the hole, but it was enough for Sammy to pull himself up and wrap his left hand around the hilt of the knife. His chest was pounding, and his lungs ached. He pushed with his boots against the side of the tunnel wall and pulled his elbows into the space inside the hole.

⸎

Joe and Annie, now knee deep in the river and in danger of being swept away themselves, pulled hard on the rope attached to Bohannon's waist. "Tom!"

⸎

Rizzo's weight balanced on the lip of the opening, his hands around the knife as it pressed into his sternum. But now he was really in a predicament. He needed to let go of the knife in order to move farther into the hole in the wall. How could he move any farther inside the hole without the danger of slipping off the lip and dropping back into the chamber?

He snuck a peek under his left armpit. The water in the chamber was rising. He needed to move.

Rizzo realized that he was still wearing his small backpack. He didn't need the extra weight. *Extra weight.* Rizzo pushed both hands down on the knife's hilt, raising his body up, and pressed his stomach hard against the handle. As he came down, he forced the hilt of the knife under the belt on his pants.

And he let go.

Rodriguez was digging the heels of his boots into the hard clay floor of the tunnel, pulling with all the strength in his arms. Annie was at his side, almost parallel to the floor as she threw her body weight against the current. Rodriguez wasn't gaining any advantage—but he wasn't losing any, either. At least not yet. Gunshots—and bullets whizzed above their heads.

As his body hung from his belt looped around the knife, Rizzo could feel the strength leeching from his arms. He willed himself to one last, great push.

His knees found the lip of the hole, and he lunged forward. The knife hilt plunged into his groin, shooting pain through his midsection, and knocking the wind out of his lungs. Rizzo reached out his hands to steady his body. They found nothing but air.

35

9:51 p.m., Babylon

Later, Bohannon would realize two things: one, as Rodriguez held fast to the rope, his brother-in-law acted as a fulcrum. Swept downstream, Bohannon's body moved in an arc, not a straight line, being pulled closer to the edge of the river the farther downstream he was pushed. Bohannon cushioned his contact with the wall of the shaft by extending his left arm and pushing off the wall. At the same time he felt a huge yank against his waist as Rodriguez began reeling in his further-battered body.

And two, whoever was chasing them wasn't getting past this river without building a bridge.

~~~

It started as a skid. Momentarily weakened by the blow to his midsection, Rizzo's hands reached for substance as his head and shoulders dipped into the descending chute. As his body started to slide down the slope, the water his boots carried from the leap inside the tunnel ran down his legs, further soaking his still damp pants. The smooth clay, worn by centuries of flowing water, became slick—like ice.

Rizzo's body picked up speed, falling headfirst, down the shaft.

Arms, legs, knees, elbows all vainly tried to act as brakes for the runaway Rizzo. For a heartbeat he slowed. Then gravity exerted its law.

"Aaaaarrrrrrggggggghhhhhhhhh!"

~~~

They were all exhausted, dripping wet, and ready to collapse. But this was no time to sit and wait. Flashlights bobbed and boots pounded on the far side of the dark. Rodriguez grabbed Bohannon's sopping shirt by the shoulders. "Let's—"

"Aaaaarrrrrrgggggggghhhhhhhhh!"

Rodriguez's ears were ringing. And for a moment he thought he was crazy. "It's Sam!"

~~~

The shaft got steeper. And Rizzo dropped into the blackness like a rock.

~~~

Hunched over in the lowering space, Rodriguez led the way as they slipped along the passage. He held Rizzo's MagLite close to his shirt, giving him a dim view of what was ahead and, hopefully, a more difficult target for their pursuers.

~~~

With the rupturing abruptness of a skidding car against a fire hydrant, Rizzo slammed to a stop. The straps of his backpack jerked his shoulders back and snapped his head into the roof of the now much-more-narrow channel.

His scream made his ears hurt.

Rizzo's head and arms had gotten through a narrowing in the shaft, but his shoulders and the pack on his back acted like emergency brakes. His shoulders throbbed from the violence of the crash. It hurt to breathe, as if he was getting stabbed in the lungs. Blood dripped into his eyes.

He fought hard to remain conscious. He forced a swallow to hold his vomit in check. He flexed his fingers, arms, and legs—just to make sure they still worked.

And he felt the steady rain of water falling down the course behind him.

"Awww, come on, will ya!" he shouted into the dark. "Give me a break!"

~~~

Rodriguez skidded to a halt, and Bohannon ran right into his back, tripped over his own feet, and fell to the wet floor of the tunnel. On his injured shoulder.

"That's Sammy! Look around. We've got to risk it. Look around."

～∧∧～

His eyes closed, Rizzo tried once again to rein in the panic attack that bubbled up in his chest like a sudden illness. He pulled in a deep breath to calm his nerves, but the shooting pain in his side pierced any growing calm and jolted his eyes wide open.

～∧∧～

"Sam! Sam, we can hear you!"

～∧∧～

Water falling like rain around him, Rizzo saw moving light through an opening at the base of the shaft. *It's Joe!* "Hey!" The yell sent a shiver of pain through Rizzo's ribs. "Oww!"

～∧∧～

At first Rodriguez thought the water on the floor was coming from the overflow of the raging river in their wake. But as he swept his MagLite in great, frantic arcs up and down the walls, he saw more water coming from an opening up ahead. The opening was down near the floor, on the right side of the shaft, like the opening of a small cave. Rodriguez threw himself on his knees and skidded to a stop just in front of the cave. He shoved his arm with the flashlight into the opening and carefully peeked under the lintel. "Sammy?"

"Will you get that stupid light out of my eyes? What, do you think you're the cave police?"

"Sammy!" A lump gathered in Rodriguez's throat, a lightness fluttered in his chest, and an urgent and grateful prayer erupted from his heart. Bohannon and his wife pressed in at the entrance while Rodriguez struggled into the cave. Rizzo was hanging upside-down, halfway through a narrow opening, maybe ten feet above Rodriguez. Steady rivulets of water rolled down Rizzo's body from several locations, falling into Rodriguez's upturned face.

"Are you hurt?"

"I think I cracked a rib. Hurts to breathe."

"Can you move?"

"My arms and legs still work, thank God. But the rest of me is stuck. I fell, and I'm wedged in here. I don't think I can move. And I feel like I've been in a car wreck."

"Okay," said Joe. "Close your eyes for a minute."

Rodriguez ran the beam from the MagLite around the space that imprisoned Rizzo. There were small openings, enough for the water to run through, but Rizzo appeared to be wedged tight against the walls on all sides. His arms and head were through the narrow opening, and his shoulders were slightly protruding. But from his collarbone back, Rizzo was stuck on the other side of the stricture. Rodriguez made note of the blood dripping from Rizzo's forehead. He turned off the light.

"Hang in there, Sam. I'll be right back."

Rodriguez heard the mumble as he pulled himself out of the opening. "Hang in there? A wise guy. Always a wise guy."

Two anxious faces, and more water moving along the tunnel, were waiting for Rodriguez.

"He's hanging upside down, stuck in a narrow portion of the shaft. His arms and head are through the narrowing, but he's stuck from his shoulders back. More water's coming down on top of him. Said he fell, but I don't know from where, or how far."

Annie reached out and touched Joe's arm. "Is he hurt?"

Rodriguez nodded his head. "Yeah. Sounds like he cracked a rib. And he's bleeding from his head somewhere. But he looks terrible. His eyes are wild looking, and his face is pale. I'd say he's not far from shock, or hypothermia, or both. We need to get him out of there."

"We need to get us out of here," said Bohannon. "I don't know what's happening with our pursuers, but this water's risen about two inches since we've been standing here. We don't have much time."

———∿∿∿———

Rizzo tried to wriggle his shoulders, but there was no movement. His arms, stuck out in front of him, were useless. Although the walls were only inches from his fingers, he couldn't reach them. There was no way for him to push himself up. No way to twist himself down.

Water ran down his back, around his ears and over his face, some getting in his nose.

He shook his head.

"Are you guys waiting for a bus? Get me out of here or I'm gonna drown while standing on my head."

⸻

Bohannon looked over Joe's shoulder at the cave opening on the floor. The water was rising into the opening.

"Can you get to him?"

Rodriguez shook his head, a grimace crossing his face. "Even if I stand up in there, and I raise my arms, I think he's going to be a couple of feet above me. But that's not the biggest problem. He can't get through the opening. He's not going back up that chute. We've got to get him on this side of the opening."

Bohannon looked into his brother-in-law's eyes. "And we need to do it now."

⸻

Rizzo watched as Rodriguez pressed himself through the opening at the base of the wall, water covering the lower half. He tried to control his breathing, tried to still the shivers running up and down his spine, tried to quell the voice declaring his impending death. He could still breathe. There was still hope.

His friends were here. He was no longer alone. And they wouldn't abandon him. Unless . . .

Rodriguez shined his MagLite up at Rizzo, blinding him for a moment.

Unless they had to run for their lives.

⸻

Joe was desperate. He examined the sides of the tunnel around Rizzo, looking for cracks . . . something to open the space wider. The water, and Rizzo's blood, kept getting into his eyes, blurring his vision. He almost missed it entirely.

Rodriguez wiped the back of his hand over his eyes, clearing the blurs for a moment. He extended his arm as far as it would go and played the beam of his light on Rizzo.

"Sam, are you wearing your pack?"

—∿∾—

Sam had turned his head away from the bright light. "Why . . . you want my pajamas?"

"*Sam!*"

Rizzo raised his head and stared into the light. "Yeah. I'd probably be dead if it hadn't cushioned the abrupt stop. Why? Wait!" Rizzo tried to see Rodriguez through the light as the reality dawned on him. "I can't reach it."

—∿∾—

Joe slid back down the shaft and splashed through the opening. He needed to grab Tom's hand to get to his feet. Annie was leaning against the far wall of the passage, holding all three of their packs out of the ankle-deep water. Joe fished into the side pocket of his pack and pulled out a pocketknife he kept to razor sharpness. He turned to Tom.

"I need you to hold me up. I need to get up to Sammy and try to cut the straps to his pack off his shoulders. Then maybe we can pull him loose."

Bohannon looked down at the rising water.

"I know. It's getting high," said Rodriguez. "I just need a couple more feet."

"Let's go."

—∿∾—

Rodriguez pushed back through the hole—where the water level now covered half the opening—with his flashlight in one hand and his knife in the other.

"I ain't gonna be some sacrifice to the water god."

"Shut up, Sam."

Rodriguez stood up and spread his legs as wide as the sides of the tunnel would allow.

"Okay, Tom."

Bohannon squeezed through the opening, but stayed on the floor. He pivoted and pushed his back against the wall facing the opening.

Rodriguez placed one boot firmly on Bohannon's left shoulder. "Ready?" he asked.

"Just do it," Tom replied.

Rodriguez stepped on his right shoulder, raising off the ground a good three feet. Joe felt a shudder underfoot as Tom moaned aloud under the pressure,

It was a tight fit that high in the tube, not much room for Rodriguez to maneuver. He switched the knife to his left hand with the flashlight and reached out with his right. He laid his right hand against Rizzo's cheek.

"Hi, Sam. Good to see you again."

"No tears, Goliath. Get me out of here. And brush your teeth."

With his right fingers Rodriguez tried to wriggle between Rizzo's left shoulder and the shoulder strap of the backpack.

"Ooowww. Oh, man . . . that hurts."

"Gotta try, Sam. That's the only way we can get you free. Here. Let me push you up a little bit. Maybe that will loosen the tension. Gonna push, Tom!"

⸺⌇⌇⸺

The boots cut into Bohannon's shoulders, bringing tears to his eyes. He ground his teeth and then bit down on his tongue to keep from screaming. What was more troublesome was the chest-high water that nearly filled the shaft's opening.

⸺⌇⌇⸺

Taking the knife into his right hand and putting his left hand against Rizzo's collarbone, Rodriguez pushed against the wedge and the force of Rizzo's body. He felt the shoulder strap go momentarily limp and darted the knife blade under the strap and sliced across its face. The cords flayed against the sharp edge.

⸺⌇⌇⸺

Bohannon desperately tried to steady himself under Rodriguez's boots, his hands hard against the walls. But when Rodriguez pushed to get closer to Rizzo, Bohannon began to slip. His right shoulder caved under Rodriguez's weight. The pressure pushed him down into the water and farther out the opening. Suddenly, the water was up to Bohannon's chin.

⸺⌇⌇⸺

The blade nearly sliced Rizzo's neck as Bohannon rocked under Rodriguez's feet. *Gotta hurry.*

This time Rodriguez needed to reach across his body, the knife in his right hand as he pushed once more against Rizzo's collarbone. Bohannon rocked some more, Rodriguez lost his balance, and the blade plunged into his left forearm.

Bohannon's mouth was open to scream. He barely had time to pull in another breath when Rodriguez pushed down onto Bohannon's shoulders once again, driving Tom's mouth and nose underwater. And the water was rising.

Rodriguez grabbed a fistful of Rizzo's shirt and held fast. He pulled the blade free from his arm and, with one swipe, sliced through both the strap on Rizzo's right shoulder and the fabric of Rizzo's shirt. A thin, red line appeared on Rizzo's shirt. But Rodriguez had no thought of possible cuts. He closed the knife against his right thigh, stuffed it into his back pants pocket, grabbed Rizzo with both hands and pulled with all the strength left in his body.

The force from Rodriguez's feet drove Bohannon's head under the surface of the water. He fought for purchase, his fingers digging against the smooth sides of the shaft, his legs thrashing as he tried to find an edge to push his boots against, torn between the need to keep Rodriguez upright enough to rescue Rizzo and his growing desperation for air.

Rodriguez was inches from Rizzo's bulging eyes. *"Pull!"*

Joe wrapped his fingers into Rizzo's shirt, tightened his muscles, and pulled hard.

When Bohannon slipped farther underwater, Rodriguez was left dangling from Rizzo's shirt.

⚬⌒⌒⌒⌒

Rizzo felt the pack break loose from his shoulders as Rodriguez's weight inched his body through the narrow opening. One shoulder popped through. Then . . . like an onrushing flood, Rizzo burst through the opening.

⚬⌒⌒⌒⌒

Tom flew out of the opening as if he was exiting a water slide, shooting across the larger passage and running into Annie's legs. He spluttered to his hands and knees in the fast-moving current, shook his head, and dove back under the water.

⚬⌒⌒⌒⌒

Like a sack of stone, Rodriguez plunged into the water. And Rizzo dropped right on top of him. Stunned by the collision, Rodriguez took in a mouthful of water. His airways blocked, he began convulsing, with Rizzo lodged against the wall by Rodriguez's bucking body.

⚬⌒⌒⌒⌒

The opening was completely covered by the rising water. Rodriguez's MagLite had fallen to the floor of the shaft under the water, but it was still on. All Bohannon could see in the swirling twilight was one leg sticking out of the opening. He tugged on the leg, but the rest of Joe's body was flailing around inside. Bohannon looked up into the hole for some way to free Rodriguez . . . and saw Rizzo, his eyes bulging, his hands twisted into the collar of Rodriguez's shirt, shaking Joe like a rag doll and screaming bubbles into the water.

Bohannon pushed against Rodriguez's leg.

⚬⌒⌒⌒⌒

The push on his leg got Joe's head back above water. He coughed out the water in his throat and sucked in some air as he steadied his feet on the floor, grabbed Rizzo under the arms, and got him right side up. "Gotta get out, Sam."

Rizzo nodded, closed his eyes, and held his nose. Joe spread his feet and lowered Sammy into the water.

〜〜〜

Bohannon needed air. His left hand steadying him against the growing current, Bohannon pushed his head above the surface, sucked in some air, and dropped back underwater to see Rizzo's legs sticking out of the opening. He pulled. Rizzo twitched, but came through the opening. Bohannon wrapped his left arm around Rizzo's waist, struggled to get his boots flat onto the floor, pushed his body up against the wall, and lifted Rizzo out of the water.

36

They were reunited, but still in mortal danger, desperate for a way out of this rapidly flooding tunnel.

Rizzo was in pain, dazed from his fall, and too weak to force his way through water that would have been up to his waist. Tom didn't know how badly Rizzo was injured, but he didn't look good. Neither did Annie—though she wouldn't say anything. And Joe was bleeding from the gash in his arm.

"Let me take the packs," said Joe. "You and Annie help Sam."

Tom knew they had to find a way out, quickly, or they would all succumb to hypothermia. He grabbed the flashlight from Annie.

"Let's go."

There was no more conversation.

Tom sloshed forward, down the tunnel, the current at his back. The tunnel was high enough to walk in. But where were they going? How were they going to get out? And what about the staff? Now that he had a moment to think, Tom took a moment to pray. *I don't understand. If you want us to find Aaron's staff, why are you making it so hard? Why are there so many obstacles?*

"Didn't you expect opposition?"

"What?" Tom glanced over his shoulder. Annie had her head down, concentrating on guiding Rizzo along the slippery clay floor, and Joe was struggling under the weight of the extra packs.

"Didn't you expect opposition? Our enemy doesn't want the staff recovered. He knows it will be used against him and will orchestrate his final defeat."

Tom's mind and emotions were reeling in a jumble of confusion. He was wet, cold, and frightened. And now . . .

"Don't be afraid."

Are you kidding? Where have you been? We're going to die down here.

"Don't be afraid. I will never leave you or forsake you. So I haven't left you now. Have faith. And stay on the right path."

He swept his flashlight back and forth through the darkness in front of him, but Tom felt no hope.

Platitudes? We don't need platitudes. We need a miracle. If you didn't bring us here to die, we need a miracle.

"We need a miracle."

Tom stumbled at the sound of the voice behind him, and almost fell into the water. He turned to find Annie close to his side.

"Tom . . . we need a miracle," she whispered. "Otherwise . . ."

"I know. We're in pretty bad shape."

Tom had his left hand braced on the side of the shaft while the flashlight in his right scanned the space in front of them. Annie was walking tight to the wall, leaning into it for traction as she tried to keep Sammy steady. The current in the river had been accelerating, and now all were struggling to keep their footing.

Tom's flashlight spotted the change coming.

The tunnel took a sharp turn to the left just ahead of them, the water sweeping around the turn in a swift current.

"Stay to the left if you can. The current is fastest on the right," Tom said over his shoulder. As he turned back to the front, his hand slipped off the wall, throwing him off balance. As Bohannon's feet were swept forward, snatched up from under him, a vision of underwater terror and a cry for help were stifled by the hands that held his shoulders steady. Bohannon's boots found the floor, and he turned to thank his rescuer. Annie and Joe were wide-eyed, both hands plastered to the left wall.

"You were falling," said Annie. "How did you stay up?"

"I know. I—" Tom's light fell against the far wall.

In the shadows, high in the wall to the right as the river made its violent swerve to the left, was the black void of a large shaft. To the right. *Stay on the right path.* He remembered the voice in his mind, the direction in his spirit, the answer to his prayer not that long ago. Tom hadn't noticed the opening earlier. He was concentrating on the water as it rushed around the corner to the left. *If I hadn't lost my balance, we may have never seen that tunnel.*

"Are you okay?" Annie placed her hand on his shoulder.

"You look like death," said Joe.

"Tom, are you all right?" Annie repeated.

He closed his eyes and carefully rolled his neck, trying to release the tension. "I don't know." He felt like a heart attack in a wet shirt—sick, in pain, cold, and clammy. He needed to sleep for a month. He forced his eyes open. "I thought I was a goner. I don't see how I stayed upright. Somebody grabbed my shoulders. It was dark and fast and frightening, and I—"

"Tom." It was Annie's voice. Soft. Calm. "You're here. You're with us. You're safe. We're going to be okay."

Tom looked up at his wife.

"I know. There's a way out."

⁓⁓⁓

Annie had the only working flashlight left between the four of them. She turned it toward the yawning shaft and wished its beam into the darkness. "How do you know? How can you be sure that's the way we should go?"

"Well, for one thing, it looks like the only real alternative. We can't go that way," Tom said, hitching his thumb toward the tube from which they could now hear the deep-throated rumble of falling water, "and I don't think going back is a viable alternative. But even if that weren't the case, I'd bet my life that is the way out. I heard a voice . . . I was told to take the right way. And that's the right way."

Annie looked over at the mouth of the shaft. *Right or wrong, did they have any choice?* "All right. But how are we going to get there?"

The opening was on the other side, across the racing water. And it was higher up the side of the tunnel, tucked inside a small alcove that made it hard to see. Twenty-five hundred years ago, the opening was probably at floor level. Not anymore.

"I know a way."

Annie turned to look into the eyes of Rizzo. He was leaning against Rodriguez, his hands holding fast to Joe's belt as he struggled against the current. He looked almost as bad as Tom, but firmness had returned to his voice.

"It's about time I pulled my own weight."

⁓⁓⁓

Rizzo hated the fact that he felt this vulnerable, this helpless, this much a captive of his small stature and limited physical ability. He knew he owed his life to Joe and Tom, and his heart ached for how much the two of them had risked rescuing him. But he was helpless then, and he felt helpless now, weakened, waterlogged, and incapable of taking care of himself. If he tried to walk in this raging torrent racing through the tunnel, he would be gone in the blink of an eye. He was a liability. Until now.

Rizzo had climbed up onto Tom's back and was tying a length of rope into a harness around the chest and shoulders of Joe. The other end of the rope was tied to a piton driven high into the wall above his head. "The harness will give your body more stability if you slip into the water, more than if you just tied it to one point, like on your belt."

"Where did you learn that?" asked Joe.

"I haven't spent my whole life playing video games, wise guy. We use that kind of a harness when we're scuba diving."

"What?"

"Keeps you more stable in the tricky currents."

"No. I mean . . . when were you scuba diving?"

"I'm not crippled, dog breath. I've been diving for the past five years. Something even you didn't know about me. It's one of the few places on the planet where I'm equal to people of average size and inferior brains, like you, Attila. Now let me get back to work."

Rizzo returned his attention to tightening the harness on Rodriguez's chest.

"Okay, big boy," Rizzo whispered. "Now it's our turn." Rizzo shifted over to Rodriguez's back. "You've got to get us across to the other side of the river and get under that opening so I can crawl up into it."

"Is that all?"

"Yeah, but it's a snap for Superman. Let's go Clarky-baby."

⚬⚬⚬

They were slightly upriver, along the left-side wall, from the alcove. Eight . . . ten feet of water. Not that far. Probably two, three long strides. Normally. Then, another eight to ten feet to the alcove and the shaft opening. Rodriguez looked down at the rushing water. It didn't seem to be rising anymore, but the water was still up to his knees. And deeper where the current was moving fastest.

There was nothing to hold on to. And he had Rizzo on his back. How was he supposed to do this?

"Bend over at the waist . . . spread your arms out in front of you. Change your center of gravity. Bend your knees. Try to get your weight distributed evenly over your hips. Now you've got two points of balance—over your knees and over your hips. When you step, keep your feet inside, between your hips and your knees. Slow, small steps."

"More scuba diving?"

"No, tae kwon do."

Incredulous, Rodriguez twisted his neck to get a look at Rizzo.

The little man held up his hands. "Remember . . . I told you once. Hands of death. Let's go."

Rodriguez looked at the water, felt foolish in the arm-pointing crouch Rizzo described, and took his first step.

37

11:09 p.m., Babylon

He was amazed. It worked. Not that crossing the rushing water was easy. Rodriguez feared every step, tried to feel the floor through his boots, searched for a telltale waver in any of his muscles. But with each step, his confidence grew and his fear subsided. Before he was fully aware of it, they were across. His outstretched hands touched the wall on the far side of the tunnel.

"Stop," Rizzo whispered. "Rest a moment. You gotta be careful here. Turning is tough. Don't let your weight rock back, or we're goners."

Careful not to tip his balance, Rodriguez rested a hand against the wall. "How do I do this? How do I keep my balance? Just go sideways?"

"Too hard," said Rizzo. "This is all about shifting your weight without losing your balance. It's what we do with kick moves. When you're ready, turn your left foot, slowly, out to a ninety degree angle. When your left foot is settled, slowly rotate your shoulders and hips to the left. About halfway through the turn, stop, and bring your right foot along. Then rotate your hips and shoulders again and extend your arms in front of you. When you turn ninety degrees, stop and rest. Then we're almost home."

～⌇∿～

Rodriguez twisted slightly from his waist so Rizzo could settle himself in a seated position on the lip of a small shelf at the entrance to the chamber at the mouth of the tunnel.

Lifting himself off the shelf sent a bolt of pain through Rizzo's side. He gritted his teeth as he untied a rope secured to Joe's harness. Walking deeper into the shaft with the lead rope in his hand, Rizzo took Joe's hammer and looked at the clay wall.

"This is going to hurt like a bleeding booger." He swung the hammer in a wide, sidearm arc, and drove one of the pitons into the clay wall. "Oh, my—" He dropped to his knees, the hammer still in his hand.

—⌇⌇⌇—

Now the lead rope stretched above the water, across to the other side of the shaft. Tom gave Annie the backpacks, lighter now that some of the equipment was in use. Hand-over-hand, Joe used the rope to cross the river once again, curled one arm around Annie's waist, and helped lead her through the river as she held the packs aloft. On the other side, they passed them up to Rizzo one at a time, then Joe cupped his hands under Annie's boot and hoisted her up onto the shelf to join Rizzo.

Then it was Tom's turn. Bohannon hooked first his right, then his left boot over the suspended rope and, pulling with his left hand, shimmied to Rodriguez's waiting arms on the far side.

Joe boosted Tom up to the opening. The three in the shaft then combined their remaining strength to help Joe scramble out of the water and up the side of the tunnel wall. When he cleared the lip, the tension on the rope suddenly slackened and sent them sprawling across the floor of this new shaft.

—⌇⌇⌇—

Tom's eyes searched into the darkness that led deeper into the earth.

"C'mon," he said as he pushed himself out of Annie's grasp and rose to his feet. "C'mon. We've got to leave."

Annie put a hand on Bohannon's arm. "Tom, please. Rest a moment at least."

"No. There's no time. We have to go," he said, taking a step forward. He turned quickly. "We've got to go. Now!"

Joe came up to his side, Rizzo in tow. "What is it?"

"I don't know," said Tom. "But we're late. Time's running and we've been delayed . . . hindered. We've gotta move."

Annie still had the final flashlight in her hand. Its beam remained strong. Tom held out his hand, took the flashlight, and turned into the tunnel, his pace rapid. He knew they would follow. But his mind wasn't dwelling on those with him. It was on those waiting for him. And they were close.

This tunnel was man-made, not water-made. The sides showed clear signs of tools. They were square at the base to the floor. The ceiling was arched, for strength, but it was worked, not worn. Tom registered the difference in the back of his consciousness, but at the moment, it was superfluous information. He searched the space ahead of him as the shaft began a slight descent. And stopped. At a door.

He stopped so fast the others piled up behind him.

"A door?" Annie was at his side. "Is it . . ."

Tom moved close. There was no doorknob . . . no handle . . . nothing. The door was large, heavy, thick wood, metal braces extending from the hinges. He laid his hand upon the weathered wood—and the door swung open, silent, on well-oiled pinions. A vast darkness lay before them, as if Bohannon stood at the threshold of the center of the earth.

He felt Annie's hand on his shoulder, her breathing on his ear. "Tom . . ."

This was it. He knew it. Somewhere out there, in that space . . . somewhere out there was the garden of God, the birthplace of the human race. And, now that he was here, he didn't know if he really wanted to get any closer.

Tom stepped forward, through the doorway, and the sun rose.

—∾∿∾—

The light was blinding after hours in the dark, only the beams of their flashlights for illumination. But this wasn't beams. It was intense, immense, all-encompassing light. So bright, Tom could feel it sizzling across the surface of his skin. It warmed his soul.

The first shock of light passed, and Tom focused on what faced him. A huge wall of blue-glazed brick dominated the far side of a massive chamber, the sides of which were invisible. The wall ran in an arc for hundreds of yards on each side until it disappeared into a twilight that swallowed the flanks of the chamber. The wall extended up into the cavernous vault above—a strange sight even in such an incredible place. It appeared as if the wall had no end, no top. The blue brick rose, and rose, and simply blended into the vaulted roof, which also seemed to have no limit.

"Oh . . . my sweet Lord," Annie breathed. "I believed . . . but I doubted, too." She wrapped her arms around Tom's left arm and pressed into his side.

"I'm bummed I don't have an iPhone with me," said Rizzo as he and Joe joined them. "Imagine this on YouTube. Going viral in a heartbeat."

"Shut up, Sam," said Joe. "Or watch out for lightning bolts from heaven."

"Holy Zappo . . . shut my mouth!"

Lowering his eyes, Tom scanned the lower reaches of the wall itself. Spaced equally along the portion of the wall's arc they could see were seven huge gates of highly polished bronze, bound by heavy timber frames and metal braces. But these were King Kong–sized gates that looked like they would need motors to move—or dozens of bodies pulling resolutely on thick ropes. The gates were intricately carved with what, from a distance, looked like a riot of stars and symbols. And each one looked unique.

"The garden is probably on the other side, through one of those gates," whispered Joe, giving voice to the thoughts in Tom's mind. "But which one?"

A vast plaza of blue-glazed brick spread before them, alive in the brilliant light, as if the sky had fallen to the floor and Tom stood with his feet in heaven. In the very center of the plaza he could see a huge circular symbol on the floor. This was it. *The starting point!*

Bohannon stepped forward, moving toward the circular symbol. He crossed the blue plaza until he stood at its edge. It was a vast sun symbol, carved into the surface of the bricks, the carved surfaces covered with what looked like gold paint. Around the circumference of the sun, rays and tongues of fire marked the points of the compass.

"Tom, what does that symbol remind you of?" asked Annie.

He stepped back and took a longer look. It did seem familiar.

"Loughcrew!" Rizzo pointed a chubby finger at the gold symbol. "That was one of the symbols that our leprechaun McDonough found on the sarcophagus at Cairn T in Loughcrew. Jeremiah's tomb, and now Jeremiah's clue."

"What now?" asked Joe. "Which gate?"

"Well, we finally know what the directions are for," said Tom.

Suddenly, a shocking dawn came to Tom's memory. He spun to face Rodriguez.

"Joe . . . the directions!"

"Safe," he said. Joe reached under his shirt, and pulled out a gold chain. A gold cross hung from it, along with a sealed plastic bag pinned to the chain. He held the chain in front of him. "Used to hold the crucifix my mother gave me. Now it holds Deirdre's cross." He opened the bag and extracted the directions. "Now we put Abiathar to the test."

Tom unfolded the paper to look at the symbols written on it—the directional clues deciphered from the leather sprockets inside the brass mezuzah—and stepped into the middle of the sun carving.

Without warning, the compass points began to spin around the circumference of the sun, slowly at first, growing to a blur until Tom felt its dizzying effects. Then the flashing compass points skidded to a halt. And changed before his eyes.

—∿∿—

There were now only six compass points. And Tom finally knew how he would follow the directions. The compass points were marked with the same Demotic symbols etched into the mezuzah's sprockets. He read what Roberta Smith believed was the first clue. Fourteen paces in the direction of that symbol . . . straight ahead. Now the directions made sense. Next was seven paces in the direction of the second symbol. But pacing off across the plaza, he would quickly lose track of the right direction.

"Joe, stand in the middle here, will you?"

Tom handed Joe the sheet of directions and stepped on the Demotic symbol at the circumference of the sun. He started pacing, Annie at his side, glued to his arm, Rizzo following close behind. Fourteen healthy steps and he stopped, turned, and faced Joe. "Which direction next?"

Rodriguez lifted his arm and was about to wave Bohannon to the left when the symbols at the circumference of the sun began to spin again. "Wait! They're moving again."

Standing still, Bohannon had a thought. *This is crazy. What am I doing here?*

"*Welcome, man of God.*"

Annie's arms closed like a vise, her breathing hard against his bicep. "Ooohhh . . ."

"What was that voice?" Rizzo whispered.

"There," Joe blurted, waving his arm to the right. "North-northeast."

But Tom wasn't moving. Seven paces north-northeast would get him closer to the wall and its gates, but the voice. The voice reverberated through his mind, turned his blood to ice. All the hunches, all the ideas, all the excitement fell away under the power of that voice. Bohannon wasn't about to move an inch.

"Onward, man of God. Follow your destiny."

Tom looked down into Annie's eyes. She nodded her head. He looked up at Joe.

He waved. "North-northeast."

⸎

Through each of the directions, Bohannon moved closer to the wall. He was heading to the left, away from the middle gate. He finished his eleven paces and turned to get his final instructions from Rodriguez.

⸎

It was a beautiful, burnished bronze, gleaming in the profuse light. Shining as if it had been polished the day before, the portal gate soared above Bohannon's head and disappeared into the twilight. The door had two panels, both sides decorated with an expanse of stars, so vividly and precisely worked into the bronze by its creator that the door looked like the night sky itself.

Tom stood on the spot of the final direction, his feet unwilling to follow Joe's urging to move straight ahead. The gate was ahead of him, third gate from the left. The last one he would have selected, but clearly his destination. But now, oh so close, Tom didn't want to move.

"The moment of truth." Annie was by his side, grasping on to his left hand until he felt like his fingers would burst. "I'm not sure why, but I'm absolutely terrified. After all we've been through, after all God's done for us and led us through to get us here, I shouldn't be frightened by anything. But looking at that gate and wondering what's behind it—what it might mean . . . to us, to everybody . . ."

Annie took a step forward and turned toward her husband. "I know it's crazy to say at this point, but we don't have to do this."

Tom looked at his wife, and he knew what was going through her mind.

"We don't know for sure what will happen," said Annie, "what we'll start by going through that gate. But I know what I think is going to happen . . . what I'm afraid we may be starting."

Tom pulled Annie close, wrapped his arms around her, and suddenly realized he was dry. Their clothes were dry. "It's already started, Annie. Once there was ritual sacrifice in the Temple, the clock started ticking. We don't know what it all means, but we know it's happening. Yeah, I think what we do next will play a part. It may accelerate the timing. But if we don't do what we've been called here to do, to open that gate—at least to try—then who knows? Will it be worse, or better? I'm scared to my bones. But I also feel this is something I must do. You do, too. I know it."

Annie pulled back and looked into his eyes. "Well, let's get it done, then."

Tom took Annie's hand once more, turned to look over his shoulder at Rizzo and Rodriguez back in the sun symbol. "Let's go."

In Bohannon's right hand he held the design the team had drawn from the clues on the sprockets. If they were correct, the combination sequence to open the gate would start with the North Star and then progress through the pattern of stars that filled the sky in Judea the night Christ was born, ending with the Star of Bethlehem. What they didn't know was how to apply that conclusion, what sequence to use in choosing the stars. What was the right way to unlock the doors to Paradise?

Drawing near the gate, Bohannon could hear the running feet of Rodriguez and Rizzo catching up with them.

Bohannon looked at the directions in his hand and faced the gate. "Where do I start?"

"What happens if you touch that gate in the wrong place?" Rizzo whispered. "How do you know you won't turn into a rotisserie chicken?"

Thanks, Sam. That helps a lot. Lord, what am I supposed to do now?

"Forward, man of God. It is for you to open the gate."

Bohannon knew the voice was an invitation. He stepped closer, found the largest star on the gate—what he hoped was the North Star—and gingerly brushed the fingers of his right hand against the edges of the design. He nearly had a stroke.

As soon as his fingers touched the bronze symbol, the surface of the star warmed and glowed. At the same time a star lower and to the left of the North Star also began to glow. Bohannon moved his right hand from the North Star to the one on the left and, immediately, the glow faded from both stars. He pressed his fingers more purposely against the second star, but nothing occurred. When

Bohannon returned his touch to the North Star, it warmed again and both stars glowed once more.

"Keep your right hand on the first star and put your left hand on the second," Annie suggested.

The left star was smaller than the first, and Tom covered it with his palm. Immediately a third star began to glow, higher and to the right. And each of the stars continued to glow as Tom moved from one to the next. Soon the door shone like the night sky, brilliant stars glimmering across its surface.

His hands rested against the carved bronze surface, reluctant to take the final steps. Should he push? Pull? And what would be waiting for him on the other side?

"Do not be afraid, appointed one."

As the voice echoed around the chamber, Bohannon shifted his weight and leaned against the gate. It swung open easily. Inside, dense fog enshrouded everything in a gray cloud.

On one side, Annie continued her lock on his left arm. On the other, Rizzo stood at an angle, looking like he was ready to run in whatever direction was necessary.

"Hey, is anybody home?" Rizzo called.

Tom took one step over the threshold and felt like he had walked into a gelatin wall. Something soft and pliable, warm, swallowed him up and surrounded him from head to toe. In the moment it took for Bohannon to register what was going on and wonder how he was going to breathe while held in this viscous cocoon, he was through and on the other side, like emerging from an eyeball.

He didn't immediately realize the other three had been stopped in their tracks.

"Oh!"

"What?"

"Hey, get your mitts off me."

The others were still standing in the gate, about three feet away. Bohannon could see them clearly enough and hear their voices. But they were on different sides of a barrier. He put out his hand and the surface gave way, like pushing on the side of a water balloon. "You can't get through?"

Annie had both hands up, leaning against the surface of the barrier. "No. It's soft, pliable, but it won't let us through. We're stuck out here."

38

With a crack like thunder, light exploded into the cavern. Not just visible light, but light sizzling like static, skipping over the molecules of the air. Bohannon spun around at the sound and saw the garden spread out before him.

Ripples in a pond, expanding out in waves, growing and building on each pulse, the light washed over the garden. At the center of the pulse stood the trees.

The light around the trees thrummed, an audible sound, as leaves sprouted on the branches of the trees and the leaves turned from white to silver . . . silver to gray . . . gray to green. As the trees came to life, the leaves sang. Bohannon marveled as the light around him joined the song. Then before him, in a flash of brilliance, the garden came alive, more lush and green than anything he could have imagined. He was astounded by the variety and the volume of growing things. Above it all, at the heart of it all, the trees stood apart. Like the core of the sun, the intense light that beat forth from the trees was blinding and spellbinding.

Then the choir of the garden joined in, its massed music rising and falling like flood waters over boulders.

Overwhelmed by what was revealed before him, Bohannon felt a presence. He looked up as an image materialized, just inside the gate, a gigantic angelic presence that morphed from voice, to vapor, to shadow—to what appeared as a being of substance. He was dressed as a warrior. A glimmering helmet covered his head but not the long, dark, flowing hair that cascaded over his shoulders. A golden breastplate, shining like the risen sun, ended at a sash of spun gold that cinched a silver girdle around his waist. Golden boots covered his feet, ankles, and calves. All this Bohannon took in with one swift glance. But his attention continued to be drawn to two things: the furled wings that rounded on either side of his head, tucked behind his broad shoulders, and the flaming sword that hung loosely from his right hand.

The angel raised the tip of the sword, the muscles of his forearm flexing, and pointed it at Bohannon.

"You are welcome here, man of God. You have been called to fulfill your purpose."

Bohannon was entranced by the beauty of the angelic being. The young man's skin was alabaster, with the incandescent glow of old pearls, and flawless. His lips were full and red, his nose long and aquiline. His hair was shiny and black, a mass of waves that tumbled around his face, framing crystal green eyes. Every movement manifested a fluid grace that failed to mask a physical strength that was formidable.

The angel's words resonated like cymbals in the cavern and spun in the air like an invitation to a dance—light and melodic. His voice was clear and firm, softly modulated. But in its words, in its breaths and pauses, it seemed like bells chimed in a far distance.

Bohannon nearly collapsed in surprised shock when the angel smiled at him. It moved closer and lowered itself to hover just over the floor.

"I am Gabriel," he said.

And Bohannon recognized the face.

He didn't know whether to cry or laugh, kneel or run. He felt secure and insane at the same time. This was the face he had seen in the *gniza* of the Ades Synagogue, the Gabriel who had spoken to him and Annie—or the young man's angelic twin—about three times the size.

"I . . . we . . ." Bohannon's lips moved, but his mind no longer worked. Every conscious cell in his body focused on the face. Not on the huge wings that now spread out before him, dimming the light. Not on the flaming sword that Gabriel held point-down, his hands resting on the hilt. On the face . . . only the face. Its radiance made the portal gate look like a candle.

Gabriel held out his left hand, palm open.

"You are most welcome. We celebrate your arrival."

Thousands of questions throttled through Bohannon's mind. None escaped.

"You are all welcome here." He gestured toward Annie, Sammy, and Joe, held behind the barrier. "Don't be afraid," said Gabriel.

"Afraid?" said Rizzo, just loud enough to be heard. "He's not the one facing a three-story angel with a flaming sword. I've felt calmer on the Bowery at midnight than I do now."

The archangel Gabriel put his hand back on the sword's grip, leaned on it, and knelt on his right knee, bringing him into closer proximity to Tom, who looked up into his dazzling beauty and felt embraced by all creation.

"You, favored one, have overcome much, learned much, persevered much to reach this point. Well done, faithful servant. We've been waiting for you. Only you could open the gate. But your calling is not yet complete."

Often rehearsed but never answered, the questions came tumbling out. "But why me?" Tom asked. "What do you need with me? You're an angel. You've got power. Why didn't you open the gate? I've been told you're the governor of Eden. So what do you need me for? Why have we been put through all this?"

Tom saw compassion and empathy in Gabriel's eyes.

"You know prayers and questions of 'why' are seldom answered in ways that are clear. Noah asked why. Abraham, David—they asked why. But even when their question of why wasn't answered, they listened and obeyed. They had faith. Faith is the substance of things hoped for, the evidence of things not seen. You have been presented with the same calling. To walk in faith and help bring forth the purposes of the Almighty. Throughout the history of creation, the Creator has called upon men to help work out his plan, because this created earth is the dominion of man. It was given to you to oversee. It was intended for your blessing.

"That plan was corrupted by the evil one who fell from heaven. And since that moment, the Creator's purpose has been to return his creation to the men for whom it was created. Many men have been called to be a part of that purpose. The Creator looks for men who have reverent awe of his presence. Not men who are perfect—there are none perfect, only one. But men who have a heart to earnestly follow the Creator's will and purpose. Men like you.

"It was man who lost his place in the garden. It must be man who reclaims that place. And it must be man who once again is entrusted with the staff of power, entrusted to bring the Creator's purpose to completion in the dominion of man.

"But understand this. The time of the Gentiles is now fulfilled. As there are seven gates to the garden, there are twelve gates to the New Jerusalem, where the One and Only King will reign for one thousand years and his scepter will unleash his power. The 144,000 will come to the Tree of Life for their reward."

Gabriel lifted up, away from the ground. He spread his wings and raised the sword before him, awesome and overwhelming.

"These words are true: 'Then he told me, "Do not seal up the words of the prophecy of this scroll, because the time is near. . . . Look, I am coming soon! My reward is with me, and I will give to each person according to what they have done. I am the Alpha and the Omega, the First and the Last, the Beginning and the End. Blessed are those who wash their robes, that they may have the right to the tree of life and may go through the gates into the city.'"

"These words are true: 'Truly I tell you, some who are standing here will not taste death before they see the Son of Man coming in his kingdom.'"

Gabriel's emerald green eyes focused on Bohannon. "Now is your time. Come. But"—Gabriel pointed his flaming sword at the others—"you may not enter. Stand fast. Do not cross the threshold of the gate. Touch this ground, and you will surely die."

"Tom—"

He turned to look into Annie's face. She was beaming. Not a trace of fear, only beatific joy and wonder. "Stay here. I'll be back."

39

Tom drew in a breath, and all his courage, and staggered forward, the message to his legs as scattered and erratic as the impressions on his mind. He felt the gate close behind him, heard the thump as its weight settled into place. But he didn't turn around. There was too much in front of him.

As soon as he stepped through the gate, he heard the song.

Not words, so much. Though the song was real, and the singers were real, and they were singing something. But not words that Tom knew or understood. Except for the Great Hallel—a hallelujah chorus that shook the foundations of the garden—that every so often rang out like exploding flames on the surface of the sun.

The song lived throughout the garden. The garden.

Impossible, but here in the bowels of the earth, a thousand feet removed from the sun, the garden was alive. Trees, bushes, shrubs, abundant grass-filled meadows, forested hills, stands of pine soaring high . . . Tom could see it all from where he stood. The green of the garden was intense and expansive, as if he had walked into a home where everything—walls, floors, furniture, curtains, everything—was deep, vibrant, pulsing green. Except the sky.

Whereas the wall and the gates disappeared up into a twilight haze in the higher reaches of the cavern, inside the garden, a bristling blue sky stretched beyond his sight, so pure it dazzled his senses—as if the sun were shining through the pristine prism of Caribbean cerulean. A breeze, strong but soft, comforting yet refreshing, invited the leaves and bushes, the blades of grass, to dance to the song.

Across the vast reaches of the garden, all living things moved. Trees remained bound by their roots but not by their molecules. It wasn't as if the garden were suffering through an earthquake, everything swaying at the mercy of the shifting earth. No, this was a choreographed expression of joy, the explosion of ecstasy in response to creation. All things were swept up in the song and its luxurious rhythm.

Tom felt himself swaying, rocking back and forth on the balls of his feet, unable to control the movement of his body in response to the invitation of the dance. The blood pulsed in his veins, keeping perfect time with the pulse of life that washed like a tide against his skin.

The light lived, a heartbeat that encompassed all. In the background of the song, the light thrummed an accompaniment, in unity of motion with the dance, in unity of spirit with the song. Dizzying, electrifying, exhilarating—the song and the ballet and the light gave glory to God and his Creation.

In the middle of it all stood the trees.

Tom couldn't tell if the trees were the source of the song, the rhythmic movement, and the light. But the trees shimmered, they pulsed, they beat like a great, cosmic heart pumping life into the far reaches of the garden.

There was no telling how long he stood there, just inside the gate, absorbing the magnificent celebration unfolding before his eyes. Content, he probably could have remained in place for a long time. A lifetime? But suddenly he felt the urgency to move forward.

Tom shifted his weight to the left, began lifting one foot—and was airborne.

Not flying. He wasn't off the ground far enough to call it flying. Skimming.

Not levitating—that signified floating in place. No, this was skimming, moving like a breeze just above the blades of grass, his feet not touching the ground, his mind dictating his direction. Slowly, languidly he drifted, drawn toward the trees.

Two of them stood in a small glade, framed by a few low, green hills. Healthy, vibrant, large-limbed trees, profuse with glossy-surfaced leaves. As Bohannon was beckoned nearer, they appeared identical. Their pulse was a symphony, sung in duet. He was at peace, all sense of dread suspended at the gate.

He settled to the grass like mist in the morning, a caress on the ground, about twenty feet away from the trees. This close, he could hear the hum and see the vibration in the trees' bark at the same time, like a giant bow string loosed. Bohannon studied the two trees, looking for the staff, looking for some way to differentiate between the Tree of Life and the Tree of the Knowledge of Good and Evil. When he saw the fruit.

Apple was not an apt description. They were round and red, yes. But, oh, so much more. Supple, luscious, crimson, dew running over their sides, heavy droplets imploding in the soft earth. The luminescence of the skin glowed like a holiday lantern. And the smell—his grandmother's apple pie just from the oven, the juice still bubbling up its side.

Tom tasted the aroma, feasted on the beauty. His mouth began salivating.

He heard a whisper on the inside of his ear. "Not for you, son of man."

A brisk breeze wafted across his eyes. Bohannon blinked, and when he looked again, the tree with the fruit had split down its middle. In the midst of the rent trunk, held fast by its host, stood the crook of a shepherd's staff. The life coming forth from the staff was abundant. It sprouted branches, and flowers budded and bloomed from every branch.

Bohannon tried to will his body to skim once more over the grass, but it wouldn't move. Every element of his consciousness fell like gravity upon that staff of wood. He was euphoric in response to the song and the dance, apprehensive in the enormity of his location, but fascinated and drawn to the reality of Aaron's staff, not twenty feet away. And he couldn't move.

Reluctant to touch anything in the wrong way, he wondered how he was to get the staff.

You receive it.

Tom felt his right arm—painless now—rise from his side until it was parallel with the ground. The fingers of his right hand opened, his palm held out before him. He stood as if beckoning to the trees, to the staff.

A shaft of brilliant sunlight fell on the staff, blinding Bohannon for an eye-blink as a thud hit his right palm and drove him back a few steps. His sight clearing, Bohannon stared at Aaron's staff, now as firmly planted in his hand as it had a heartbeat before been planted in the Tree of the Knowledge of Good and Evil. The staff felt warm, a fading sizzle withdrawing into its supple bark. As he watched spellbound, the budding and blooming branches of Aaron's staff withered and receded, some fell to the ground. And the staff died in his hand.

He turned it over, as if there might be some other result on the opposite side, but the staff had not only fallen dormant, it was dead. Not only withered, but also dried, cracked, a knot hole opening just below the crook, a fissure opening a third of the way down the bark and running half its length. It felt, and looked, thousands of years old—heavy, yet brittle. More like stone than wood.

Bohannon brought the staff to his chest and held it securely, both hands cradling its length and supporting its weight.

He looked up to the trees, and realized the song had ended. The light was fading. The pulse of the dance slowed to a stop. As he watched, the staff tight in his grasp, the garden of God became vapor before his eyes. The hills evaporated. The meadows floated away in a swirling mist. Alone, twilight closing around them, the trees began to eject their leaves in great explosions of green.

⌁∧∿⌁

They waited outside the gate and, every so often, touched the invisible barrier that barred their way to the garden. Annie stood quietly, her hands resting against the barrier, her eyes closed, praying for her husband's safety, while Joe prowled a tight circle, anxiety showing in every step.

"How can you be so calm?" Joe said as he passed Annie on one of his circuits.

Annie glanced over her shoulder at his passing. "Because Tom is in God's hands—more now than ever before in his life. If I can't trust God to keep my husband safe now, when can I? Where can I?"

Joe stopped with a jolt. His head down, he ran a hand across his face, then he turned to Annie. "But how can you be sure? I mean . . . I believe there's a God." He waved his hand. "How could I ever doubt what the Bible says now? But disasters happen. People get sick and die. There's evil in the world. I believe there's a God, but how can I be sure enough to trust him all of the time?"

"That's one of the gifts of prayer, Joe. Peace. A peace that surpasses circumstances. I was really anxious when we came up to the gate, too. I've been anxious and frightened for months. But now? Now I'm peaceful. As long as I'm praying, I'm peaceful. It doesn't—

"Ooohhh." Annie glanced up as the light in the cavern began to fade, as if someone was using a master dimmer switch—even affecting Joe's flashlight. Twilight was descending rapidly, promising imminent darkness.

"Oh, this is not good," said Rizzo.

40

Before he could blink, utter darkness engulfed him. Tom stood rooted to the spot. He didn't know what to do next. It was as if he had lost his sight in some cataclysmic accident, the blindness was so complete. How could he take a step? Which direction could he go?

"Annie, can you see anything?"

Joe's voice—close.

"Where are you?"

Annie's voice!

"Annie?"

If it hadn't been for the voices, when the hand touched his shoulder he probably would have suffered a heart attack from fright. Holding fast to the staff, Tom swept out with his left hand toward Annie's voice and almost immediately felt his fingers against her cheek.

Their words jumbled over each other as they came together in a knot, hugging each other tightly.

"How did you get here?"

"Where is here?"

"Did you find it?"

"Did God give you a free pass to heaven? I might need it."

"I've got it."

"I can feel it," said Annie.

"Where's the flashlight?"

"Kaput."

"Well, the staff is kaput, too. It was alive in the tree. But now it's dead and dried—like it's been petrified." He could feel Rodriguez's hand on his shoulder. "Now what?"

"Now would be a good time for the marines," said Rizzo. "Except they couldn't find us. Hey, Tom, maybe you could part the darkness with that magic stick of yours."

"I'm not waving this at anything or anybody, I don't care how dead it looks. Listen, does anybody have any matches?"

"Oh, man. What a doofus," said Rizzo. "Wait a minute. I've got a lighter in my pocket, if it's still there. Low tech. You're a genius."

The shaft of flame seared Bohannon's eyes as Rizzo held up the cheap lighter. "Left over from a U2 concert," said Rizzo. "They were pretty good, so I've got no clue how much fuel is left. Can anybody see anything?"

———

"Can you see anything?"

Michael Papa, standing on the Land Rover's hood, scanned the darkness with his night-vision binoculars. "Nothing. There's nothing moving over there."

It had been too long. Whalen knew that. After he and Atkins, double-timing on foot, made it back to the rally point on the far side of the gaping square that was once the Tower of Babel's foundation, he wrestled with what to do next. He and his men were exposed, sitting next to this hole in the ground. The crew had converged on the rally point and decided to wait, and hope, for some kind of contact with Bohannon and the others. Time was running out.

"Somebody is going to wander down this way sooner or later," said Papa.

Whalen walked over to the verge of the huge, square hole that fell away into the depths of the desert and sat on an earthen mound that rimmed the foundation. They still had a couple of hours before the sun came up, but he wanted to be long gone from here by then. He didn't want to be anywhere in the open when it got light.

Sal Molluzzo, the mechanic, drifted over next to Whalen, planted his boot on the dirt rim, and leaned against his thigh. "One of the Rovers has a puncture in the gas tank. I've plugged it for now."

"Okay . . . thanks. Everything else in shape?"

"For a bunch of beat-up old beasts, these vehicles are—Hey! What's that?"

Molluzzo was looking past Whalen's shoulder, down into the hole of the foundation. Whalen swung his legs around to the other side of the mound and followed Molluzzo's gaze into the black below them.

"Do you see it?" asked Molluzzo.

Far below, a speck in the dark void, but a visible speck—a wavering light breaking the darkness. "That's a flame. Sal, get the sealed beam."

⟞⟋⟍⟍⟞

"Here, Sammy. Let me hold it up higher," said Rodriguez. He took the lighter and held it high over his head. "It doesn't throw much light. I can't see anything except my feet."

"Those boats—who could miss them? I think . . ."

⟞⟋⟍⟍⟞

"Do you think it's them?"

Atkins was hovering over the hole with the rest of the team at his side. "Could be the bad guys."

"Gotta take the chance," said Whalen. "Who else would be deep under Babylon in the middle of the night? Sal, do you have the hood secure on that beam?"

Molluzzo was lying flat on the ground, his arms extended into the open foundation. The sealed-beam light was held at arm's length and had a fiberboard hood around it—like blinders on a racehorse. The light would shine down, but very little of it would be visible above the hole . . . or a half-mile away in Babylon. "Set to go."

"Hit it."

He snapped on the high-beam spotlight that the *National Geographic* crew often used on night shoots and directed the beam into the famous tower's foundation, toward where they had seen the flickering light.

⟞⟋⟍⟍⟞

A bright bolt of light from above split the darkness and covered them with a shimmering twilight. Joe looked up, waiting for judgment.

⟞⟋⟍⟍⟞

Whalen strained his eyes to see something, strained his ears to hear anything.

"Flash the light, Fred. Two long, three short."

———〜〜〜———

"That's them! That's Whalen." Annie squeezed Bohannon's arm. "It's a night signal we used to use on shoots. It means 'good to go.' Joe, three long, two short to respond."

———〜〜〜———

"Bingo. That's them. Grant, do we still have that block-and-tackle gear?"

"Yeah. It's stowed in my Rover."

"Get it. Quick. We need to move."

———〜〜〜———

The spotlight was now shining into the foundation, reflecting off the walls and providing a diffused, gray twilight where Bohannon and his team waited at the bottom of the deep hole.

"How did we get here?" asked Rodriguez. "I mean, it doesn't really matter, does it? But still. We didn't move after the lights went out. And we sure weren't standing under that opening. But without moving, here we are?"

Bohannon looked up at the rim of the opening, so far above. "I'm more concerned about how they're going to get us out of here. That's a long way."

"Maybe we'll just take the elevator," said Rizzo. "They can beam me up, feet first, for all I care. As long as I don't have to ride the rapids again."

Bohannon kept his eyes on the opening, mumbling to himself. "Elevator. That's what I'm afraid of."

———〜〜〜———

Whalen finished printing his instructions, rolled up the paper, fastened it with some twine, and then tied it to the bosun's seat swinging from the end of the rope that was threaded through the assembled block-and-tackle. Normally, this rig was used for dropping a photographer over a cliff, or off a wall—somewhere you couldn't get to by walking or climbing. The other end stretched back to the nearest Rover and passed through a pair of pulleys, Bowman and Vordenberg ready to lower and hoist as needed.

"What are you telling them?" asked James Leonard.

"One at a time, sit in the middle of the seat, don't move around a lot, and Annie should come out first. Something else?"

"Yeah," said the Brit. "Don't dawdle."

———

Annie and Joe got up without a hitch and Rizzo was singing an aria as he was pulled up through the foundation. Bohannon was checking out his body, trying to figure out what worked and what didn't.

He imagined he looked like Bruce Willis near the end of a *Die Hard* movie. Both his knees ached from his collision with the cave wall as he was washed along the underground river. His head hurt from hitting something, his wrists were sore, and his right shoulder was a mess—worse after Joe had pushed down with his 220 pounds, trying to free Rizzo. Before she was lifted out, Annie fashioned a rudimentary sling from some strips of cloth, and Tom tried to keep his right forearm against his chest to minimize the pain. Joe had offered to carry the staff when he was pulled up to the surface, but Tom already felt a strong attachment to this stick and wasn't about to let it out of his sight. He had crossed his left arm over his right, cradling his right elbow in his left hand, the staff resting in a left-to-right angle between his two arms.

Now he felt pretty foolish for refusing Rodriguez's offer.

———

"Where's the line for the Log Flume ride?" Rizzo was swaying above the hole in the earth, his head bobbing and his legs flapping. "And after that, the Mad Tea Party ride."

Rizzo flipped Whalen the lead cord and the ex-SEAL pulled him over to solid ground.

"C'mon. Move it. We need to get Bohannon out of that hole and get ourselves out of town."

Vordenberg pulled Rizzo from the bosun's chair and swung the arm back out over the foundation hole. "Go ahead. Drop it down."

———

If he kept his thoughts on his aches and pains, Bohannon didn't have to worry his mind or kick in his fear of what was coming next.

Rizzo's singing had faded, and then stopped, as he got near the rim of the foundation.

Bohannon looked up. The harness was dropping like a stone. In a flash his heartbeat started racing, his breathing became labored, and he broke out in a clammy sweat that gave his body the shivers. He couldn't remember how long he had been terrified of heights or why it had started. But he knew the next ten minutes would probably be the longest of his life.

The note was still tied to the cross-hatch of canvas strips that made up the bosun's seat, but he remembered what it said without reading it again: *Sit still. Don't move around. Stay in the middle of the seat.* "God, help me."

Bohannon had the staff tightly pressed to his chest as he tried to hold every muscle in his body fixed in place. Eyes closed, he was thinking of anything to keep his mind off the ascent and what was below. Whether the Phillies' aging lineup could manufacture one more run at the World Series, whether it was possible to make an ice cream better than Ben & Jerry's chocolate, whether Jimmy Fallon could live up to the legacy of Jay Leno or Johnny Carson. It was working. Bohannon's mind was half-a-world away. Maybe he nodded out. It had been a long time since any of them slept. Didn't matter. He started back to consciousness, half in and half out of the harness. As he reached out with his left hand and grabbed the side of the harness, his right hand lost its grip on the staff, and it started to slide. His eyes flew open.

There was no substance, no structure to the bosun's seat harness, just strips of canvas. Nothing to hold his body steady. Even the motion of reaching out with his left hand made the harness unstable.

All this in the split second it took for two things to happen: Bohannon clamped his knees on the staff like vise grips. And his open eyes stared into the void far below. Enough light to see the deep, not enough to see the bottom. Far. Down. His body tripped into a state he had visited many times before, whether he was watching a movie or standing on the edge of a cliff.

An electric current ran a loop between his shoulder blades and sent shivers of shock down his spine and into his legs. At the same moment, a wave of nausea filled his throat, and behind his eyes vertigo made him light-headed. They all combined to make Bohannon feel certain that he was about to launch himself, hurtling and screaming, into the pit.

Forget sitting still. Forget everything. Bohannon wrestled with dual reali-
ties of critical importance that flashed through his thoughts but supplanted his
reason. Save the staff! Save yourself! *God, help me.*

"Hey!" came a shout from above. "Grab the rope!"

The rope!

It was a moment of selfless decision. He let go with both hands. As his right
hand grabbed hold of the shaft of Aaron's staff, Bohannon's left hand shot up,
flailed about, then seized the knot where the rope was secured to the bosun's
seat . . . the rope to the surface . . . the rope that was secure. The seat rocked violently from the two desperate stabs that generated force in opposite directions.
Bohannon still imagined himself falling into the abyss, but he strained every
muscle in his left arm to pull himself deeper into the bosun's chair, hand and
knees squeezing the staff hard against his body.

Bohannon pressed his eyes shut, shivered in a breath, and held fast not only
to the rope, but also to his lifeline. *Thank you, Lord.*

⌇⌇⌇

A light breeze added to the chill of the desert night, and once Molluzzo switched
off the sealed beam, only the stars and a crescent moon filtered the darkness.

Whalen helped Tom regain his balance, Annie on his opposite side, cradling Tom's right arm, as he slipped out of the bosun's chair at the rim of the
foundation.

"We almost lost you there."

"No sweat." But Bohannon's throat was as dry as the wadi that hid their
tents. His voice croaked, and his words caught.

"You got him?"

"Yes, and I'm not letting go," said Annie.

"Okay. We gotta get moving. James, break down the rig. I don't want to
leave any trace, anything that could be followed. Grant, night lights. Steve,
pull out two of the H&K MP7s, one in the front vehicle with us, the other in
the rear vehicle with Fred. Grab that 357-magnum Desert Eagle for you—we
may need the punch. And give one of the longer gun cases to Bohannon for
that stick."

⌇⌇⌇

Gamal prepared his men as best he could. Three were with him, a few hundred meters south of the provincial police outpost at the main entrance to Babylon, Saddam Hussein's re-creation of the Ishtar Gate. They were behind a small mound of sand, each on one knee. Their car sat behind them, the engine idling. One had come on a small motorcycle.

Two other men were at the back gate, though there were grave questions about the reliability of the battered Jeep they drove. And two were mobile, circling the ancient city on an all-terrain vehicle stolen from the police supply depot, but focusing primarily on the northern perimeter—the direction they expected the *National Geographic* team to take once they left the city.

Gamal cursed the dark, and the lazy police who failed to demand that the American photographers follow the rules and leave Babylon at dusk. The dark was as heavy as the heat of day, impenetrable where there was no light. But it was the lights that Gamal hoped for, the lights of the Americans' vehicles leaving the city. The lights he would follow to their camp.

—∿〰—

They gathered in a small knot between the first and second Rover, Whalen and his crew. Vordenberg and Atkins finished wiping down and oiling the guns, James Leonard was handing out charged batteries for the radios, and Molluzzo was done with his final check of the Rovers. The civilians were at the back of the last vehicle, surrounding Bohannon and staring at Aaron's staff.

"We going to make a run for it?" asked Bowman.

"I don't think so," said Whalen, keeping the volume of his voice down. "Most of our gear is still at camp, and that belongs to *NG*. Besides, we can navigate back to camp because we know its coordinates."

"Whoever was chasing these guys knows we're around here somewhere," said Atkins. "And this is their turf, not ours. The sooner we're outta here the better."

Whalen nodded his head. "I know, I know. But, look . . . we're not going anywhere but camp until it gets light. The last thing we want is to be wandering around in this desert in the middle of the night, looking for a way to escape. We can't use the roads. We don't know if there is any chance of getting Bohannon and his team back to Baghdad. Even if we knew where we were going for sure, there are ISIS bands out there, marauding tribal raiders, and now more military. Civil war is about to engulf this country. Yes, we need to get out of here, and we need to get out quickly. The problem is figuring the right way to do that without getting us all killed in the process. So we get back to camp, try to get some sleep, wait until it's light, and hope no camel-jockey stumbles across us in the dark. We need to understand our options and then try to pick the best one. For now, let's see if we can get back to camp without picking a fight."

⸎

Gamal toggled his radio. "Do you see anything?"

"Nothing has come through the back gate. No one has even come near it," said a weary voice. "How long do we wait?"

"Until I tell you!" Gamal's nerves were rattled, his anxiety growing. There had been no word from his men on Procession Street since they reported something moving in the shadows of twilight. They were good men. They would have contacted him if . . .

He radioed to the men in the all-terrain vehicle. "Hassan, do you see anything?"

"I would have called you if I did. We've been around the city twice, up and down this side countless times. We've seen nothing, no lights, no vehicles, no movement at all. As if the ruins have gone back to sleep."

"Well you had best remain awake. Take another sweep around the city. Move slowly. Check for tire tracks. They didn't come out this way, either. They must be somewhere, but it's not here. Look closely. We must find them." His voice lowered, almost to a whisper, as if the words were only for him. "We must."

⸎

The red night-vision lights welded to the front bumper of the Land Rover turned the ruined clay brick walls into a nightmarish landscape as Mike Whalen threaded his way through the most dilapidated and ignored streets of ancient Babylon, south of the palace and Procession Street. The light was low to the ground and illuminated only a small arc around the front of the Rover, but it was enough to guide Whalen and his team along the rubble-strewn streets until they emerged into the unmarked desert.

Atkins watched the GPS screen, hooded with cardboard to minimize the light emitted. Whalen would drive, but it was Atkins's job to concentrate on the GPS and guide them in the right direction. South, away from Babylon and farther away from Hillah and Baghdad, deep into the desert, where they would not be expected to hide.

41

After being transformed into the Clemente Soto Velez Cultural & Educational Center, the old PS 160 school at the southwest corner of Suffolk and Rivington Streets on the Lower East Side of New York City got a new lease on life, but little else. It took up half a city block and, except for its community center designation, would have long ago succumbed to the wrecking ball, making way for another modern apartment tower. But neither the community nor the myriad poor arts groups that used it—nor the city itself—had the necessary disposable funds to fix its roof or improve its heating system or to do anything about saving the elaborately carved, but deteriorating, granite façade. Still . . . it survived.

A small but well-reviewed acting troupe, the American Bard Theater Company, was staging its final performance of *As You Like It* that night. So as the several-dozen friends, fans, and family lingered in the lobby prior to the performance, Rory O'Neill led Connor Bohannon and Stew Manthey around the edge of the theatergoers into a hallway and up a flight of stairs to the second floor. O'Neill turned to his left at the top of the stairs and walked to the front of the building, entering a room that spanned the southwest corner.

Inside the room, two men dressed for the Lower East Side—old jeans, ratty tee shirts, worn sneakers, needing a shave—stood by the windows, binoculars to their eyes as they scanned the streets, both talking into filament microphones that looped over their ears and held receivers in place.

"I think the two of you have suffered enough that you've earned the right to be here," said O'Neill, the New York City police commissioner. "I just don't want you on the street."

O'Neill walked to the window on the right, the one that looked down into Suffolk Street, and stood on the opposite side of the officer with the binoculars. He motioned Connor to join him and for Stew to take up station in the other window.

"Try to stay out of sight, but take a look into the street below and tell me everything you see."

Connor peered around the side of the window looking south, down Suffolk, and then stretched his neck to look uptown. The sun was still an hour from setting, and even though shadows were growing longer, there was still enough light for good visibility on the street. "Two women, Hispanic looking, talking on the far side of the street, shopping carts by their sides. A taxicab, looks like he's waiting for a fare. At the corner, a UPS truck—double-parked—the driver making a delivery to the corner bodega. And a lot of pedestrians."

O'Neill nodded his head and looked over at Manthey. "Stew?"

"Mr. Softee truck down below—I'd know that music anywhere—and a corner vendor's truck selling pita and falafel. Mailman walking down the street. And a—"

"Site two has eyes on Clinton at Stanton. Walking south," said the officer across the window from Connor.

O'Neill tipped his head toward the window. "Watch."

Connor shifted so he could watch north on Clinton Street. A bicycle-riding messenger came south on Clinton.

"Messenger, double back and ride west on Rivington," crackled out of a radio.

The messenger turned left on Rivington and, halfway down the block, made a U-turn and waited on the sidewalk.

"Postman, north on Clinton."

The mailman turned left, north on Clinton.

"Ladies to the bodega."

"Subjects have crossed Clinton to the east side," said the other officer. "Still walking south."

Connor watched as the ballet continued outside his window. Then he saw two men walking south on the east side of Clinton. They looked like merchant sailors, sea bags slung over their shoulders. And they looked familiar.

"Hey," and he pointed.

"Yeah," said O'Neill, "those are your boys. Keep your eyes open."

"And joggers south on Clinton."

The two men approached the corner of Clinton and Rivington, where the bodega was situated.

"Bring up the bus. UPS into the truck."

Approaching from Rivington, heading east, an Access-a-Ride van—the city's on-call transportation system for the disabled—slowly approached the Clinton intersection.

The two men turned the corner onto Rivington Street, walking east.

"Ladies out . . . joggers pass 'em . . ."

The white-and-blue Access-a-Ride van slowed to a crawl as the joggers ran past the two men, the ladies with the shopping carts came up behind, and the UPS driver came out of his truck.

"Out of sight . . . take 'em now."

If Connor hadn't been keenly watching each move, even he might have missed what happened next. In near flawless choreography, the joggers turned abruptly and ran straight at the two men, who stopped in their tracks and were bowled over by the shopping carts. Before they could fall to the sidewalk, the two joggers latched on to one of the men, the two ladies—who now lost their wigs—manhandled the second, while the UPS man threw open the side doors of the Access-a-Ride van. The two men with the sea bags were inside the van along with their captors, the doors closed, before Connor could react.

"Whoa!"

"Not over yet," said O'Neill.

"Postman, take the door. Messenger, the back alley."

"Halfway up the block on Clinton," said O'Neill, "Keep an eye on the building they came from. C'mon over to this side."

Connor switched to the far side of the window and looked up Clinton.

An old black car with a Domino's Pizza sign suction-cupped to the roof pulled up in front of the same building the postman approached. A very big man jumped out, reached in the back of the car, pulled out a stack of pizza boxes, and bounded up the steps of the five-story walkup.

The taxi pulled up Clinton Street and stopped in the middle, blocking traffic. Two men in Mr. Softee uniforms ran up the sidewalk. The taxi driver and the ice-cream peddlers rushed up the stairs behind the pizza delivery.

"Con Ed, cover the back. Third floor."

A high-flying helicopter materialized from someplace west and stopped, hovering over the building.

"*Go.*"

Connor looked at O'Neill. "Who are these guys?"

The officer on the far side of the window looked over at Connor and smiled. "We call ourselves the Army of the Invisible," he said, turning his attention back to the operation taking place up the street. "You see us every day, but you don't know we're there. NYPD has thirty-five thousand uniformed officers. There are almost—"

The officer put the binoculars up to his eyes. He must have been getting a message.

"*There were five. Con Ed, we've got one on the loose. Be careful. All units, cordon off the area.*"

Connor watched as individuals he hadn't noticed before came out of the community center, out of the bodega, out of an auto garage on the far side of Rivington Street. They all converged on the center of Clinton Street, taking different routes.

"*Two in hand, sir. One running . . . no . . . got 'em coming down the fire escape. All five in hand, sir.*"

"Good job, Captain," said O'Neill. "Split 'em up. Different cars. Take them to the holding center, separate cells. I think we got them all, but bring in the interrogators, just in case."

O'Neill turned from the window, put his hand on Connor's back. "That's it. Not your TV cop drama, but efficient. You don't have to worry about the Prophet's Guard anymore, at least not here in New York."

Manthey fell in alongside them as they left the room and walked into the hall. "How did you find them?"

"A tip. We got the word out again after they attacked the two of you in the taxicab. Those two were planning to leave the country. They contacted somebody for help. That individual has helped us out before."

The theater lobby was empty as they crossed to the front door of the Clemente Center. "Now what?" asked Manthey.

"Now they go to jail for a very long time."

42

Tuesday, September 1

6:12 a.m., the desert, south of Hillah, Iraq

Under the flaps of the black tent, morning light was a dim intention yet to express itself. Annie Bohannon sat on the edge of a canvas stool, holding the hand and strengthening the soul of her friend, Latiffa Naouri, who had stumbled into camp in the last darkness of night, battered, bruised, and bewildered. But alive. Holding Latiffa's hand, Annie allowed her fingers to linger over her wrist. Her pulse was heavy, rugged, and irregular. But calmer than ten minutes ago.

"I didn't expect to live. I don't think I understand why they let me live."

"Take deep breaths," said Annie. "Tell me what happened."

———∿∿∿———

Latiffa was on her way back to her apartment in Baghdad when the road was blocked by two black SUVs. A third closed from behind when her driver slowed down. "They wanted to know where you were, where your camp was," said Latiffa, as slim fingers of sunlight began to transform the dusky desert floor into subtle hues of tan and blue. "That's all they cared about. I think I gave them directions to the dunes south of al Qasim. I believe . . . I don't know. It's all so blurry. But I didn't want to give you away. I don't think I told them the Wadi Defenneh. I hope not." Her eyes glazed over as she stared into the distance.

"They stopped hitting me. That's when I thought—"

"Shh . . . here, drink some water." Annie handed Latiffa a canteen and used the moment to assess the damage in the growing light. The left side of Latiffa's face was ruined. Wide purple-and-red welts were interspersed with sickly yellow streaks of puffy, swollen skin. Her left eye had been pummeled closed, the eyelid bulging out beyond her left eyebrow. Her nose was traveling in a new direction, and her upper lip had been ripped into two gashes. Annie held a wet cloth to a golf-ball-sized bump, with a bleeding cut, just above Latiffa's temple.

The beating had shattered Naouri's face, but not her resolve.

"One of them must have gotten a message because he came back and told the others that you were in Babylon.

"The men, they left quickly when they got the message. One stayed. But there was a fight. My driver, I think, tried to rescue me. I passed out. There were two bodies by the side of the road when I became conscious." She buried her battered face with shaking hands. "My driver—he had three children. Somehow, I drove here."

"It's a good thing you came back here and not back to Baghdad," said Annie. She pulled a gauze pad and a roll of bandage from the first-aid kit by her feet and carefully cared for the wound above Latiffa's temple. "I don't think you would have made it home." Annie fastened the bandage. "Do you have any idea who these men were?"

Latiffa closed her eyes. The movement of her head back and forth was nearly imperceptible, as if avoiding any further damage. "Special Apparatus . . . the Brotherhood . . . agents from the Prophet's Guard—I don't know. Whoever it is, they are determined to find you. And I'm afraid I may have put you in even more danger. It's possible now they know where to look."

Latiffa swept a handful of hair from her face, back over her head, away from the wound. She turned in Annie's direction. "They lost you in the desert last night. But they will return today. You have no way out."

As she returned the remaining bandage to the first-aid kit, Annie felt a stab of fear about their chances for escape, but then a strengthening determination.

"Annie, you should come over here."

At Tom's voice, her head jerked up. She looked over Naouri's shoulder into the center of the camp and the mounds of gritty desert to the west. In the strengthening light, a long line of camels crested the ridgeline of the deep desert defile that defined the Wadi Deffeneh.

"*You have no way out,*" echoed in her head. Her voice was almost a whisper even to her own ear. "Perhaps we do."

With a purposeful, undulating gait, the camel line flowed along the rim of the ridge, a tide of grunts and tawny fur breaking upon the dawn. A group of riders, some on horses, broke away from the camel caravan, raced down the face of the ridge, and galloped toward the encampment.

Annie got to her feet and stepped from within the shelter of the tent. To her left, looking like they just rolled out of their sleeping bags, Tom, Joe, and two of the *National Geographic* crew were leaning across the hoods of two Land Rovers, high-powered rifles cradled in their arms. *Sweet. Always the protector.*

"Don't shoot . . . it's okay," she said, waving her left hand in Tom's direction. "It's okay."

The palm of her right hand shading her eyes, Annie started walking forward, toward the oncoming riders, not giving Tom a chance to challenge either her or the riders. She felt the thunder of the heavy hooves closing fast, a pungent perfume of musk and camel droppings enveloping her in a swirling cloud of grit and sand that filled her nostrils and covered her hair.

Like a dirt shower falling from the sky, the billows of sand settled around Annie, revealing a glistening, black stallion with heavily muscled haunches. It stopped inches from her face. "Welcome, Wind of the Desert," said Annie as she stood in the shade of the lead rider.

In a flourish of robes, his face still covered by the long tail of his keffiyeh, the rider slipped off the gleaming black stallion and approached Annie. "Welcome back, Lily of the River," he said. "I never thought I would see you again."

—⁓⁓—

"I don't care if he's the Grand Wazoo of Turkmenistan," Tom exploded, "we're not going to tell this guy why we're here. I don't know him. Why should I trust him?"

Annie sat in a camp chair on the other side of the tent, a canteen in her hand, halfway to her mouth. Joe and Rizzo were on her right, Latiffa Naouri stretched out on a cot, and Mike Whalen on her left.

"Because *I* trust him." Annie pushed the words out between her clenched teeth. Her grip on the canteen tightened as her anger and frustration increased. "For the last thirty years, Kabir's tribe has been the only law and order in the western Iraqi desert. He's commander of the Anbar Awakening militia that fought against Al Qaeda and shoulder-to-shoulder with US Marines, driving both the terrorists and the bandits from this section of the country. Kabir bows his knee to no man—certainly not the Prophet's Guard, or the Muslim Brotherhood, or ISIS, or any other group of power-hungry crazies."

Tom paced across the length of the tent. He stopped suddenly and turned to face Annie. "And how do you know so much about this guy who just materialized out of the desert?"

Annie took a long, slow drink from the canteen, selecting her words as if they were ingredients in a recipe. She wiped her lips on her sleeve as she shot a glance toward Sammy. From the look on his face, he appeared to be enjoying the show. She got up from the chair, walked over to Tom, and offered him the canteen.

"I was here at the beginning of my career, doing a photo shoot in Ur. It was before I met you, Tom. Kabir had just driven the worst bandits out of Anbar Province. We asked him for protection. His father was sheik then, but it was Kabir who led the fighters of the Awakening. We spent a lot of time together, then. And he didn't just materialize. I contacted Kabir before we left Jerusalem. Told him where we were headed. And asked for his help."

For an eternal moment, Bohannon felt like his stomach had dropped to the floor and bounced back up into his throat. But then Annie took his left hand, wrapped his arm around her waist, and pressed into his side. There was a twinkle in her eyes. "I'm flattered, sweetie. But that was a long time ago, a long time before you. We were friends. That's all I could offer him."

Annie kissed him. Full and warm, her fingers slipping into the hair at his neck. Doubt . . . fear . . . melted away as his heart began to trip faster. She pulled back and stared into his eyes. "But thanks for the moment, my hero."

He didn't realize Mike Whalen had come up to his side.

"Tom," Whalen whispered, taking Bohannon by the elbow, "come outside for a minute. There's something I want to tell you."

His lips still tasted Annie's as he followed Whalen outside the tent. The *National Geographic* crew leader leaned against one of the Land Rovers and pulled a battered, half-smoked cigar out of his shirt pocket. He pointed the cigar at Bohannon. "You need to understand something about what's going on out here," he said, before tucking the cigar into the right corner of his mouth.

"Back in oh-five, the marines out in this part of Iraq were getting pounded. Fallujah and Ramadi were strongholds of the Sunni militias who opposed both the ouster of their patron Saddam and the American occupation. You gotta remember that Saddam was Sunni and he kept the Sunnis, a minority in Iraq, in power by oppressing the Shiite majority. When Saddam fell and Americans occupied Iraq, it left a power vacuum. One of the biggest mistakes President Bush made was to disband the Iraqi Army and outlaw the top leadership levels of the Baath Party, the Sunnis. Iraq was left without a functioning government and without a functioning military to enforce the law.

"It didn't take long for Al Qaeda to show up. There was an Al Qaeda terror group of fundamental Islamists in Syria. When Saddam fell, Al Qaeda flooded across the Syrian border into Iraq, into the cities of Fallujah and Ramadi. For all intents, Al Qaeda became the rulers of western Iraq. At least, until the tribes rose."

Whalen took the stub of cigar out of his mouth and pointed its mangled, chewed-on end in Bohannon's direction. "The Albu Mahals, a tribe that moved with impunity across the borders of Jordan, Syria, Iraq, and Saudi Arabia, called together the leaders of the tribes of Anbar Province. They were Sunni, but they hated Al Qaeda more than they distrusted the Shi'a. Sheik Abdul led the Anbar Awakening. They called themselves the Sons of Iraq and joined forces with US marines to fight against Al Qaeda. The battle for Anbar Province was one of the most brutal and intense of the Iraq war but, between the marines and the Awakening, they beat the living daylights out of Al Qaeda and the militias and drove them back into Syria. By 2008, the Anbar Awakening was an army of over fifty thousand strong, and the west was secure."

Back in his mouth, the cigar bounced around like moving punctuation. "Today, the situation out here is ten times worse. When the United States pulled its troops out of Iraq in 2011, sectarian violence escalated, and Al Qaeda—now merged with an even more radical group of Syrian jihadists—returned with a vengeance. You know, forty-five hundred American soldiers lost their lives in the eight-year war with Iraq. Well, last year alone over eight thousand Iraqis were killed in this sectarian civil war. Eight thousand in just one year. Just a few weeks ago, this new incarnation of Al Qaeda—ISIS, the Islamic State of Iraq and al-Sham—overran both Fallujah and Ramadi once again and took control of the cities from government troops. Al Qaeda is threatening to cut this country in half. And this guy"—he gestured with his thumb in the direction of Kabir, who was overseeing the care of his camel caravan—"I've heard of him before. Sheik Abdul was his uncle. This guy is now the head of the Anbar Awakening. And he is a fearless enemy of Al Qaeda."

Whalen pushed off the side of the Land Rover and stepped closer to Tom.

"Listen. If Naouri is right, you are not going back to Baghdad, and you are not going back to Israel on some comfortable airplane. If you want to get that package of yours out of here and back to Jerusalem safely, then you better put any concern you have about Kabir aside. Because I think this guy may be the only ticket you have—hey, the only ticket any of us have. If we don't get out of here soon, I can almost guarantee we'll be in a firefight right on this spot. So suck it up Tom, and let's listen to what this guy has to say. And"—he put his hand on Tom's shoulder—"give your wife a break."

Tom grunted. "Let's go talk to the man."

43

Standing in the entrance to the tent, he blocked the light like a robed eclipse. Sheikh Khalid al-Kabir wore the ubiquitous keffiyeh headdress of the Arab male, red-and-white checked, with twin black ropes wrapped around his head to keep it in place, their ends hanging down his back. But the rest of his wardrobe was an anachronism. An open, white muslin robe hung from his shoulders, but it covered a black dress shirt and well-worn blue jeans. A pair of supple, sagging leather boots had lost most of their color to the scoring wind of the desert.

Kabir was taller than Bohannon, his thick, curly, jet-black hair and beard streaked with the gray of leadership and hardship. He was broad shouldered and solidly muscled. Even standing still, Sheik Kabir commanded attention and evoked respect.

Behind the sheikh stood two imposing Bedouin fighters, Kabir's lieutenants. The three of them created a formidable presence. Bohannon felt a shiver of apprehension.

"Hey, Chief." Rizzo sidled up to the surprised Arab. "You got any genies stuffed away in your saddle bags? You know, three wishes and we can all be sipping piña coladas in Barbados?"

A smile on his face, Kabir leaned over toward Rizzo. "You are most fortunate to be a friend of Ann's. Perhaps, I will deal with you later. But first . . ."

Kabir stepped across the tent and stood in front of Bohannon. He looked at the sling once again encasing Bohannon's right arm and offered his right hand.

"Mr. Bohannon, forgive me. In our culture, it is an insult to offer the left hand. I'm grateful for the opportunity to meet you. A man worthy of Ann's love is a man I would be proud to call friend."

Bohannon searched Kabir's face for sarcasm. After a heartbeat, he stepped closer and gingerly grasped the sheik's right hand. A volume of life's experience could be conveyed in a man's handshake. True hearts and trustworthy character are communicated in an instant. Or their opposite. Kabir's hand was rough and calloused, but his handshake was warm, firm, and sincere. In that moment, he won Tom's trust.

"My men and I are at your service," said Kabir. "Tell me, how can we be of assistance?"

"How about making breakfast?" Rizzo was straightening his rumpled shirt. "Pancakes would be great."

‒‒‸‸⌒‸‸‒

Over the next hour, in a surreal summit meeting with the extended members of the team present, Tom and Annie told Kabir and his lieutenants their story of the mezuzah, its secret messages, how it cost some their lives, and why it was still pursued with such violent determination by the Prophet's Guard and the Muslim Brotherhood. They told him about Aaron's staff and what they believed they were called to do now that it had been found.

"But why," asked Kabir, "would God want to remove such a powerful weapon from the garden, where it's been safe for over two thousand years, and bring it back into a world as unstable as this one, into a country as close to anarchy as Iraq?"

"Good question," said Rodriguez. "One we've been asking ourselves. But over the last couple of months, we've been doing a lot of things we didn't understand. Even a biblical scholar wouldn't be able to give us a reasonable answer to that question. It's just pretty clear we've been led to this time, this place, and this responsibility . . . if you can believe that."

Kabir opened his arms and looked down at the long robe covering his jeans. "Because of my clothes, and where I live, you think me a Muslim. That is understandable. But I am not. I am Coptic."

Sitting on the floor, propped up against his pack, Rizzo was now cleaning the dried clay out of his fingernails with the smaller blade of his Swiss Army knife. "Another Coptic? Do you know those guys over in Egypt who are bringing pantaloons back in fashion? The Temple Guard. They saved my butt once."

"Perhaps they had no other choice?"

"Another wise guy. Say, you and Mr. Hilarious Rodriguez should get together sometime for a comedy jam. Slim Jim and the Camel Jockey. Sounds like a fun act. But I've got more important work to do," he said, digging under another crusted nail.

"Most people of our tribe are Coptic Christians," said Kabir. "Copts are the largest population of Christians in the Middle East. Our ancestors originally wandered into Assyria from Egypt. So I am fully aware of the meaning associated with ritual Jewish sacrifice returning to the Temple. You think the staff has a part to play in this final age?"

"When I saw the staff in the garden, when it was still implanted in the Tree of the Knowledge of Good and Evil, it was alive, budding," said Tom. "It glowed and shimmered—pulsed, really—like the entire tree around it. But when it flew out of the tree and into my hand, it deteriorated into a weathered old stick. Our rabbi friend back in Jerusalem said Jewish tradition believed Aaron's staff would become the ruling scepter of their Messiah in the Millennium. For me, that's just too far off, too much to consider. All I know is, after all we've been through, all that's been revealed to us, I believe—we believe—that we've been called to find the staff, to bring it back to Israel, and to leave it someplace safe. We think the Israel Museum. They've kept the Dead Sea Scrolls safe; they should be able to keep this safe."

Sheik Khalid al-Kabir nodded his head. "Then we need to get you to Israel as quickly and safely as possible. Do you have a plan?"

"Our plan ended when the Baghdad airport closed to us," said Tom.

"Then we need a new plan."

⌘

Gamal clutched the Russian-made machine gun close to his chest, the oil smell from the gun barrel competing for supremacy with the dry, desert dust that clogged his nostrils. He felt out of place with these warriors, certainly awkward, because his knowledge of the terrain made him their de facto leader, which increased his unease. He had no trouble directing the efforts of the poor and ignorant local Iraqis who joined their cause. But these men, a dozen heavily armed agents of the Muslim Brotherhood's Special Apparatus unit, professional killers who were flown into Baghdad last night, were trained in terror and torture. Last night, they had ambushed Naouri and beaten out of her the location of the Americans. Normally, the Apparatus operated in smaller teams.

But his leader had brought these men together because of the urgency of the moment and the demands of the one who guided them all. The Americans must be found. He had failed last night. He must not fail today.

Naouri didn't hold up long under the beating, and her directions to the Americans' camp, farther east than he would have imagined, were clear and precise. Even in the barren wastes of the desert, without roads or signs, Gamal and his men had no difficulty following the landmarks Naouri remembered and the direction she mapped out.

His men moved in the shadows at the base of the high-desert dunes, dark within dark evolving across the face of the sand. These Americans must be stopped, but not before they revealed what they knew or surrendered what they had discovered.

They rounded the end of a dune. A huge, hulking shape appeared to Gamal's left. A massive, sandstone pillar, it looked like a giant of a man about to strike a blow. In spite of himself and the directions that led him to this place, Gamal stopped and took a step back. *Left from here, she said. Down the wadi between the dunes.*

He inclined his head to the left and stepped around the rock, the black-clad assassins in his wake.

———— ⌇⌇ ————

Whalen pulled a rolled-up pack of maps out of his Land Rover and spread two out over the vehicle's hood. Rizzo clambered up onto a fender by using the tire as a ladder. Kabir laughed and motioned him closer. "Over here, my feisty friend." He bent over the maps as the others gathered around. He pointed to the large map of the central Middle East. Iraq was an irregular triangle, pointed down—its bottom edge the border with Saudi Arabia, the bottom right point at the Persian Gulf, its right flank bordered by Iran, its left flank bordered by Syria, and Jordan at the blunted lower left point.

"This is the Euphrates, slicing diagonally through Iraq from northwest to southeast and the gulf. On the east, fertile land. On the west"—Kabir's hand moved across one-third of the map—"all the way to the Jordanian highlands and the Lebanon Mountains is the great Anbar desert." He pulled the bottom, more detailed map, to the top.

"You have a few options—none of them good," said Kabir, glancing up at the others. "There are over ten thousand ISIS fighters north of here around Fallujah and Ramadi, and the army is massing a force up there for a counterattack. Obviously, we can't get to Israel by going east into Iran, and traveling south into Saudi Arabia would double the distance for no rational reason. So one possibility is to go west through the desert. Al Anbar is vast and lifeless, larger than the state of California. Crossing that desert in a camel caravan is the safest way. We will never be discovered."

Rizzo looked over at the camels, which the sheik's men were attending. "Hundreds of miles on one of those things? I'll stay here and get chopped into baba ghanoush, thank you."

"How long will that take, by caravan?" asked Annie.

"Two or three weeks, perhaps more."

"Do we have that much time?"

"If you'd ask me, I'd doubt it," said Whalen. "So far, we've been lucky, but it can't last. I think you need to get outta here now, and get as far away from here as possible, as quickly as possible. And I don't think those camels will do it."

Sheik Kabir looked over at Bohannon. Someone would need to decide.

"The longer we possess the staff, the longer we're in danger," said Bohannon. "We get the staff to the museum, and it's over. We're done."

"Very well," said Kabir, "then we do one of two things—we drive west, through the desert, eight hundred kilometers, through Iraq, Saudi Arabia, and Jordan, try to navigate the Karak Gorge and cross the Israeli border illegally, south of the Dead Sea."

Rizzo twisted around on the fender and looked at Kabir as if he'd just spoken Japanese. "Are you a loon? Why don't we just shoot each other in the head?"

Nodding his head, Kabir placed a hand on Rizzo's shoulder. "And you won't like the next option, either." He looked over his shoulder at Bohannon. "Your friend's private jet . . . is it still in Baghdad?"

Startled for a moment, Bohannon shook his head. "I don't know. He said he would send it back if he could." He looked at the powered down satellite phone he'd received from Sam Reynolds strapped to his left wrist. "But if I can reach him with this . . ." He held up his arm.

A quizzical look on his face, Kabir shrugged his shoulders. "Then, here is what I propose. About 250 kilometers northwest of here is the abandoned

Al Asad air base. The air base is massive—twenty-five kilometers across with six runways. It was the headquarters of the Iraqi Air Force and, after the second invasion, the primary land base for Allied air forces. It's been abandoned since 2011, but the runways are in perfect shape. There is a small unit of Iraqi defense corps whose primary job is to patrol the perimeter fence. They have been known to turn a blind eye in the past, for the right consideration. If you can get your friend's jet to Al Asad, it will have no trouble landing on the runway farthest from the tower.

"To reach Al Asad, the most direct route would take us on the main highways, along the path of the Euphrates, through the middle of Fallujah and Ramadi. Not a good idea."

"So far," said Rizzo, "all of your ideas are registering a zero on the Rizz-Man meter. What else do you have up your burnoose, Ahab?"

Kabir looked at Rizzo his eyebrows arched high, and his hand on the curved dagger that he incongruously kept tucked in his belt. "What was it you wanted to be chopped into?"

"Hundred dollar bills? Okay, okay. I get the point."

Kabir nodded and a grin slowly spread to his eyes. "There are two bridges over the western branch of the Euphrates, one north of us at Hindiyah and another about twenty kilometers south. Instead of going north, we'll run south to that bridge, then cut due west, cross country, another twenty kilometers."

He pointed at two vertical lines running north and south along the length of the river on the west bank, opposite Babylon.

"This is the Najaf road," he said, pointing to the road closest to the river. "It would be a good route north. But too obvious and too well-traveled. Over here"—he pointed to the line further west—"is a road with no name, no number. Not a bad road, but less traveled. It passes west of Karbala, east of Lake Razzaza, bypassing both Fallujah and Ramadi. It is our best chance.

"Altogether, over three hundred kilometers—two hundred miles—give or take. With good luck, we should cover the distance in six hours."

"Great," said Rizzo. "Good luck has been as plentiful around here as pickled cobra venom."

"With your permission," Kabir said, nodding toward Whalen, "we make a trade. My camels for your Land Rovers. Two Rovers we send back to Baghdad. One takes Ms. Naouri to get medical attention. The other, with your photo equipment, goes to the airport—in case Tom's magic phone doesn't work—and finds out if the jet was sent back. Tom, can you give them a way to identify themselves that would get your friend to send the plane to Al Asad?"

"I can do that."

"Good. Then the other two vehicles we transform." Kabir turned to his men and spoke a few words of Arabic. They immediately left the tent. He turned back to the assembled team. "We make them disappear. Let's get to work."

———

While Whalen's team struck camp, breaking down the tents and packing their gear in the two Land Rovers, Kabir's men were vigorously working with a concerted purpose, transferring wildly diverse material from the camel caravan to the Land Rovers. Tents and carpets were piled on roofs and hoods, pots and tent poles hung from the sides, making the Rovers look like a Bedouin camp on the move.

"By the way, how did you find us?" Bohannon asked.

"You were given something before you left Jerusalem. Something from an old friend. So you wouldn't get lost."

"Fischoff? You know Fischoff?"

"Well, let's just say the sergeant and I have fought together against the same enemies," said Kabir, "and at times on the same soil. He contacted me after you disappeared from the Tel Aviv airport and asked if my men would watch for your arrival. I told him of the phone call from Ann. That's when he asked if I still had the transponder. We've been closing in on your signal since yesterday."

———

"I would like to take as many of my men as possible," said Kabir. "They know the desert, and they know the way. If anything should happen—"

"It would be best to have as many men as possible," Whalen interrupted. "I know . . . I understand. But I don't think that's the wisest course.

"This isn't a military operation," said Whalen, "it's an escape. Our job is to help get Bohannon, his team, and his package safely out of the country. It's not our mission to take on the Iraqi militias, or ISIS, or anyone else with a gun. If we have to fight our way through to Al Asad we're in big trouble, no matter how many men we can squeeze into those Rovers."

"But these people who are pursuing us, pursuing the staff, will not give up," said Bohannon. "They are determined and ruthless."

"And they will probably pick up our trail, sooner or later," said Whalen. "But I think our best chance is to draw as little attention to ourselves as possible, to blend in, look anonymous, and move as fast as we possibly can—outrun them to Al Asad and hope that the plane is waiting for us when we get there."

Whalen turned and checked the location of the sun, then looked back at Kabir. "I don't think it's healthy for us to hang around here."

"I understand," said Kabir, "but it would be prudent to cross Highway One, the road that connects Fallujah and Ramadi, after the sun goes down."

Bohannon regarded the other two men, the serious but determined looks on their faces. "So, when do we leave?"

Whalen looked at his watch. "Five minutes. We worry about Fallujah when we get there."

—————

Gamal knew it wasn't far now. They were close, perhaps over the next dune. He held up his right hand and turned to the men behind him, putting an index finger to his lips. Twelve heads nodded in response.

The desert here was more pounded grit, tawny brown sandstone ground to coarse pebbles, than the white sand of the Sahara. Gamal split his men into two groups. One group he sent around the dune to approach the Americans' camp from behind. His group would go over the ridge. But they needed to be very careful with their footing.

He checked his watch again. Enough time. He started up the dune, the machine gun held aloft in his left hand, his right hand helping keep his balance on the loose gravel. As he got near the ridge, he knelt on the ground and ventured a peek over the edge. And he could see . . . nothing.

He hoped the woman wasn't dead yet so he could crush her throat with his own hands and watch the light fade from her eyes.

44

The speed—or lack of it—wasn't the driver's fault. Kabir had told him to keep the speed down as they traveled south on Route 70. But the relatively slow pace was eating away at Bohannon's nerves like fingernails on a blackboard. The bridge they were heading for crossed the western fork of the twin-branched Euphrates between Al-Kifl and Qaryat Aqtab, about twenty kilometers south of Hillah. Route 70 was a well-traveled road compared to most in western Iraq, and Kabir made it clear that an extended Bedouin family traveling from one location to another would be in no hurry.

They looked the part of Bedouin nomads.

Each of the men in the Land Rovers wore the ubiquitous keffiyeh. Kabir's bodyguard was driving the lead Land Rover, with Kabir riding beside him. Whalen, Vordenberg, and Atkins were squeezed into the back seat.

A concession to Kabir was to have one of his desert-wise men drive the second Rover. Rodriguez was riding shotgun, a well-worn red-checked keffiyeh making him look like the driver's brother.

Even Rizzo, whose dark features and hooked nose made him ideal for the part, had the scarf affixed to his head with dual bands of thin, black rope, the agal. He sat on a couple of sleeping rugs on the back seat of the second Rover, next to Annie. She was covered head-to-toe in a black burnoose and a light, black veil covered the lower half of her face. It was hot, but it was necessary. Above everything, they wanted to blend in as much as possible, to be invisible to the people around them. Tom was next to Annie, a sweat-stained ghutra, the white version of the checked keffiyeh, on his head.

Bohannon was anything but relaxed. For the first time in months, they were completely dependent on someone else. Aaron's staff was stashed carefully in the back, in a padded weapons carrier, but Bohannon kept glancing over his shoulder to make sure it was still there and to make sure there was no lightning bolt from heaven or angelic death ray shooting out from the bag. He felt like he was riding in the Nitro Express. Slowly.

This was going to be a long day.

11:22 a.m., Riyadh, Saudi Arabia

Saudi King Abbudin had already been surprised once this day. He didn't like surprises, particularly such monumental ones.

The first surprise came when the Swiss and Chinese agreed. It was rare for Switzerland and China to agree on anything. But today, Geneva and Peking agreed to rescue the world's economy. The Swiss bailed out the European Union with an infusion of one billion euros into the European Central Bank, staving off the imminent bankruptcy of half a dozen nations. And the Chinese bought debt around the globe, stabilizing shaky markets from New York to Tokyo.

Abbudin was conferring with his minister of finance and the head of the Saudi Central Bank—both cousins of the family Saud—when his son Faisal brought news of a second surprise.

Crown Prince Faisal, Abbudin's heir and pride, was barely through the door when he began to speak, a breach of etiquette but one his father tolerated on this day. "The Americans are moving swiftly," Faisal declared. "President Whitestone has removed all limits on pumping from the Alaskan oil fields, and he has offered licenses for off-shore drilling and for more drilling in Alaska to American-owned companies only."

Faisal came to the side of the table where his father sat with his ministers. "Even more surprising, the Russians have opened up a new oil field—the Mamontovskoye Field—for the express use of Europe. The field was unknown to us, but it is fully prepared for production. It sits right along the Trans-Siberian pipeline. They can be pumping oil into the pipeline in three days."

A portrait of his father hung over a mantel across the room from where Abbudin sat. He gazed at it with questioning eyes. *What would you think?* His father had dreamed of a moment in time like this, a moment to throw the arrogant Americans under his feet. *What would you do now?*

King Abbudin turned his gaze to his son. "We have lost the initiative and the element of surprise. We have one chance to regain it. Has there been word from Baghdad?"

"I wish there was." Faisal sat at the table on his father's right. "Somehow the Americans have disappeared again. Operatives of the Brotherhood were closing in on them yesterday evening in the ruins of Babylon. Then they vanished, along with some of our men."

"Underground?"

"Perhaps . . . likely."

"How long ago did they vanish?"

"Eighteen hours?"

"Then we must assume they found the garden," said Abbudin. "If they surface—when they surface—we must be prepared to act as if they found the staff and have it in their possession. Get word to all the ISIS commanders to turn the attention of all their men to finding this team of Americans. Tell them to look for the dwarf. And tell the Brotherhood faithful to take to the streets, the roads, the bridges. Find these infidels. Find the staff, and we still have a chance."

Abbudin looked at the portrait once more. *We are so close, Father. So close.*

11:35 a.m., Baghdad, Iraq

The old man in the tobacco shop had never been so frightened. His hands were wrapped together in a knot around the telephone pressed to his ear. The urgency of the demands coming from Riyadh, and the threats that underlay that urgency, once again made him doubt the wisdom of this alliance he'd formed with the Brotherhood.

"We have agents at the airport in both the commercial and private terminals." His explanations sounded like pleas for mercy. "We have teams of men at every bus station, every railway terminal. We've dispatched fighting squads to every major highway intersection and others patrol almost every secondary road."

He listened to the voice on the other end of the phone connection. "No, Your Excellency. We captured one of their contacts yesterday and beat her until we got the information we sought. But she lied to us and then escaped. We surrounded their hiding place, only to find it empty. We will kill her when we find her again."

He listened.

"No. We have no other leads."

The old man wondered if he would see another moon. Unless he succeeded, it was unlikely. His grandson would have only a memory.

"Yes, Your Excellency. We will not give up."

11:54 a.m., Al-Kifl, Iraq

They turned off the approach road and onto the bridge across the Euphrates. Immediately Rodriguez spotted the militia. There were loiterers around the bridge entrance, which concerned him, but a few yards onto the bridge itself, two Jeeps were parked on either side of the bridge, men in ragged, mismatched camouflage and holding automatic weapons standing on the hoods to get a better look at any passing vehicle.

"Don't look."

Rizzo swung his head toward the urgency of Rodriguez's voice, and his gaze drifted past Rodriguez and out the window, toward the men standing on the Jeep along the side of the road. For one fleeting moment, his eyes locked with one of the men.

❦

Kabir turned in the seat and looked over his left shoulder, out the back window of the Land Rover, as they gained speed on the down slope of the bridge. He couldn't see much, or for long. But he noticed that the men who had been standing on the hoods of the Jeeps were gone.

"Faster," he said to the driver.

❦

He was a baker, his shop a prosperous one in the southeast fringe of Baghdad. He owed much to the Muslim Brotherhood, including his bakery. But he was annoyed at being pulled away from his work and his family for this "emergency." At times he wondered if he had bargained with the devil.

The concrete was hot under his feet. Two of his men were on the far side of the road, inspecting the unpaved track that crossed this unnamed highway at right angles and continued into the western desert. He and his men had chased the Land Rovers from the bridge. He feared they had lost the trail at the Najaf Road, but after much delay, one of his men noticed the tire marks in a desolate, unpaved track that led into the desert. Whether by intuition, experience, or the will of Allah, they had followed this far and he had stopped the Jeeps short of the road. On foot, they found the faint residue of desert grit, a number of tire tracks turning off the unpaved east-west trail onto the north-south road.

His driver walked quickly across the road. "There are no tire tracks on the other side, sir."

"They turned north."

"Why would they do that? If these men were taking the Americans across the desert, why turn north?" asked the driver. "There is no benefit to that."

"Unless their destination is in the north. Their way of escape is in the north."

The two men looked up the long ribbon of road. They had worked side by side for nearly three years, occasionally fighting together, and knew each other well. "There is nothing north," said the driver, "except . . ." He looked at his commander. "Al Asad?"

"I don't know," said the commander. "But if I were trying to escape the country, escape detection, this would be a good plan. West is a thousand kilometers of wasteland. South the same. They are not traveling to Fallujah or Ramadi, and they must know they can no longer leave from Baghdad. What does that leave them?"

"But I would not drive on this road past Ramadi," said the driver. "It would be foolish."

"Perhaps. Gashur!"

The driver of the second Jeep trotted up to the road. "It appears that their destination is not west through the desert, after all. We believe they run for Al Asad. Take your Jeep and one of your men and drive quickly to Karbala. Contact Baghdad and tell the leader what we believe. Have him dispatch as many units as possible from Ramadi, some up the Euphrates road, some the interior road, and others into the desert along the wadis. Have some units go directly to Al Asad. Try to reach the air base before them. We may have them in a trap. Go. Quickly."

4:05 p.m., north of Ramadi, Iraq

The lead vehicle on the interior road west of the Euphrates was a well-worn, four-wheel-drive Subaru station wagon with 267,000 miles on its odometer, a hole ripped in the roof above its rear cargo compartment, a heavy-caliber machine gun mounted on the floor and protruding through the hole in the roof.

Kalil Unifa was small and dark, an enigma to his men and a terror to his enemies. An ISIS cell leader from its infancy in Syria, he read the Quran morning and evening and Tom Clancy novels before he went to sleep. He preached benevolence to the poor and death to the infidel with the same passion. And he was fiercely loyal, obedient to death.

"If you were trying to reach Al Asad undetected," Unifa asked his driver, "which way would you go?"

"Wadi Al-Ubayyid," the driver answered without hesitation. "Dry, flat, off the road. It reaches nearly all the way to Al Asad. It would be the best way."

"And if you wanted to intercept these people in the wadi?"

"There is a good place to the north where a rocky hill reaches into, and over, the wadi below. We would see them coming—have good lines of fire," said the driver.

"Excellent. Quickly."

5:44 p.m., Wadi Al-Ubayyid, Iraq

The Subaru pulled onto the low promontory that hung like a nose over the Wadi Al-Ubayyid and stopped well short of the edge. The other two cars came up on his flanks and came to a halt. They held eight men, and only a cursory glance would reveal they were fighters. Green fatigue jackets bleached by the sun barely covered massive shoulders and biceps. They all wore cargo pants of differing hues of gray and boots so battered by the desert and their duty that they were more scuff and scratch than shoes. They wore no hats, but their heads were covered with thick, curly masses of hair, dusted with the residue of the dunes.

Unifa pulled a night-vision scope from his gun bag and surveyed the wadi below. It would be dark soon. He put his hand on the left shoulder of Varun and passed the scope to him. "Do you see that place where the wadi narrows and the large mound is in the middle? Cross the wadi to the far side. Take some of the dynamite and the RPG launcher. Set your charges along the far-side track. Your task is not to harm them or their vehicles, but to chase them to us."

Two men followed Varun as he gathered up the gear and disappeared into the wadi.

He turned to his muscled driver. "Uncouple the fifty. Take it about halfway down the hill. Don't open up until Varun sets off his charges. If they refuse to stop or get through our blockade, destroy the engine of the first vehicle, not the people inside. Be very careful. Do not incur the wrath of the leader."

His mind visualizing the coming encounter, Unifa retraced his steps to the Subaru and opened the rear door. He unloaded three Swiss-made machine pistols and handed those to the men behind him, then pulled out a long, heavy sniper rifle, affixed the 10X scope onto its stock, and lifted it onto his shoulder.

"Scour the hillside. Find any large stones or wild brush and bring them to the floor of the wadi. We will build a barricade on the near side. We will stop them and hold them until the leader arrives. Go."

45

Tom jumped out of his sleep, wrestling to find a way out of the blackness. Fear ripped through him. Memories of the cave crashed through his mind.

"It's okay." Joe's voice. "We're just slowing down."

Tom drew in a hot breath of the desert, drying his mouth even more, and tried to focus his eyes. The Rovers were covered by the false twilight cast by a sharp narrowing of the wadi's walls, the dry riverbed twisting through a series of tight turns. He must have dozed somewhere after they turned off the road. The Rovers pulled to stop, tightly hugging one of the walls. Bohannon opened the door and stepped out. He was so sore, even his eyes hurt. He leaned over, his hands on his knees, and tried to stretch out the aches.

"Where are we?"

Whalen's voice to his left.

"Just below the oasis."

Curiosity gnawed at Tom. Above them was Abraham's Oasis, a long, thin ribbon of green grasses, palm trees, and marshland surrounding a small, still lake. Kabir provided the oasis's history, an unproven legend of speculation that Abraham and his family—at that time more than three hundred trained fighting men, along with camels, goats, dogs, and women, children, and elderly— had stopped at this oasis on their journey from Ur of the Chaldees to Canaan. This oasis sat astride the main caravan route from Ur and was one of the few known oases between Ur and Haran, making it a likely resting place for any travelers heading west.

Perhaps fanciful conjecture, but the local Bedouins believed the legend and passed it down as gospel from generation to generation.

Whether Abram ever drank from this pond or rested under its palm trees was less critical than discovering what occupied the space now.

"Let's take a look."

Tom pushed his body upright, stretching out the hurts. "I'm going, too."

They climbed the steep sides of the wadi along a track that was more likely intended for goats. Below the summit, Kabir stopped and peeked over the edge. Tom watched as Kabir's body visibly tensed. He waved them forward with exaggerated caution, which is when Tom noticed that Rizzo was right on his heels.

"I'm not going to miss this," Rizzo whispered.

Tom raised his head above the lip of the desert floor and was surprised that the sky was purpling in the west, the sun gashes of orange behind low clouds. Maybe it was because he slept, but he thought it was early to be getting dark.

Kabir pointed off into the distance and passed the binoculars to Whalen.

"Three vehicles . . . I could see only two men," said Kabir.

"There must be others waiting for us," said Whalen. "Where would they be hiding?"

"They would expect us to come along the main channel of the Wadi Al-Ubayyid, over there to the west where they are."

"Can we get around them?"

Kabir touched Whalen on his left shoulder and pointed farther south. "The militia is not our only problem."

Bohannon looked to the south. The low clouds he had noticed to the west obscured the sun. Then he looked closer. The clouds were boiling along the surface of the desert, not dipping from the sky. They covered the horizon, left and right, for as far as he could see in either direction. They were brown. And they were advancing.

"The Great Anbar Storm. The last one I encountered was fifteen hundred kilometers high, almost a mile," said Kabir.

Tom's eyes could not break from the roiling mass rolling in their direction.

"Sandstorm." Rizzo was by his side. "I saw one, almost got eaten by it, in Egypt. This one looks pretty ticked."

"How far away?" asked Whalen.

"Thirty minutes, perhaps less," said Kabir.

"Looks like a brown ocean. Can we outrun it?"

"No."

⸺∿∾⸺

"Commander!"

"Yes, I see it. A little sand. Tell the men to stand fast."

⸺∿∾⸺

Kabir's men, the two drivers, were quick and precise, wrapping the two engines in rugs that had been strapped to the cars. Kabir and Whalen's men rigged the tents to extend from the wadi's walls, over the Rovers, and down the far side. Tom, Annie, Joe, and Rizzo had sparingly used their precious water to wet down torn cloth and then stuffed it into every vent and over every window, which were cranked up tight. Not impervious to the coming sandstorm, but better protected. The wind was growing in ferocity, and they could hear a thick rumble coming closer and closer as they piled into the vehicles and took cover.

Their driver, silent most of the trip, climbed in last, took a length of cloth, and wrapped it over his nose and mouth, motioning for each of them to follow suit.

"Hey, Lone Ranger, are the masks necessary?" Rizzo wrapped his cloth strip around his forehead. "Yo, I'm Rambo!"

The driver looked at Rizzo in the rearview mirror. "The sand will suck the oxygen out of the air and out of your body. Be careful, or you may turn to stone."

"I've always wanted to be immortalized," said Rizzo. But he quickly pulled the strip off his forehead to cover his mouth. "Hey, Abdul, how many—"

The wind-driven sand slammed into the far wall of the wadi with the thunder of a passing freight train, rolled back over the floor of the gorge, and rocked the Rover with such force that the left side of the vehicle was thrown into the wadi's bank. The desert's brown grit pummeled the Land Rover on three sides, invading the Rover's interior through unknown openings. Soon, the silt-like particles were falling like rain inside the car.

Tom had taken off his chamois shirt and draped it over Annie's head, supplementing the robe and veil she had worn through most of the trip, and now had his arms wrapped around her shoulders, trying to protect her in any way possible. He figured his wife must be getting awfully hot under there as the temperature in the car continued to climb.

"Does it always get hotter inside a sandstorm?" Joe asked.

"Never," mumbled the driver, barely audible beneath the deafening din.

"Then why does it feel like a sauna in here? The heat is just pouring out from the back of the car."

Tom could feel the temperature rise dramatically on the back of his neck, like the heat of a sunburn. He put one hand at the base of his skull and was assailed by the acrid smell as the hair on his fingers was singed. He pulled Annie away from the back of the seat, fearful that a fire had erupted in the rear of the Land Rover. "Hey—"

The sandstorm stopped.

And the heat disappeared.

Silence.

"It's over?"

"Impossible," mumbled the driver.

"But there's no noise . . . no wind," said Joe.

"No sand," said Rizzo.

Tom heard the conversation, and while he realized that the fury of the storm had subsided, his eyes weren't on the others in the car. Instead he was looking in the back of the car past Annie's head. Blackened spots seeped through the gun bag that held Aaron's staff, and the plastic storage bin alongside the bag was melting along its length.

"Impossible," repeated the driver. "These storms last for hours."

Tom withdrew his shirt from Annie's head and nodded toward the back of the car. "Maybe not. C'mon, Annie, let's get out and take a look around."

⟿⟿

Kalil Unifa knelt in the lee of his car, his jacket wrapped tightly around his head. Varun pressed as tightly into the metal as his leader.

"We can see nothing, Kalil," Varun shouted near his ear. "Bring the men in."

The jacket was poor protection. Unifa had a mouthful of sand particles, his ears were stopped up, and visibility was long gone. "No, find the goggles. We must keep looking."

⟿⟿

Sand fell onto his head as he pushed open the back door of the Rover, but it was the deposit of the storm, not its presence. Bohannon leaned his shoulders out the door and looked up, between a break in the tent. The sky above was blue and bright. He looked forward, past the front Rover. Twenty feet beyond where the Rovers were parked, the sandstorm raged. Tom ducked back into the vehicle, looking first at Annie, then at the weapons bag in the back. "You're not going to believe this."

⌇⌇⌇

They stood between the two vehicles, their heads craned backward, looking in all directions. Surrounding them, on all sides, was a roiling wall of wind-blown brown grit. But where they stood was quiet, peaceful, separate.

Tom held the gun bag by its strap, dangling it in front of him, afraid to touch it lest—what?

Rizzo came up to Tom's side. "Hey, why don't you check out the stick, Tom?"

Looking down, Tom held the gun bag out toward Rizzo. "Curious? Here."

"Yo. I'm already short. I don't need to be deaf and dumb, too. You touch it."

The idea came unbidden, but clear as the sky above them. Tom looked at the bag, took a breath. *God, help me.* Then he started walking away from the Rovers, toward the storm. With each step he took, the storm got no closer. Ten, twelve, fourteen steps and still the wildly whipping waves of sand remained as far in front of him as they had when he started.

Annie was at his side.

"Tom!"

"I know." He turned to the others, open-mouthed between the Land Rovers. "Come on. Let's get moving while we can. I have no idea how long this might last."

⌇⌇⌇

Bohannon's Land Rover was now in the lead, Kabir's close behind, almost knit to the back bumper. And the calm in the midst of the storm traveled with them. It was like driving in a tunnel. Even the sky above them was obliterated by the roaring storm. But down here, as they exited the wadi and swung west following the compass, around the edges of Abraham's Oasis toward Al Asad, a miraculous calm enveloped both the cars and the people in them. And the faster they drove, the faster the storm opened in front of them.

The driver demanded Bohannon sit in the back of the vehicle, not next to him. "Don't point that thing anywhere near me."

But as they raced across the desert flats toward the air base, Rizzo on one side, Annie on the other, Rodriguez draped over the back of the front seat, Bohannon held the gun bag gingerly in his lap. He looked up at his wife. "What do you think?"

"I'm dying to see what's inside," said Annie.

Rizzo bent over and peeked around Tom, his eyes wide. "How soon do you want to get your wish?"

"Sammy, if the staff was a danger to us, we all would be dead by now," she responded. "Go ahead, Tom. Open it. We've got to know."

⌁⌁⌁

The old Subaru's engine cranked in paroxysms of grinding protest, as if ripping itself apart from the inside. Kalil Unifa coughed violently and punched the steering wheel. Even if he knew where to go, even if he knew where the rest of his men were at this moment, he wasn't going anywhere. Building in intensity, the wind buffeted the car even more viciously, and new, thicker clouds of sand streamed in through unprotected openings, replacing more and more of the vanishing oxygen.

Kalil called out to Allah, cursed his luck, coughed up blood, and dreaded his next breath.

⌁⌁⌁

Images from the Bible dashed through Bohannon's mind as he inched open the zipper on the weapons bag. What would he find inside? A budding almond tree? A slithering snake? *I hate snakes!*

As he pulled back the flap of the bag, Bohannon tried to prepare for almost anything. Except this.

It was still a stick. Dead. Petrified like a stone.

"Doesn't look very powerful, does it?" Rizzo leaned a hand toward the shaft, then stopped. "Well, maybe I'll let you handle Moses's missile launcher . . . just in case."

"There's the air base," said Joe.

Bohannon looked up as the perimeter fence of Al Asad emerged from the blowing brown of the sandstorm. As they came closer to the fence, the area clear of the sandstorm now extended before them in an ever-lengthening avenue of early evening sunshine and blue sky.

"Over there," Bohannon pointed over the driver's shoulder. "It's a gate."

He felt the heat just as Rizzo opened his mouth. "How are we . . ."

The jolt of heat raced through Bohannon's right hand and up his arm just as the two halves of the cyclone fence gate blasted inward, off their hinges. The Land Rovers continued moving at high speed toward the long strip of concrete that opened before them. The sandstorm was still raging, but now it was raging on either side of this long runway. The rest of the base, even the control tower, was invisible.

Annie screamed when the voice came from Bohannon's wrist.

"Tom, is that you in those Land Rovers?"

Krupp!

"Alex?"

"Yeah. Thank God you guys got here. We would have been forced to turn back soon. So what happened down there? That sandstorm had everything absolutely obliterated. Then, all of a sudden, you guys just appeared. You made it look like Charlton Heston in *The Ten Commandments*. That sandstorm opened up just like the parting of the Red Sea. Pretty cool special effect. Something tells me I know how you pulled it off. Found it, didn't you?"

"Alex, we've got a lot to talk about. But how about you get us out of here?"

"We're on our way. Wait for us at the western end of the runway. We'll be down in less than two minutes."

⌇⌇⌇

Kabir's driver pulled up to the concrete about two-thirds of the way down, his vehicle facing the runway. Bohannon noticed that Whalen's car continued on another twenty or thirty yards and came to a stop with its front windshield facing away from the runway. *Precautions. Just like Whalen.*

As they all piled out of the Rovers, Tom could see the jet turning into its approach run to the air base from the east. There wasn't a lot of time. Rodriguez was pulling gear out of the car. "Go ahead. Say goodbye," said Joe. "I'll be there in a minute." Tom, Annie, and Rizzo walked toward the other Land Rover.

Mike Whalen met Tom halfway as Annie and Rizzo continued toward Kabir. Tom turned toward the ex–Navy SEAL, another man to whom they owed their lives.

"Don't think about it," said Whalen, reading Bohannon's thoughts. "It's what we trained for." Whalen grasped Bohannon's left shoulder with a level of intensity and sincerity that sent a powerful message. "It's been a pleasure, Tom. A pleasure to play even a small role in what God's got cooking here. And a pleasure to know you. You're a good man, Bohannon. A man after God's own heart. He can do a lot with that. I'll be praying for you."

His eyes blinking, perplexed, Tom tried to absorb the significance of all Whalen just shared when Steve Vordenberg and Fred Atkins joined their boss.

"Good luck, Bohannon," said Atkins. "Stay safe."

"And ask Annie to put in a good word with Vince Kasper," said Vordenberg. "I could use a long vacation after all this excitement."

"Oh! Wait," said Whalen, turning and jogging back to their Rover. Tom looked over his shoulder. He didn't see what he expected. Annie, saying goodbye to Kabir. Instead, Annie was waiting, right behind him. "I already said goodbye," she grabbed his hand as she looked into the sky at the approaching jet. "Oh, Tom. *Are* we finally going home?"

It was Rizzo talking with Kabir. Kabir pulled his curved dagger from its scabbard and, with it laying across his open palms, handed it to Rizzo, who promptly slashed it through the air while dancing around the sheik. Kabir's laughter echoed off the walls of sand.

"Annie . . . here . . ." Whalen called from the other Rover. "You can't forget these."

Hanging from his raised fist Whalen was holding her camera bag. Annie walked over to the Rover while Tom went in Kabir's direction.

"Who knows what images you've got in your cameras," said Whalen, "maybe another cover."

Annie took the cameras in her left hand and threw her right arm around Whalen.

"Thanks, Mike. I owe you big-time."

"Great. Just get me a credit when you score that next cover. Comes with a nice bonus, you know?"

Rizzo was just walking away, still waving the dagger above his head, when Tom came up to Kabir.

Sometimes, words fail a man. Even in those most crucial moments. When the depth of a heart can only be shared by the sincerity of a look. Kabir shared one of those looks with Bohannon and communicated a lifetime.

"I would have enjoyed meeting you earlier, too," said the sheik, stealing the words from Tom's mind. His fingers touched his heart then his lips as he bowed his head in Tom's direction. "May the miles be good to you and bring you safely home."

In the distance, they heard the screech of tires on concrete. Time was short. "Thanks for taking care of Annie when—"

Mayhem made a landing with the Gulfstream.

46

Thump. Thump. Thump. The pounding noise shocked their ears and joined in the ripping rattle of death that advanced down the runway.

Bohannon's head snapped to the east as two attack helicopters swept out of the edges of the storm, their cannons drowning out the *whomp* of the rotor blades, tearing up the concrete at a couple hundred rounds per minute as they advanced on the still rolling form of the Gulfstream.

"Militia!"

It sounded like a hundred muffled voices shouting at once while everything and everyone was moving at the same time. "Take cover. Get off the runway. Get to the airplane."

───≈∿≈───

"Get down," Joe yelled, grabbing Sammy by the shoulder and pulling him into the lee of the Land Rover. Rizzo skidded along the concrete on his knees, crashing into the rear tire with his left hip, pain rushing down his legs like runaway electricity. But as soon as he hit the tire, Rizzo was back up on his feet, peering through the Rover's window as the choppers swept past, their cannons pumping lead.

───≈∿≈───

Spinning on his heel, Tom shot a frantic glance down the runway as he began to run west, not toward the Gulfstream, but toward the Land Rover. Whalen had grabbed Annie and pushed her down against the flank of the vehicle, away from the oncoming choppers, while he joined Vordenberg and Atkins pulling weapons from a compartment underneath the vehicle's floor. Before Tom could call Annie's name, the three combat veterans were launching a fusillade at the swooping choppers. The fury and intensity of their onslaught forced the helicopters to peel away from the landing strip in opposite directions, but the pilots kept their cannons churning, and Tom kept running, as cannon rounds ripped across the back of the Land Rover, shattering glass and shredding metal as the vehicle shook like a dishtowel in a hurricane.

Reaching the Rover, Tom launched himself, covering Annie's body with his own as the roaring fury of the helicopters moved away from the airstrip and the world around them slipped from bedlam to terror. Raising his head, Bohannon saw Kabir's body lying on the runway, blood bubbling from a series of wounds on his back. He started to rise, to run to Kabir's aid, when the helicopters banked hard for a return run.

⚯

"Stay down," Joe roared. "I'm going to help." He was off, running toward Kabir's bloody body.

"Fat chance of that," Rizzo mumbled to himself. *Are there any of those weapons in this car?* Rizzo pulled open the back door of the Land Rover. In the distance he could see the helicopters making wide turns inward, turning back toward the airstrip as the Gulfstream pulled into an open hangar halfway down the concrete. He jumped on the back seat and steadied himself on the seatback with his left hand as he reached down and tried to pull up the floor of the Rover. A pulsing heat passed through his left hand and along his arm. Rizzo turned to his left where his hand was resting on *the* gun bag. "Holy guacamole, Moses's missile launcher."

Rizzo grabbed the pulsing bag and dragged it behind him as he crawled along the seat to the far side, pushed open the door, and jumped down to the runway.

Thump. Thump. Thump. The helicopters had straightened out and were bearing down on the hangar, cannons blazing away nonstop.

Running to the front of the Rover, Rizzo pulled the bag to his chest.

One of the choppers fired off two rockets that slammed into the concrete runway on either side of the hangar, its cannons shredding a third of the metal building into twisted knots.

The bag was longer than he was tall. Rizzo reached up and yanked on the zippers and the flaps of the bag fell away.

Rizzo quickly looked around. Joe was leaning over Kabir. Whalen had come out from behind the Rover with some big gun planted on his hip and was blasting away at the oncoming choppers.

Rizzo grabbed Aaron's staff, long and unwieldy, by the crook and pulled it into his side, his left hand trying to balance its surprising weight while his entire body infused with heat.

His hands began to glow.

"You don't mess with Moses."

The helicopter to the right, pounding out incessant cannon fire, was also taking the full brunt of Whalen's onslaught. It turned violently away from the airstrip, smoke and fire pouring out of it. Rizzo gave his full attention to the one bearing down on him like a dragon from the pit of hell. *What do I do?*

He had no clue. There was no trigger, no button to push.

"God, help me!"

Rizzo was driven back against the front of the Rover as if he had been on the wrong end of a missile launch at Cape Canaveral. A blinding white streak of light leaped from the entire length of the staff and shot into the sky, slamming into the front of the attacking chopper. For a heartbeat the helicopter shimmered and lit up like a light bulb. All the air sucked toward the copter as if the world had taken a deep breath. Then it erupted into a million tiny, flaming pieces.

"Sammy!" The voice came from down the runway.

Shaken like a rag doll, Rizzo was now sitting on the concrete runway, as he looked at his left hand for scorch marks. His fingers tingled, but there were no burns.

"I'mmm . . ."

Rizzo had a hard time coherently connecting his brain to his tongue. "Ooookaay," was all he could manage. But his eyes were on this marvelous stick that now lay across his lap, as cold and inert as the bones of a dinosaur in the Natural History Museum. "Ooookaay."

His eyes bouncing back and forth from Kabir's bleeding body to Rizzo's pale white face, Tom was shaken into the present when Atkins grabbed him by the shirt and started running down the airstrip. Whalen had joined Joe next to Kabir, and Vordenberg and Annie were running in their direction with a large, first-aid kit. "Kabir's got plenty of help," Atkins called over his shoulder, "but the plane . . ."

Tom looked to the west as he started running in Atkins's wake. The far hangar was smoldering, a good third of it molten metal girders and shredded steel skin.

Home. Alex!

Before he could process his fear, Tom saw Krupp run out a side door of the hangar and race in their direction.

"Get one of the trucks," Krupp called. "We've got to pull some of the debris away from the plane."

—∽∿∾—

A few minutes later, the surviving Land Rover had pulled aside piles of twisted metal, freeing the Gulfstream from its prison at the back of the hangar. The jet taxied downwind, to the end of the runway, as Bohannon and Atkins drove the vehicle back to the knot around Kabir. Rizzo sat on the back seat, Aaron's staff resting across his lap, a look of shock and awe on his face. Annie was on her feet and moving toward them.

"Kabir's going to be okay," she said through the driver's window. "Shrapnel wounds in his back, but Mike stopped the bleeding and there doesn't appear to be any internal damage."

Tom opened the door and swung his legs out.

"Don't get out," shouted Whalen. He was jogging toward them, Vordenberg helping Kabir to his feet. "Grab what you can of your gear, and you're getting on that plane before we have any other visitors."

Up the runway, Joe had swept up the small pile of packs he'd gathered earlier and was hustling in their direction, but Tom pushed the door open farther and stepped out. "Hang on a minute, Mike." With Annie at his shoulder, he moved toward Kabir, who was hurting and hobbled, but still had a smile on his face. Tom searched his eyes. "Are you—"

"Hurts, but I'll be fine. You need to get moving."

Tom reached out with his right hand and grasped Kabir's bicep. "Thank you. We won't forget what you did."

———

The goodbyes were rushed but heartfelt as the two teams parted ways, Bohannon and his gang climbing aboard the Gulfstream whose engines were still running hot. Annie had her cameras; Rodriguez had the packs in one hand and was using his other hand to help Rizzo up onto the high, first step into the jet; Tom had the staff back in the gun bag and slung over his left shoulder as he came up beside Whalen.

"You saved our lives," he said, matter-of-factly. "Again."

"Part of the job, going all the way back to 'Nam," said Whalen, his smile bringing one to Bohannon's lips. "No man left behind, eh? Goes with the territory. But I'm glad the guys and I could be of some service. Really glad we got you all here in one piece. And thrilled that you're taking that nasty stick away from here."

"Come with us," said Bohannon. "It's too dangerous for you here."

"Wish we could," Whalen responded. "But some of my crew are still out there. Once we meet up in Baghdad and we're all on a plane together, I can relax. Not before. I gave up writing those letters to widows years ago. C'mon. Get moving. We'll take care of Kabir. He'll be okay. And you take a vacation. Just not anywhere near us, okay?"

Annie was waiting in the doorway of the plane as Tom climbed the steps. He had to pull the gun bag from his shoulder and slip it through the hatch. As he did, he noticed Kabir, steadied by Vordenberg and Atkins, had his right hand up in farewell. Annie's eyes were out the door, but she turned to Tom, smiled, slipped her arm into his. "Let's go home."

47

THURSDAY, SEPTEMBER 3

2:12 p.m., Riyadh, Saudi Arabia

"Twenty thousand were in the streets yesterday." Prince Faisal was looking out one of the few windows of King Abuddin's palace that afforded a view of life outside the Saud family compound in Riyadh. "There will be double that today. Aramco has closed all its facilities indefinitely. They say it's because the pumping stations have been destroyed and there's not enough oil flowing to keep their operations open."

"So the Arab Spring comes to our nation, to our doors," said Abbudin as he joined his son at the window. "Whitestone is shrewd. He uses our own plot against us. And there will be one hundred thousand in the streets today."

King Abbudin was sixth of the Saudi kings, fifth son of Abdul Aziz al Saud to rule the absolute monarchy since his father consolidated power and created the nation in 1932. Six years later, oil was discovered under the rolling sand of the Arabian peninsula, leading to unprecedented wealth and unparalleled luxury for the family Saud, its friends, and the army officers who helped keep it in power.

But despite the $364 billion in export revenue that poured into Saudi Arabia each year, ninety percent from its oil exports, and despite the fact that education was free for Saudi nationals and that Saudi Arabia had twice the per capita income of Egypt, Iraq, or Iran, little of this monumental wealth filtered down to the twenty-three million native Saudis. Over eight million people were employed in Saudi Arabia, but more than eighty percent of those were foreign nationals. Unemployment was reported by the government at eleven percent, nearly thirty percent of its youth, but independent sources reported only ten percent of the native population had jobs and more than twenty percent of all Saudis lived in poverty.

Abbudin crossed the small room, sat in one of the deeply cushioned chairs, and picked up the telephone from the small, carved olive wood table to his right.

"Yes, Cousin, have the planes fully prepared for takeoff. Keep them in the hangars until we arrive. I want no warning. Family members will begin arriving soon, in FedEx delivery trucks. There will be much luggage. It will be heavy. You must deal with it as you can. I will contact you after my speech."

He gently replaced the phone in its cradle, leaned back in the chair, and closed his eyes. "Have all the transfers been made?"

Faisal's voice came from the window. "Yes. A little over twenty billion has been moved as you desired—the Cayman Islands, Tokyo, Switzerland."

"Yes, the Swiss," said Abuddin, his head back in the cushions, his eyes still closed. "We will have to make some trouble for the Swiss one day soon. The diamonds?"

"We carry with us. There will be no immigration checks when we reach Paraguay."

Suddenly Abuddin realized his son was beside him. Abuddin opened his eyes. Faisal had one knee on the floor, his hands on the arm of the chair. "Father, we can fight. We can resist. Send in the army and the police. Rout these protestors from the streets. We still have all the power. Why run?"

Abbudin, now the last of the Saudi kings, placed his hand on his son's. "My dearest wish, Faisal, is to see you and your sons sit on the throne of Saud. But that hope will no longer be realized. Mubarak tried to resist the rising of the people. Qaddafi tried. Even with all of the military power at their disposal, even with ruthlessly effective secret police and death squads, neither survived. Mubarak is dying in prison. Qaddafi, like Saddam, was found hiding in a hole in the ground. This is not the fate I have in mind—either for me, or for you, or for any of my sons. We can stay and fight, perhaps gain some time. But you know the truth, Faisal. Once the people turned, once they believed they had a voice and someone was listening, our time was over. Even more so, now, with Mossad and CIA agents stirring up the revolt, pouring in money and weapons. No one will come to our aid, Faisal. We dared take on the West. We dared too much. We raised the banner of jihad for Allah, but this time, fate was not on our side. We could stay here and fight—and die. Perhaps be tortured, perhaps imprisoned, perhaps, if the unwashed break through these walls while we remain, perhaps your sisters defiled?

"No, my son. We leave. Tonight. And we all will continue to live in luxury and safety. My counsel will still be heard at the table of the Muslim Brotherhood. We live, and we wait, and we prepare. This is one day. Another day will come. And you, Faisal, you will be ready."

4:37 p.m., Plain of Megiddo, Israel

Rabbi Ronald Fineman stood on the ruins of the city of Megiddo, a stiff breeze flapping his robe and making a mockery of the last time he brushed his hair. He stood on the brow of a high escarpment, balanced on the edge of a foundation wall, looking out over the vast valley to the east, stretching north and south as far as his eyes could see—the Plain of Megiddo, biblical location of the prophesied battle of Armageddon. The Bohannons, Rizzo, and Rodriguez stood at Fineman's side, waiting for him to move. The crate holding Aaron's staff lay unopened at his feet.

"All of a sudden, I don't know if this is such a good idea," said Fineman, his gaze fixed on the vast plain, covered by haze in the distance. "I just thought it fitting to bring it out here, you know, to test it out? If the staff is ever going to be used again as a weapon, this is probably where it will be used. Maybe this is the weapon that allows God to strike down all of the invading armies of Revelation. I don't know. It's pretty desolate out here, but . . . but . . ."

"But what if it goes off again?" asked Bohannon.

"Absolutely," agreed Fineman. "What if this thing starts shooting off lightning bolts as it did for Mr. Rizzo? Or causes an earthquake? Or sends out a death ray that kills everyone for one hundred kilometers?"

"Don't get carried away, Padre," said Rizzo. "I don't think it's got any juice left. Believe me, ever since we got rescued from the sandstorm and that helicopter got obliterated—"

"Which could have been caused by Whalen and his guys blasting away," reminded Rodriguez."

"Yeah. We're not sure. But I've been trying to get it to heat up again ever since. Nothing . . . nada . . . zippo . . . bubkes . . . you get my drift? I think she's kaputski!"

Rodriguez moved over closer to the crate and the rabbi, and sat on a raised portion of the foundation wall. "But you're forgetting one thing, Sammy," said Rodriguez. "None of us has the power, the authority, to use the staff."

After returning to Jerusalem, Bohannon and his team decided to keep the existence of Aaron's staff a secret, at least until they could carry out one crucial test. They wanted to see what the staff would do in the hands of an Aaronite priest, a rabbi in the line of Aaron. Having a priest wield the staff would be the best way to discern if the staff still held any supernatural power.

And Ronald Fineman was their willing guinea pig.

"Well, we're not going to find out anything standing here in the breeze," said the rabbi. He opened the padded crate and looked down at something as outlandish as the Loch Ness monster. It was still a dried out, gnarled stick. *Sort of looks like me—old, bent, and brittle.*

Fineman gently withdrew the staff from the crate. Rodriguez helped him stand to his feet. Fineman stepped out to the brow of the escarpment and lifted the stick over his head, pointing up. *If the lightning bolts start flying, at least they'll be flying back into the sky.*

Nothing happened.

Slowly, putting a strain on his aging muscles, closing his eyes, Fineman lowered the staff until it was pointing over the Megiddo plain. He felt nothing. He heard nothing. He opened his eyes. "Nothing?"

"Other than scaring a few birds and boring me to death, you're as bubkes as I was, Padre. Do you know any magic prayers? Anything in the Torah about turning on the juice?"

"Prayer is a good suggestion, Samuel. Prayer is always powerful."

Fineman stood at the brow of the hill and swung the staff back and forth over the plain. He began with Shema Yisrael.

Thirty minutes later, his arms and his prayers exhausted, Fineman gladly gave the staff back to Rodriguez, who returned it to the crate.

"Maybe it needs the Ark to come alive again," said Annie. "Maybe your life needs to be in danger."

"Maybe," said Bohannon. "But if it has no power now, then nobody needs to be chasing it anymore. Maybe we can finally go home."

Rodriguez closed the lid on the crate. "Wait a minute. We can't forget what happened in the desert. The staff got hot, it separated the sandstorm so we could escape, it opened a way for Krupp's jet to land. Maybe it even wiped out the helicopter. The staff had power then."

Bohannon held his ground. "Did it?" he asked. "Yeah, the staff got warm—hot, really. But it never changed. It's never exhibited any indication of life. It's been the same dried-out hardwood since we found it."

"Or it found you," said Fineman.

"Yeah, but now, here, with a priest in the line of Aaron, there is still no glimmer of life or power in the stick. I don't know, none of us do, for sure. Only God knows what he wants to do with Aaron's staff. But I think we've done what we've been called to do. I really believe it's over for us. Our task is completed."

10:44 p.m., Riyadh, Saudi Arabia

The ancient yellow Volkswagen, the color of desert afternoons, went into a sideways skid as it cleared the empty stalls of the bazaar, empty since the street protests began three days ago. The car's tires spun wildly for purchase on the sandy street.

Fouquari Yesid squeezed the steering wheel so hard, his fingers throbbed and cramped. The VW shot forward, and Yesid wrestled for control, slamming on the brakes as he squeezed into a tight, dark alley in the peasant section of Riyadh.

In spite of his excitement and urgency, Yesid halted in front of the door to the crumbling concrete-block building and took a deep breath to slow his heart and a moment to remember that day's code—one long knock, a pause, then three quick knocks—and he was through the door.

Israel was in the first of the two small rooms, an Uzi—comfortably ready to blast whomever entered—in his capable hands. Peter would be in the rear, working on the devices.

"He leaves tonight, after the address. The airplanes are being prepared."

Israel Klein was second-generation Sabra and Mossad's chief in Saudi Arabia. A broad, bald man of limited speech and less joy. "We will be ready."

"Where?" Peter Carver came out of the back room, his tiny, square-rimmed glasses pushed down to the end of his nose. Klein's counterpart in Riyadh's CIA office, Carver spoke even less than Klein.

"The main highway. He has no fear of being discovered," said Yesid.

"Good."

Defiant and combative in his television address to the nation, Abuddin had vowed to destroy those who protested and preached, demanding the death of the Saud dynasty. It was good theater, and Abuddin was confident his performance would provide the time needed for him and his family to complete their rape of the Saudi treasury. It appeared to work.

But the soon-no-longer king was anything but defiant as he sat on a hard, wooden bench bolted to the side of the hastily refurbished FedEx delivery truck. He desired to travel to the airport in a phalanx of black, armored limousines— one last act of royal prerogative—but wiser counsel prevailed. He and his family were widely dispersed in various forms of delivery trucks. Only Faisal and his brothers were with Abuddin.

⟨⟨⟨∿∿⟩⟩⟩

Yesid watched, a smile on his face, joyful anticipation in his heart, as Carver completed placement of the devices. It was only a small bridge spanning a dry wadi, but enough to set and conceal six devices—two at each end, two in the middle of the bridge. Carver joined Yesid and Klein behind the sand dune to the east of the bridge.

A cell phone to his ear, Yesid said, "They are coming."

⟨⟨⟨∿∿⟩⟩⟩

"When we arrive in Asunción," said Abbudin, "contact the bank immediately, perhaps go there personally, and begin the second set of transfers. Three should be enough to cause the necessary confusion until we get the funds secured."

Faisal was bored. He wanted to get on with his new life away from the constraints, mostly ignored, of restrictive Islamic law. "How much—"

⟨⟨⟨∿∿⟩⟩⟩

The light was blinding, the noise deafening, the impact catastrophically destructive. The explosive force on the ends of the bridge would likely destroy the FedEx truck. The two in the middle were just to be certain. The truck was crushed from the front and back, and the bridge obliterated at the same time, but the two central charges cleaved the truck in two across its midsection, allowing the fire ball created by the explosives to not only roll over the length and breadth of the truck, but also to rush into its interior.

———

"The world may not know who," said Klein, "but those who call for jihad will know why." He turned to Carver. "What did your colonials have on their flag?"

Carver was stuffing the transmitter and his gear into a small bag. He stopped and looked at Klein. "'Don't Tread on Me.' Is that what you mean?"

"'Don't Tread on Me.' My people should borrow that flag. It's a good one. Do not try to assassinate our prime minister. Or your president."

"Or try to take over the world," said Carver, closing the bag and standing up. "That's not a very wise prescription for your future health."

Carver looked to the west.

His work had been deadly efficient. The king of the Saud and his future kings had returned, in a flash, to the desert sand from which they sprang.

PART THREE

PURPOSE
FULFILLED

48

SATURDAY, SEPTEMBER 26

4:44 p.m., New York City

Prior to the turn of the twenty-first century, the last significant renovation of the Bowery Mission took place just after World War II. When Tom Bohannon began his tenure, the Mission was well worn.

There hadn't been much disposable income in New York City in the seventies and eighties. That was the era when most folks used the words *New York City* and *bankrupt* in the same sentence. During those decades, it was tough enough for the Mission to find donors willing to provide thirty thousand nights of shelter and a quarter-million meals each year for homeless men addicted to drugs, alcohol, and the myth that freedom slept on the streets. There wasn't much left over for sprucing up the buildings.

But at the turn of the century, that changed. Bohannon and one of his directors had taken a walk around the three buildings that comprised the Bowery Mission, the third-oldest rescue mission in the United States, and it didn't take much to convince Bohannon they needed to act.

So the Mission leadership joined together with the board and some key donors and embarked on what became a five-year rebuilding project. First the men's dorms—where eighty men enrolled in the Mission's recovery program lived for nine months while they took their first steps of sobriety—were gut renovated, one floor a year. Then the overnight dorm, with forty beds for men still on the street, allocated by lottery each afternoon, was moved from the basement of one building to a newly renovated space, with windows, on the second floor of an adjacent building.

Then the real work began.

Coming close to its hundredth anniversary, the Mission embarked on a historic renovation of its 1909 landmark building and a major overhaul, modernization, and renovation of nearly every other square inch of its space.

It took years. It took millions. It took determination and vision. And it turned out magnificently.

Back in the old days, the Bowery Mission chapel was a long, narrow, hulking kind of place, darkness surrounding its rafters, century-old wooden pews filling its space, deep burgundy terra-cotta tile floor and stone walls offering little in the way of warmth.

Bohannon stood on the platform that late Saturday afternoon of Labor Day weekend and soaked in the view. The lighting changed everything.

In the old chapel, the lights hung down from the rafters and lit the chapel space below. The rafters, and the space above them, were painted black, emulating the empty void of a dark cave, giving the chapel a claustrophobic feel. With the renovation, new lights were installed to shine up into the vault, which was painted a deep crimson, and to illuminate the beautifully carved ornamental rafters that were painted a rich, bright gray. The chapel looked bigger, glowed brighter, and felt warmer than it had in five decades.

Facing Bowery, the massive fifteen-by-thirty-foot Tiffany window of the Prodigal Son story was removed, taken apart, cleaned, repaired, and reassembled. And the famous organ pipes were renovated back to their original luster and design.

On the structure's façade, an architecturally beautiful building had emerged from decades of paint and neglect.

The transformation of the Bowery Mission was nothing less than awesome. And Bohannon's heart was moved every time he looked at it.

Today his heart was moved for another reason. It was time to say goodbye.

Bohannon was in the aisle in the rear of the Bowery Mission chapel, leaning against the last large, wooden pew on the left side. The chapel was empty. It was thirty minutes before the doors would open for the evening service, followed by dinner for the poor and homeless people—probably more than one hundred—who crossed the Mission's threshold three times a day.

His eyes on the organ pipes above the platform, at the far end of the long chapel, Bohannon shook his head. How much his life had changed. How grateful he was to still be alive. They had grieved and released Winthrop, then

Doc, now Kallie. He ran his hand over the worn but polished wood along the top of the pew. His heart ached for the loss.

Bohannon took a deep sigh of a breath and looked over the work of a decade. Like many of the men who would kneel at its altar rail, the Bowery Mission had been reborn. And a verse came to mind. *Well done, good and faithful servant.*

It was time.

49

It was a tight fit getting all five of them—Tom and Annie, Joe and Deirdre, and Sammy—seated at the round table in the front window of Paesano's Restaurant along Mulberry Street in New York City's Little Italy. It was the Bohannons' favorite table in their favorite restaurant, and it was the first time the team had been fully reunited in three weeks. Even though the price had steadily risen from the "$7.95 Pasta Special" the Bohannons first found twelve years earlier, Paesano's still served some of the best dishes in Little Italy.

Looking like it had been rescued from a 1940s movie, Paesano's was what an old Italian restaurant should look like. Straw-bound Chianti bottles hung from old, dark oak beams, lined with fake grapevines. Antique opera posters dotted the white plaster walls, green-checked cloths covered the tables, and Sinatra, Martin, and Como dominated the background music.

"Please don't give away my secret," Bohannon whispered into his wife's ear, "but I admit I've even missed Rizzo."

"I can hear you, Houdini. And I've missed you too, as long as you're going to pick up the check. Yo guys"—Rizzo took two breadsticks from the bread basket and inserted them between his upper teeth and gums—"ever see a walrus?"

Bohannon was about to skewer Rizzo's table manners when he looked into Alejandro's eyes, his favorite waiter standing to the side of the table with his notebook and pen in the air, but his eyes as big as pizzas. "You're scaring the staff, Samuel."

"I'm scaring myself. This feels good," he said as he twirled the still-implanted breadsticks. He glanced over at Alejandro. "More bread, please."

That wicked Rizzo-smile flooded his face as Alejandro beat a hasty retreat to the kitchen.

"Sammy," said Rodriguez, sitting to Rizzo's right, "you are going to have a tough time adjusting to real life again."

"Who says I want to?"

"C'mon, Sam. Our reality has changed, again, now that we're back from the Mideast. We need to change, too."

"Why? This place hasn't changed a lick since Columbus served spumoni on the *Santa Maria*, and they're doing fine."

Tom had another moment of concern for Rizzo. In a way, he had lost more than any of them. Kallie's death had broken his heart. Rizzo must have seen the concern in Bohannon's eyes.

"No, seriously," said Rizzo, pulling the breadsticks and pushing himself back in his chair. "I'm not going back to normal. I don't think I can ever go back to *normal*, whatever that is."

"Sam, what is it?" Annie asked, putting her hand on his.

"I've resigned my position with the library," Rizzo said, holding Annie's gaze. "I'm leaving New York."

"Don't be—"

"Wait," Annie said in Joe's direction. Then turned again to Rizzo. "Why?"

"Kallie and I had a lot of long talks in those few days we were here in New York, between our trips to Jerusalem. One of the dreams we shared was to open a dive shop in the town of St. Croix in the US Virgin Islands. You know that I've done a lot of diving. Underwater, I'm the same as anyone else, no matter what size. And Kallie loved the sea, loved the reefs. If she couldn't be in the Red Sea, she wanted to be in the Caribbean. I think I can be closer to her there."

For a moment, each of them appeared to be lost in thought. Then Deirdre leaned forward and reached out a hand to Rizzo.

"Just don't be rash, Sam," she said.

"That's what I was going to say!" said Joe.

"I don't think he's being rash," said Annie. "Tom and I have made a decision, too."

"You're opening a dive shop?" said Rizzo, feigning alarm. "We're going to be competitors?"

"No dive shop," said Tom. "But we're leaving New York City, too."

"What!" Joe's back arched, his shoulders were thrown back, and his head twisted so fast that Tom thought he heard Joe's neck snap. "What are you talking about?"

Tom reached to his right and grasped Annie's hand in his. "Time is short. Life is fleeting, and we want to experience it together, every minute. We've talked to the kids, and they are all for it. Annie and I have come up with a plan that will allow us to work together in parts of the world that are most in need of peace and God's love."

"You're going to be the new Mother Teresa?"

"No, Sam. I've taken a position with Global Compassion, a faith-based organization that finds sponsorships for children, helps build communities, and works for social justice in the poorest, most ravished and tumultuous areas of the world. My job will be to create and implement strategies that will enable peace and reconciliation to occur in countries most in need, including the United States and Ireland."

"When does all this happen?" Joe sounded like a ten-year-old who had his Christmas toys repossessed.

"Soon. Annie is going to travel with me, working as a freelance photographer, contributing photos to *National Geographic* and international photo services, but also for Salvation Army, Global Compassion, World Vision, and other humanitarian agencies operating in the areas where I'm assigned."

Joe looked from face to face, his eyes blinking in Morse code the questions that must have been in his mind. "Just like that? You're going to chuck it all in, leave the kids behind, and go off to save the world? Haven't you had enough of that the last couple of months?" He pushed his chair back and headed toward the restrooms.

Tom watched him walk away. *I guess we could have announced that better.*

"Joe's been offered his dream job at the library," said Deirdre, breaking into Tom's thoughts. "I think they realized how much they needed him while he was away. With all of you leaving, he's probably feeling guilty because we're not going to the ends of the earth, too. He's going to lose his best friends to boot and, now—" Deirdre put her hand on her brother's arm. "Tom, the Joe who came back with you is a changed man. Something happened to him over there, something that I've been praying for years to see happen. There's a new peace about Joe. But now, suddenly, you guys are going to be gone. He probably feels abandoned."

Alejandro returned with three plates of steaming pasta, another waiter in his wake with the other two orders. And a new basket of bread, which he put on the table, as far from Rizzo as possible.

Joe returned, but didn't sit. He stood between Tom and Annie and put a hand on each of their shoulders. "I'm sorry. I'm going to miss you." He returned to his chair and pulled close to the table, his eyes still on Tom. "It's just I—does it have to be so soon?"

Starting with Annie, Tom looked at each of the faces around the table—most of the people he loved were with him tonight. "Annie and I have talked about it a lot, wondering the same thing. Maybe we should just wait awhile. Take a break. Rest after what we've been through. But we kept coming back to one key principle."

Bohannon turned his full attention toward Rizzo. "Sam, what do you think this has all been about?"

"About I'm going to fall over dead if I don't eat this food soon."

Tom wasn't going to let Rizzo get away with wisecracks now. "Come on, Sam. Humor me. Why have we gone through all of it? What's the point?"

Rizzo intently studied his ravioli, his fork tapping a rhythm on the tabletop. "God at work." His voice was barely audible. Rizzo raised his head. "There is something going on, something cosmic and eternal. I know I probably sound like some quack televangelist, but for a reason only the Almighty can under-stand, it certainly looks like we've been God's instruments in bringing forward a time that has been prophesied for over three thousand years. The beginning of the end of what the devil started in the garden of Eden, and all that."

Bohannon smiled and Rizzo smiled back. "Thanks, Sam. So you understand, then—why we can't sit back." He turned to Joe. "If finding the Temple and the priests holding ritual sacrifice was another switch turning on God's prophetic clock, if bringing Aaron's staff back to Israel is another harbinger of 'last-days revelation,' then time is short. The clock is ticking. There is only so much time left, only so much time to get the message out. To bring the hope of salvation to those in the world who most desperately need to hear it.

"While there is still time, we want to offer other people the gift of grace and spread the hope of salvation. If we are in the last days of earth as we know it, which Annie and I believe, then it's up to us to do everything we can to share the truth, as we know it."

Tom grabbed a breadstick and pointed across the table. "And I intend to start with you, Samuel. Let me tell you a story."

50

Benji Propolski turned his thermos upside down, and still no tea escaped into his cup.

I'm going to fall asleep, here. Melda, this is your fault.

His wife, Melda, had been preoccupied the previous evening as Propolski prepared to leave for his overnight security shift at the Israel Museum. Twenty-six years he had been doing this job . . . twenty-six years, and the routine was always the same. Melda made his lunch while he dressed in his uniform. She boiled water and made sure he had a full, steaming thermos of strong tea to get him through the night.

But not last evening. No, Melda was too preoccupied, too glued to the television to remember Benji's lunch or his tea.

War with the Arabs had been averted. That fool Meir Kandel had been driven from office. General Orhlon seemed to have everything in order. Peace was ready to return to Jerusalem. Until the TV woke him up.

"Look, Benji, what they found." His Melda wasn't even on the sofa. She had pulled a chair right in front of the TV screen, her elbows on her knees, her eyes as wide as her amazement. "Under the Mount it is."

Benji Propolski and his family had emigrated from Poland when Benji was ten. His grandfather's shoe repair shop had been firebombed, *Juden* painted on the largest chunks of the ruins. It had been time to leave. But now he was an Israeli. Not a devout Jew, but a Jew nonetheless. So even Benji understood what so fascinated Melda.

"Look, the German engineers were doing a magnetic test something or other to make sure the rest of the Kotel didn't collapse," said Melda. "And they saw the image of a room, buried near the Kotel wall, near the Warren's Gate. They say there is something—here, look. They are again showing it."

Benji had to get to work. But he took a quick look over Melda's shoulder. Inside the image of the room, a box, with two figures above it, what looked like two kneeling angels, their wings outstretched, touching each other.

He kissed Melda on the top of her head. "I'll get lunch from the truck."

Melda didn't hear him leave.

⸺⸺⸺

Benji was tired of reading about the playoffs in the Israeli basketball league, so he threw the newspaper on top of the metal desk in the corner of the security post inside the Shrine of the Book. He was tired, period. No tea can leave you heavy-lidded.

Security Officer Propolski got up from the poorly cushioned metal chair, stretched to release the knots of arthritis in his back, and prepared for his rounds of the building. *Rounds, it's a good word.* The building itself was round, its roofline representing the end of a scroll holder, a mezuzah, the spindle of the shaft extending above the roof. It represented the contents of the Shrine of the Book—the oldest extant copies of the Talmud, the Dead Sea Scrolls, and the partial Aleppo Codex.

Propolski's job, as it had been for the past twenty-six years, was to protect the safety and sanctity of these sacred documents. Not that he'd ever read them. Propolski didn't read Aramaic nor did he understand the ancient Hebrew of the codex. So what? He didn't need to read it. He needed to protect it. He knew that was important.

Before leaving the security post, Propolski checked the security cameras and the alarm system. All were green. There were no alarms on the motion detectors, no reports from the sensors in the floors that would detect the steps of even the lightest of men. Security had always been extensive, but the levels had increased even more when Aaron's staff was added to the exhibit a week earlier.

Officer Propolski took his time as he wandered the outer rim of the building, ensuring all the doors were secure. He checked all the staircases, walking up and down them despite his arthritic knees, and opened the doors to the few offices in the shrine building.

As he entered the massive, round rotunda in the midst of the building, where the Dead Sea Scrolls were displayed in a muted, eternal twilight, Propolski's thoughts returned to his stomach—the lousy lunch he bought at the truck, the cold tea—and he wondered if Melda was still watching television. He walked around the rim wall, with the story of the Dead Sea Scrolls and reproductions of many of the scrolls themselves. In the center of the room, elevated, surrounded by a platform with a railing at its rim, the room was dominated by a large, spoke-like display case within which was mounted the original Book of Jeremiah, over two thousand years old, removed from a clay jar in the Negev Desert.

The room was quiet, as it should be. None of the precious exhibits were disturbed.

Without warning or cause, brilliant shafts of light shot from the two circular stairways on opposite sides of the center display case that led down into the museum area underneath Jeremiah's book. The lower area housed the Aleppo Codex and the display case holding Aaron's staff. There were no lights in that area that could come close to producing the radiant light coming from the stairways.

Officer Propolski's adrenaline level spiked, his heartbeat began pounding through his veins. He hesitated for a moment. Would he appear foolish? Was he simply tired? No. He clicked the small microphone attached to his uniform shirt at the left shoulder. "Code Red. Shrine of the Book," he whispered. He descended the stairs and walked cautiously toward the nearly blinding light.

Housed in a specially designed, clear-sided security case, Aaron's staff stood straight up, apparently not supported by anything. It shimmered and vibrated. It thrummed, a sound emitted by the shimmering vibrations, a sound that Propolski could feel painlessly moving his bones. White-blue light pulsed from within the staff. And it was budding. This five-thousand-year-old stick, now throbbing with a light that sounded like music, was growing, flowering, coming back to life right before his shielded eyes.

AUTHOR'S NOTE

While *The Aleppo Code* is a work of fiction, several plot elements are based on fact.

The Aleppo Codex—safe in a vault in Jerusalem's Israel Museum—is, in fact, the oldest, most accurate, and most comprehensive compilation of the Hebrew scriptures. It is written as a Masoretic text, meaning notes were added in the margins of the text to help with pronunciation and to provide explanation. Its history as presented in this book is true—begun by a group of rabbinical scholars in Tiberias, near the Sea of Galilee, the codex was completed around AD 930, captured by the crusaders, ransomed to the Jewish community in Alexandria, Egypt, and in the fourteenth century, taken to Aleppo, Syria, where it was hidden in a cave below the Great Aleppo Synagogue.

But only half of the codex now resides in the Israel Museum. The most fascinating element of the codex's history is what became of it after a riot in 1947 destroyed the Aleppo Synagogue. Was part of the codex destroyed in a fire? Or were parts of the codex stolen by those who conspired to return the codex to Israel? That mystery remains unsolved and is at the center of a book written by Canadian-Israeli journalist Matti Friedman, *The Aleppo Codex: A True Story of Obsession, Faith, and the Pursuit of an Ancient Bible*. In 2012, the *New York Times Magazine* ran a fascinating story about the codex and Friedman's research—"A High Holy Whodunit" by Ronen Bergman, http://www.nytimes.com/2012/07/29/magazine/the-aleppo-codex-mystery.html?pagewanted=all&_r=0.

⌁〰〰⌁

The Great Synagogue Ades of the Glorious Aleppo Community actually exists in the Nahla'ot neighborhood of Jerusalem, just west of the Old City. Nondescript on the outside, the interior of the Ades Synagogue, founded in 1901 by Jews emigrating from Aleppo, Syria, is ornately decorated.

⟞⟝⟞⟝

The biblical history of Aaron's staff and the tradition and teaching of Jewish scholars is faithfully communicated in the book, including the literature that asserts Aaron's staff is a fragment from the Tree of the Knowledge of Good and Evil in the garden of Eden and that it is to be used as a scepter of authority when Messiah arrives. There is nothing in Scripture or in Judeo-Christian teaching, however, which asserts that Aaron's staff, or even the Ark of the Covenant, contained a power that was exclusively its own. The staff and the ark are only objects. God used these objects to display his power . . . but it is always God's power at work through his created objects. Aaron's staff, were it ever to be found, would not be the most powerful weapon in the history of the world. It would be a really old stick.

⟞⟝⟞⟝

Sir General Charles Warren was a larger-than-life character who, in fact, had an incredible impact on the lore of nineteenth-century England. Both a war hero and a criticized military leader, General Warren commanded the British military forces in Singapore and later the Thames District outside London. But his two most memorable exploits were his clandestine tunneling under Jerusalem's Temple Mount in 1867 and his three-year service as commissioner of the Metropolitan Police Service (Scotland Yard) in London during the Jack the Ripper murders. London newspapers at one time even theorized that Warren himself was a suspect in the serial killings.

⟞⟝⟞⟝

The US Navy has actually deployed its Laser Weapons System (LaWS) on the warship USS *Ponce*, the navy's first Afloat Forward Staging Base, which patrols in the Persian Gulf. The Laser Weapons System marks, illuminates, and obliterates its targets within seconds.

⟞⟝⟞⟝

The Jewish prophets Jeremiah, Ezekiel, and Daniel were all in Babylon at the same time, while Daniel was chancellor to the great Chaldean Emperor, Nebuchadnezzar, who ordered the great tower to be built near his palace in Babylon. The foundation pit of the "Tower of Babylon" is visible from the air today.

⌒⌒⌒

In 2006, thirty Sunni tribes who called the Great Anbar Desert in western Iraq their home, rose up in opposition to a radical, Islamic terror group—Al Qaeda in Iraq—and its violently fanatic religious extremism. Led by the Albu Mahals, the Sons of Iraq, as they called themselves, allied with US Marines. For the next three years, the Sunni fighters of the Anbar Awakening engaged in some of the bloodiest and brutal battles of the Iraq war and were critical to the marines driving Al Qaeda in Iraq over into Syria. Al Qaeda in Iraq merged with Syrian jihadists and became known as the Islamic State in Iraq and al-Sham (ISIS).

⌒⌒⌒

The Bowery Mission (http://bowery.org) has served the lost, the least, and the lonely of New York City since 1878. It is the third-oldest rescue mission in the United States and one of its most effective. Besides serving more than 250,000 meals yearly to the homeless and poor, the Bowery Mission's nine-month, faith-based residential recovery program has guided thousands of men in transforming themselves from addiction and hopelessness to productive and healthy lives. There are more than three hundred rescue missions in the United States helping the poor and homeless with a combined one million donors and more than four hundred thousand volunteers. Most of them belong to the Association of Gospel Rescue Missions (http://agrm.org).

⌒⌒⌒

Charles Haddon Spurgeon (1834–92) was England's best-known preacher for most of the second half of the nineteenth century and pastor of London's famed New Park Street Chapel. Spurgeon's *All of Grace* was the first book published by Moody Press and is still its all-time bestseller. Three of his works have sold more than one million copies, and there is more of Spurgeon's work in print than any other Christian author (http://www.pilgrimpublications.com).

Spurgeon's London publication, *The Sword and the Trowel*, was replicated in New York City in 1878 by his cousin, Joseph Spurgeon, as *The Christian Herald and Signs of Our Times*. Dr. Louis Klopsch purchased the magazine in 1890 and was instrumental in preventing the Bowery Mission from closing its doors by purchasing the rescue mission from the Rev. A. G. Ruliffson in 1895 after its original superintendent passed away.

⌘

Now extinct, Demotic is the third language inscribed on the Rosetta Stone. First a spoken language then a written language it was extensively used in Egypt for more than one thousand years, from 660 BC to 425 AD. University of Chicago's Oriental Institute recently completed its nearly forty-year Demotic Dictionary Project (http://oi.uchicago.edu/research/projects/dem), cataloguing and deciphering the twenty-seven Demotic letters. As noted in the book, because Demotic was first a spoken language, each of its letters carries hundreds—if not thousands—of potential definitions. The current Demotic Dictionary contains more than two thousand pages of possible meanings for words associated with those letters or combinations of those letters.

In 2012, the *New York Times* wrote an article about the completion of the Institute's Demotic Dictionary Project: http://www.nytimes.com/2012/09/18/science/new-demotic-dictionary-translates-lives-of-ancient-egyptians.html.

⌘

Sir Edward Elgar (1857–1934) was an English romantic composer most notable for his many compositions of *Pomp and Circumstance* and his orchestral work the "Enigma" Variations. Elgar was also a devotee of codes, puzzles, and ciphers. On July 14, 1897, Elgar sent a letter to a young friend, Miss Dora Penny, the twenty-two-year-old daughter of the Rev. Alfred Penny, rector of St Peter's, Wolverhampton—the now famous Dorabella Cipher.

The cipher consists of eighty-seven characters, apparently constructed from an alphabet of twenty-four symbols. The symbols are arranged in three lines, contain one, two, or three semicircles, and are oriented in one of eight directions. A small dot appears after the fifth character on the third line. No one has yet deciphered its meaning. Dora Penny died in 1964.

Temple Mount in Jerusalem is a platform supported by a series of arches built by Herod the Great. The Mount is a formation of karstic limestone, which has been eroded over time by water, creating a honeycomb of cisterns, tunnels, and caverns. Other than the unofficial diggings of Charles Warren in the nineteenth century, there has been virtually no archaeological study of the space under the Temple Mount platform.

St. Antony's Monastery actually exists. St. Antony was a Coptic Christian monk and the father of monasticism. The monastery is, in fact, the oldest inhabited Christian monastery in the world, being continually occupied by monks since its founding in AD 356. The monastery itself was plundered a number of times by the Bedouins. In response to these attacks, a fortress-like structure was built around the monastery for its protection.

The modern monastery (http://stantonymonastery.com/) is a self-contained village in the Oasis Dayr al Qiddis deep in the Red Sea wilderness with gardens, a mill, a bakery, and five churches. The walls are adorned with paintings of knights in bright colors and hermits in more subdued colors, and the oldest date to the seventh and eighth centuries. The monastery also has a library with more than seventeen hundred handwritten manuscripts. The library probably contained many more volumes but was significantly reduced by the plundering.

Other than the basic facts and associated research listed above, the rest of *The Aleppo Code* is a result of the author's imagination. Any "errors of fact" are a result of that imagination.

ABOUT THE AUTHOR

Terry Brennan's twenty-two-year career in journalism included leading *The Mercury* of Pottstown, Pennsylvania, as its editor, to a Pulitzer Prize in Editorial Writing; serving as executive editor of a multinational newspaper firm—Ingersoll Publications—with papers in the United States, England, and Ireland; and earning the Valley Forge Award for editorial writing from the Freedoms Foundation.

In 1996 Brennan transferred to the nonprofit sector and served for twelve yeas as vice president of operations for the Christian Herald Association, Inc., the parent organization of four New York City ministries, including the Bowery Mission.

He now serves as chief administrative officer for Care for the Homeless, a New York City nonprofit that delivers medical teams to serve homeless people in shelters, soup kitchens, and drop-in centers. Two of his adult sons and their families live in Pennsylvania. Terry and his wife, Andrea, their two adult children, son-in-law, and a precious granddaughter live in the New York City area.